Carnival of Lies

D. V. Bishop is the pseudonym of award-winning writer David Bishop. His love for the city of Florence and the Renaissance period meant there could be only one setting for his historical thrillers. The first Cesare Aldo novel, *City of Vengeance*, won the Pitch Perfect competition at the Bloody Scotland crime writing festival and the NZ Booklovers Award for Best Adult Fiction Book. Book two in the series, *The Darkest Sin*, won the prestigious Crime Writers' Association Historical Dagger. The third Aldo novel, *Ritual of Fire*, won the Ngaio Marsh Award for Best Novel, while the fourth in the series, *A Divine Fury*, was a finalist for the McIlvanney Award. He teaches creative writing at Edinburgh Napier University. *Carnival of Lies* is the fifth novel in the Cesare Aldo series, following *A Divine Fury*.

BY D. V. BISHOP

City of Vengeance
The Darkest Sin
Ritual of Fire
A Divine Fury
Carnival of Lies

'I loved the story, in particular the Venice setting and the Contessa! What an excellent sparring partner for Aldo'   Lin Anderson

'David Bishop is a gifted writer of historical crime. *Carnival of Lies* is an immersive, fascinating journey through Renaissance Venice. The city is so vividly drawn, it almost becomes a character within the story'   Kate Rhodes

'A very exciting read, great plot with tension maintained right up until the end. The Contessa was truly superb, and so was Venice. The picture of a treacherous, dark bureaucracy grinding along behind the masks and parties was quite chilling'   Fiona Forsyth

'An absolutely astounding book. [David is] so skilled at bringing [his] characters to life'   Joanna Wallace

'D. V. Bishop has such tremendous flair for a thrilling plot, a gruesome mystery and engaging, relatable characters . . . this is the very finest in historical thriller storytelling'   Kate Foster

'It's hard to think of a better guide than D. V. Bishop to the brutality and glamour of Renaissance Florence. Religion and lust? Money and politics? It's all here, combined into a murderous brew'   Andrew Taylor

'He is fast becoming a serious rival to C. J. Sansom and S. J. Parris with his page-turning novels. Highly recommended'
Historical Novel Society

'A deft and engrossing historical thriller set in Renaissance Florence drawing on the fascinating and troubling legacy of Girolamo Savonarola. I thoroughly enjoyed the latest – and I think best – in D. V. Bishop's brilliant series'   Anna Mazzola

'Aldo is a magnificent creation'   Vaseem Khan

'A great insight into Renaissance Florence. What I love about these books is the seamless weaving of factual history with a great story'   Abir Mukherjee

'Bishop builds the suspense well, masterfully connecting the disparate strands of the story' *Crime Fiction Lover*

'Impressive' *Literary Review*

'History, mystery and the eternal mystique of Renaissance Florence in perfect harmony!' *Lancashire Evening Post*

'Atmospheric . . . this fourth volume in the Cesare Aldo series is full of dash and atmosphere' *The Times*

'A complex, intriguing plot which weaves its way through the treacherous streets of sixteenth-century Florence, encountering danger at every dark corner' Sarah Maine

'In Cesare Aldo, Bishop has created a character with the cunning, bravery and balls of steel to take on the twisty, toxic politics of the Medicis with panache. I can't wait for his next outing'
Alison Belsham

'This atmospheric murder mystery is packed with political intrigue and questionable morality. Secrets and conspiracies abound, danger is ever present and tension rises within the complex plotting'
Choice

'Dramatic and compelling, a great example of quality historical crime fiction . . . But the crowning glory of the book has to be the character of Cesare Aldo: bold, disquieting and complex; beautifully crafted with a deep and sensitive understanding of human frailty' Laura Carlin, author of *The Wicked Cometh*

'This dramatic and compelling book, with the larger-than-life, complex, charismatic and enduring and towering figure of Aldo holding it all together, is for all who enjoy well-written and enthralling historical mysteries' *Crime Review*

'Rich in atmosphere, and chilling in its authenticity, Bishop paints a vivid image of sixteenth-century Italy' *Scottish Field*

'Bishop has an impressive command of Florence's history, its beauty, ambition and taste for violence' *Publishers Weekly*

Carnival of Lies

D. V. BISHOP

PAN BOOKS

First published 2025 by Macmillan

This paperback edition first published 2026 by Pan Books
an imprint of Pan Macmillan
The Smithson, 6 Briset Street, London EC1M 5NR
EU representative: Macmillan Publishers Ireland Ltd, 1st Floor,
The Liffey Trust Centre, 117-126 Sheriff Street Upper,
Dublin 1 D01 YC43
Associated companies throughout the world

ISBN 978-1-0350-4196-1

Copyright © D. V. Bishop 2025

The right of D. V. Bishop to be identified as the author of this work has been asserted in accordance with the Copyright, Designs and Patents Act 1988.

All rights reserved. No part of this publication may be reproduced, stored in a retrieval system, or transmitted, in any form, or by any means (including, without limitation, electronic, mechanical, photocopying, recording or otherwise) without the prior written permission of the publisher.

Pan Macmillan does not have any control over, or any responsibility for, any author or third party websites (including, without limitation, URLs, emails and QR codes) referred to in or on this book.

1 3 5 7 9 8 6 4 2

A CIP catalogue record for this book is available from the British Library.
Map artwork by Neil Gower

Typeset in Adobe Caslon Pro by Palimpsest Book Production Ltd,
Falkirk, Stirlingshire
Printed and bound in the UK using 100% Renewable Electricity by CPI Group (UK) Ltd

This book is sold subject to the condition that it shall not, by way of trade or otherwise, be lent, hired out, or otherwise circulated without the publisher's prior consent in any form of binding or cover other than that in which it is published and without a similar condition including this condition being imposed on the subsequent purchaser. The publisher does not authorize the use or reproduction of any part of this book in any manner for the purpose of training artificial intelligence technologies or systems. The publisher expressly reserves this book from the Text and Data Mining exception in accordance with Article 4(3) of the European Union Digital Single Market Directive 2019/790.

Visit **www.panmacmillan.com** to read more about all our books
and to buy them.

*For my editor, Alex Saunders,
and everything he does for my stories*

*It is better to be adventurous than cautious,
because fortune is a woman.*

Niccolò Machiavelli, *The Prince*
Translated by W. K. Marriott (1908)

Author's Note

During this period, the new calendar year in Florence and Venice started during March. All the days in January and February 1540 (as we would think of them now) were then considered to be part of 1539.

Monday, February 12th 1539

The room around Aldo was murky, thin light seeping past the edges of battered wooden shutters in one wall. There was no furniture, there were no adornments to hint at where he might be. Something fast scuttled across the floor, keeping close to the far wall: a rat. It paused to stare at Aldo, nose twitching, before squeezing under the door and scampering away.

He was lying on an uneven straw mattress, without blanket or bedsheets. His toes were cold, limbs stiff and sore. He could make out voices murmuring nearby. In the distance were cries of greeting, sharp calls which were familiar but which he had not heard in years. Another noise sipped at the air, close and insistent: the lapping of water.

He couldn't be here. Not again. Not now.

Aldo struggled to his feet, legs protesting. He inhaled his own stale sweat, sour fear mingled with the ripe smell of horse. His satchel was missing, probably still—

It all came back in a rush. Now he had to know, had to be sure.

Aldo marched to the shutters, throwing them open.

A gondola floated by on the canal outside.

His worst fears were confirmed.

He was in Venice.
'Palle!'

Chapter One

Wednesday, February 7th 1539 (five days earlier)

Aldo was more intimate with the sights, sounds and smells of a bordello than almost any man in Florence. The bored faces of the women who worked there were all too familiar to him, as were their feigned cries of ecstasy while pleasing a man, and the aromas that lingered long after the last visitor had come and gone. It was legal for women to sell sex in Florence so long as they complied with the Office of Decency's regulations. The men who went to a bordello craved guilty pleasures and exciting sins . . . Aldo sought those elsewhere.

His knowledge came from living at Signora Tessa Robustelli's bordello for the past seven years. Aldo slept in a back room upstairs at the humble house south of the river Arno. The bordello gave him a place to rest and store his few belongings. Residing there also deflected questions about why Aldo was neither married nor a widower despite having seen more than forty summers. But it was a mutually beneficial arrangement.

In return for his lodgings Aldo helped Robustelli and her women with anyone who caused trouble at the bordello. Some visitors outstayed their welcome, such as drunkards unwilling or unable to leave. Other men were eager to inflict pain on the women, which Aldo and Robustelli abhorred. Lastly, there were those who came to offer protection from other criminals in return for coin. Aldo's residency had banished most of these threats.

Tonight, he was in a different bordello, one north of the river near the Mercato Vecchio. It was run by Signorina Nardi, a woman with generous curves, dark ringlets and a shrewd business mind. Where Robustelli's bordello was decorated in a simple and rustic style, Nardi favoured lurid frescoes of naked bodies and lustful faces. Golden statues of nubile women writhed in recesses, while aromas of musk and sandalwood spiced the air. But behind all of these were the familiar sights, sounds and smells of every bordello in the city.

Aldo lounged in Nardi's ufficio where the matrona was sipping wine and counting coin at a sturdy table. It was positioned to give her a clear view of the front door; nobody came or went without Nardi knowing. Aldo sat across from her, a hand resting on the stiletto tucked in his left boot. The last customer had scuttled away as bells across the city chimed to announce the start of the evening curfew. At least two more hours had passed since, the long wait testing Aldo's patience. He had spurned an earlier offer of wine, wanting all his wits when the expected trouble arrived. But if the unwelcome visitors didn't come soon . . .

A heavy fist hammered at the front door, making Nardi jump. Her face had been that of a purring seductress when dealing with guests, and a cold-eyed merchant when accepting the profits of those transactions. This was the first time Aldo had seen her afraid.

'Let them in,' he said, retreating to stand by a wooden screen in a corner, out of sight of the front door. 'Have them talk first. I can't intervene until I've heard their demands.'

Nardi gave a quick nod, her hands trembling as she pushed all her coin into a small chest atop the table. The matrona locked it and hid the key in the deep valley between her breasts. She straightened her back and raised her chin before striding from the ufficio. Aldo listened as Nardi opened the front door, welcoming two visitors inside.

'Have you got our coin?' a gruff male voice demanded.

'Your coin?' Nardi replied, all trace of her fear hidden.

'You heard,' another man sneered, his words an ugly nasal whine.

'We had an agreement,' the first man said. 'You give us half of everything this place makes from now on, and we don't shut you down.'

'You can't do that,' Nardi insisted, 'not without good cause—'

The slap of a hand across a face was unmistakeable, as was her cry of pain.

'We're the Office of Decency,' the sneering man said. 'That's all the cause we need. Now, are you going to give us what we want, or do we have to take it by force?'

Having heard enough, Aldo pulled the stiletto from his boot but held it behind his back. Better ready than on show. Brandishing the weapon would only invite violence.

Nardi returned to her ufficio, putting the table between her and the men following. One was tall and lean, a bushy brown beard in stark contrast to his shaved scalp. He was not known to Aldo, but the Office of Decency was notorious for how few men stayed long in its service. The other man leading the way was small and cocky, his features pinched as if caught in a cold wind. Aldo recognized this one: Presa, a man who carried a thwarted entitlement with him everywhere. It was no surprise that he was involved.

'Well, where is it?' Presa demanded. 'Where's the coin?'

'There is none,' Aldo said from where he stood. 'Not for the likes of you.'

Presa and his companion twisted round, anger swiftly replacing the surprise on their faces. 'Aldo? What are you doing here?' Presa demanded.

'I should have thought that obvious, even for someone of your stunted abilities.'

'Answer the question,' the taller man warned.

'You two have been using your positions at the Office of Decency to extort coin from bordelli,' Aldo replied. 'That ends here. Tonight.'

Presa laughed, but there was no amusement in his face. 'When Benedetto moved over from the Otto, he told me that you'd stopped working for the court months ago. You've got no authority here, no authority anywhere. You're just another citizen now.'

'True,' Aldo agreed before producing the stiletto from behind his back. 'But my blade can still cut you, even if I no longer serve the Otto.'

'There are two of us,' Presa persisted, 'and only one of you.'

'Don't worry, I'll make sure there's enough pain for . . .' Aldo looked past Presa to the other man. 'Sorry, I don't know your name?'

'Don't tell him, Sasso,' Presa snapped.

'Ahh, Sasso,' Aldo said. 'Well, don't worry, there'll be pain enough for both of you.' It was a statement intended to goad and enrage them, but he meant every word.

Presa attacked first, his face twisted by anger. Aldo snapped the stiletto hilt up into Presa's nose with a sharp crack. Presa sank to the floor, blood gushing down his chin. Sasso roared before lunging forwards, helpfully giving Aldo a moment's warning. He stepped to one side and Sasso dove past him, flying head-first into the heavy wooden screen. Sasso crumpled into a heap, the shattered screen collapsing on top of him. This revealed a burly figure who had been waiting behind the screen, hidden from view.

Aldo stood his ground, ready in case either attacker came at him again. But Presa was too busy muttering curses and nursing a broken nose, while Sasso had lost his senses to the wooden screen. Satisfied they were no longer a threat, Aldo arched an eyebrow at the man who'd been watching the confrontation. 'You didn't want to help with those two?'

Constable Manuffi of the Otto di Guardia e Balia shrugged and shook his head. 'You said I was only here as an observer. Besides, they didn't cause you much trouble.' He was a large, imposing figure. Most men were too intimidated by Manuffi's physical presence to take him on in a fight, yet his nature was gentle and genial.

Nardi came from behind her table to stand over Presa. 'Men who hurt women deserve to have that pain returned to them three-fold,' she hissed before kicking him hard in the palle. Presa folded forwards, hands cupping his groin, broken nose apparently forgotten. Nardi spat on him, muttering a few curses that were new even to Aldo, before stepping away.

Presa had chosen the wrong bordello for his extortion strategia, but he had been right about one thing. Aldo held no official authority since leaving the Otto three months ago. That was why he had brought Manuffi to observe. Accusations of corruption made by an ordinary citizen against men from the Office of Decency were unlikely to be given much weight. But corruption witnessed by a constable of the Otto – the city's most feared and powerful criminal court – was far more compelling. Presa stopped threatening to charge Aldo with assault after learning who Manuffi was.

'Should I arrest them now?' the constable asked, smiling down at the witless Sasso.

'Soon,' Aldo said. 'First, we need Presa to sign a confession. Help me get him up.' They dragged the bloody figure to the chair where Aldo had waited earlier. 'Signorina, do you have any cord? Something strong enough to bind Sasso before he regains his senses.'

'It's a bordello,' Nardi replied with a smirk. 'We have many ways of tying men up.'

The Venetian listened with interest as his informer described the daily routine of Duke Cosimo de' Medici. The ruler of Florence resided at Palazzo Medici, a sturdy stone residence a short stroll north of the Duomo. There had been rumours he would move elsewhere after his marriage the previous summer, especially as his young bride was expecting their first child soon. Palazzo Medici was perfectly acceptable for a Florentine famiglia, the informant observed, but lacked the grandeur that the duke's Spanish wife Eleonora seemed to expect. To raise bambini in the same place where Cosimo was leading the city of Florence . . . it was unsatisfactory.

Gossip and rumour often contained some of the truth, but these speculations were of little help to the Venetian. 'Tell me more about Palazzo Medici.'

Guards stood sentry outside the front and rear entrances day and night, the informer revealed, with all visitors needing permission before being allowed inside while the duke was present. Even if entry could be gained, the target would still be difficult to reach. 'Cosimo has learned from his predecessors' mistakes,' the informer said. 'He is always guarded, even inside his residence. Getting out alive after an attack would be difficult, perhaps impossible.'

Then it must happen while the duke was outside the palazzo, the Venetian concluded. The task would be no easier, but escape was more likely. Of course, he did not share that with the informer.

The fewer who knew what was planned, the better. 'How often does Cosimo leave his palazzo?'

'He does most days,' the informer replied. 'Cosimo is fond of hunting, and frequently takes a party of men outside the city walls. They tend to leave not long after dawn, when the streets are emptier and the duke has more chance of good sport. Eleonora accompanied him on these trips for several months – even after she was already with child – but that has now stopped on orders from her physician, I've heard.'

'And how many men accompany the duke when he hunts?'

'Fewer than when Eleonora went along – she always has her Spanish ladies in waiting and often male relatives close by – but the duke still has at least six guards accompany him, and several servants. A strike against him would need overwhelming numbers or great stealth for the attackers to succeed and escape alive.'

The Venetian nodded. It was to be expected. But he had a plan for that.

'What else can you tell me?'

It took an hour to persuade Presa that signing a confession was the right thing to do. Nardi delivering several more kicks to his tenderer parts while Aldo drafted the document did not help. It was Aldo offering to testify on Presa's behalf that made the difference. Aldo was lying, of course – he had no intention of standing before the Otto again, and certainly not to offer mitigation for such a repulsive parasite – but Presa was not to know that.

Sasso had recovered enough to stand. Manuffi bound both prisoners' hands behind their backs for the walk to Palazzo del Podestà, the headquarters of the Otto. Aldo secured a gag across the mouths of both men to keep them silent for the journey. The good people of Florence deserved peace and quiet, plus it put an end to Presa's whining.

Outside the bordello, the night was cold and dark, but enough moonlight slipped between clouds to show the way ahead. 'Grazie for doing this,' Aldo said to Manuffi as they pushed the prisoners in front of them, heading east through the city. 'There are plenty of men working for the Otto who would not be so generous with their time.'

Manuffi shrugged. 'It was interesting being inside a bordello.'

'You'd never been to one before?'

'Why would I?'

Aldo hid his smile. The constable had a charming innocence despite working for the Otto, a job that often involved meeting the worst things that people did to each other.

'And what did you think of Signorina Nardi's establishment?'

Manuffi took a moment before replying, as if deep in thought. 'It was full of aromas.'

Aldo waited, expecting more – but nothing came. 'Aromas?'

'Yes.'

'I see. Was there anything else you noticed?'

'Well, the women . . .'

'Yes?'

'Do you think they don't feel the cold?'

'I . . .' Aldo found himself short of words for once.

'It's just they all seemed happy to bounce around with almost nothing on,' Manuffi said. 'I would certainly get cold if I did that.'

'Certainly. But I believe they are quite . . . busy . . . most of the time. With their visitors. So, they don't get much chance to feel the cold.'

'Ahh.' Manuffi nodded. 'That must be it.'

The hulking silhouette of the Podestà soon loomed ahead of

them, the stone fortress no less forbidding in moonlight. Aldo had given many years of service to the Otto, struggling to see justice done while enforcing its unjust laws – many of which he regularly broke. Leaving the court had lifted a great weight, something he only realized once it was no longer pressing on him. To set foot back inside this building . . . No. That he would not do.

'Are you happy to take these two in?' Aldo asked.

'Of course,' Manuffi replied. 'But this is as much your arrest as mine.'

'Perhaps, but I no longer serve the Otto.'

'There might be a reward . . .'

Aldo doubted that. The evidence of what Presa and Sasso had been doing was beyond doubt, but two men from the Office of Decency extorting coin would not help its reputation. A quiet arrangement to have the pair charged and sentenced without word of what they had done escaping the Podestà was more likely. 'If there is a reward, you can keep it.'

'That's very generous,' Manuffi said.

'You earned it, standing behind that screen for so long.' Aldo hesitated before asking a last question. 'How is Strocchi? I heard that Tomasia lost the bambino she was carrying.'

The constable nodded, his face falling. 'Carlo's on leave. Took the famiglia to stay with his mama in Ponte a Signa while Tomasia recovers.'

'And Bindi was happy with that?' The Otto was largely run by Massimo Bindi, its administrative segretario. He was a self-important bully who expected all those at his command to be ready day and night for orders, despite his own craven indolence.

'I don't think Carlo gave him any choice.'

'Good,' Aldo said. It was pleasing to hear Strocchi had stood up for himself. After such a tragedy, the famiglia deserved a chance to heal in peace. Giving birth was a dangerous time for both woman and child. Indeed, Aldo's own mama had died bringing him into the world. Losing a bambino or bambina was sadly common, but at least Tomasia had not died too. 'Well, grazie again for helping,' Aldo said before strolling away. 'Buona notte.'

'Buona notte,' Manuffi replied.

Aldo gave a final wave before strolling south, careful to avoid the roads habitually taken by the night patrol. Having spent more than a year on those purgatorial shifts himself, he knew their patterns well. Besides, he was too tired to bother explaining why he was out after curfew without authority. Better to get back to Robustelli's unseen and untroubled.

Soon Aldo was striding up the curving stone arch of Ponte Vecchio, ignoring the closed butcher shops and other stalls on either side. He paused at a gap between buildings in the middle of the bridge, stopping to look at the Arno flowing underneath. Clouds had shrouded the moon once more, leaving the river in inky darkness. Yet Aldo could still make out occasional movements and hear water pushing past the stone foundations. He shivered, recalling the sound a body had made as it tumbled into the Arno. If that ever happened to him, he would surely drown. There was no need to learn how to swim in Florence, and the one place he had spent time where a comfort with water was essential . . .

Well, he was never going back there again.

Aldo blew into his hands as he strolled down the other side of the bridge, heading home. It was tempting to pay a visit to Saul, but the good doctor would not thank him for coming in from the wintry cold at this late hour. Besides, they had agreed to be more careful about Aldo's comings and goings on via dei Giudei. The narrow dirt alley was home to most of the Jews in Florence, many of whom were Saul's patients. A few might be willing to forgive their doctor for taking a man to his bed, such was the quality of care that Saul gave. But most would never understand nor condone such behaviour.

Eventually, Aldo reached Robustelli's bordello, stumbling in through the door to find the buxom matrona waiting, her little dog Piccolo under one arm. 'Well?' she asked.

'It's done,' he replied. 'Both men have been arrested and one of them admitted to what they've been doing and signed a confession. The Otto will send them to prison. Neither will have a job with the Office of Decency when they are eventually released from Le Stinche.'

'Grazie!' Robustelli said, enveloping Aldo in a perfumed embrace. Piccolo barked in protest at being squeezed between them. 'Grazie mille!'

'Prego,' Aldo said when finally she let him go. 'Now, it's been a long night . . .'

'Of course, of course! Off you go to bed,' she agreed, waving towards the stairs. 'I'll make sure none of my women disturb you in the morning. No matter what happens, you will be able to sleep all day tomorrow, if you wish!'

But it would not even be dawn when he was dragged from his slumbers.

Chapter Two

Thursday, February 8th 1539

Aldo knows he is dreaming when a familiar masked figure in a billowing crimson cloak beckons him towards the alley. He breaks away from the crowd of revellers, leaving behind their lanterns and laughter, following his beloved into the darkness.

'Quick, before anyone sees us,' Vincenzo whispers from the shadows. Aldo hurries to that husky, lusty voice he knows so well.

The darkness swallows him.

Then he's alone with Vincenzo, urgent hands pulling at each other's clothing, lifting tunics and pulling down hose. Their mouths meet – kissing, tasting, wanting. Finally, after so long, they can sate their longing for each other, can truly know each other. A strong hand takes hold of him and—

Aldo snapped awake. 'What? What is it?' Robustelli leaned over him, clutching a lantern.

'There's someone waiting downstairs,' she whispered, 'demanding to see you. They woke poor Piccolo with their banging at the front door.'

Aldo squinted at the shutters above his bed. It was still dark outside. 'Now? Curfew can't have ended yet.'

'That's what I said, but they insisted.'

He pulled himself upright, adjusting the bedclothes to cover his erect cazzo. 'Who is it? What name did they give?'

Robustelli shook her head. 'Wouldn't say, but he's definitely a servant for somebody rich, judging by the silk tunic and good boots. Whoever wants you is outside in a carriage.'

'You see a crest on it?'

'Too dark.'

'Did the servant say anything else?'

'That they'd heard about you helping those the law ignores or who are too poor to get its attention. Didn't mention you also work for those outside the law—'

'Doesn't mean they don't know about that,' he muttered. A suspicion was growing about who might be waiting for him in the carriage.

'Anyway, the servant says she knows you.'

'She? It's a woman in the carriage?'

'Seems so.'

That removed all doubt. Aldo could name only one woman who might venture south of the Arno during curfew to seek his services or his attention: Contessa Valentine Coltello. For her to have come at this hour could only mean trouble, and plenty of it. 'Very well. Tell this servant I'll be down once I've had a chance to wash and dress.'

'He wanted you to come immediately. Very demanding, he was.'

And that sounded like Coltello's maggiordomo, Pozzo. 'Nevertheless, he can wait. I'm sure the woman in the carriage would rather I made myself presentable first.'

The matrona shrugged. 'Your funeral,' she said, turning away.

Hopefully not.

Aldo hauled himself out of bed, the last remnants of his dream slipping away in the shivering cold of early morning. It was years since he'd thought about Vincenzo, not since meeting Saul. Some lovers were best forgotten, otherwise the wounds they'd left never healed. Besides, there was a far more urgent problem outside: the contessa.

Coltello had entered Aldo's world a few months ago, when he was still working for the Otto. She was the Venetian spymaster in Florence, a role Coltello inherited from her late husband, reporting to the Council of Ten and its Inquisitori di Stato in Venice on any and all matters that might be of interest to the Serene Republic. But having a woman in such a significant post had been deemed unsatisfactory and a boorish brute called Grossolano was sent to replace her. Coltello responded by having him murdered and placing the blame on another Venetian. In doing so, the contessa secured her own position and ensured another successor could not easily be installed. All of this had been achieved with an effortless elegance and the warmest of smiles.

That smile . . . Being in the contessa's presence bewitched Aldo in ways he couldn't explain. In all his years, no woman had never caught his eye. He could appreciate their wit and intelligence, could admire the bravery of those who stood their ground against forces far stronger than themselves. But no woman had caused Aldo the slightest twinge of attraction – until the contessa. To learn something new about himself, so at odds with everything he believed to be true . . . it was both disturbing and exciting.

Coltello was perhaps the most dangerous woman in Florence. She could teach tricks to military strategists that would leave their enemies bewildered. And only the contessa would be so bold as to visit the bordello this early, while the city was still under curfew.

But what did she want from Aldo, and how perilous might it be?

Having washed and dressed, he strode down the stairs to greet the waiting servant. But it was not Pozzo scowling by the front door, nor anyone else Aldo recognized. When he stepped out into Piazza della Passera, the crest on the carriage was not that of Coltello. Yet there was something familiar about the driver tending to the two horses.

The servant pushed past him to open the door, beckoning Aldo nearer.

When he did, the passenger within was unexpected and welcoming.

'Isabella?' Aldo asked. 'What are you doing here?'

She smiled at him. 'Get in and I'll tell you.'

Isabella Potenza had spent days deciding whether to call on Aldo. Most choices she made in a moment, without doubt or hesitation. Mama always said that proved how similar Isabella was to her nonna, but Isabella couldn't see it. For most of her life Lucrezia Fioravanti had been a fearsome strega, with eyes full of judgement and a tongue dipped in poison. Being compared to her . . . That was an insult, though Mama insisted it was a good thing in some ways. 'You will always know your own mind, Isabella, and never let anyone get the better of you.'

Perhaps there was some truth in that.

Having decided to visit Aldo, the next challenge was finding him. He was her uncle – well, step-uncle to people who cared about such things – but had been estranged from the famiglia for more than a decade. Isabella met him by chance when she was fifteen, and a student at the Convent of Santa Maria Magdalena. Aldo had come there investigating reports of an intruder. A naked male corpse was found within the convent, stabbed dozens of times and covered in blood. Isabella had helped Aldo uncover those responsible for the killing, though he would probably disagree with that (her uncle could be very stubborn).

To find Aldo, Isabella sent her maid to the Podestà with a letter for him, knowing Nucca could be trusted with any errand. Yet she returned carrying the document still sealed, bringing word that Aldo no longer worked for the court. One of the guards claimed Aldo slept in a bordello south of the Arno, and even provided a description of its location. Nucca had dismissed that as the guard making mischief, but Isabella recalled Aldo saying he did indeed reside in such a place. Certainly, her experiences of Aldo suggested he paid little attention to those who might be dismayed by such an arrangement. The guard had also told Nucca that Aldo now spent his days assisting those the Otto could not or would not help. That sounded like the man Isabella knew three years ago. She doubted he had changed much in the time since . . .

Her final challenge was deciding when and how to approach Aldo. She could not send Nucca to a bordello, that was too much to ask, and what needed to be said was too important to entrust to any other servant. Most were still new to Isabella and she wasn't sure of them yet. Besides, Aldo would never agree to her request if it came through an intermediary. No, she had to speak with him directly, and that meant going to the bordello herself. But if she was seen stepping inside such an establishment . . . Well, that wouldn't do. Ultimately, there was only one solution: to go during curfew, when nobody could witness the visit.

Her sour-faced maggiordomo Calabi had objected to venturing out at such an hour, of course. What if the night patrol stopped them? But Isabella insisted and Calabi begrudgingly gave in to her wishes. The journey south from Palazzo Potenza was brisk and uninterrupted, but waiting in her carriage outside the bordello seemed to go on for ever. Eventually, footsteps approached and Calabi opened the door, ushering a figure towards it.

Isabella could not help smiling when she saw Aldo, enjoying the surprise on his face. He spluttered some words as she invited him into the carriage. Once he was sitting opposite her, she called for the driver to take them back across the river. 'Try to avoid the Otto's night patrols,' she added. The carriage jolted forwards, and Isabella settled back to look at Aldo. He had not changed much. A few more lines around the eyes, perhaps, some extra grey in the stubble. But he remained lithe and lean, a man not enslaved by vices that thickened the belly and slowed the wits. His eyes were piercing as ever, studying her as she did him. Isabella wondered what he saw. Her circumstances were much changed since their last encounter, but how much of that was visible to his steady gaze? How much did it show in her?

'You know which roads the night patrols usually take?' Aldo asked.

'My driver was a constable for the Otto two years ago. He spent several unhappy weeks on night patrol, so he knows which roads and alleys they tend to follow.'

'I thought I knew his face. But it isn't the Fioravanti famiglia crest on this carriage.'

'No. It belonged to my husband, Stefano Potenza.'

'The wool merchant. So, you're a signora now? The last time we met you ran away to a convent to avoid getting married.'

Isabella smiled. 'I was only fifteen then.'

'Many become wives younger than that in this city.'

'True. I eventually agreed to a wedding so long as Nonna let me have some say in the choice of my husband.'

Aldo grimaced at her mention of Nonna Fioravanti. 'That

explains why you're in this particular carriage, but not why you called on me before dawn.'

'I could hardly come to a bordello during the day.'

'No, not now you're a respectable married woman.' He paused, his brow furrowing. 'You said this carriage belonged to your husband, meaning . . .'

'Yes, I'm a widow.'

Aldo arched an eyebrow at her. 'How long were you . . . ?'

'Three days.' Isabella shrugged. 'Three rather wonderful days. I'll admit there was some awkwardness on our first night, but once I discovered the pleasure to be had in our marriage bed . . .' She looked down at her hands, avoiding Aldo's gaze. 'Alas, it seems my . . . enthusiasm . . . was too much for poor Stefano. He had a good heart, but also a weak one.'

Aldo burst out laughing. Isabella leaned across to smack his hands.

'Don't you dare laugh at me! You've no idea what it was like.'

'I'm sorry,' Aldo said. 'You're right. But honestly . . .'

'I know,' she replied, letting a smile play across her lips. 'It sounds so comical. I did my best to appear sad at his funeral but, if I'm honest, I never really loved him.'

'Loved him? In three days? You hardly knew him.'

'True. And he did die with a smile on his face. But that's all in the past now. Besides, I've found being a widow quite liberating. My marriage helped to secure the future of Papa's wool-import business, and Stefano left me a considerable fortune. I am free to do as I please.'

'Then I congratulate you, Isabella. Most young women live their lives without a tiny piece of your good fortune. But I still don't know why you've called on me.'

'I need to tell you something, and ask you something,' she said.

'Very well. What do you wish to tell me?'

'Nonna is dying.'

Aldo's smile vanished. 'That cagna has been dying since before you were born.'

'That's what everyone tells me, but she truly is close to the end now.'

'Good.'

Isabella recoiled at the hatred in his voice. 'How can you say that?'

'I have my reasons.'

'I know Nonna has a vicious tongue in her mouth most days—'

'You know nothing about that woman,' Aldo snapped. 'Any hint of affection she shows is simply a mask. Everything Lucrezia says and does is calculated to advance her wishes, nothing more. Trust me, I lived at Palazzo Fioravanti until I was twelve, and every day she would—' He stopped and shook his head, refusing to go on. His hands clenched tight, the knuckles stark white against his skin.

Isabella had never seen him so consumed by anger. Coming had been a mistake, that was obvious. Still, better to say what she must and let Aldo decide what he would do with that. 'I know Nonna treated you badly, but she's an old, wizened woman now. When she speaks, her words sound like a dried-out poppy in the wind.'

Aldo did not reply. The carriage gently rocked the two of them as it rolled onwards, the creaking of wheels and horses' hooves on the street the only sounds to be heard.

'Every breath Nonna takes could be her last,' Isabella persisted, 'and she knows it.'

'That only makes her more dangerous.'

She peered at him, unsure what Aldo meant. 'How?'

'Because Lucrezia has nothing left to lose. She craves one last chance to inflict pain on me, and I won't give her that satisfaction.'

They went on in silence a while, Isabella waiting for his anger to recede. Bells rang in the distance, announcing the end of curfew. 'Was there anything else?' Aldo asked.

Isabella wasn't sure if she should tell him, but he deserved to know. 'The closer Nonna gets to death, the more it loosens her tongue.'

Aldo gave a bitter laugh. 'She's never had a problem speaking her mind.'

'True, but Nonna has lost control of her thoughts too. She called Papa curses I'd never heard before, and told Mama to marry again as soon as he died. She keeps muttering about someone called Ginevra . . .'

That got Aldo's attention. 'What does she say about her?'

Isabella hesitated. 'She called her sister, but I didn't think Nonna had any sisters.'

'Ginevra wasn't Lucrezia's sister.'

'Then who was she?'

'A servant girl who worked for the famiglia, but she died in childbirth.'

'I don't understand,' Isabella said. 'Why would Nonna call a servant girl her sister?'

'To trick me into coming back to that palazzo before she dies.'

Isabella frowned. What did he mean?

'Lucrezia has spent a lifetime punishing me one way or another for my papa's unfaithfulness. Now that death is finally about to take her, she hopes mentioning Ginevra will bring me back.' Aldo banged a fist twice against the carriage roof. 'Stop here,' he called to the driver. 'I'm getting out.'

Isabella grabbed his arm. 'Wait, I don't—'

'Let me go,' Aldo said, a cold warning in his voice. She did as he demanded. Aldo jumped out, already reaching for the door to close it. 'I know you didn't come here of your own choice. She tricked you into doing this, into being her messenger. But don't come back again or send anyone to fetch me until Lucrezia is dead and cold. Understand?'

Isabella nodded. 'Please, tell me one thing: who was Ginevra?'

'She was my mama.'

The Venetian emerged onto the streets of Florence as bells rang across the city for the end of curfew. He wanted to observe for himself Duke Cosimo's movements to and from Palazzo Medici. What the informer had said was useful, but it was always wiser to test the veracity of such statements. Trusting without question those who took coin to betray their masters was foolhardy; better to make certain than regret it at the end of a noose.

Bringing a servant gave the Venetian reason to linger in a doorway that offered a good view of the palazzo's main entrance. A lone individual keeping watch would soon bring attention from the guards outside the ducal residence, but two men talking drew little notice. The Venetian had arranged for a different servant to join him each hour during the morning; that should be enough to confirm what the informer had reported.

'What should we talk about?' the first servant asked, their back to the palazzo.

'Nothing of consequence,' the Venetian replied, nodding to a merchant as he strolled by. 'All we need do is appear occupied by our conversation.'

'Very well.' The servant set to the task but the Venetian paid little heed to the words spoken, aside from nodding and making occasional noises of interest. All his attention was focused on Palazzo Medici, assessing the security of the ducal residence.

The informer's report was proving quite accurate. Two guards stood sentry outside the main entrance. When merchants and administrators approached them, the guards directed visitors to wait while their names and purpose were confirmed. Some were turned away while others were allowed inside. A few men and women – often dressed in more audacious clothes – were admitted with a brisk nod.

These visitors wore distinctive dresses, cloaks and doublets, confirming what the Venetian had heard about the duke's wife. Eleonora kept Spanish servants and associates close by at all times while she awaited her first child. It must be an anxious time for Cosimo and his bride. Having a legitimate heir was essential to ensure the succession of Medici rule over Florence. Once Cosimo had a son, his hold on the city would be strengthened; until then, he remained vulnerable to attack.

The informer's claim that Cosimo often left early to go hunting proved accurate, too. The guards outside the entrance were soon joined by half a dozen more men, all carrying different weapons. A selection of stable hands approached on foot, leading horses ready to be ridden. Most of the guards climbed into the saddles, but two waited, looking expectantly at the palazzo entrance.

A single figure strode from the palazzo, full of certainty and vigour. One of the guards moved to assist him into the saddle but was dismissed with a gesture. This man had no need of help. He swung himself atop the horse and straightened up, giving the Venetian a better view. He was muscular of build, with chestnut hair cropped close to the scalp and the hint of a beard across his lower face. A short cloak trimmed with sable was draped across his shoulders, with a leather jerkin, black doublet and dark hose visible beneath that. The way he held himself, the certainty and imperiousness of his manner... This was Duke Cosimo de' Medici, the ruler of Florence.

One of the nearby horses chose that moment to piss all over the street in front of the palazzo. Cosimo made a comment, bringing laughter from his guards. He had an ease about him, appearing comfortable as a leader. The duke would not be an easy man to bring down, not if his attackers hoped to escape alive.

Cosimo twisted round on the horse, his eyes searching the street to assess those who had stopped to watch him emerge from the palazzo. That gaze paused for a moment when it reached the Venetian, the duke's eyes narrowing a little.

The Venetian gave a respectful bow, hiding his face from the duke.

When the Venetian looked up Cosimo was riding away, guards on horses in front, behind and at either side. Had the duke realized a threat was close? No, it was impossible. Few knew of the Venetian's presence in the city, and none had the full story of what he intended, what was to come. Even his master at the Inquisitori di Stato, Signor Bragadin, was unaware of the stratagemma – for now. If it succeeded, no doubt Bragadin would get much of the praise, but the Venetian was confident his boldness would also be recognized.

It was the least he deserved.

Chapter Three

Aldo stalked south as the city awoke around him. Workers stumbled out of homes into the cold air to face another day's labour. Servants hurried to fulfil the first command of the morning from their masters. Shopkeepers opened for business, hanging wares from hooks and shutters to catch early trade. Farmers shuffled to the mercato with baskets of tired brassica and other frost-wizened vegetables. Aldo paid little heed to any of them except those who lurched into his path, forcing him to leap across the channel of foul waste running down the road. He was too busy turning over what Isabella had said.

Perhaps Lucrezia was dying; if so, he would celebrate the day when it finally came. For years he had striven to keep the old cagna in the past, refusing to let her sneering voice and vindictive cruelties linger in his head. That was successful for the most part, but Aldo knew she still cast a long shadow. Hatred of Lucrezia was probably why he felt obliged to antagonize anyone who used their authority to torment those who couldn't fight back. But now the vicious strega was in his thoughts again, her petty victories brought back to life.

It had been tempting to tell Isabella the truth about her nonna, to say why he despised Lucrezia so much. The twelve years she spent hissing bastardo at him after his papa insisted Aldo be raised as one of the famiglia. The joy she took in discovering Aldo kissing another boy because it gave her a fresh excuse for the hatred in her cold, dead heart. The triumph on Lucrezia's face as she banished him from the palazzo an hour after the death of his papa, her husband. She forbade Aldo from taking anything with him – no clothes, no coin, none of his few possessions. As a final twist of the knife, Lucrezia had demanded he sign a letter stating he would never use the famiglia name. She promised to let him say goodbye to his little stepsister Teresa in return – and then reneged on that too.

Once Lucrezia was lying in the Fioravanti crypt, Aldo intended to prise open her tomb and piss on the rotting corpse inside. Then he would be done with her. Then he could see Teresa again, spend time with her and Isabella. After so long alone, surviving on the streets as a boy and living in cold rented rooms as a man, he might have somewhere to call home . . .

Aldo crossed the Arno at Ponte alla Carraia before turning east towards the bordello. It was the closest thing to a home he had known in recent years. He had lived there longer than most of Robustelli's women, yet it still seemed temporary. Leaving would be the work of moments, and all memory of his presence would soon be forgotten. Then again, that was true of most lives. Without children or some other legacy to live on after a person was dead, all were destined to go unremembered once the ground claimed their bones.

A man was pacing outside Robustelli's bordello as Aldo approached. Curfew was not long over yet this visitor seemed eager to satisfy his lust. If so, he would be waiting some time; the bordello did not open for business until most Florentines were eating in the middle of the day. Aldo was about to send the man away when he recognized the lone figure.

It was Pozzo, the maggiordomo to Contessa Coltello.

Aldo almost laughed. He had thought of the contessa, and now it seemed she wanted something of him. Good. It would take his mind off other matters. Dealing with dolts like Presa and Sasso offered little challenge, while a simple conversation with Coltello was an opportunity to match wits with someone worthy of his best. Whatever she had in mind, it would be dangerous and wrapped in deceptions. Perhaps half the words that slipped from her lips might be true, while the rest were a lure for the unwary.

On his first visit to the contessa's palazzo Aldo had irritated her maggiordomo by refusing to leave until she invited Aldo to her salone. Pozzo had made no effort to hide his disdain ever since. The contessa sending her most trusted servant across the Arno to find Aldo so soon after curfew meant it must be a matter of importance, otherwise she would have simply despatched a messenger. As an added extra, it would have made Pozzo even sourer than usual. Good. The maggiordomo enjoyed using his authority inside Palazzo Coltello to vex others. But now he was on Aldo's territory.

'If your palle are in need of emptying, you've come too soon,' Aldo called out, the words loud enough to echo around Piazza della Passera. Shutters overlooking the small square swung open, residents peering out to see whom Aldo was addressing. 'The bordello doesn't open for several hours yet.'

Pozzo swung round, his face livid. 'I'm not here for a woman,' he hissed, keeping his voice quiet so it couldn't be heard by anyone else.

'Oh, you're not interested in women?' Aldo announced, still booming out the words. 'Well, if you'd prefer a man's touch, better to visit via tra' Pellicciai. But you want to go there at the end of the day, not the start. I've heard that's the best time to find a . . . friend.'

Pozzo strode to Aldo until they were within fighting distance. 'Lower your voice,' the maggiordomo warned. 'I am here on behalf of the contessa, as you well know. She does not appreciate her servants being made to look foolish.'

Aldo smiled, knowing it would enrage Pozzo further, but did reply more quietly. 'I suspect she would find it very amusing, but I will do as you ask. Now, what you did want?'

The maggiordomo grimaced. 'The contessa wishes to speak with you.'

'Now? I'm surprised she rises this early.'

'When the contessa rises or sleeps is no concern of yours.'

'Ahh, so she prefers a more languid start to her day. Much like the women inside here,' Aldo said, nodding towards the bordello.

Anger twisted Pozzo's face. 'Are you comparing her to a common puttana?'

'Of course not. Besides, there is nothing common about Signora Robustelli or her women.' Aldo glanced at the humble building. 'When does Coltello wish to see me?'

Pozzo shrugged. 'The middle of the day will do.'

'Very well. Tell the contessa I shall present myself for an audience later today.' He smiled at Pozzo. 'You may go.'

'I—'

'Unless there was anything else?'

Pozzo twisted on his heels and stamped away, muttering curses under his breath. Aldo strolled to the bordello while considering the contessa's summons. He had not spoken with her since the murders of Grossolano and two other men during November. Aldo sought a favour from Coltello at the time, deliberately placing himself in her debt. But she had not acted upon that, neither calling on him for assistance nor demanding he divulge any secrets. Now the contessa wished to see him. Why?

Making Pozzo deliver the invitation so early suggested it was important, yet she did not require Aldo's presence immediately. That could be a *stratagemma* – Coltello was fond of those – or it might indicate the matter was not urgent. Whatever she wished to say, Duke Cosimo would need to be informed of the meeting. Since leaving the Otto, Aldo had received a small retainer from the duke for information about potential threats to the city. An invitation to meet with Venice's spymaster in Florence must be declared in advance to the duke and a full report of what transpired be given afterwards. The contessa knew that too, of course.

When dealing with Valentine Coltello, there was always courtly intrigue. Every truth was hidden behind a mask, while every smile disguised the thrust of a dagger.

The challenge was emerging from such encounters unscathed.

Isabella had her driver take the carriage on a slow journey through the streets of Florence. She had no wish to return home to an empty palazzo. What she had told Aldo was true; Stefano's death left her independently wealthy and without need to marry again, unlike many widows. But most of her acquaintances were now wives and mothers, their days filled with the joys and duties that brought. Even her best friend Chola – now Signora Ridolfi – was busy preparing for the arrival of her first child. Being free to do whatever she wished was pleasing, but without anyone to share the experience there seemed less joy in such things.

It was Mama who had suggested keeping Nonna company for an hour every few days. That was how she fell into the trap, Isabella realized. Nonna had used her to get to Aldo, knowing he would dismiss any direct message from Palazzo Fioravanti.

But what to do next?

She could go to Palazzo Fioravanti and tell Nonna what to do with her *stratagemma*. Antagonizing her was enjoyable, yet it came with risks. Lucrezia might be close to death, but she could still make the lives of others a misery. Isabella could say what she wished and stroll away without consequences, but Mama would suffer in her stead, and that was unfair. No, there was another way of dealing with this . . .

Isabella rapped on the carriage ceiling. 'Take me to Palazzo Fioravanti,' she called.

'We're not far from there now,' Calabi replied. He was riding with the driver, as usual refusing to travel inside the carriage. Calabi was an exemplary servant but even older than her late husband, and poor Stefano had been forty when he died. Worse still, Calabi lacked any sense of fun. Try as she might, Isabella had been unable to provoke a smile from him. She might have to find another *maggiordomo*, one nearer her own age.

The carriage rolled to a halt, and Calabi opened the door to help Isabella climb down. She jumped out onto the street, preferring to do such things for herself. 'Signora Potenza,' he whispered, 'you should allow me to assist you.'

Isabella shook her head, but smiled to show there no was anger involved. 'I shall be inside for a while. Why don't you take the carriage back to Palazzo Potenza? I'll send a messenger when I'm ready.'

'Very well, signora.' Calabi bowed at the waist, eyes cast down.

'You could ride inside the carriage, if you wished,' she said.

'But . . . that would not be proper.'

Isabella fought the urge to roll her eyes. 'How about this, then? I was uncomfortable today. Ride inside the carriage and see whether you agree it needs repairing.'

'Of course, signora – whatever you wish.'

'Grazie,' she replied before strolling into the palazzo. No sooner was she inside her former home than a sharp, bitter voice cut through the air.

'Where is she? Where is that cunning little volpe?'

Somehow Lucrezia always knew when anyone arrived. Isabella went upstairs to Nonna's bedchamber, making the sign of the cross before going in. Better safe than sorry.

When Aldo presented himself at Palazzo Medici there was only a single guard at the main entrance. That indicated the duke was not inside, as there was less need for security while Cosimo was away from his residence. Nonetheless, it was some time before Aldo was given permission to enter and, even then, he was accompanied by a servant. They led him up to the middle level, ushering Aldo into the small ufficio of Campana, a private segretario to the duke. Cosimo had several assistants, but Campana was the most trusted.

He was a sober figure at the best of times, yet seemed both weary and wary to Aldo's gaze. Campana wore the habitual black robes of an administrator, his drawn face appearing hollow-cheeked and near exhaustion. 'What do you want?' Campana demanded as he wrote, not looking up from the papers scattered across his table.

'Buon giorno,' Aldo said, meeting hostility with civility. 'If this is not a good time . . .'

'It's the only time I have, so, whatever you are here to report, make it brisk.'

'Of course.' Aldo gave a brief summary of his encounter with Pozzo.

Campana continued writing. If Aldo had been standing before the segretario of the Otto, this would be a ploy by Bindi to demonstrate his importance. But here it simply showed how busy Campana was.

'Is there anything I should know before visiting the contessa?' Aldo asked.

'Yes,' Campana replied, finally glancing up. 'Be careful.'

'Of course.'

The segretario returned to his papers.

'Nothing more?'

'That will do for now,' Campana said. 'In this, the less you know, the better.'

Aldo waited for any further explanation, but all he got was a wave of dismissal from Campana's left hand. The meeting was at an end. 'Grazie, signor.' Aldo bowed on his way out. The servant who had escorted him up was waiting in the hallway and ushered Aldo to the rear entrance. He asked a few gentle questions, hoping to prompt the servant into talking, but got nothing except silence. He left the palazzo more worried than when he first went in.

Why had Campana been so unwilling to share what he knew or suspected about Coltello requesting a meeting? Yes, visiting the contessa in a state of ignorance prevented Aldo divulging anything, but it was also insulting. He had proven his ability to withstand Coltello's intrigues, unlike other men sent to meet her. The reluctance of Campana to talk suggested there was strong cause for concern. Aldo knew he was almost certainly walking into a test or a trap, and now Campana was expecting him to do so blindfolded.

Emerging from his encounter with the contessa unscathed was forgotten.

Now it was a matter of getting out alive.

* * *

The contessa studied herself in the looking glass while maids fussed all around. She wished to be her most irresistible for the man coming to her palazzo. Coltello knew Aldo had little interest in women, but this made teasing and tormenting him all the more delightful. To tempt someone who preferred a good, hard cazzo to the exquisite pleasures she could offer was a true challenge for her skills, and it wasn't often she encountered one.

Her skin remained pale and flawless, offering no hint of her age, while a golden net studded with tiny emeralds held back her fine hair. The gown she had chosen was made of the finest silk, embroidered with delicate patterns. Its bodice both enhanced and drew attention to the swell of her breasts. That might be wasted on Aldo, but the pretence must be maintained. Letting the unspoken speak for itself saved them time and needless chatter.

In truth, she might be disappointed if Aldo ever did succumb to her charms. As with so many things, the anticipation of savouring a delicious morsel was far more entertaining than the thing itself. Once attained, the impossible soon became tawdry and tiresome. Better that she and Aldo remain the best of enemies, moving in slow circles around one another, coming close to a kiss or more without ever touching lips. But this didn't stop her imagining what it would be like to know him intimately. He doubtless possessed skills she did not, and any woman who forsook a chance to increase her knowledge was a very dull creature.

People called Coltello many things, but she prided herself on never being dull.

Her green eyes glittered when Pozzo knocked at the dressing-room door to announce Aldo's arrival downstairs. 'Very good,' she replied. 'Escort him to the salone and remain with our guest. I shall be there presently.'

'Of course,' the maggiordomo replied.

For most meetings Coltello preferred to keep a visitor waiting to make them more nervous and easier to manipulate. But Aldo was too shrewd for such an obvious stratagemma. Instead, she swept into the salone mere moments after Pozzo had brought Aldo there, dismissing the maggiordomo with a flick of her gaze. Once alone with Aldo she sank onto a chair to stare at him. He remained firm of posture and trim of waist, his flinty gaze as piercing as ever. 'What a pleasure to see you again,' she began.

He bowed, a smile playing about his lips. 'And you.' His eyes took in the gown, a flicker of recognition settling on him. 'Is that the work of . . . ?'

'Renato Patricio? Yes, it is. I understand he's an old friend of yours.' She knew much more than that, of course. Her informants had mentioned Aldo's acquaintance with Patricio, so she had commissioned a new gown from the dressmaker as a means of learning what, if anything, he knew. She had expected to hate the gown but instead it was a triumph, while the discomfort this was now causing Aldo only enhanced its success.

'I understand you have departed the Otto?'

'Yes, not long after our last encounter. It seemed that my . . . talents were not fully appreciated there. Now I offer my services to those whom the Otto would ignore.'

'Including Duke Cosimo, I hear.'

Aldo gave a small nod of acknowledgement. 'Your sources within Palazzo Medici are impeccable, as ever.' She appreciated his tendency to admit the truth whenever possible. This made discerning the deceptions amid his words all the more enjoyable.

'I must say being free of that fool Bindi seems to agree with you,' Coltello observed, and meant it. Aldo looked better rested than before, with more colour in his face.

'Grazie mille,' he replied. 'And you are as radiant as ever.'

'Naturally.' She patted the chair beside her own. 'Come, sit with me. There is much for us to discuss.' He did as he was told, but chose not to ask the obvious question: why had he been summoned? What a pity so few men had the wit to remain as silent in her company, especially since most found little of interest to say. The bedchamber was the only place she wished a man to truly exercise his tongue . . . but that was a thought for another occasion.

'Knowing as I do that the duke sometimes employs you on his behalf,' she said, 'I felt certain he would wish to hear an urgent matter which has reached my attention. But the position I hold here in the city does not allow me to approach Duke Cosimo myself.'

'Indeed.' One of Aldo's eyebrows arched a little.

He was intrigued. Good.

'So, I decided to have Pozzo call on you and offer an invitation to visit. You must forgive the earliness of his arrival, but it was . . . necessary.'

'Of course,' her guest replied. 'Fortunately, I was already up when Pozzo called. It was most enjoyable to witness his dismay in delivering your message at the bordello. Grazie.'

'Prego.' The contessa let concern seep into her face. 'But I fear there is nothing enjoyable in what I must now say.' She placed a hand to her chest, as if overcome by worry. 'You see, I believe someone plans to murder Duke Cosimo de' Medici.'

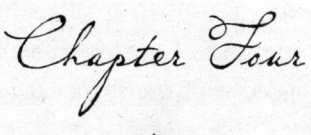

Aldo could not keep the surprise from his face. Coltello had arranged all of this to see how he would respond, so he let his surprise linger a moment before drawing it back into himself. 'I see. And do you have any further details of this attack on the duke? A time, perhaps, when it will happen, or a particular location?'

'Perhaps . . .' she said, rising from her chair to approach the nearest shutters – 'but I'm not sure how accurate my information is.'

Aldo remained where he was. Hurrying after the contessa would show weakness and a desperation to hear what she knew. This was not the way to entice from her intriguing lips the secrets she had brought him here to share. All encounters with Coltello were a joust, a game that must be played by her rules, and to her satisfaction.

'I understand,' he replied. 'It is difficult to obtain reliable intelligence these days.'

'Quite.' She looked down at Piazza Santa Trinita outside. Another of her games.

'Might I assist you in some way?' Aldo offered, rising to his feet. 'If you shared a little of what has reached your ears, perhaps I could help sift the truth from the gossip.'

'That would be most generous of you,' the contessa said, still staring through the shutters, 'but hardly necessary. I can make such determinations for myself.'

'Of course.' He strolled to her, close enough to inhale a sweet hint of jasmine mingled with the sharp tang of limone. As ever, she smelled exquisite. 'I am at your service.'

Coltello slowly turned until Aldo could see the tiny flecks of hazel in those bewitching green eyes. She reached up, stroking her fingertips down his right cheek with the lightest of touches. 'I would expect nothing less, Cesare.'

Was that the first time the contessa had used his given name? Aldo believed it might be. But before he could respond she swept past him, a sad smile of regret passing across her face. 'Very well,' she announced, returning to her seat. 'I shall tell you what I have heard. Let Cosimo decide for himself which parts he wishes to believe.'

Aldo let his gaze follow her but remained where he stood, hands behind his back.

'I'm told there is a disquiet among Florentine exiles in Venice,' the contessa said. 'They long for the days when this city was a republic, before the famiglia Medici reclaimed power here. Some of them had believed the selection of Cosimo – a callow youth of seventeen, after all, when he was made leader – was an opportunity to put an end to the Medici hold on Florence. That proved to be false.'

So far Coltello had said nothing which was not common knowledge. The exiles did launch an armed campaign to reclaim Florence not long after Cosimo's election, but their forces were defeated by his men without reaching the city walls. That was several summers past; had the anti-Medici faction in Venice regrouped enough to try again?

'The exiles now recognize they lack the means to attempt

another overthrow by force of arms,' the contessa continued. 'Instead, they're plotting to kill the duke by stealth in the hope it will persuade people to rise up and restore their city to a republic.'

Her words reminded Aldo of a conversation he once had with the man responsible for the downfall of Cosimo's predecessor. Lorenzino de' Medici claimed he and his accomplices had plotted against Duke Alessandro to liberate Florence from tyranny. Yet they fled the city under cover of darkness to escape capture, more concerned with saving themselves than with restoring the republic. Cosimo had sent Aldo to find Lorenzino and warn him never to return to Florence; if the traitor Medici did, he would be arrested, tried and executed. That was three years ago. Was Lorenzino behind this new stratagemma?

'How is the duke's cousin these days?' Aldo asked. 'Still winning friends in Venice thanks to his reputation as the Brutus of Florence?'

The contessa gave a nod of appreciation. 'I did not realize you were such a keen observer in such matters. Bravo, it's not what one expects from a former constable of the Otto. Yes, I believe Lorenzino is residing in Venice at present. But he is not involved with this, not according to my sources in the Serenissima.'

Aldo returned to sit beside her. 'Then, if I may be so bold as to ask, who is?'

'Someone close to the Council of Ten's new tribunal, the Inquisitori di Stato. Alas, I can tell you no more than that. My friends in Venice have been less forthcoming of late. It seems some within the tribunal blame me for the death of Signor Tito Grossolano.'

She had been responsible for the man's death, but Aldo knew better than to mention this. 'How unfortunate,' he said instead. 'And unfair. Grossolano's demise – while a tragedy to anyone who cared about him – served the interests of Venice by keeping you in your present position. But that may not yet be apparent to some within the tribunal.'

'Quite.' The contessa smiled. 'I'm so glad you understand.'

He nodded, letting his silence ask the question that he could not.

'It seems a handful of exiles have returned to Florence,' Coltello went on, 'claiming to have made peace with Cosimo's leadership. But these men are, in fact, intent upon taking the duke's life. They are being assisted by a Venetian, someone who purports to be acting on behalf of the Inquisitori di Stato, but I know little more about this particular individual.'

That helped to explain Campana's earlier evasiveness. Aldo knew the Inquisitori di Stato had been formed a few months earlier to protect Venice's secrets and gather counterintelligence on its enemies and allies. Cosimo and his private segretario must have heard whispers of this fresh plot, and were taking measures to guard against it. All information would be held in a closed circle of only the most trusted advisers to ensure Cosimo's safety. This was wise, as few Medici leaders died from old age; more often, they departed this life at the edge of a blade.

'And you cannot ask for more information about this Venetian,' Aldo said, 'not without appearing disloyal to the council and its tribunal.'

Now it was the contessa who did not speak, her green eyes studying Aldo, a hint of mischief curling up the corners of her mouth. That meant Coltello was tempted to share what else she knew; equally, she might choose to withhold it as a tease.

'When will this happen?' Aldo asked.

The warmth seeped from her face, leaving disapproval in its place. 'Oh dear,' she said. 'I find men who ask too much of me rather tiresome.' One hand rose to her mouth as she turned aside, appearing to stifle a small yawn. 'Besides, being up so early is not at all my preference. I fear that I shall have to rest now.'

Aldo gave a small nod, cursing himself for being too eager, too impatient. No woman enjoys the company of a man who rushes to satisfy his own needs first, Robustelli often said, and so it was with the contessa. 'Of course,' Aldo replied, preparing to leave. 'Please forgive me for taking up your time. I will withdraw at once.'

'Grazie.' She did not look at him, her face turning towards a particular tapestry. The scene it depicted – members of the nobility attending a masked ball – was unremarkable, yet it had claimed her attention several times during their meeting.

Aldo went to the salone door but paused to bow on his way out. 'Contessa.'

The merest flutter of her fingers acknowledged him, but no more.

He was dismissed.

The Venetian slipped into Coltello's salone after Aldo left, having watched the meeting through a spyhole. The contessa had toyed with her visitor as a cat might a captive mouse, teasing Aldo before punishing his attempt to question her dominance.

'Brava,' the Venetian said. 'Grazie.'

'Prego,' she replied.

'When this matter is at an end, I shall be certain to tell my master at the tribunal of your talents.'

The contessa acknowledged his praise but said no more.

'However, I noticed you chose not to say when the exiles plan to attack.'

Coltello smiled. 'That would have been too easy. Aldo distrusts any information that comes without difficulty or is too freely offered.'

Her intermediary was of no importance to the Venetian, yet he noticed a hint of admiration in the way she described this Aldo. 'It seems you know him well.'

'Well enough to be certain he will take what I have said to the duke.'

'Good. The exiles are ready and eager. The attack will be tomorrow, as planned.'

The contessa nodded, but a frown appeared on her face for a moment.

'You are wondering why I wish Cosimo to be forewarned?' the Venetian asked.

'I'm sure you have good reason.'

'Yes, I do.' The Venetian bowed on his way out. 'Again, grazie for your assistance in this matter. Perhaps it is as well Signor Bragadin has summoned you back to the Serenissima to answer to the Inquisitori di Stato. Should the exiles succeed, Florence would be a difficult place to live for those representing the interests of Venice. Buon giorno, Contessa.' He was at the salone door when Coltello spoke.

'Please give my regards to your cousin,' she said.

The Venetian paused to glance back. The contessa was smiling once more, mischief twinkling in those green eyes. So, she knew more about his plans than had been apparent. No wonder Bragadin was so wary of her. 'I shall. Buon giorno.'

Aldo strode north from Palazzo Coltello, but his thoughts were still with the contessa. There had been something false about their meeting, as if she were playing a part at the teatro. Of course, everything the contessa said or did was a performance, yet he sensed a difference between their usual jousting and the way she had treated him today. It was almost dismissive, and she had been even more evasive than usual – why?

Then there was the way she volunteered information about this apparent threat to the duke. Aldo believed much of what Coltello had said was true, though knowing which parts to trust was always a challenge with her. The contessa might be willing to share interesting morsels, but she always expected something in return for such generosity.

This time she asked for nothing, and gave him no chance to offer.

That was akin to seeing black smoke rising in the countryside.

It was a warning sign of trouble ahead.

Aldo paused outside the church of San Lorenzo, where the bodies of many Medici lay in the crypt. It was essential to bring what Coltello had said to the duke, otherwise Cosimo might also soon spend eternity lying beneath this church. If there was an attack and it later emerged a warning had been withheld, the consequences for those who kept silent would be fatal. Better to tell the duke of something which did not come to pass, and be diminished in his esteem. That could be rebuilt, in time. Besides, Cosimo was quite capable of determining for himself how much importance to place on what Coltello had said.

Turning east, Aldo hurried on towards Palazzo Medici. He passed two courtesans strolling around a piazza in the weak afternoon sun. One was a slender woman with a hawkish face; the second was younger and more voluptuous. Though they were walking arm in arm, each was busy watching to see if any man paid them attention. It was a frequent ritual on some streets, a way for such women to attract the eye of potential visitors and benefactors. Mass on Sundays was another place where courtesans went to be seen, so much so that some churches used a coarse curtain to separate unmarried women from men during services.

Aldo smiled; of course! The contessa's behaviour today was not for his eyes; she had been performing for another's gaze. Aldo always expected to be observed while inside her palazzo; the maggiordomo Pozzo was usually close by. It made sense that Coltello had a concealed spyhole, enabling the contessa or her servants to keep an eye on visitors. The more Aldo considered this, the more certain he became: someone had been watching his meeting with her, most likely from behind the tapestry of a masked ball.

She would not bother to perform for her own servants. That meant the observer was someone else. Coltello had many informants in Florence, along with those she manipulated into helping her, but few allies. For a person to be watching inside her palazzo, and the way she had behaved for them . . . that indicated the observer was from outside the city.

She had said the exiles were being assisted by a Venetian, someone who claimed to be acting on behalf of the Inquisitori di Stato. Aldo suspected it was this unnamed Venetian who had been watching them. Was that why Coltello did not demand anything in exchange for her information? Had she been signalling what was happening, knowing she could not say so out loud? It was an elaborate stratagemma, but typical of her. In Aldo's experience of the contessa, everything was a game within a game.

Aldo presented himself at the back entrance of Palazzo Medici, not wishing to stand at the front with the merchants and those seeking favours from Cosimo. If an attack on the duke's life was imminent, telling him so could not wait. One of the guards at the rear door went to see if Aldo should be admitted while the other remained standing sentry.

'Why two of you?' Aldo asked. 'Most days you're alone.'

The guard shrugged. 'Orders from Campana.'

The other man soon returned with a courtier Aldo recognized but could not name. The man wore a gaudy silk tunic, perhaps to distract from the dullness of his face and receding hair. Yet all it succeeded in doing was to draw attention to his bulging belly and poor taste in fabrics. 'You wish to speak with His Grace?' the courtier sniffed.

Aldo nodded.

'Name?'

'Cesare Aldo. Is the duke back from hunting?'

The courtier ignored the question. 'Why should you be brought before His Grace?'

'Tell Campana I'm here. He will want to see me, even if the duke is occupied.'

'I need a better reason than that. His Grace and Signor Campana are always busy.'

Aldo was losing patience with this officious official. He beckoned the courtier close, then closer still, until the man was almost standing on Aldo's boots. 'Tell Campana I'm here,' Aldo whispered before adding a threat involving the sharp end of a stiletto and the courtier's palle. Aldo stepped back, smiling warmly. 'Is that enough of a reason?'

The courtier gave a quick nod, his face ashen.

'Well? Why are you waiting?'

The courtier scuttled back inside, his rapid retreat amusing both guards. 'That's the fastest I've seen him move in a long time,' one said.

'Who is that fool?' Aldo asked.

'Federico Dandolo.'

Ahh, that was his name! Dandolo was a minor functionary in the ducal court who had unwisely let himself be tempted by an overture from Coltello a few months ago. She did so in a deliberately clumsy way to get the duke's attention and distract him from her true sources inside Palazzo Medici. Dandolo had told Campana about Coltello's approach, which was probably the only reason the courtier still had a position at the ducal residence.

Dandolo soon returned, gesturing for Aldo to follow. The courtier escorted him to the middle level of the palazzo, taking Aldo to Campana's ufficio. Dandolo opened the door but remained outside when Aldo entered, closing the door after him. Campana was waiting within, all his attention on Aldo this time. 'Well? What did the contessa have to say?'

Aldo gave a brief summary of the meeting. Before he finished, Campana was already opening another door. 'Come with me. His Grace will want to hear this, every word of it.'

The duke was working at a table in his private ufficio but he set aside the papers when Campana brought Aldo in. Cosimo had not yet changed out of his hunting clothes, a thick leather jerkin worn over a silk doublet. He had the thin beard of a young man, but the duke possessed a shrewd mind far beyond his twenty years.

'Is it true?' Cosimo asked. 'Are these exiles planning to kill me?'

Aldo was not surprised the duke already knew of this plot. He had spies and informants in most parts of Florentine society, from the grandest palazzo to the lowliest hovel. Cosimo also had guards at each porta, requiring them to provide a summary of all those entering and leaving the city. Exiles returning to Florence after years away would have been noticed, even if they came in through different gates, their arrivals spread over several days.

'Yes, Your Grace,' Aldo replied.

The duke nodded to his segretario. Campana went out a different door, leaving Aldo alone with Cosimo – a sign of trust. 'Tell me everything.'

Aldo repeated what he'd shared with Campana, adding his suspicion that someone had been observing the meeting. 'It could well be this Venetian the contessa mentioned. She said he claimed to be acting on behalf of the Inquisitori di Stato. For her to mention that . . .'

'It suggests this had not been sanctioned by the tribunal,' Cosimo said.

'Yes, that was my conclusion.'

As Aldo finished speaking, Campana returned with a bold-faced man who had close-cropped dark hair and a confident stride. He wore the clothes of a guard, but had a sheathed sword on one hip and a pistol tucked in his belt. Campana introduced Aldo but the newcomer ignored this, instead bowing to Cosimo. 'You sent for me, Your Grace?'

'We now have confirmation that a group of exiles plans to murder me in the coming days. Where and when would you expect them to strike, Ottone?'

Aldo knew the name, but this was his first encounter with the duke's new head of security. Once a leader in the Florentine militia, Alvise Ottone was notorious for his brutality. Aldo knew citizens who had suffered at the hands of Ottone and his men. Cosimo employing Ottone as his protector indicated how significant the threat was. A near insurrection two summers past had proven the need for Cosimo to be better guarded. His personal safety – and that of his heavily pregnant wife – was crucial to the future of Florence.

Ottone carried himself with an implacable severity. Aldo had known such men when riding as a mercenary. Few prisoners survived in their company.

'Well?' Cosimo asked.

'It depends on their intentions,' Ottone said. 'If one exile is willing to give his life to take yours, the attack could come anywhere at any time. Are these men ready to die?'

Cosimo gestured to his segretario. Campana read out a list of names: Marco Talenti, Gian Quercia, Bertoldo Nasi, Pazzo Rovere and Ugo Piacenza. 'There may be others, but we are certain of these five.'

'I knew these men before they fled the city,' Aldo said. 'Several served as magistrates with the Otto. Piacenza, Quercia and Rovere must all be at least fifty. The others – Nasi and Talenti – are younger, but both have seen close to forty summers. All five were merchants or politicians when they lived in Florence, not soldiers.'

'A man need not be a soldier to hold a blade or fire a gun,' Ottone said.

'True, but it makes his hand steadier and his aim truer,' Aldo replied. 'If any of these men was willing to die for their beliefs, they would have done so long before now. The fact that they haven't suggests each values his own life more.'

Cosimo nodded. 'You may be right. And, as you say, Ottone, it is near impossible to defend against a lone attacker who is willing to die trying. So let us assume these men wish me dead but hope to survive the attempt. When and where would that happen?'

Ottone scowled. 'An attack in this palazzo is unlikely, Your Grace, not without at least a dozen men at arms. You are more vulnerable outside the walls of Palazzo Medici but, so long as you have guards around you when riding through the streets, that risk is still small. A skilled marksman with a superior weapon could shoot from a building as you pass . . .'

'But these exiles do not seem to be such men,' Cosimo said.

'Perhaps not,' Ottone replied. 'Let us hope Aldo's information about them is correct.'

His response made it clear where the blame would fall if someone did kill the duke.

Chapter Five

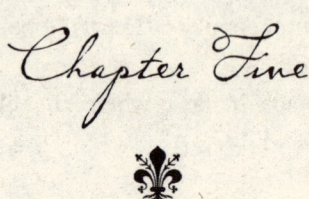

Aldo refused to be threatened by Ottone. If the exiles did murder Cosimo, there would be blame for everyone to share. Protecting the city was the priority, and that meant keeping Cosimo alive. 'To kill Your Grace inside the walls of Florence would carry a greater risk for the exiles,' Aldo said. 'It limits their hope of escape, especially now you are forewarned.'

Cosimo smiled, a wry amusement in his eyes. 'I must remember this conversation the next time I complain how onerous it is being duke. Discussing your own potential murder makes you look kindly on less . . . fatal problems.'

'I must agree with Aldo on one thing,' Ottone said. 'Outside the city is the most likely place for an attack, especially when you go hunting. If you were to forgo these outings for several weeks, it would give us time to hunt down these exiles.'

'It might, but I refuse to be a prisoner in my own residence,' the duke replied. 'I will not cower from attacks, nor will I alter my behaviour. If there is to be an attempt on my life, better that happens outside the city so none of its people are put in danger. It is your task to keep me alive, Ottone. If you are incapable of this, I must employ someone who can.'

Cosimo's head of security bristled. 'There is no need for that, Your Grace.'

'Then the matter's settled.' The duke regarded Campana. 'I

intend to go out on another hunting trip tomorrow. I shall be a lure to draw out these would-be killers. You must find ways to keep me safe from them. Is that clear?'

'Yes, Your Grace.'

'Furthermore, I am employing Aldo to help until this threat is ended. He shall work alongside you, Ottone, to ensure my safety.'

Aldo had no wish to see Cosimo dead, but the prospect of working with Ottone was not inviting. He was the sort of man who met any problem with brute force or violence; more elegant solutions were beyond his thinking. But Cosimo had given no choice in the matter. The duke's decision was final. 'Grazie, Your Grace.'

Ottone seemed too angry to speak, his face flushed crimson.

'Campana, add Aldo to the ducal staff,' Cosimo said.

'As you wish,' the segretario replied, bowing.

'Your Grace,' Ottone finally protested, 'I do not think—'

'Is it your life these exiles are trying to end?' the duke cut in.

Ottone had no answer for that. Instead, he shook his head.

'Then the question is settled,' Cosimo said. 'Now, I have other matters requiring my attention.' He pointed to a rough pile of papers and slim journal bound in red leather at one corner of his table. 'Campana, can you make sure these are locked away?'

'Yes, Your Grace,' the segretario replied. He gathered the documents and ledgers in his arms before leading Ottone and Aldo from the chamber.

Once all three were in Campana's nearby ufficio Ottone returned to arguing against Aldo being involved. 'This man has no experience of the militia. How can he be part of our efforts to protect the duke?'

Campana kept himself busy sorting through Cosimo's papers. 'I'm sure Aldo has other experiences which will be of value in the days to come.'

Ottone swung round, sneering. 'Do you?'

Aldo chose not to detail his time riding with Cosimo's papa, the condottiere Giovanni delle Bande Nere. Nor did he mention his years investigating crime and enforcing laws for the Otto. Ottone's arrogance deserved no such response. 'The duke has chosen to put his trust in me as well as you and your men. That is all you need to know.'

Ottone seethed but did not deny the truth of those words. Instead, he glared at Campana, who gave a regretful shrug. Ottone stalked from the ufficio, slamming the door on his way out. The sound of his stamping feet was gone in moments.

'Well,' Aldo said. 'I've made a new friend there.'

Campana rolled his eyes. 'An unerring ability to antagonize those with power will be the death of you,' the segretario said. 'And you should be especially careful around Ottone. He may be effective as a weapon and blunt of manner, yet the ground is full of men who got in his way.'

'Then I am safer at his side than beneath his boots. When does the duke usually leave the palazzo to go hunting?'

'Early,' Campana said. 'He believes the sport is better before the sun gets too high.' The segretario opened a small casket atop his table and took out an ornate key. He used that to open a large, upright cabinet tucked in a corner of the ufficio.

'Does the duke have any more outside engagements today?' Aldo asked.

Shaking his head, Campana put the duke's papers in a neat stack on the top shelf, while the red journal was placed on the next shelf down. 'I've been having most of his meetings here in the palazzo since word of these exiles reached me.'

'I noticed you have doubled the guards at the front and rear entrances too.'

'It seemed prudent. His Grace would not approve of that if asked, but he pays little attention to such arrangements. Some rulers need protecting from their own . . . boldness.'

One of Cosimo's predecessors had died violently after refusing to heed warnings by Campana and others. For days afterwards the fate of Florence had hung in the balance until another Medici was found to be made ruler. Should these exiles succeed in killing Cosimo, preserving peace in the city would be even harder this time.

Aldo gave a small bow to Campana before leaving the segretario to his paperwork. When Aldo withdrew from the ufficio, Dandolo was waiting outside the door. The courtier scowled at Aldo before hurrying in to speak with Campana, no doubt eager to complain about what had happened earlier. The segretario seemed to spend much of his time soothing the self-important or listening to their woes; a thankless task.

Aldo descended the nearest staircase, intending to leave through the rear entrance. Ottone was waiting below, a foul face suggesting his mood was no better.

'Do you plan to join the hunting party tomorrow?' Ottone demanded.

'Of course. As you noted, the duke is most vulnerable when outside the city.'

'Very well,' Ottone said, 'but I must warn you that such expeditions are dangerous. It is not unknown for arrows and bolts to go astray, or weapons to misfire. Sometimes game birds are not the only things shot beyond the walls of Florence.'

'It sounds as if your men struggle to hit their target or have a tendency to fire too soon when excited,' Aldo replied. 'Or were you talking about yourself? I have heard that is a problem for men of a certain age. Should that be the case, you could consider visiting an apothecary to ask them for a remedy.'

Ottone stepped so close the stench of stale garlic on his breath invaded Aldo's nostrils. 'I'm quite capable of hitting any target I wish.'

'Then the duke's life is in safe hands. Buon giorno.' Aldo stepped around Ottone and strolled from the palazzo, muttered curses following him out.

Campana was right, of course. Antagonizing those with power or too many weapons at their command was a dangerous game – but also an enjoyable one.

The Venetian was not impressed by the exiles. Yes, he had recruited them, persuading and cajoling the five men to leave their comfortable residences in Venice for this vainglorious mission. He knew that none of them had experience as men at arms; most were merchants when they still lived in Florence, before each man fled the city after the Medici took control. In the years since they had grown soft, enjoying the luxuries offered by their new home in the Serenissima. But the Venetian had hoped that returning the exiles to Florence and putting weapons in their hands would turn them into warriors. His hopes had been foolish.

Nonetheless, these five men planned to kill Cosimo tomorrow. And it was just what the Venetian needed.

'I have consulted with my informant inside Palazzo Medici. It seems the duke may know of your return to the city—'

'What? How does he know? When did he learn this? Who told him?' The five were all shouting at once, fear and anger battling for control on their faces.

'This was inevitable,' the Venetian replied in a voice full of soothing reassurance. 'Your names are well known here. How else could we have secured this palazzo as a place to plan and prepare? Yes, you have been away, yet you are still true Florentines. When you strike down the duke, people will rise up to celebrate you and reclaim their republic. That is why you came, is it not? To free your city from the Medici?'

'It's true,' Pazzo Rovere said, nodding his approval. He was the most bellicose of the five, a blowhard with a crooked nose. He claimed it had been broken fighting in the exiles' last campaign to topple Cosimo; the Venetian knew a fall after too much wine was the true cause. Rovere was the most determined of the five, even if his courage came from a bottle. 'The duke might know we are here, but not why. His complacency is our strength!'

The man beside Rovere cracked the knuckles of one hand inside a fist. 'He's right,' Ugo Piacenza said. 'Surprise will be the undoing of this Medici brat.' Piacenza had been a fighter in his youth before taking over the famiglia business as a silk merchant, an unlikely profession for such a man. He still carried himself like someone spoiling for combat, but his belly had long ago surrendered to fat. Piacenza was easily led, following the last strong voice in his ears. He would go where the others went.

'If you can surprise the duke, you will succeed,' the Venetian agreed. He knew any chance of that was lost, thanks to his own intervention. But some sacrifices were necessary.

'If the duke knows we are here, won't Cosimo and his acolytes suspect why we have come?' Bertoldo Nasi asked. He was the youngest of the five, and the most fearful. Nasi was a knot of anxiety, worry evident in his clasping hands. 'Each of us proclaimed we would never return to Florence until the malign leadership of the Medici could be swept away. Coming back to the city, even one by one as we did . . . They must suspect us, yes?'

The Venetian smiled. 'We spoke about this before each of you left the Serenissima. I have been coming to Florence for three months to make everything ready for this moment.'

'You told us you were carrying messages for the Inquisitori di Stato,' Nasi said.

'That was the official reason for my journeys,' the Venetian replied. 'But I used those trips here to prepare the way for you. These last few days I have been watching Palazzo Medici on your behalf, and receiving reports from my informant inside it. The duke goes out hunting most mornings. If he knew the five of you intended to kill him, the man would be a fool to ride beyond the city walls in search of sport – yet he persists. What does this tell you?'

'That the so-called duke has no idea what we are planning for him,' Gian Quercia replied, a satisfied smirk obvious despite a fulsome beard. 'Or he is a greater fool than we think!' Beside him Marco Talenti nodded. The last exile rarely spoke, letting his best friend Quercia talk for him. That influence should be enough.

'Then it is agreed,' the Venetian said. 'You will strike when the duke goes hunting in the morning, before the significance of your return to Florence becomes apparent.'

Nasi noticed what the others had not. 'We will strike? Meaning you are not going to stand with us when the time comes?'

'Regrettably, I cannot,' the Venetian said. 'Far better that the duke is brought down by true Florentines, which all of you are. Nobody can doubt why you are doing this, nor can anyone question your loyalty to this city. If an outsider like myself was among you, it would suggest that Venice is responsible for the downfall of this Medici pretender. Rather than the people of Florence striking back against their own oppressor, Cosimo's supporters could claim your bold act was a declaration of war by one city against another.'

'That makes sense,' Rovere agreed, before emptying his cup of wine. 'To reclaim our city, only true Florentines can hold the weapon that kills Cosimo.'

'Where will you be when we are confronting the duke?' Nasi asked.

'I shall remain here in the palazzo,' the Venetian replied, 'waiting to celebrate your triumph.' It was a lie, of course, but no trace of that reached his face. As a true Venetian he was used to wearing masks. 'Gentlemen, let us drink to what the morning will bring. Fill your cups and raise your voices.' The five did as he bid. 'Here's to the end of Medici tyranny,' the Venetian said, 'and to a new dawn for all who live here. For Florence!'

'For Florence!' the exiles shouted and drained their cups.

The light was fading as Aldo waited for the last patient to leave Doctor Orvieto's home on via dei Giudei. Saul was a gentle, caring man who had devoted his life to looking after others. That was the reason Saul always gave when asked why he never married, and there was some truth in his reply. But another truth was hidden behind that: Saul preferred the company of a man in his bed, a choice forbidden by his faith and the law.

Aldo's and Saul's nights together had been infrequent since their first meeting three years ago. Not long after that events drove them apart. No sooner had they found a way back to one another than Aldo went to the Tuscan countryside for a year on behalf of the Otto. When finally he returned, Aldo spent seventeen months on night patrols, which made seeing Saul all but impossible as they could only meet in private after dark.

Those long separations were one of the reasons Aldo left the Otto. He and Saul had spent more nights together in the past three months than in the previous three years. Yet they still had to be careful, especially now Aldo could no longer claim to be visiting on court business. A few knew and were happy to see Saul happy; others were willing to ignore such matters as he was a good doctor. But most would never approve or understand.

The last patient emerged from the doorway, accompanied by Saul's student Rebecca Levi. She had been studying at his side for two years, observing the remedies and treatments, getting to know his patients and their needs. A female physician was uncommon, but not unknown. The Jewish commune in Florence was small, perhaps a hundred all told. They needed a doctor among them, and Saul was approaching fifty, so training a replacement was sensible. And Rebecca had displayed a talent for it. Not just in learning the medicines but in how she treated people, especially other women. Saul was sympathetic, but he could never share their experiences as Rebecca did. Indeed, it was Rebecca who first alerted Aldo to men from the Office of Decency extorting coin from bordelli. Women who worked in such places came to Rebecca for help, seeking assistance no male physician could or would offer them.

Once the patient had gone, Rebecca smiled at Aldo. 'You can come in now.'

He followed her inside and along the hallway to the back of the building, where Saul treated those in need. The physician was scrubbing his hands in a bowl of water. 'I hear you've been busy,' Saul said. 'One of the women who comes to see Rebecca couldn't wait to tell us about the fight at Signorina Nardi's.'

Aldo sank into a simple chair by the long wooden table as Rebecca brought two steaming bowls of stew in from the kitchen. 'The women are all grateful for what you did,' she said. 'They sent two bottles of good wine as thanks.'

'Very kind of them, but I will not be drinking tonight.'

Saul stopped drying his hands. 'Not drinking? Are you unwell?'

Aldo laughed, shaking his head. He and Saul often ate an evening meal together, Rebecca staying with them to prevent neighbours gossiping. It had become common to share a bottle of wine and discuss the day, a habit as comfortable as well-worn boot. 'No, but I was out much of the night and got called from my bed this morning before curfew ended. I must be up before dawn again tomorrow, and will need a clear head.'

Saul sat next to him, reaching for one of the bottles Rebecca had brought in. 'You don't mind if we . . . ?'

'No, of course not.' Aldo described his day, the apparent threat from exiles to murder Cosimo and the duke's insistence on acting as a lure for his would-be killers.

'Do you think these exiles could succeed?' Rebecca asked.

'I knew them a little before they left Florence, and none had experience of war or battle. I doubt years of comfortable living in Venice will have transformed them into killers. Taking a life is not easy, especially the first time.'

'Then they are not a threat,' Saul said between sips of wine.

Aldo pushed a spoon round inside his bowl of stew. 'They shouldn't be. If anything, the duke is in more danger from Ottone and his men being too eager to prove themselves. Yet a single lucky shot is still enough to kill.'

Saul studied him. 'Something else is bothering you, Cesare.'

'Am I that obvious?'

'Know a person long enough, you recognize their moods.'

Aldo pushed the food aside. 'All of this – the contessa giving me a warning, the way the exiles returned to Florence – is too straightforward. Another aim is behind all of it.'

'You mentioned a Venetian,' Rebecca said.

'Someone is pushing the exiles into action, and has probably given them weapons and information about where best to attack the duke. But why do this now? It is more than three years since Cosimo was chosen to lead the city.'

'Once he has an heir, it will be that much harder to usurp the Medici,' Saul observed.

'Perhaps you're right,' Aldo agreed. Yet he wasn't convinced. Something else was lurking in the shadows.

But what was it?

Chapter Six

Friday, February 9th 1539

Aldo rose before dawn, having come back to Robustelli's bordello after eating with Saul and Rebecca. Better to get out of his own bed at this hour instead of waking Saul. Aldo emptied his bladder and washed, pulling on a clean tunic, hose and his best boots. Rubbing a hand across his jaw proved the need for a shave, but doing so in inky darkness was asking for cuts and pain. The task ahead was liable to be bloody and brutal; greying bristles could wait.

He crept down the bordello stairs, avoiding those that creaked loudest, and slipped out onto Piazza della Passera. The small square was empty, the sky overhead the colours of an angry bruise as distant bells announced the end of curfew. Aldo hurried north-east to Ponte Vecchio, boots slipping on the frosty stones of the bridge, his breath fogging the air. At least the cold morning suppressed the usual ripe aromas from the butcher shops and fish stalls.

By the time Aldo was in sight of the ducal residence, a handful of guards were already on horses outside the main entrance. He quickened his stride, determined to be there when the duke emerged. Getting closer, Aldo could see Ottone with five guards, while two stable hands were waiting with Cosimo's horse. Two servants stood to one side, one carrying a crossbow and bolts, the other a musket and bag. The surrounding street was almost empty, aside from a large-nosed merchant with shoulder-length brown hair who was arguing with his servant in a nearby doorway. Some men were never satisfied with their lot in life, despite having all the luxuries and help they would ever need.

The duke strode from Palazzo Medici as Aldo reached the gathering. Cosimo climbed atop his mount with ease, nodding to Ottone and the guards before noticing Aldo standing to one side. 'No horse?' the duke asked. Aldo shook his head.

'He can run behind us,' Ottone said. 'With the servants.'

Aldo kept the anger from his face, refusing to give Ottone the satisfaction of seeing that. The true sign of a bully was how much pleasure they took from meaningless victories. Denying Ottone that pleasure was more effective than protesting or pouting.

'Very well,' Cosimo announced. 'Today we will be going out through Porta Romana.' The duke urged his horse forwards and it trotted south, towards the Duomo. Ottone brought his mount alongside Cosimo, with another guard on the other side. Two men rode ahead of the duke, the other two behind. The servants ran after them, scurrying to keep pace.

Aldo shook his head. 'Palle,' he muttered before hurrying to catch up.

The Venetian watched Aldo running after the duke and his guards, all of them on horseback. They were riding south towards the Arno. Once the hunting party had crossed the river it would continue on to Porta Romana, the most southerly gate. That was where travellers departed the city on their way to Rome. Some went by way of Siena, others through Perugia. But Cosimo would venture no more than a mile or two beyond the outer wall of

Florence, if the Venetian's informant was correct. So far, there had been no reason for doubt.

Aldo had looked at the Venetian twice in his brief time outside Palazzo Medici; once when he was hurrying to join the hunting party, and again as the duke rode away. Both times the Venetian nodded to Aldo, acknowledging his gaze. To look aside or avoid an enquiring stare was an admission of guilt, inviting suspicion. Better to hold that gaze, show there was nothing to fear and nothing of interest. The Venetian was wearing the guise of an impatient merchant, berating their servant for some slight or another. It was enough to escape the notice of most men. The duke's head of security had paid the Venetian no heed, nor had the guards. Yet Aldo had shown a sharp eye, and a keener mind. That demonstrated why the contessa held this man in such regard. It was as well that Aldo would be occupied with the duke's protection. He might die when the exiles attacked, or he might help to save Cosimo. Whatever occurred, Aldo and the others would be busy for the morning, if not longer.

Everything was going as planned, yet the Venetian still had a squirm of fear in his belly. This stratagemma with the exiles, it was far beyond the simple task Signor Bragadin had sent him to undertake in Florence. Should things go awry, the consequences could be ruinous, even fatal. But if it succeeded . . . The Venetian smiled. His true worth would be recognized at last. Of that he was certain.

Aldo was gasping as Cosimo's hunting party crossed the Arno. By the time the duke and his guards approached Porta Romana, it seemed someone had lit a fire inside Aldo's chest, while his breathing was reduced to a dry rasp of desperation. Thankfully there was a cart blocking the southern gate, forcing Cosimo and his protectors to stop. Aldo used the pause to get his wind back, but wondered why no progress was being made.

Knowing the cart might be a ploy to enable an ambush, Aldo pushed between the horses to see who or what was causing the problem. The answer was innocent: a farmer arguing with guards who refused to let him further into the city without proof of his name or residence.

'What is it?' Cosimo called out.

'A simple dispute,' Aldo replied. 'Let me resolve this for you.'

'Make it swift,' Ottone said. 'His Grace has no wish to be kept waiting.'

Aldo took the head guard at the gate aside for a few words, pointing at the duke atop his horse. Within moments the guards were bustling the farmer back onto his cart and out of the way, allowing the hunting party to pass through the gate.

Beyond Porta Romana was a dirt road heading south. To the west was open land, unpromising for anyone eager to hunt. But to the east a hill rose up, its side thick with trees and bushes. Those would provide plenty of shelter for game, birds – and also for exiles intent on murdering the duke.

'Where to today, Your Grace?' Ottone asked.

'Up the hillside,' Cosimo replied, gesturing at the wooded slope.

'Of course. Let your guards go first, to be certain it is safe.'

'If your men go blundering in, they'll scare off anything worth hunting.'

Aldo stepped forwards. 'I must agree with Ottone, Your Grace. It may cost you some sport, but better that than being an easy target.'

Cosimo's face darkened. 'No. You are charged with keeping me safe, all of you. Do your jobs and there should be no danger. Is that clear?' Aldo nodded and Ottone did the same, but the duke was giving them no other choice.

'Perhaps I could go first?' Aldo suggested. 'One man moving quietly is less likely to frighten game or birds than two bold warriors with weapons.'

Cosimo chewed on that a moment before nodding. 'But be quick as well as quiet.'

Leaving the hunting party behind, Aldo strode towards the wooded hillside. If exiles lurking amid the trees had any sense, they would not kill him. Far better to wait until Cosimo was making his way up the slope before launching an attack, using the trees and bushes as cover until the last moment. Nonetheless, Aldo crouched to retrieve the trusty stiletto from the sheath inside his left boot. Only a fool faced an enemy with their weapon tucked away.

Clutching the stiletto, Aldo stepped into the trees.

Coltello rose early – early for her, at least. Getting out of bed before most Florentines were eating their midday meal was unwelcome for any person of wit. But some days had peculiar demands and this was such a day. Adding a silk shawl atop her nightgown, she emerged from her bedchamber calling for Pozzo. The maggiordomo appeared in moments.

'Contessa? Forgive me, I had not expected—'

'Yes, yes,' she said, dismissing his apologies. 'I am leaving for Venice.'

'Of course. And when do you wish to depart?'

'Within the hour, if not sooner.'

'Within—' Pozzo stopped himself. 'As you wish. I will let the other servants know, and send a message to the stables that your carriage be made ready at once.'

Coltello nodded. She expected no less.

'May I ask the intended length of this visit? It would help your maids to know how much they should pack, and which gowns you might require.'

'The journey will no doubt take several dreary days,' she sighed, 'though I will not need to be at my most resplendent for that. As for how long I might remain in Venice . . . I do not know. It will depend upon matters over which even I have limited control.'

'I understand,' Pozzo replied.

'Let us say seven days in Venice and then several days for the return trip.' Coltello forced a smile. Bearing in mind what she knew, the worst should also be prepared for. 'If all is not well, then I shall have greater causes for concern than the paucity of my wardrobe. Should an extended stay there be required, I can always have my gowns cleaned and made ready to wear again, though that would be less acceptable.'

'Indeed. And how many maids do you wish to accompany you?'

It was an apt question. To look her best she required the assistance of several servants, but the nature of this journey meant taking that many was impractical. 'Agnese will have to do. The others shall remain here. They can help prepare the palazzo and my wardrobe for the new season. The worst of winter is behind us. Soon we shall be entertaining again.'

'Very good, Contessa.'

'You will be coming with me, Pozzo.'

That seemed to surprise him more than finding her up. 'I will?'

'Yes. I need those I can trust close to me in the coming days. Your counterpart in Venice is quite effective in his own way, but . . .' The count had retained his palazzo in the Serenissima, intending to see out his last days by the lagoon. Alas, a fatal hunting accident near Florence proved the death of him and such plans. The contessa had been avoiding the question of what to do about the palazzo in Venice. It needed a smaller staff when she was not in residence, but was still a significant burden. The maggiordomo there was Amaro, an astringent servant whose loyalties were only to the late count.

'Of course,' Pozzo agreed. Like her, he had no time for Amaro, though that might have been as much a matter of professional rivalry. Pozzo was a jealous man.

She stared at the maggiordomo. 'Well? Get to it!'

He bowed once more before hurrying away. The sudden haste and capriciousness of her decision to depart would do him good. He was an excellent servant, but sometimes it was as if Pozzo believed himself the true master of this particular palazzo. 'Oh, and Pozzo?'

He stopped to face her again. 'Yes, Contessa?'

'Have Agnese come and attend me at once.' She held open her shawl, revealing the flimsy nightgown underneath. 'After all, I can hardly travel to Venice looking like this.'

'No, Contessa,' he agreed, his gaze fixed on her face.

She laughed as Pozzo hurried off. Teasing him was cruel, yet it offered amusement and a momentary diversione from what was happening elsewhere.

Returning to her bedchamber, the contessa strolled to the shutters and pulled them open. Outside, the city was alive with noise, an aroma of baking bread drifting on the crisp air. People passed on the street below, unaware that all of Florence was at risk. If the exiles succeeded in killing Cosimo, it would cause great uncertainty for the rich and the poor, merchants and workers alike. Ending the duke's life could well end Medici rule over the city. Whoever emerged as leader might be a far more dangerous threat to her position.

The involvement of the Venetian was vexing, particularly the high-handed way he had involved her. Yet his closeness to the Inquisitori di Stato had left her with little choice in that, while the letter he brought from Signor Bragadin gave her no choice about where she must go: back to Venice, where the Inquisitori di Stato had questions she must answer.

Knowing what was planned, having to leave Florence was the best path at this moment. Whatever happened in the next few hours, it would certainly involve somebody's blood being spilled. But what awaited her in Venice might be even more dangerous . . .

Aldo had edged his way up the hillside, squinting to see in the dimmer light beneath trees, stopping and listening several times for noises not caused by animals or birds. The wooded hill was recovering from winter, branches that lost their leaves in the coldest months coming back to life. Breezes made them shift and creak.

Twice he caught sight of movement among the branches and bushes – but in neither case was it an exile intent on murder. The first was a young deer stretching up to eat early growth on a low-hanging branch. It stared at Aldo a moment before bounding away. The second movement was a pair of game birds throwing themselves into the air, eager to escape. Good. The fewer creatures there were on the hillside, the less likely that Ottone or one of his men had cause to open fire with their weapons.

Duke Cosimo was as much at risk from his protectors as the exiles if an attack came.

Eventually Aldo reached the top of the hill, a clearing in the trees giving an unbroken view back down to the clearing in front of Porta Romana, the city's wall and then the majesty of Florence beyond it. Smoke from chimneys billowed above terracotta roofs, forming a grey haze in the air, but that could not conceal the beauty of this place. At its heart stood the Duomo, that magnificent cupola a symbol of achievement and aspiration, its construction an apparent impossibility yet solid and reassuring. While that stood, the heart of Florence would always remain, no matter who ruled over its people.

Aldo moved to one side, peering down between the treetops. Yes, he could just see the duke and hunting party, waiting in front of the wooded hill. Their horses were shuffling around, no doubt restless at doing nothing. Behind the hunting party a cart was emerging from Porta Romana, two men leading its horse. Loose hay was piled atop the cart, far more than was sensible. A strong gust of wind would send it flying.

That made no sense to Aldo. Why would anyone be bringing loose hay out of the city, let alone this early? And there was no need for two men—

Palle!

Aldo hurled himself down the hillside, running and shouting at those below.

'That cart! The exiles are with that cart!'

The distant crack of a shot echoed in the air.

The last thing Aldo saw before trees blocked his view was the duke falling.

Chapter Seven

Aldo spat curses while running down the hill. He could hear more shots below: pistols and arquebuses firing, the dull clash of blades accompanied by roars of anger and cries of pain. Through the trees he caught glimpses of the battle below: men reloading their weapons, others attacking foes. One guard still on his horse was charging forwards, trampling a man beneath the hooves. Where was Cosimo? Aldo saw a body face-down on the ground, but couldn't tell if that was the duke. Ottone stood over the prone figure, a pistol in one hand, a blade in the other. Then the trees were too dense to—

Someone was coming up the hill towards Aldo.

Not one of the guards.

An exile.

The man seemed terrified, his eyes wide, blood on both hands and smeared across one cheek. He had a pistol in his grasp but was making no effort to reload or aim it. His attention was split between scrambling up the steep slope and glancing back to see if anyone was following. The man's boots slipped on dew-damp grass and he fell to one knee, gasping for breath, mouth hanging open, sweat soaking his tunic as he got back up.

Aldo stepped behind a tree, letting the exile get closer but staying out of sight in case that pistol was ready to fire. He did not recognize the man's blotchy face, meaning the exile was either

Talenti or Nasi; the other three Aldo knew from past meetings. The exile was getting nearer, his breath a ragged wheeze of panic and fear. He staggered level with Aldo, eyes scouring his surroundings for—

'Buon giorno,' Aldo said, startling the exile.

The man twisted around . . .

. . . and Aldo punched him in the face.

The exile staggered back, arms flailing as he struggled to stay upright.

Aldo hit him again, this time hard in the throat.

The exile dropped his pistol, choking and gurgling.

His legs failed and he went tumbling back down the hill.

Picking up the pistol, Aldo found it loaded and ready. The barrel held no heat, nor any whiff of gunpowder. Somehow the exile had come through the confronto below without being hurt – it must be another man's blood on his face and hands – and never having opened fire. Instead, he sought escape by clambering up the hill.

The exile's rapid descent stopped when his torso slammed into a tree, arms and legs wrapping around the trunk. The sounds of battle below were dying, but Aldo couldn't see who – if anyone – had prevailed. Picking his steps carefully, he went down to the fallen man, pistol ready. As Aldo got closer the exile rolled back from the tree, one arm nursing his torso, the other clasping at his throat.

'Up,' Aldo said, gesturing with the pistol.

The exile shook his head.

'Get up,' Aldo warned, 'or die where you are.' He had no intention of shooting, but it was an effective threat. The exile dragged himself halfway upright before collapsing back against the tree. He coughed twice, still struggling to speak.

'Name,' Aldo demanded, aiming the pistol at him.

The exile frowned, bewildered.

'What's your name?'

'Bertoldo Nasi,' he rasped in reply.

'Signor Nasi,' Aldo said, 'I want you to listen.'

'Listen? To what?'

Aldo held a finger to his lips. The last sounds of the *confronto* had fallen silent. 'Hear that? All the other exiles are dead or dying. You're the last one.'

'You can't know that,' Nasi said.

'Well, if your fellow conspirators had succeeded, we would hear them celebrating, congratulating each other. Triumphant men bellow out their victories; dead men don't.'

The exile shook his head but seemed less certain Aldo was wrong.

'You have no weapon, no escape. If you live long enough to stand trial for today's incident, the sentence will almost certainly be death. It's more likely you will be killed in a small, dank cell at the Podestà, a priest giving the last rites as someone throttles the life from you. There'll be no official record of this, no history written that mentions you or the others. Nobody will recall you, Talenti, Piacenza, Rovere or Quercia, nor what you tried to do.'

Confusion furrowed Nasi's brow. 'You knew our names?'

'Of course.'

'And what we were going to do?'

Aldo nodded.

'But . . . why did you let it happen?'

'That wasn't my decision. The duke knows it is sometimes wiser to let an enemy show themselves so their threat can be met and vanquished. Far easier to fight a foe who stands before you than to find one that skulks in the shadows. The duke made himself a target to draw you out – and it worked.'

Nasi's head dropped to his chest. 'I told them it was madness.'

'Who convinced you to do this?' Aldo asked. 'And why now?'

'Does it matter?'

'There could still be a way out of this for you.'

That got the exile's attention. 'How?'

'Answer my questions and I'll ask the duke to show clemency. Tell me what I need to know and Cosimo might be convinced simply to banish you for life.'

Nasi hesitated. '*Might be* isn't much of a promise.'

'After today, it's the only hope you've got.' Aldo crouched down in the grass to meet the exile's gaze at his level. 'Who convinced you to do this? And why now?'

There was a long silence before Nasi replied. 'It was a Venetian, someone close to the Inquisitori di Stato. He told us the duke remained vulnerable until there was a Medici heir. This was our last chance to restore the city to a republic.'

This confirmed Aldo's suspicions, but he needed more. 'And what is the name of this Venetian? Who was it that brought you here, gave you weapons, got you ready to kill?'

'I was never going to kill,' Nasi protested. 'I never even fired my pistol!'

'That's the only reason you're alive,' Aldo said. 'Now, tell me this Venetian's name.'

The Venetian waited near the main entrance of Palazzo Medici. His informant had agreed to usher him inside soon after the duke left. That was some time past, yet the informant had not appeared. This was what came of needing help from those lacking courage or clarity of mind.

That the Venetian's informant was also his cousin . . . well, there was a reason why this fool resided in Florence, rather than the Serenissima. He was from the junior branch of the famiglia, one that had brought disgrace upon itself. The Venetian's cousin had fled to Florence in search of redemption, knowing he could probably never achieve any position of significance in Venice. That he had attained a minor post within the Medici ducal residence made the cousin useful, but also showed how low standards were in Florence.

Finally, the informant emerged, murmuring to the guards before beckoning the Venetian inside. 'What took you so long?' the Venetian demanded in a whisper while keeping his face bland and pleasant.

'The segretario had me making copies of letters for the duke,' the informant replied. 'Campana insists on duplicates of all correspondence as a safety measure.' He nodded and smiled to a passing courtier. 'We must not linger,' the informant said once the courtier was out of hearing. 'I told the segretario he was needed at Palazzo della Signoria, but Campana will soon discover this was a lie.'

'A few moments are all I need,' the Venetian insisted.

The informant led him up a wide stone staircase to the middle level, turning left towards the rear of the palazzo. The informant produced a small key to unlock an ufficio door. The Venetian heard footsteps and a woman came round the corner, clad in the grand clothes of a Spanish noblewoman. He had been told how Eleonora de Toledo looked. This woman matched the duke's wife in appearance and was heavy with child.

The Venetian had a blade concealed inside his right sleeve. A crossbow was his weapon of choice, one with which he was quite adept, surpassing the skills of his three older brothers. But a blade was far more useful in close quarters. The Venetian reached into his sleeve as Eleonora came closer, smiling at her. He could cut the Medici bride down before she had time to cry out, and the duke's heir would die with her . . .

Aldo marched Nasi down the hillside, keeping the pistol in the exile's back to stop him fleeing. When they emerged from the trees Aldo's prediction proved correct: three of Nasi's fellow conspirators were dead, their bloody bodies lying in the dirt. But the confronto had also claimed two guards and several horses had bolted. The two remaining mounts were being tended by Cosimo's servants. An acrid smell hung in the air: gunpowder.

The exile who had survived the confronto was bleeding heavily from the belly. His face was ashen, but Aldo still knew him: Pazzo Rovere. He would not survive the day, judging by his wounds. Aldo was more concerned to see Cosimo on the ground, Ottone and his surviving men gathered around the duke. There was blood on the duke's head, and no movement from him. Palle, had the exiles succeeded?

'Where were you?' Ottone demanded as Aldo approached with Nasi.

'The duke, is he . . . ?'

Cosimo stirred, his eyes opening. 'Not dead,' he said. 'Not yet.' Ottone helped the duke to his feet. 'Horse threw me when the first shot went past,' Cosimo went on. He put a hand to the back of his head, wincing at the blood he found. 'Must have hit a rock when I fell.' The duke looked around. 'Which of my men did they kill?'

'Moretti and Giordano,' Ottone replied.

Cosimo glared at Aldo's prisoner. 'Who's this?'

'Bertoldo Nasi,' Aldo replied. 'He fled up the hill.'

The duke moved closer, fixing his gaze on Nasi. 'Who sent you?'

The prisoner did not reply. Fear rather than defiance had probably taken Nasi's tongue, but the result was the same. 'He claimed it was a Venetian,' Aldo volunteered. 'Someone close to the Inquisitori di Stato.'

'Does this Venetian have a name?' Cosimo asked.

'Nasi refused to say it.'

The duke scowled. 'Very well. Ottone, take the surviving exiles to the Podestà. Use whatever means are necessary to make them talk.'

'Yes, Your Grace,' Ottone replied.

'You mean torture,' Rovere snarled from nearby. 'You'll torture us to get answers.' He struggled to his feet, one hand clutched to the bloody mess of his belly. Rovere lurched towards Cosimo, red flecking his teeth as he snarled accusations. 'I'd expect nothing more from a Medici—'

A single shot fired by Ottone killed the exile, a hole appearing in his forehead like a third, unblinking eye. Ottone spat at Rovere's corpse. 'No torture for you.'

'Oh God,' Nasi whispered, a wet stain appearing on his hose. The smell of fresh, warm piss blossomed from him.

'Last chance to talk,' Aldo said.

Cosimo glared at Nasi. 'Well?'

'It's true, we had help,' Nasi whimpered. 'The Venetian got our blood up.'

'Is he close to the Inquisitori di Stato?' the duke asked.

'So he said, but we were acting for the people of Florence, not for Venice.'

'Obviously,' Ottone sneered. 'If Venice wanted His Grace dead, it would use trained killers, not five fools.'

'The Venetian sent you to die,' Cosimo said. 'Why?'

'I don't understand,' Nasi mumbled, confusion troubling his brow.

'His Grace believes you were a distraction,' Aldo replied, 'a stratagemma intended to demand his attention while another plan was enacted.'

'Exactly,' Cosimo agreed. 'Who or what is the Venetian's true target?'

'I don't know,' Nasi said, shaking his head.

Ottone thrust a blade against the prisoner's neck. 'Tell us!'

'I don't know!' Tears brimmed in Nasi's eyes.

'Then tell us this Venetian's name,' Cosimo said.

'Dandolo. His name is Armando Dandolo.'

Aldo recalled his clash with the courtier Federico Dandolo. Someone working inside Palazzo Medici with the same famiglia name as this Venetian – that couldn't be happenstance.

The duke had a similar conclusion, judging by worry in his face. 'Eleonora . . .'

Aldo gestured at the two servants. 'Bring the horses here. Now!'

Ottone was still holding his blade to Nasi's neck. 'What is it?'

The duke clambered atop a horse while a servant helped Aldo onto another. 'This was all a ruse,' Cosimo snarled. 'The true attack was not here – it's at my residence!'

'But how—?'

'The Venetian has a man inside Palazzo Medici,' Aldo said. Cosimo was already riding fast towards the city gate. Aldo urged his horse after the duke. He heard a cry behind him and glanced back. Nasi was crumpling to the dirt, hands clutching at his face, blood seeping between his fingers. Ottone stood over the exile, his blade red.

Aldo willed his horse to keep up with the racing Cosimo.

If they didn't reach Palazzo Medici in time . . .

More blood would be shed today.

* * *

Armando Dandolo rode north, away from Florence. Alongside him on a second horse was his cousin Federico. Dandolo had sought his cousin out on a previous visit to Florence, and found a willing ally. Federico was a man of frustrated self-importance who believed himself overlooked and undervalued. Would he be willing to help a distant member of his famiglia? The promise of plentiful coin and a new position within the Doge's palazzo in Venice had proven too tempting to resist. Both were lies, of course, but Federico wanted to believe them.

Securing an informant in Palazzo Medici was essential for Dandolo's stratagemma. For months he had been befriending Florentine exiles in Venice. Most of their leading figures perished in a foolhardy attempt to reclaim Florence in 1537, but that had been to Dandolo's advantage. It meant those who remained were less forceful and far more easily led. They were embittered, fearing any chance to rebuild Florence as a republic was gone. Dandolo offered them glory, and none of the five questioned it out loud. He knew some carried doubts – Nasi, in particular, had required additional reassurance – but good wine and rich promises were enough to overcome their hesitation. The chance to overthrow the Medici was too tempting.

Once Dandolo was confident of having the exiles' trust, he offered to be a messenger for the Inquisitori di Stato, taking coded letters to and from their spymasters in Florence and Bologna. That gave him access to reports from those cities, which was how he had learned of Federico's position within Palazzo Medici. That put more parts in place for the stratagemma.

The final piece was supplied by Dandolo's master, Signor Bragadin. He sent Dandolo to Florence with an urgent letter for Contessa Coltello, summoning her back to Venice. Bragadin had idly suggested Dandolo look into ways of retrieving a stolen book of Venetian ciphers which was believed to be in the possession of Duke Cosimo, but dealing with Coltello was the principal task. It was all the opportunity Dandolo had needed.

He rode on, urging his horse to go faster. The exiles had served their purpose in drawing out the duke, making Cosimo believe he was outwitting them by letting himself be attacked. Had one of the five killed the Medici leader? It was unlikely. If they had, the Florentines would be too busy deciding who should succeed Cosimo or battling republican forces within their city to worry about where this insurrection had its origins. Far more probable was the exiles' failure, each of them dying in the attempt or being executed for their involvement afterwards. One might name the Venetian who had helped them, but by then . . .

It would be too late.

It already was.

Dandolo's plan had succeeded. His master might object to the methods used, but even the scowling Bragadin could not deny the results or their value to Venice.

'You're bleeding,' Federico shouted from atop his horse.

'What?' Dandolo called back.

'You are bleeding,' Federico repeated, pointing at Dandolo's right hand. Blood was soaking through the hasty binding wrapped round it after his blade had slipped inside Palazzo Medici. But that was a small wound, one which should heal soon enough.

The blow he had struck against Cosimo de' Medici?

That would hurt for far longer.

Chapter Eight

Aldo struggled to keep pace with Cosimo as they raced through the city. The duke rode most days, but it was a far less frequent event for Aldo. Twice he was almost jolted from his mount; once when they charged up and over Ponte Vecchio, citizens throwing themselves aside to avoid being ridden down, and again when rounding the Duomo as exhaustion was stealing the strength from Aldo's thighs. He clung on, knowing how close they were to Palazzo Medici, but feared what they would find there.

The duke's segretario Campana stood by the entrance as they approached, his face grave. 'Where is Eleonora?' Cosimo shouted as his horse clattered to a stop. 'Is she . . . ?'

'Your wife is unhurt,' Campana said as the duke dismounted. 'Shaken, but unhurt. She is resting now.'

'What about Dandolo?' Aldo asked as he slid from his horse. 'Federico Dandolo, is he still here?'

'No,' Campana replied. 'He left with the other man, the Venetian.'

'What happened?' Cosimo demanded.

'Better to have this conversation in your residence,' Aldo suggested, 'not out here.'

The duke looked around at the people who had stopped to watch his sudden arrival. 'Very well, but I want a full report at once.'

'Of course,' Campana said.

Aldo watched them go inside. Should he follow? The duke had employed him to stop the exiles' attack or provide protection if it happened. That was over now. His job was done.

A stable hand dashed from the palazzo to take care of the horses. 'Are you Cesare Aldo? If so, the duke is calling for you.' He pointed inside.

Not done yet, it seemed.

Willing his legs to stop trembling, Aldo hurried into Palazzo Medici. Cosimo and Campana were in the courtyard, the duke scowling while his segretario talked. 'The Venetian was brought into the palazzo by one of your courtiers, Federico Dandolo—'

'Yes, yes,' Cosimo snapped. 'I know that already. The Venetian's name is Armando Dandolo. He and the courtier must be related.'

'We knew Federico Dandolo had famiglia in Venice,' Campana said, 'but he was a minor functionary who posed no obvious threat to Your Grace.'

'Where were you while the Venetian was here?' Aldo asked.

'At Palazzo della Signoria,' Campana said. 'Dandolo – our Dandolo – had brought me a message stating I was urgently required there. By the time I discovered it was a ruse . . .'

'What did these two men do in your ufficio?' Cosimo demanded.

'It's easier to show you.' Campana led them upstairs and along the corridor, pausing outside the door to his ufficio. 'This was where Eleonora met them. The Venetian approached her but was called in here by the other Dandolo.'

'Did they threaten Eleonora, or harm her in any way?' the duke demanded.

'No, but she glimpsed a blade half hidden in the Venetian's sleeve.'

Cosimo roared a curse that echoed around the walls. Aldo had never seen the duke this angry. Neither Dandolo would live long if captured, but the pain inflicted on them before they died was likely to be excruciating. When the duke had composed himself, Campana pushed open the ufficio door and Cosimo stalked inside. Aldo followed, exchanging a look with the fearful segretario. Who else might suffer the duke's wrath?

Campana's ufficio was usually clean and orderly, a small casket atop the table often the sole possession. Now the ufficio looked like a tempest had blown through it.

The small casket had been smashed open, scattering ink, quills and other items. The table was pushed aside, and one of the chairs toppled. But it was the cabinet in the corner that had suffered most. The doors were hanging open, and many of the neatly stacked papers Aldo had seen on its top shelf the previous day were now strewn across the floor. All the ledgers were missing from the middle section, and the bottom shelf was equally empty.

'What's missing from inside this cabinet?' the duke asked.

'I am still trying to determine that,' Campana replied. 'Many of your official papers are gone, along with the ledgers and other items you entrusted to me for safekeeping.'

That got Cosimo's attention. 'The book of ciphers?'

'Yes. I suspect that is what the intruder came to steal.'

Aldo hesitated before speaking, but the duke had demanded his presence, so it made sense to ask. 'This book of ciphers, was it Venetian?'

Campana nodded. 'One of our sources close to the Inquisitori di Stato obtained the book some months ago, making it possible to read intercepted letters from the tribunal.'

'A valuable acquisition,' Aldo said.

'Our man in Venice was murdered because of it,' Cosimo revealed.

'That explains why Armando Dandolo went to such lengths to

get it back,' Aldo observed. 'Goading and persuading the exiles into attacking you, using them as a diversione so his relative could smuggle him inside your residence . . . a high-risk stratagemma.'

'But an effective one,' the duke sighed.

'I fear it is worse than that, Your Grace,' Campana said. 'I believe the thieves may also have taken your private journal . . .' He hesitated, eyes shifting from Cosimo to Aldo.

'To recover these items,' the duke said, 'Aldo needs to know what he seeks.'

'Very well.' Campana took a deep breath before continuing. 'His Grace writes his most private thoughts and plans in one particular book. Plain red binding, a small black C stamped on the top-left corner of the cover. In this he writes about our enemies and allies, their strengths and weaknesses, potential strategia for dealing with them.'

This explained why the segretario was so fearful. The loss of the cipher book was troublesome, while Cosimo's personal papers being stolen away by another city-state was even more unfortunate. But the theft of this journal could be far more important.

'How private were these writings?' Aldo asked.

Cosimo glowered. 'Very.'

'If you could give me an example . . .'

Campana cleared his throat. 'Most recently His Grace was musing about the Holy Roman Emperor, and what it would take to escape his hold over Florence. There may also have been some unflattering comments about His Holiness, the Pope . . .'

'I see.'

'His Grace uses a cipher of his own devising in this journal,' Campana added, 'to prevent someone chancing on it being easily able to read its contents. But those experienced in decrypting codes would soon unlock its secrets.'

Aldo nodded. If such a book reached the Inquisitori di Stato or the Council of Ten, they could use it to humiliate the duke, even exert influence over his decisions, such as demanding Florence support Venice in its battle for control of the Mediterranean. Should Cosimo's private journal reach Charles V, it would be even more devastating. The Holy Roman Emperor could withdraw his support from Florence, making it vulnerable to attack from all sides. That the duke had ever written such things down, even in code, was folly – every Florentine capable of writing knew never to put ink to paper unless it was unavoidable – but for this book to be locked away in nothing more secure than a cabinet in an ufficio . . .

Recriminations and accusations could wait. Recovering the journal or destroying it was all that mattered now, and certainly the only pathway forwards.

'We need a plan to recover what has been stolen,' Cosimo announced, 'but I can't think in here.' He led them along the short connecting corridor to his ufficio at the rear of the palazzo. Once there, the duke paced as he often did while weighing a choice. 'The first task must be determining whether these thieves are still within the city walls.'

'When I discovered what was missing,' Campana replied, 'I sent messengers to each city gate to learn whether the two Dandolos had fled and, if so, in which direction. Those messengers should return soon, Your Grace.'

'These thieves will be long gone if they have any sense,' Cosimo said. 'And we know they didn't depart through Porta Romana, otherwise we would have seen them.'

'I expect that the messengers will tell us both men are heading north towards Venice,' Aldo said. 'If so, the question is whether they go via Bologna or take the direct but more difficult road to Venice.'

'Do we know how long ago the Dandolos left the palazzo?' the duke asked.

'I understand the Venetian came in soon after Your Grace left to go hunting,' Campana replied. 'They were not here long, a few minutes at most.'

This meant the two Dandolos had been gone for at least an hour, Aldo estimated, perhaps more. If the thieves were riding hard and fast away from Florence, they could well have fresh horses waiting at intervals along the road. Aldo knew hunting such a quarry would not be easy. Most horses kept a similar pace, so overtaking the thieves was likely to be difficult. He had to hope they stopped to rest often, or believed themselves beyond reach and slowed their journey north. Even if the Dandolos were less than an hour ahead, catching them could still take days.

Aldo was sharing this with Cosimo when a rapid knock at the ufficio door summoned Campana away. He returned with reports from the messengers. Men matching the Dandolos had departed the city an hour after curfew ended, leaving through the northern gate, Porta San Gallo. They were on horseback, last seen riding towards Bologna.

No sooner had the segretario revealed this than Ottone strode into the ufficio, his face flushed from exertion, a triumphant gleam in his eyes. 'I can confirm all five exiles are dead, Your Grace. The last one was thoroughly questioned before he perished. There are no more exiles lying in wait, and the threat to your life has been averted. This is a good day!'

'This is far from a good day,' Cosimo replied through gritted teeth. 'But for the poor tactics and worse aim of my enemies, I would be dead now. What does that say about the qualities of your men? And while I was being attacked within sight of my own city, thieves came inside this palazzo and got close enough to kill my wife.'

Ottone's face fell. 'I didn't know . . . how could I . . .'

In other circumstances, seeing the boastful head of security chastened would be a joy for Aldo. But there were more important problems to resolve. 'These thieves stole valuable documents,' Aldo said. 'Private papers belonging to the duke are being carried to Venice as we stand here, including a journal that – in the wrong hands – threatens all of Florence.'

'Is this true?' Ottone asked Campana. The segretario nodded. 'Then we must set out at once to hunt the thieves down and retrieve these papers. I will lead the pursuit myself—'

'No,' Cosimo cut in. 'Any pursuit of the thieves must be properly planned. They are some distance away already. Haste alone will not be enough to catch them, it will require cunning. You need someone who has insight into the minds of such men. Someone with experience in finding and stopping criminals.'

Ottone kept his gaze on the duke, still refusing to look at or acknowledge Aldo. 'Your Grace, my men and I are quite capable of capturing these—'

'Enough,' Cosimo snapped. 'You and Aldo will ride together. Take two of your men as well, but I want you to treat Aldo as your equal. Yes?'

Ottone gave a curt nod, his triumph replaced by cold fury when he glared at Aldo. 'We leave from outside this palazzo in an hour. Do you have your own horse?'

'No.'

'The stables shall provide one,' Cosimo said. 'Make sure it is among our finest.'

'Of course, Your Grace.'

Aldo cleared his throat. 'May I ask for a description of Armando Dandolo? Neither I nor Ottone have met him. It will be an easier hunt if we know what he looks like.'

'A good question,' Cosimo agreed. 'Campana?'

'According to those who encountered him inside the palazzo,' the segretario replied, 'he has a prominent nose and shoulder-length brown hair.'

Campana's words made Aldo frown. He had seen such a man earlier, but where . . . ?

'Is something causing you pain?' Ottone asked.

'No,' Aldo said, his recollection returning. 'But I witnessed a man with a large nose and hair like Campana describes this morning. He was outside when the hunting party set off, dressed as a merchant and arguing with someone who appeared to be his servant. I suspect it was Armando Dandolo, waiting to be brought inside.'

'I want this Armando Dandolo captured or killed. And let me be quite clear about this: neither of you may return to Florence unless you have reclaimed my private journal or destroyed it. Is that understood?'

'Of course,' Aldo replied, bowing to the duke.

Cosimo glared at his head of security. 'Well?'

'Yes, Your Grace.' Ottone bowed before stalking out.

'How long will it take to catch up to the thieves?' Cosimo asked Aldo.

'It might be days,' he replied. 'We could reach them before Bologna, but that depends how hard and long they ride, not to mention how much help they have waiting on the road.'

Cosimo frowned. 'Campana, fetch ink and paper for me.'

'Yes, Your Grace.' The segretario hurried out, leaving Aldo alone with the duke.

'Do you think it's possible this pursuit might take you all the way to Venice?'

'I hope not,' Aldo admitted. He had sworn never to return

there, but the duke did not need to know the reasons for that. 'If we cannot stop their thieves before they reach the lagoon, our chances of finding them in that city would be all but naught.'

'I take it you've been to Venice?'

'I spent some time there, in my younger days.'

The duke nodded. 'As I recall, you rode with my papa.'

'Giovanni delle Bande Nere was my condottieri,' Aldo said. 'It was an honour.'

'Before he died, Papa was friends with someone who now resides in Venice. This man was a writer and a troublemaker; probably still is. But he also sends many letters, and has written to me several times since I became duke.'

Aldo wasn't certain why Cosimo was revealing this; in such circumstances it was better to stay quiet and let those speaking explain themselves.

'This intrusion into my palazzo is an outrage, yet the Venetian authorities might claim it is a justified response to the theft of their cipher book. We cannot risk further clashes with the Serenissima in this matter. If your pursuit takes you all the way to Venice and you are arrested there, I will deny any claim you might make to represent myself or the city of Florence. You shall have no authority there, no support from me, and you would be surrounded at all times by enemies.'

Aldo nodded. If arrested in Venice, he faced execution or spending the rest of his days in a cell beneath the Doge's palazzo. Execution would be quick, at least.

Campana returned, bringing paper and ink for the duke.

'I will write you a letter of introduction to this man I mentioned,' Cosimo said while writing at his table. 'He might be an ally should all else fail. But, if you are in danger of arrest, you must destroy this document before being taken. Otherwise, it will probably cost you your life.' The duke sealed the letter with wax. 'If the pursuit does take you to Venice, Ottone cannot accompany you there.'

Aldo nodded his understanding as he accepted the letter, tucking it in his tunic before leaving the ufficio. Striding down a stone staircase to the lower level of Palazzo Medici, Aldo wished he'd never accepted the contessa's invitation to visit her. Now he must ride with a violent man who distrusted him in pursuit of well-prepared thieves. If circumstances took him all the way to Venice, the prospects there were even worse. It was a hostile city where he struggled to speak the local dialect, and would be hunting two men amid a hundred and fifty thousand citizens. Should he fail, Aldo faced banishment for life.

'Palle,' he muttered under his breath.

It was an impossible mission.

Aldo went to Palazzo Coltello first, but the contessa was not in residence. Nor was Pozzo, her maggiordomo. That told Aldo more than the servant who refused to let him inside. Short trips did not require a maggiordomo; Coltello taking Pozzo with her indicated that she would be out of the city for some time. Clearly the contessa had known when the exiles would attack Cosimo and had left Florence to escape the consequences of that.

It was a wise choice, but made her complicity more apparent.

Aldo crossed the river and headed east to via dei Giudei. He needed to see Saul before leaving, needed to explain. But the doctor was too busy with patients and sent Rebecca outside to offer his apologies. Perhaps Aldo could come back later? If only he could! Aldo stalked to Robustelli's bordello, frustration getting the better of him. He stamped up the stairs to his room and threw a change of clothes into a satchel, along with a short cloak. It would be cold the further north they went, and it was hard to sleep while shivering. But another thought was scratching at him, like a nail caught in a boot. Ottone would not wait, yet Saul deserved to know why Aldo was leaving in such haste.

He found paper and ink in Robustelli's ufficio. Taking it to his room, he scratched out a few brief sentences. The words could not express his regrets at leaving, nor say how he felt about Saul – committing that to paper would be leaving evidence that might see the doctor imprisoned, even executed if discovered. But Saul already knew the contents of Aldo's heart. A few words in ink could add nothing more to that.

Retrieving a pouch of coin from a hiding place in his room, Aldo took it downstairs for Robustelli. He found her cleaning up after Piccolo. For such a small creature, the dog was an impressive excreter.

'This is rent for my room,' he said, putting the pouch on a table.

'But you don't pay rent,' the matrona replied. 'You being here in the bordello keeps trouble away. That's more useful than coin.'

'I won't be here for a few days. Perhaps longer.'

'A week?'

Aldo shrugged.

Robustelli took the coin, and nodded. 'Your room will be waiting when you return. But make sure you do come back, Cesare.'

He gave her a kiss on the cheek before leaving.

Aldo pressed the unsealed letter into Rebecca's grasp. 'Please, give this to Saul. Tell him . . .' But there were not enough words and there was not enough time to say all he wanted. Rebecca glanced at what was written on the page. She squeezed Aldo's hand.

'I'll tell him. He will understand.'

'Grazie.'

Rebecca went back into Saul's home. Aldo lingered on via dei Giudei. He studied the narrow street around him. It was little more than a dirt alley, humble homes huddled close on either side. Twice men had been murdered in the houses here, years apart, yet this place had also brought him friendship and joy. Knowing he might not see it again—

No. Enough.

Aldo strode north, away from the good doctor's doorstep. Better to be gone, not wallowing in regrets that could not be undone, losses that could not be avoided.

'Cesare!'

Saul came hurrying after him, clutching the brief letter. 'You're going? Now?'

Aldo nodded, aware of the doctor's neighbours in the houses around them.

'You don't know for how long?'

'No.'

Those warm hazel eyes gazed at Aldo, sadness at their edges. 'Then Rebecca and I shall miss you when you leave.' Saul clasped Aldo's hands in his own. '*Nesiyah tovah.*'

Aldo nodded again, not trusting himself to speak.

Then he left Saul behind.

Chapter Nine

When Aldo returned to Palazzo Medici he found Ottone and two guards about to leave. Ottone was atop a handsome chestnut with heavy leather bags slung over its back and an arquebus strapped to the saddle, while his men were checking their mounts for the journey. One man had a crossbow strapped to his back, the other a pistol at his side. Aldo had only the stiletto in his left boot, but that usually served him well enough.

'Leaving without me?' Aldo asked.

'His Grace decided we should go sooner,' Ottone replied. This was an obvious lie, yet he made no effort to hide it. 'You are welcome to confirm that inside, if you wish.'

'No, I'm sure you are correct. But I will be needing a horse.'

Ottone snapped his fingers. A young stable hand hurried away to fetch another mount. 'Make it quick!' Ottone shouted after him.

Aldo eyed the two guards. One was thick of build but it all seemed to be muscle. He glared from beneath a heavy brow, his face set in a permanent scowl. Working for Ottone would do that to anyone, Aldo supposed. He introduced himself. 'Bandoni,' the man replied.

The other guard was thinner, yet bristled with anger. His long, dark flowing hair was quite handsome, but his lips were a disdainful sneer. 'Guerra,' he muttered.

Riding with these three would be a chore in most circumstances.

Going outside the city with them – and potentially beyond Cosimo's dominion – was also dangerous. Ottone had already shown he did not hesitate to kill anyone he saw as an enemy, or a threat. Once out in the countryside where witnesses were few, Aldo knew his life would be in constant peril. Ottone could kill him and blame the thieves they were pursuing or claim an attack by banditi without fear of contradiction. Irritating Ottone had been an enjoyable diversione the previous day, but making an enemy of him could now prove fatal.

The stable hand returned with a dappled grey, saddled and ready to ride. Aldo moved round the animal, admiring its calm strength and good condition. This horse would carry him well, but its colouring was a stark contrast to the others, all shades of chestnut. If they were attacked from a distance, his mount would be the easiest target. Aldo suspected Ottone had chosen it for that reason, but did not object. There was probably a far less able animal being kept in reserve if he complained that this one was too conspicuous.

Aldo stroked a gentle hand across the horse, careful not to pass close behind it in case the hooves kicked out. He stopped at the head to murmur in a soothing voice. 'We have many miles ahead of us today. I will do all I can to keep you safe.'

The beast responded to his voice, nudging against him. The young stable hand held the horse steady as Aldo climbed into the saddle. 'Take care of this one,' the stable hand said.

Aldo smiled. 'I will.'

Ottone leaned forwards on his horse, yawning loudly. 'Ready yet?'

Aldo glanced up at the middle level of Palazzo Medici. Campana was watching through the shutters, concern evident in his hunched posture. Aldo nodded. 'Ready.'

Ottone urged his horse forwards and the two guards followed him. Aldo took the rear position as they rode towards Porta San Gallo. After pausing at the northern gate to report their leaving, they galloped away from Florence towards the rising hills.

Aldo looked back over a shoulder. Behind him the city receded, a low cloud of smoke and winter fog obscuring the Duomo's cupola. He was not one for religion; his faith had been lost while a mercenary. But he offered a silent prayer to whatever god might be listening: let this not be the last time he saw Florence . . .

They rode hard for several hours, up into the hills north of the city and onto difficult, rougher tracks that forced a slower pace. Aldo's legs were aching and his lower back throbbed with pain. Having not been atop a horse in a long time, riding like this twice in a day was close to agony. He didn't want to consider how stiff and sore he would be the next morning. Tomorrow could take care of itself; besides, he had to be alive to see it.

There was no sight of the thieves and no evidence they had come this way, but Aldo had not expected any. The Dandolos had too much of a lead to be easily overtaken. This was the most direct road north, whether a rider was heading for Bologna or Venice. The next significant village ahead was Scarperia, which should be within reach before nightfall. But fresh horses would be needed there to sustain the pursuit into another day.

A difficult decision awaited them if they continued beyond Scarperia. The dirt road split in two some distance beyond the village, one path going to Bologna while the other was a harder, more direct track towards Venice. If the pursuit had not caught the thieves by then, someone had to choose which way to go on. Aldo doubted Ottone would leave that to others. A wise man would divide the four into two pairs, doubling their chances of finding the thieves and retrieving the stolen ledger.

Persuading Ottone of that wisdom was another problem for tomorrow.

The duke's head of security had drifted back as the pursuit wore on, letting his two men take turns in the lead. Bandoni was at the front as the dirt road narrowed to pass between two steep stone slopes. Ottone rode his horse close to that of Guerra, enabling them to talk in hushed whispers without being overheard. Guerra glared back at Aldo, his face creasing into a smirk before he nodded. The cold, calculating way Guerra studied him gave Aldo reason to slip a hand down to the stiletto in his boot.

Birdsong had accompanied them before, but it died away now as the dirt road became steeper. Up ahead Bandoni was slowing his horse to a walk, picking a path between broken rocks and boulders. Had these fallen from the sheer rockfaces on either side, leaving debris across the track? Aldo could see no sign of that. Further ahead, the stone slope on one side of the track had cracked and fractured, a large pile of broken rock beneath the fissure. Yet the track around it was clear, whereas the part they were crossing was scattered with hazards, forcing them to go that much slower . . .

Aldo glimpsed movement ahead. They were being watched.

A cold shiver ran up his back, dread and recognition making his belly squirm. He had been here before. Three years earlier, on the way back from Bologna, he'd been attacked by banditi eager to kill the man under Aldo's protection.

'We need to turn back,' he said.

'Why?' Ottone twisted round in his saddle. 'You struggling to keep up?'

A sudden cry silenced Ottone. Ahead of him Bandoni slumped

sideways, falling from his mount onto broken rocks. He had a crossbow bolt buried in his throat.

'Palle!' Aldo slid from his horse, keeping hold of the reins. As he did a second bolt fizzed past, slicing the air where he had been moments before. 'Take cover!'

Ottone was already on the ground, unstrapping the arquebus from his horse, but Guerra made the mistake of pulling his pistol before dismounting. A gunshot rang out and a spatter of red burst from Guerra's left arm. He toppled to the dirt and rocks, howling in pain.

'Guerra!' Ottone called out.

Aldo studied their surroundings. The crossbow was firing at them from eye level. This meant their foe must be ahead of them, not atop the steep stone slopes on either side. That was fortunate, as there was little defence against weapons firing down from above. But the attackers still had an advantage. The broken rocks and boulders had not fallen on this part of the track by chance. That showed cunning and foresight.

'Is it the thieves?' Ottone hissed, his arquebus now free and ready to fire.

'I don't think so,' Aldo replied. 'There are at least two attackers out there, one with an arquebus, the other a crossbow. The Venetian might be good with either weapon, but the Dandolo who worked for the duke was a fool, not a soldier. I think our foes are banditi.'

Ottone gave a curt nod. 'We have to turn back, find another way round.'

He spoke with the authority of someone used to commanding others, but his tactics were poor. Ottone might be the duke's head of security, but he clearly lacked battlefield experience. Any retreat would be difficult in such terrain. It meant turning their backs on the enemy – an invitation to be shot – or retreating backwards down the track, which would be slow and treacherous. Even if they left Bandoni's body behind, Guerra was wounded and in need of bandaging before going forwards or back.

'Too dangerous,' Aldo said. 'Besides, that would add hours to our journey.'

'Then what do you suggest?' Guerra sneered, his face pale and soaked with sweat, a hand clasping his wounded arm.

Aldo crept forwards, keeping low to the ground. There was a flash ahead by a pile of broken rocks and a shot fizzed past him, little more than a hair's breadth away. Aldo dropped to his knees, crawling over Guerra, ignoring curses from the wounded man. Bandoni's crossbow and bolts were close by, and they needed every weapon available.

Another bolt flew at them, passing Ottone. The attackers were getting bolder, emerging from behind the rock pile to fire, knowing their targets were pinned down. Ottone swore and fired back with his arquebus. There was a cry of pain, and the sound of someone falling to the dirt. 'Got one!' Ottone snarled.

He might not know tactics, but Ottone was a skilled shot.

Aldo squinted at the steep slope above their attackers. It was fractured, cracks and crevices visible, large pieces of rock clinging to the hill at precarious angles. 'Shoot at the stone slope,' he hissed.

'Don't be a fool,' Ottone replied. 'I can pick them off one by one!'

Another bolt flew past Aldo, thudding into Guerra's hand where it was clasping the wounded arm. He cried out in anguish, howling blasphemies at the sky.

'Our attackers can do the same,' Aldo said. 'Soon enough they will realize doing that is taking too long, and shoot our horses instead.'

'They would do that?' Ottone was happy to kill any man that

stood in his way, but the notion of harming a horse seemed to surprise him.

'Shoot at the stone slope above our enemy,' Aldo urged. 'If we're lucky, that will bring rocks down on top of them.' He didn't say what might happen if they were unlucky: either the shots would have no effect, or might trigger a larger rockfall that buried them all. 'Do it,' Aldo said, reaching for Bandoni's crossbow. 'I'll keep them in place.'

Ottone shifted his aim from the attackers to the broken, fractured stone above them. He fired once, reloaded and fired again.

Nothing happened.

One of the attackers lifted his head from behind the rubble. 'You shoot worse than my nonna,' he cackled, 'and she's been dead for—'

Aldo fired the crossbow, aiming for the eyes, but put a bolt through his target's left ear instead. The man went down screaming.

'Were you saying something?' Aldo called. 'Sorry, I can't hear you!'

The curses that followed would have shamed a sailor.

Ottone reloaded his arquebus and fired again. At first it seemed there was still no effect, then a cracking, creaking noise began. The rocks above their attackers were shifting, small fragments of stone tumbling down . . . and then one of the large pieces tipped forwards.

Two of the attackers rose up, one clutching a bloody ear.

Aldo fired again, forcing them back.

The large piece of stone fell from above.

For a moment all was silence, the stone twisting as it tumbled down.

Then there was a heavy, wet splutch as the stone crushed what was beneath it.

A man screamed, his agony high-pitched and unnerving.

More rocks fell, smaller pieces of stone.

But the rest of the slope stayed still.

Ottone rose to his feet but Aldo stayed where he was.

Only when the screaming became sobs and whimpers did he get up.

'Are those bastardi dead?' Guerra asked, his face ashen, sweat soaking through his tunic. A crossbow bolt was buried in his right hand, pinning it to his upper left arm.

'If not, they soon will be,' Ottone replied, taking Guerra's pistol before marching up the dirt track. Aldo hurried after, throwing the crossbow to one side. It would be little use while face to face with their foes.

'We can't question dead men,' he warned.

But Ottone did not reply.

Aldo could smell piss and merda before reaching their attackers. One of the men was already dead, crushed by the large boulder, and his body had emptied itself of waste. The other – the one Aldo had shot through the ear – was trapped, a foot pinned beneath the boulder. His leg had shattered, stark white bones protruding through his hose. He was retching in the dirt, unable to look at his shattered limb.

'Tell us what we want to know and we can help you,' Aldo said.

The reply was a tirade of curses and insults.

Ottone rested a boot against the bandito's leg. 'How about this? Tell us what we want to know . . .' he leaned his boot into the broken bones, forcing out fresh screams of agony – 'and we won't make your suffering worse.'

Aldo placed a hand on Ottone's shoulder, easing him back. 'Let me.'

Ottone removed his boot but spat in the bandito's face before stepping aside. Aldo crouched by the man. 'You're a bandito, yes?' The trapped man glared at Ottone, muttering insults. 'I can keep him away, but only if you answer my questions. What's your name?'

'Does it matter?'

'Probably not, but I've always thought knowing a man's name makes it harder to kill him. He seems more of a person, less of an enemy.'

'Astuzia, Fredo Astuzia.'

'Grazie, Fredo. You were waiting for us, weren't you?'

'How did you . . . ?'

'Few travellers pass this way in winter, and fewer banditi wait in these hills for prey. That means you knew we were coming. Someone paid you to attack us, yes?'

Astuzia nodded. He could not be much older than thirty, but he was stretched taut by pain that was adding years to his pallid face. 'A Venetian gave us coin to slow you down. Said if we killed you, whatever we found on your bodies was ours to keep.'

'What did he look like?'

'Brown hair down to his shoulders, and a big nose.'

'Was he alone?'

'No, someone was with him, but they didn't speak. Wore an ugly tunic.'

Federico Dandolo. That meant the two thieves were still together. Ottone was pacing back and forth close to Aldo, his impatience more apparent by the moment.

'Did they say where they were going?' Ottone demanded.

Astuzia shook his head. 'But they rode north.'

'Towards Bologna?'

'Yes.'

Ottone frowned. 'We shall have to go on without Guerra, he will slow us down.'

'You're leaving me like this?' Astuzia wailed.

'Of course not,' Ottone replied. 'You might bleed to death.'

'Grazie a Dio,' the bandit said. 'Grazie mille.'

'There's only one way to be certain you never attack anyone else,' Ottone went on. Before Aldo could intervene, he shot Astuzia in the head.

'Was that necessary?' Aldo asked. 'He could have told us more.'

'Such as?'

'What weapons the thieves are carrying, for a start. How far ahead they are.'

Ottone shrugged. 'Perhaps, but you cannot trust the word of a killer.' He spat on the dead bandit. 'That's for killing Bandoni.' Ottone marched back down the dirt track.

Aldo searched Astuzia's clothes, finding a pouch of Bolognese coin. That could help pay for fresh horses if they reached Scarperia before night fell. The banditi probably had horses nearby, but searching for them would take valuable time. Aldo strode after Ottone, planning to retrieve Bandoni's crossbow. Yet when he reached it, he saw that the weapon was broken and beyond easy repair. Aldo had not thrown the crossbow aside with enough force to cause this much damage. Ottone must have stamped on it on his way past, sacrificing a good weapon to keep it out of Aldo's hands.

By the horses, Guerra had pulled himself into a sitting position. 'Let me come with you,' he said.

Ottone grabbed the wooden bolt embedded in Guerra's arm and snapped it in two, making his man cry out in pain. 'You're no use to me like this. We'll tie Bandoni to his horse, get you on yours and you can take them back to Florence.'

Guerra gave a reluctant nod. Ottone was a ruthless, murderous bastardo, but he seemed to inspire strong loyalty in his men.

* * *

It was dusk when Aldo and Ottone rode into Scarperia, the scent of spruce thick in the early evening air. The Tuscan village was best known for the quality of its blades and knives. Smoke rose from a few workshop chimneys as night consumed day. The artisans were working late, judging by the sounds of iron being tempered.

Ottone had brooded on their way to Scarperia, responding with grunts and shakes of his head when asked a question. Aldo was grateful to only be on his guard against one man now, rather than three. It was in Ottone's interest to have Aldo alive to assist with the pursuit. Working together, they stood a far better chance of finding the Dandolos and retrieving Cosimo's private journal. They would also need fewer fresh horses.

Aldo found a stable willing to care for their mounts overnight in case it was necessary to ride them again the next day. Scarperia was a small village, and only one inn had a room. Ottone took that, sending Aldo back to the stable to sleep alongside the horses.

That suited Aldo fine; he had no wish to share a room or a bed with Ottone.

But no matter how well Aldo settled himself in the hay, his thoughts would not lie still. How far ahead must the thieves be? Might they have reached Bologna if fresh horses had been waiting for them in Scarperia? It seemed unlikely, but the two Dandolos had a lead of perhaps half a day. The pursuit might be lost already.

Aldo went to the doorway of the stable and stared up at the stars overhead. The sky was clear of clouds, making the air colder than in Florence at night. There the fires of the city helped keep people warm. Out here there was nothing but the heavens and the darkness . . .

Chapter Ten

Saturday, February 10th 1539

Aldo woke before dawn. It was a habit born from years riding as a mercenary; today it was born of pain from a day of riding a horse. His lower back and legs ached, while his palle and seat were saddle-sore. Sharing a stable might be preferable to a night with Ottone, but lumpy hay and a rough blanket had made sleep fitful at best. A hot bath would be a blessing, but there was little prospect of that.

After emptying his bladder, Aldo searched for water in which to wash. He found a half-barrel outside the stable used to catch rain from the roof; that would have to do. The sky was shrouded by mist, while the winter air was cold and bitter. He stripped bare and washed himself with a discarded lump of soap. On a shelf near the stable door Aldo found an earthenware jar sealed with a wide cork stopper. He prised it open and was assailed by an eye-watering aroma from the thick paste inside: horse liniment. It would ease his aching body, but he would stink to the highest of heavens. Better that than a day's agony.

Breathing through his mouth, Aldo smeared the paste on his lower back and inside his thighs, with a generous handful rubbed beneath his palle. He was pulling on his spare hose when a stable hand came in, yawning and scratching at a thick brown beard.

He arched an eyebrow as Aldo finished dressing, but made no comment.

'How long is the ride to Bologna?' Aldo asked.

'From here, with your horses?' The stable hand set to sweeping the dirt floor. 'A full day, if you make an early start.'

'Would fresh horses quicken the journey?'

'Yes, but there aren't any in the village. That Venetian who came through yesterday bought the only two good horses left in Scarperia. Paid more than they were worth, as well. He and his companion must have ridden here like the diavolo himself was following, because the horses they left behind will need days to recover.' The stable hand gestured at two haggard, careworn animals standing in a corner.

Aldo was more interested in the men who had ridden them. 'This Venetian, did he have brown hair that reached his shoulders, and a big nose?'

The stable hand laughed. 'Biggest I've seen! You could shelter under it in a rainstorm and not get wet.' It was amusing, but something else he'd said before interested Aldo more.

'Why would a village the size of Scarperia only have two good horses?'

'Someone else bought all the others a few days ago.'

'The Venetian?'

The stable hand resumed sweeping. 'No, another man. Short-arsed little runt. I remember him because he paid with coin from Bologna, just like the Venetian.'

'You get a lot of that?'

'No, almost never.'

That meant whoever bought the other horses was probably working with Dandolo, securing fresh mounts for the thieves or making sure nobody else could have any.

Aldo dug out the coin he'd taken from Astuzia. 'Where can I find something to eat and drink this early? I haven't had a meal since we left Florence.'

Ottone was saddling his horse when Aldo returned to the stable. Morning sun was burning through the mist to reveal a bright blue sky but it was still a cold start.

'What's that stench?' Ottone demanded.

'Horse liniment.' Aldo shared what the stable hand had revealed, but Ottone did not seem to grasp the significance of it.

'If there are no fresh horses,' he said, 'we must continue on our own. Both mounts should be good for another day's ride.'

'True, but there is more to know here. The two Dandolos have someone else helping them. That means we may face three men, if we catch up to them. Perhaps more.'

They rode north out of Scarperia, leaving behind the artisan workshops and smoking chimneys. Being back in the saddle was agony at first, but Aldo's body became accustomed to it soon enough, the pain subsiding to a dull throb. He chose not to hide his suffering from Ottone; better to let the man think him weak and incapable. It would fuel Ottone's arrogance, but also make him more complacent and self-assured. That might be useful later.

After an hour the dirt road reached a division, splitting into two tracks. One was wider and looked far more frequently used; that was the road north to Bologna. The other was narrower, cutting away to the north-east. It would be a more direct road to Venice, but also more difficult. There would be fewer settlements on the way, less places to seek help.

Ottone did not even ask which way they should go, urging his horse along the road to Bologna. Aldo stopped, calling at Ottone to do the same. 'How do you know they went straight on to Bologna?' Aldo asked.

'The innkeeper in Scarperia told me that's where our thieves were headed next. Besides, it is what I would do if I was them. Only a fool takes the harder road.'

'Only a fool, or a man who knows that is the obvious conclusion of another fool.'

Ottone bristled. 'You're calling me a fool?'

'No, I'm suggesting the thieves went north-east because it is unexpected. Besides, how do you know they didn't pay the innkeeper to lie? That's what I would do.'

Ottone seemed to consider this a moment before replying. 'Then you're the fool here. I intend to ride north, to Bologna. You can follow whatever road you wish. But the two of us together have a better chance of recovering the duke's private journal. Alone, we will probably both fail. Come with me or don't, that is your choice. But I am going towards Bologna.' He snapped his reins and his horse took the road north.

'Palle,' Aldo muttered. Ottone was right. Alone, they would fail. Together was their best hope. He urged his horse to follow Ottone.

The contessa enjoyed her first night outside Florence far more than the day which preceded it. The carriage journey north with only a maid for company soon proved as dreary as Coltello had feared. Pozzo rode up alongside the driver, a loaded pistol ready if banditi should be foolish enough to attempt a robbery. That left Agnese as Coltello's sole companion inside the carriage. True, the maid possessed a keen ear for gossip and a sharp eye in observing the follies and indiscretions of others. Her bountiful collection of rumours was a helpful diversione for the first few hours, but this supply of tall tales and wilder allegations eventually ran dry. After that the journey continued in a yawning silence, the jolt of carriage wheels and passing an occasional village the only respites.

Happily, Coltello had not been obliged to spend the night in some regrettable roadside tavern. Travelling back and forth to Venice twice a year had shown the value of cultivating friendships with the wives of minor nobility and rich merchants on estates in the countryside and Venice. As a consequence, the contessa had gathered invitations to call on several such women when passing their respective villas. Her journey to Venice was long and tiresome, so she shuddered to imagine how much more of a chore it must be to live every day stuck in the outskirts of Tuscany or places beyond the dominion. But a surprise visit by a seemingly reputable signora who brought with her a sparkling wit and certain wicked appetites . . .

Well, that would improve anyone's day – and especially their night.

Coltello received a splendid reception when she arrived at the home of comely widow Signora Masina Rosso not long before dusk. Rosso's husband had been a wealthy importer of fabrics from the Low Countries who married late in life to a bride twenty years his junior. He retired to his country estate and died a few months later, stranding Rosso there. But she had discovered new aspects of herself since, often with the contessa's guidance.

Coltello sent Agnese, Pozzo and their driver to find lodgings in the servants' quarters, leaving her alone with Signora Rosso. They entertained one another for several hours in the sala and then in a bedchamber before the contessa fell into a splendid, dreamless sleep. She awoke refreshed and enjoyed a brief but torrid farewell with Rosso before eventually setting back out on her journey north-east. The scent of those happy hours was still lingering on Coltello's fingertips, but her thoughts inevitably flew ahead to what welcome she might expect in Venice. It was unlikely to be so . . . enthusiastic.

Her position as spymaster in Florence had been in doubt ever since she succeeded her late husband. In truth he was a spymaster in name only; all the Florentine sources he supposedly fostered belonged to her, all the information he reported had been obtained by her efforts. After his demise the Council of Ten and then its new tribunal, the Inquisitori di Stato, had tolerated her, allowing her to act as a temporary replacement for the late count. But a few months ago the wholly unsuitable Grossolano was sent to take over her position.

The man proved himself to be a fool, a bore and a lecher with an opinion of his own genius that was the exact reverse of his actual abilities. Naturally, the contessa had arranged for his murder within hours of that unwelcome arrival; Grossolano could no more represent the best interests of the Serenissima than she could grow a beard. An initial attempt to make his death appear the work of a killer then claiming lives in Florence proved ineffective due to the perceptiveness of Cesare Aldo. Instead, she had the blame placed on another Venetian, Gonzalo Zilio, the man responsible for managing Venice's spies in rival city-states. The Otto, the most powerful criminal court in Florence, helpfully convicted Zilio in his absence of Grossolano's murder and – at the behest of Duke Cosimo de' Medici – issued a standing warrant for the arrest of Zilio should he attempt to re-enter the city.

All of which had secured the contessa another three months as spymaster, but those came with a cost: she was no longer trusted. The Inquisitori di Stato had sent a letter – written in cipher, of course – demanding she return to Venice and explain herself at the earliest opportunity. Armando Dandolo had delivered the letter to her personally, meaning she could not claim it had gone missing on the way to Florence or been intercepted by rival forces.

She had other problems to face in Venice, such as the unfortunate state of her late husband's crumbling palazzo. Generations of the famiglia Coltello were guilty of neglecting the grand building. Like much of Venice, the palazzo was in danger of slowly sinking into the water. But where other structures had a thick layer of marble to protect the ground floor, the builders who'd constructed Palazzo Coltello had substituted other, far less suitable stone in many places to cut costs, making the lowest level almost uninhabitable. Meanwhile repairs on the top floor had made the roof worse, not better.

All of that might have been overcome if addressed sooner. But gambling debts left by the count's papa swallowed all available coin. Rather than plunge any further funds into a drowning home, the count had fled to Florence with his new wife. There were no canals there, no acqua alta. Yes, Florence did flood when the Arno burst its banks, but that was an exceptional event, not an almost annual one. If the contessa was ever to make Venice her home again, the future of Palazzo Coltello had to be addressed.

Her other problems were something she could never surmount. The contessa would forever be an outsider in a city which resented being sneered at for its origins amid marsh and mud. A person could live in Venice every day of their lives but the first, and still not be considered a true Venetian. Its citizens had a special insult for outsiders: they were not born in the salty water. No matter what service she offered the Inquisitori di Stato, suspicion would remain about her motives and her loyalties.

The fact that she was a woman only made matters worse. Venice was governed by old men, all of them patricians from the noble class. Rare was the individual under fifty who was chosen for the

Council of Ten. Venice was led by the Doge, a man elected to that position for life, but few doges were less than seventy when elevated to the role. The Council of Ten was all men, of course, as was the Inquisitori di Stato. Being a woman meant she was tolerated at most, no matter how well she proved her worth, and could never expect to be truly valued.

Did the three tribunal members suspect her of arranging Grossolano's death? Perhaps.

Could they prove it? No.

But his murder was another black mark against her.

It could not be helped that Grossolano had been a nephew of Signor Bragadin, the Doge's personal representative on the Inquisitori di Stato, but it was unfortunate. Now she was on her way to stand before the tribunal, knowing one of its three members had reason to hate her. Finding ways to win over the other two would require all her considerable skills, and more besides. But she had a plan for that, and a second plan if her first should fail.

Coltello rapped her knuckles on the carriage ceiling. 'Faster!' she called out. 'We lingered too long at the Rosso estate.'

There was a fierce crack of a whip and the carriage jolted forwards, gathering speed.

The sun was overhead when Aldo noticed two listless horses waiting by the side of the road. The animals were standing in the shade of a tree, yet did not look as if they belonged there. The ground on either side of the road was broken and rough, giving no sign that anyone lived nearby or was farming this land. As he and Ottone rode closer, Aldo could see the horses were tired but well kept. Why were such fine mounts out here in the countryside, far from any village or farmhouse? Aldo called for Ottone to stop.

'Why?'

'Those horses don't belong there.'

'And?' Ottone kept riding, but Aldo slowed his mount to a halt. He slipped down from the saddle, legs weak when they hit the ground. Moving gingerly, Aldo led his horse towards those under the tree. One animal showed more signs of tiredness, its head drooping down, but otherwise both were in good condition. He could see marks left by saddles, proof that they had been ridden recently, yet there were no saddles in sight.

What Aldo found behind the tree removed all doubt.

Ottone rode back, his face a scowl. 'We don't have time to stop,' he sneered. 'You can rest when this is over.'

'These horses were ridden here,' Aldo replied, pointing to the saddle marks. 'And someone was waiting for them.' He showed Ottone an empty wine bottle, scraps of food and a discarded cloth next to the stamped-out remnants of a fire.

'What makes you think anyone was waiting? We know there were two thieves. They could have stopped here to eat and drink.'

'True, but why make a fire? You only do that if you plan to stay some time.' Aldo pointed to a length of flattened grass beneath the tree. 'Whoever was here fell asleep while they were waiting. And look at the horses they left behind.' He gestured at the two animals. 'Both had saddles on all morning, but one of them is far more tired.'

Ottone shook his head, not bothering to hide his impatience. 'Meaning?'

'I think a single person rode from Scarperia, bringing the second horse without a rider on it. He met someone who had been waiting here with fresh horses, perhaps overnight. They ate, drank and rode on towards Bologna, leaving the spent horses behind.'

'We're pursuing two thieves, not one.'

'Indeed. If only one of these horses was ridden here, it means the two Dandolos split up on the road from Scarperia. I suspect one of them is riding direct to Venice.' Ottone didn't reply. 'It makes sense of what's here, at least.'

'All I see are two horses and parts of a meal. Could have been left days ago.'

Aldo held a hand over the stamped-out fire. 'These embers are still warm. It was burning not long ago.' This changed Ottone's attitude.

'If you're right, it means they're not far ahead of us.' He twisted round to look at the road north. 'We could still ride them down before they reach Bologna!'

Armando Dandolo smiled as his horse ambled north, the leather satchels slung across it bulging with papers and bound volumes from Palazzo Medici. He was well beyond the jurisdiction of Florence now. In the unlikely event that pursuers from there caught up with him, they no longer had any right of arrest. He could kill them on the open road, claim self-defence and face no punishment. His escape was now assured.

The five exiles had provided a fruitful *diversione* while he attained his true target. Paying the *banditi* to lie in wait on the hill path north of Florence had been inspired, too. Those men had shown no hesitation when asked to kill for coin. Anyone coming north would have to get by the *banditi* – an unlikely achievement – or take another road around the hills. The first meant bloodshed, while the second was a slow journey to failure.

Lastly, there was his masterstroke: taking one track north of Scarperia while sending his cousin Federico along the other. Anyone pursuing them faced a final dilemma: the road that wound its way towards Bologna, or the more direct, more difficult track to Venice?

Dandolo doubted there was anyone still hunting him. Men of sense would abandon the chase and turn back towards Florence. But, if some fools kept coming, that last choice would certainly be their undoing . . .

A rumbling sound behind Dandolo made him pause. Was that thunder in the distance? The weather had looked fair when he set out that morning, no sign of storms on the horizon. He twisted round in his saddle but there were no clouds to be seen, an earlier mist having burned away to reveal a clear blue sky. After a lifetime in the Serenissima, he was used to the gentle slap of water against stone and the warning calls of gondoliers as they approached a corner on the canals. Florence had been a cacophonous babble, the sounds of people, horses, carts and carriage wheels bouncing off the stone walls of palazzi and churches. Out here in the countryside, it was far quieter; the gentle clip-clop of his horse's hooves, the whispering breezes across fields, and the occasional cries of birds in the air had been all he heard for hours. But that rumbling sound was new . . . and getting louder.

Dandolo looked again, doubt nagging at him.

Impossibile! Someone was following.

And they were getting closer.

Chapter Eleven

Aldo saw their quarry first. He and Ottone had been riding hard all afternoon, determined to confront the thieves before Bologna. But the horses were slowing, strength failing them as the sun sank towards the horizon. Aldo was suffering as well; back and crotch torturing him, each jolt of the ride another agony. It was a relief when he spied riders ahead. 'There!'

Ottone spat out a curse. 'We must be near Bologna by now. If they enter the city, we'll never find them.' He whipped at his horse's flanks to make it go faster. The animal almost threw Ottone off but he clung on and it raced forwards. Aldo urged his dappled grey on, striving to keep up with Ottone but not wanting the animal to suffer. If the horse was half as exhausted as him, it must be close to collapse.

Their targets disappeared over the brow of a low hill as Ottone and Aldo got closer. Ottone charged up the hill, pulling his exhausted horse to a halt at the top. By the time Aldo reached him Ottone had untied his arquebus from the saddle and was aiming at the pair below. They were on a dirt road, the city wall of Bologna visible beyond them.

'You'll never hit those men from here,' Aldo gasped, every part of him aching.

'I don't have to,' Ottone replied. 'As you said yesterday, shoot the horses instead.'

'That's not what I meant,' Aldo protested. 'You can't—'

Ottone pulled the trigger.

A moment later one of the thieves' horses staggered sideways before falling into the other, sending both animals sprawling and throwing their riders to the ground.

'Yes!' Ottone snarled. He galloped his mount down the hillside. Aldo followed, ashamed to be riding with Ottone. The sooner this unwanted partnership ended, the better.

When they reached the men one horse had got up and trotted away, seeming no worse for its tumble. The other animal stayed down, its legs thrashing at the air, unable to rise. Ottone ignored the horse's misery; his only interest was the fallen riders. One of them was lying beside the downed horse, whimpering in pain, while the second – Federico Dandolo – clambered to his feet, appearing dazed but otherwise unhurt. Aldo did not recognize the man on the ground, who looked nothing like the Venetian.

'You shot at our horses?' Dandolo spluttered. 'You could have killed us!'

Ottone stayed on his mount, using the extra height to his advantage. He discarded his arquebus, pulling a pistol from his belt and aiming that at the courtier instead. 'I still can. And I will, unless you surrender what you stole from Palazzo Medici.'

'I never stole anything—' Dandolo began to reply.

A single shot cut off his words. The man beside the downed horse lay still, a neat hole replacing his left eye. Dandolo screamed, stumbling backwards before emptying his belly onto the stony ground.

Aldo moved his tired horse alongside Ottone. 'Was that necessary?'

'I've no intention of taking them both back to Florence. Now Signor Dandolo knows the kind of men he is facing, he will be more willing to give us answers.'

Dandolo was still bent over, retching and spitting. They would get no sense from him for a few moments yet. Aldo eased himself down to the ground, legs quaking before they straightened. He went to the wounded horse, which was no longer kicking or fighting to get up. The ground beneath it was wet with blood, too much for the animal to survive. Aldo crouched by the horse, whispering to it in a soothing voice while stroking its mane. 'Hush,' he said. 'You can rest now.'

As the animal gave in to death, Aldo noted there were no satchels or bags slung across its saddle or lying nearby. The other horse had been equally unladen. That meant the journal stolen from Palazzo Medici must be elsewhere. 'We've been chasing the wrong Dandolo,' Aldo said once the wounded horse was still. 'This man is not the Venetian, and neither of these two have any of the duke's papers with them.'

'How do you—' Ottone hissed a curse. He jumped from his horse, stalking towards Dandolo. 'Where is he?' Ottone demanded. 'Where's Armando?'

'I don't know who that—'

Ottone slapped Dandolo's face. 'Where?'

'I don't—'

Another slap.

Aldo got to his feet.

'Where?' Ottone snarled. A third slap.

Dandolo sank to his knees. 'Please, I don't know,' he whimpered, tears streaming down his cheeks. 'I don't . . . I swear to you, I don't.'

Ottone was about to strike Dandolo again, but Aldo caught hold of his arm. 'Enough,' Aldo said. 'He's telling the truth. Look at him.'

Ottone glared at Dandolo cowering on the ground.

'Let me try,' Aldo suggested. 'See if I can find out what he knows.'

Ottone gave a curt nod before striding away to reclaim his discarded arquebus.

Aldo crouched by Dandolo. The courtier was a weeping mess, his face reddened, and vomit staining his tunic. 'You're safe,' Aldo said. 'I won't let him hurt you again.'

Dandolo stared past Aldo to Ottone glowering by his horse. 'Grazie.'

'Now, tell me, who was the man you were riding with? You don't have to look at him. Just tell me his name, if you know it.'

'Pesce. His name was Pesce.'

'Good, that's good. Where did you meet him?'

'North of Scarperia. He was waiting with fresh horses.'

That confirmed Aldo's suspicions. 'How did you know he would be there?'

'Armando told me,' Dandolo said. His head sank to his chest. 'I didn't want any part of this. But Armando claimed a good position was waiting for me at the Doge's palazzo. He said I'd be a hero in Venice if I helped him.'

'He made you promises.'

'Yes.'

'And has he kept any of them?'

Dandolo hesitated before replying. 'No.'

Aldo could hear Ottone pacing, but ignored that. Dandolo wanted to confess his sins and ask for forgiveness. All they needed to do was to be patient. 'Tell me about Armando . . .'

The truth came tumbling out of Federico Dandolo, or at least his recollection of it. How he came to Florence years earlier after his branch of the famiglia Dandolo fell into disgrace. How he struggled to attain a position at Palazzo Medici and, when he did, was often ignored or belittled as an outsider. How the contessa's attempt to recruit him a few months ago saw his hopes pushed even further aside. Dandolo had been ripe for recruitment when his cousin first approached him outside Palazzo Medici one day.

Armando was interested in Dandolo, wanting to know all about him. Armando agreed it was a scandal how others were stopping Dandolo from getting the recognition he deserved. At first Armando did not ask anything of his cousin, and spoke little of himself. But a few days ago he revealed how Cosimo's spies had stolen an important cipher book from Venice, spiriting it away to Florence. Armando claimed he had been held responsible for that loss despite others being at fault, and that threatened his prospects within the Doge's palazzo – just as Dandolo was being unjustly punished for matters beyond his control.

If only there was a way the two cousins could help each other . . .

Once Dandolo agreed to that, the snare soon closed on him. Armando took his cousin drinking at a tavern, and then a bordello. Dandolo had far too much wine and boasted about things he shouldn't: the locked cabinet where the duke's private segretario secured important documents. Next day, Dandolo asked Armando to keep this secret between them. His cousin agreed, but said they could not be so certain of the bordello women who had been with them . . . Dandolo was trapped, forced to be a servant of two masters.

'Enough whining,' Ottone snapped. He had returned to listen while Dandolo spoke, lurking close behind Aldo. 'Where's Armando now?'

'Ignore him,' Aldo said. 'What happened yesterday?'

Dandolo claimed he had intervened to stop his cousin attacking the duke's wife, Eleonora. 'She is heavy with child. To kill her, that would be the worst of sins . . .'

'Yes, yes,' Ottone sighed. 'But what happened?'

Dandolo said he was opening the door to Campana's ufficio for Armando when ill chance brought Eleonora towards them. Dandolo saw his cousin pulling out a blade to attack her. 'In truth, I do not know if he would go through with such a barbaric act. But his blood was up, and anything could have happened. I grabbed his sleeve with the blade inside it and pulled Armando into the ufficio.' Dandolo shook his head. 'I have never been so afraid.'

He unlocked the cabinet in Campana's ufficio and Armando tore through the contents, shoving some of them into satchels he had brought. He was in such a hurry Armando didn't have time to read what was taken. Aldo glanced at Ottone, who nodded his understanding. They must hope Armando had not taken time since to study the items. 'What did you do next?'

Dandolo and his cousin left the ducal residence and were soon riding north, away from the city. They bought fresh horses at Scarperia before riding on. But Armando left his cousin not long after, taking the more direct track towards Venice while sending Dandolo along the other road to Bologna. 'Armando took the satchels I had been carrying. He said they would be safer with him.'

Aldo cursed Ottone for not listening earlier. Armando had used his cousin as another diversione, and Ottone had risen to the lure. If they had taken the harder road to Venice, Armando and the duke's private journal could be within their grasp by now. But going all the way back would add another day to their journey, and attempting to cross rough country between the two tracks was even more foolish. Any chance of overtaking Armando was gone, lost to Ottone's stubbornness.

'How did Armando persuade you to take the road to Bologna?' Aldo asked. Dandolo was a fool, but not such an idiota he would fail to realize the dangers involved.

'He promised a warm welcome in Bologna,' Dandolo replied. 'A comfortable bed in a palazzo. A hot meal with good wine, and fresh horses the next morning.'

'Your cousin plans to meet you in Bologna?' Ottone asked.

'No, we were to meet him after, closer to Venice.'

That meant there was still hope . . .

'Where?' Aldo asked.

'I don't know,' Dandolo replied.

'Liar.' Ottone was so close behind Aldo now, his breath soured the air.

'I promise, I don't know,' Dandolo insisted.

Ottone pushed by Aldo to shove his pistol in Dandolo's face. 'Tell me!'

'I swear on the Blessed Madonna,' Dandolo pleaded. 'Armando said someone would come to the palazzo just before curfew and give us instructions on where to meet him.'

Aldo glanced at the setting sun. They didn't have long left in the day.

'Who was coming to the palazzo?' Ottone demanded.

'G-Giovanni degli Scozzesi,' Dandolo whispered, fear whitening his face.

That name was familiar to Aldo. As a mercenary he had ridden with a flame-haired bear of a man for several months whose strange accent and stranger ways baffled most. He was called Giovanni degli Scozzesi, but said he preferred the name John of Scotland.

'Have you met this man before?' Aldo asked.

Dandolo shook his head. 'Pesce knew him, not me.'

Aldo lifted a hand to nudge Ottone's pistol aside. It was unlikely Dandolo would be alive much longer, judging by the ruthlessness of Ottone, but they still needed answers. 'Well done, Federico. It can't have been easy admitting all of this. There's just one more thing we need to know: which palazzo did Armando say you should go to when you reach Bologna?'

Dandolo gave a weak smile, his gratitude for the praise as evident as it was feeble. 'Cavaticcio, near the centre of the city. It's—'

The pistol shot was a thunderclap by Aldo's right ear, an explosion of noise, smoke and light. He jerked his head away, squeezing both eyes shut. The taste of burnt gunpowder was bitter on his tongue, its smell violating his nostrils. The shot kept repeating itself in his ears, as if echoing inside his head. When that eventually faded, he opened his eyes and saw Dandolo's corpse splayed on the ground.

Ottone was strolling back to his horse, pistol in one hand, arquebus in the other.

'You didn't have to do that,' Aldo said, clambering to his feet.

'He'd told us all he knew. We could hardly take him to Bologna. Besides, he was a traitor. He allowed a spy into Palazzo Medici, stole secret documents, and put the duke's wife in danger. If we took Dandolo back to Florence, he would have been executed.' Ottone lashed the arquebus alongside his saddle. 'I saved us the trouble of keeping him alive until then.'

Aldo refused to give Ottone the satisfaction of admitting he was right. The prospect of more riding was unwelcome, but they had to reach the palazzo in Bologna before nightfall.

'Have you been to this city?' Aldo asked while searching the corpses of Dandolo and Pesce for anything of use.

'Once,' Ottone replied. 'It's an ugly city, no match for the beauty of Florence.'

On that Aldo agreed with him. Pesce had been carrying a pouch of Bolognese coin, which Aldo took. It was always better to spend local coin, it attracted less attention. He found nothing of help on Dandolo. The dead courtier's horse had fled after its former rider was shot. Hopefully it would find safety elsewhere. Aldo stood between the bodies of Dandolo, Pesce and the dead horse. Ottone would kill anything that ceased being useful.

Staying alive in his company was a dangerous pursuit.

Aldo and Ottone rode the short distance to Bologna and entrusted their exhausted horses to the first stable they saw inside the city. A handful of coin bought guidance on how to find Palazzo Cavaticcio, and the landmarks that would lead them there. Aldo was grateful to be on foot, but his body was still sore and weary from two days of hard riding. He struggled to keep pace with Ottone, who had grudgingly agreed to wrap a blanket round his arquebus while they were in Bologna. There were laws against carrying weapons in Florence without written permission, so it was safer to assume the same was true here.

When they reached Palazzo Cavaticcio, the sun had dropped behind nearby buildings, the air getting colder as dusk settled over Bologna. The palazzo was not grand, its outer walls far more rustic than the elegant homes of rich merchants in Florence, but after two days on horseback and a night in a stable it was good enough for Aldo.

Ottone strode towards the entrance but Aldo stopped him. 'Which one will you be?'

'What?'

'Dandolo or Pesce, which one will you be? Whoever is inside here is expecting the men you killed, not us. Dandolo hadn't been here before, but Pesce could well have. We need a plan before marching in there.'

Ottone frowned. Despite being responsible for protecting the ruler of Florence, at times he did not seem much troubled by thinking. Violence and brute force were more his strengths. 'One of us could be Dandolo. But neither of us will pass for Pesce.'

'Agreed. We'll say there was a change of plan, and—'

'Cesare Aldo, is that you?' a coarse male voice roared. Aldo swung round in time to see a burly red-haired figure running at him. Then he was being lifted into the air, two mighty arms crushing him in an embrace. 'What the fuck are you doing here?'

'You're squeezing the life out of me,' Aldo gasped. 'Put me down!' The newcomer let go and Aldo dropped to the ground, legs almost crumpling beneath him. When he got his breath back, Aldo gestured at Ottone beside him. 'Giovanni degli Scozzesi, this is Federico Dandolo. Federico, this is Giovanni degli Scozzesi.'

'You wee merda,' the newcomer laughed, his smile apparent despite an impressively bushy beard. He thrust a meaty hand at Ottone. 'Good to meet you. Any laddie of Aldo's can call me John. John of Scotland was good enough for my papa and his papa, it'll do for you.'

Ottone accepted the vigorous handshake but seemed baffled by John's broad accent and tendency to lurch from the Tuscan tongue to his own language and back again. 'What is this man saying to me?' Ottone whispered.

'He's making us welcome,' Aldo replied.

'Aye!' John nodded. 'But where's yon Pesce? He was supposed to be meeting me here with your man Dandolo.'

'I had to take his place,' Aldo said.

'Did you now? Well, no skin off my bahookie. Let's go in!' John strode towards the palazzo, his arms swinging through the air like a child playing soldier. It was years since he'd ridden with John, but the burly Scot hadn't changed.

'I can't follow half the words that come out of his mouth,' Ottone said.

Aldo nodded. He wasn't understanding all of it, but wouldn't admit that to Ottone. Years of riding with mercenaries had taught him enough of other languages to grasp what was being said in many situations. John had insisted on teaching Aldo how to curse and order drinks in English, while peppering that with plenty of his own tongue. Together they had drunk more taverns dry than Aldo could recall. 'Don't try to keep up if John offers wine,' Aldo warned Ottone. 'The man could out-drink a sailor and still be thirsty the next morning.'

They followed John into the palazzo. The interior was cold and rather austere, with a grand marble floor inside and a sneering maggiordomo. John introduced them to the servant, insisting they be given good rooms on the middle level.

'You don't own all of this, do you?' Aldo asked as the servant hurried away.

John roared with laughter. 'Don't be daft, man! It belongs to a Venetian famiglia but I keep an eye on it when none of them is in residence. One of them lived here before moving to Florence a few months back. Poor bastardo got murdered the same day he arrived. But his famiglia has kept the place open for now.'

That meant the palazzo's previous occupant was Tito Grossolano, the man sent to replace Coltello in Florence. Aldo was fast coming to the conclusion that happenstance was amusing itself today. First it engineered his unlikely reunion with John of Scotland; now he would be spending the night in the former home of a man whose murder he had investigated.

'Is that what you do, work for the famiglia?'

'Away, man! I'm a Bologna constable, like my papa and his papa. I settled here when I got too old for being a man at arms. But a constable doesn't get paid much, so I also offer my services to those with the coin to pay. What about you? Still a mercenary?'

'Not these days.' Aldo had to stop himself saying he worked for the Otto. After so many years with the court, the habitual answer was hard to overcome. 'I'm guarding Federico on the road to a meeting with his cousin. Pesce said you knew where we needed to go.'

'Aye, that's right,' John agreed.

Ottone had been listening to them carefully. 'Well? Where are we to meet him?'

'It's a wee village near the Po,' John replied. 'About halfway to Venice from here. There's a coach house where the wealthy often stop for the night. Place is called—'

'Le Casette?' Aldo asked.

'You know it?' John and Ottone replied in unison.

'I've been there before.' Aldo wondered at how this journey kept bringing him back to his past. Three years ago, he had confronted Lorenzino de'Medici at Le Casette, warning the traitor never to return to Florence. Now events were leading back to that village again.

Yes, happenstance was certainly enjoying itself today.

Chapter Twelve

Sunday, February 11th 1539

Aldo woke early at Palazzo Cavaticcio – and regretted it. His head was pounding, his tongue seemed to have been replaced in the night with a thick flap of coarse cloth, and his bladder was near bursting. He found a pot beside the bed and pissed into that, the stream lasting so long he feared an overflow. It was years since he had known a morning this bad, and the last one was also due to John of Scotland.

The Bologna constable had persuaded Aldo and Ottone to go with him to a tavern near the palazzo. Aldo wasn't sure why Ottone agreed to accompany them, but he proved unwilling to heed warnings about matching John's thirst. One tavern became a second and a third, and more followed. Being with a constable meant they could ignore curfew laws and the innkeepers were happy to provide whatever the big, burly Scot wanted. Aldo had hoped drink might loosen Ottone's tongue, revealing more about the man. Instead, he became silent and moody, withdrawing into himself. Eventually, John led both his guests back to the palazzo, vowing to return in the morning for a final farewell.

Aldo found water for washing and put on the tunic and hose he'd worn two days before. The clothes stank of stale sweat but yesterday's garments were even worse. There was no time to wash any of them before leaving, and riding away from Bologna in wet clothes on a winter's morning was asking for a fever. He would simply have to stink.

Aldo stumbled down to the palazzo entrance, squinting at the bright sunshine pouring in. It appeared warm but the air was cold, making him shiver as he stretched and yawned.

'You look like you need the water of life,' John called, marching inside.

Aldo shrugged; he had no notion what the Scot was saying.

'Whisky,' John said, slapping him on the back. 'Good spirits revive you!'

'I drank enough last night to flood the Arno.' Aldo's belly threatened to rebel, so he changed the subject. 'What can you tell me about the Venetian that owns this palazzo?'

'Girolamo Bragadin? He's not a man you want to cross without an army at your side. His cousin led the Venetian forces that withstood a Turkish siege for months. They're that kind of famiglia.'

'You seem to know a lot for a Bologna constable.'

John grinned. 'Being a constable is only one of my jobs, you might say.'

'Along with keeping an eye on this palazzo.'

'And sometimes Bragadin summons me to Venice when he needs help.'

'Help his own men cannot provide?'

'Well, you know, once a mercenary . . .'

Aldo did know. The skills he learned as a man at arms had saved his life many times. Having someone like John of Scotland ready to answer a summons must be useful for Bragadin. An outsider could achieve things those who lived in a city would not, and they faced far fewer consequences, as Armando Dandolo had proven.

'I'm going to Venice again soon,' John continued. 'A messenger from Bragadin left a summons for me last night, while I was drinking with you and your compagno.'

Aldo shook his head. 'Trust me, Federico Dandolo is nobody's compagno. We're doing a job together, that's all.'

'If you say so! I'd ride with the two of you to Le Casette, but I can't go for another day or two. I have duties here.'

Aldo and Ottone left Bologna on fresh horses by mid-morning, with enough supplies to sustain them for the journey to Le Casette and back. Ottone's mood was even sourer and more abrasive than previous days. Aldo exchanged few words with him as they rode east, using a crude map drawn by John that showed landmarks to track their progress. The sun had passed its peak when Ottone pointed ahead to a huddle of trees not far from the dirt track.

'We should stop there,' he said, 'get something in our bellies.'

Aldo nodded, grateful for a chance to rest.

Once the horses were secured to a tree, Aldo settled down to eat while Ottone was fussing with his arquebus. The stiletto in Aldo's left boot had been rubbing at him so he pulled it out and stuck the blade into the ground. He had few doubts what might – no, probably would – happen if they successfully confronted Dandolo. Ottone had shown no hesitation in killing when he deemed that necessary. It didn't hurt to remind him he wasn't the only one carrying a weapon.

'You never mentioned having been a mercenary,' Ottone said. 'Our companion last night couldn't wait to tell me about that.'

Aldo shrugged. 'What I did in the past belongs there.'

'He claimed you rode with Giovanni delle Bande Nere.'

'That was a long time ago,' Aldo replied between mouthfuls of bread and cheese. 'I was as young then as the duke is now when I rode alongside his papa.'

'Giovanni – John – said other things about you when you went for a piss.'

Aldo put the food to one side, resting his hand on the stiletto hilt instead. 'Did he?'

Ottone stared at Aldo, his eyes cold and calculating. 'Indeed.'

'Never believe a man worse for wine. Many a tale grows taller once drink is supped.'

'In my experience, most men only reveal the truth after drinking.'

Aldo returned Ottone's gaze, letting that be a warning. 'And what is your truth?'

'That I will do whatever it takes to recover the duke's private journal, and anyone who stands in my way shall suffer the consequences. That is all you need know of me.'

'Indeed.'

Ottone's eyes slid to where Aldo was resting his hand on the stiletto. 'You've been to Le Casette before. Tell me about it. The more we both know, the easier it should be for us.'

'Three years have passed since I was last there, but I doubt the village has changed. It has a few simple, single-level homes close to an easy place for fording the Po. The tallest building is a church with a bell tower. Across the dirt road stands a coach house with stables. Travellers between Venice and Bologna often sleep there.'

'The bell tower would be a good place to watch over the village,' Ottone said.

'Yes, but if Armando Dandolo reaches Le Casette first, he can use the bell tower to see us coming long before we get there. He will be expecting Federico and Pesce, so two of us approaching might not alarm him. But Dandolo was outside Palazzo Medici when we left with the duke's hunting party, so he knows what we both look like. Once he sees our faces . . .'

'He will realize what has happened.'

'That's if we get near enough,' Aldo said. Even approaching Le Casette was a danger should Dandolo already be there. They would be easy targets if he had skill with an arquebus or other weapons that were potent across distance. A good crossbow was deadly in experienced hands, and they had no armour or other means of stopping such bolts.

'Then we must get there first,' Ottone replied. 'We've come too far to fail now.'

Aldo and Ottone were close to Le Casette by late afternoon. As they approached the ford in the river Po, Ottone pulled his horse back, letting Aldo go first. But when they were both across, Ottone did not urge his mount forwards again. Instead, Aldo heard a sound familiar from his years as a mercenary: that of a weapon being readied to fire. He twisted round to see Ottone aiming a pistol at him.

'We agreed to ride into the village together,' Aldo said.

'We will,' Ottone replied, 'but you first. That way, if Dandolo fires . . .'

'I'm his target.'

'So good of you to understand.'

'That pistol doesn't leave me much choice.'

Le Casette was up a slight rise from the riverbank. It looked much as Aldo recalled, the church's bell tower casting a long shadow as the sun dipped lower in the sky. The few homes around it were humble dwellings, plain plaster walls and tiled roofs. Most of the parishioners would be farmers and their famiglia who came into the village for Mass. Only the coach house opposite the church had two levels.

Aldo squeezed both thighs together and his horse ambled up the gentle slope, Ottone not far behind. They passed the first two homes at the edge of Le Casette. Each house had its front door closed and shutters pulled to stop anyone seeing in or out. In a village like this where everyone knew each other's business, there was no point hiding away. Shutters were usually closed for the hottest part of the day, and at night – but not as dusk approached.

'Keep going,' Ottone said, his voice an urgent whisper.

Aldo peered at the bell tower. He had climbed inside it on his previous visit, using the height to see quarry coming before they arrived. But there was no movement, nothing to catch the late afternoon sun. To his right the stable doors stood open, several horses tethered there. Something man-made lurked deep in the shadows – was that a cart, or a carriage? If the latter, it was standing end-on, denying him a glimpse of any crest on the doors.

'Keep going,' Ottone repeated.

Aldo rode on, slowly passing the coach house. Aside from the stable, no other doors stood open in all of Le Casette. It was as if the village had been abandoned, residents having fled. Ahead of Aldo a single shutter on a house creaked in the breeze. A hand reached from inside to pull it shut. So, Le Casette had not been abandoned. Its people were in their homes, unwilling to be part of this . . .

A bolt flew past Aldo, and he heard a thud behind him. He swung round to see the bolt buried in Ottone's chest. The pistol slipped from his fingers, falling to the dirt as he stared at his wound with bewilderment. Ottone was a dead man, he just didn't believe it.

Aldo threw himself from the saddle, tumbling to the ground

in an awkward heap. His horse trotted away, leaving him exposed in the middle of the dirt road. Had the bolt been aimed at him or Ottone? Whatever the answer, he needed to get out of sight. Whoever fired would be readying their crossbow to shoot again. Aldo crawled to the door of the coach house, keeping as close to the ground as he could.

There was a heavy thump as Ottone fell to the ground, one hand clutching at the bolt in his chest. 'Help . . .' he rasped. 'Help . . . me.'

Aldo ignored him. There was no point both of them dying here. Reaching the coach-house door, he stretched up to open it. A fresh bolt thundered into the wood just above his hand. Palle! Knowing it would take a few moments to make the crossbow ready for firing, Aldo scuttled towards the stable. But as he neared the door it closed in front of him, somebody pulling the heavy wood back and closing it. 'Let me in!' he hissed.

'No,' a male voice replied. It sounded familiar, but Aldo couldn't place it.

Twisting round, he could spy no easy escape. Ottone's horse had followed the other along the road, abandoning their riders. He scrambled over to Ottone, and pulled the dying man up so he was sitting on the ground. 'What . . . are you . . . doing?' Ottone gasped.

'When Dandolo fires again,' Aldo said, 'you can be my shield.'

Ottone spat a curse about Aldo's mama.

'That'd be difficult,' he replied. 'She's been dead more than forty years.'

Another bolt fizzed through the air, silencing Ottone for ever. It was no loss to Aldo.

He used the moments between bolts to grab Ottone's discarded pistol and dash to the left, diving between the church and the home next to it. Aldo lay there catching his breath, struggling to remember the back of these buildings. Could he come round behind whoever was firing the crossbow, catch them unawares? Maybe. But if they saw him flee this way, they would be ready for that.

A single bird flew overhead, a plaintive cry clear over the flap of its wings. Clear as a bell . . . Of course! Aldo hurried to the church's back door. He recalled little within worth stealing. Yes, it was unlocked. He slipped inside, closing the door behind him, and strode to the ladder fixed beneath the bell tower.

Aldo climbed fast, not wanting to be caught on the ladder if his enemy came into the church. By the time he reached the bell tower, Aldo was gasping for air, his chest burning. Careful to stay in the shadows, he squinted down at the village.

There was nobody on the street below, aside from Ottone's corpse. Both horses had trotted to the edge of the village and stopped by the last home. Aldo knew somebody was inside the stable, but they seemed intent on protecting their own life, not taking his.

A single figure emerged from the lengthening shadows between buildings, creeping along the dirt road, crossbow ready to fire in their hands. Aldo waited for them to get closer; shooting a borrowed pistol from an elevated position was not easy, as the target was far smaller. The furtive figure was male, with shoulder-length brown hair hiding his face. He wore a tunic, hose and boots, all dusty from travelling. It was probably Dandolo, but Aldo needed to be sure. The Venetian could have sent a villager out in his place . . .

There was one way to be certain.

'Armando!' Aldo called out.

The man's head tilted towards the bell tower, revealing his prominent nose: Dandolo. His arms brought the crossbow up—

Aldo shot first, hitting Dandolo at the top of his left shoulder. But the Venetian also fired his weapon, the bolt flying at Aldo. He flung himself backwards –

– and fell towards the entry hole in the bell-tower floor.

Aldo teetered on its edge, arms flailing.

He managed to loop one arm round the ladder –

– then fell through the hole.

His shoulder wrenched, threatening to tear itself apart.

But he clung on for dear life.

He clung on.

'Come down,' a voice soon called from inside the church. 'You can't stay up there for ever.'

Aldo had dragged himself back from the hole in the bell-tower floor, but his right arm was throbbing with pain. 'Better than a bolt in the head,' he replied.

'I promise not to kill you,' Dandolo said.

'Not sure Ottone would believe that.'

'Is that your friend out in the dirt?'

'Friend? No, not exactly.'

'True. He had a pistol on you all the way.'

Dandolo had good eyes to see that.

'He was Duke Cosimo's head of security, yes?'

'You're well informed.'

'Perhaps, but I didn't expect anyone to pursue me all the way here.'

'Ottone was a very stubborn man,' Aldo said, looking round for the pistol.

'Your weapon fell down into the church, by the way.'

'I wondered where that had gone.'

'Needs repairing now, too.'

'Ahh. That's a pity.'

'Isn't it?' Dandolo was moving around below, but Aldo didn't risk looking. 'Tell me, what happened to my cousin? Or little Pesce?'

'Dead. Both shot by Ottone, not far from Bologna.'

'So, you took their place and stayed the night at Palazzo Cavaticcio? Well, Federico is no loss. He always was a disappointment to the famiglia, that's why he was sent away to Florence. But I will miss Pesce, a most helpful sort of scoundrel.'

'These things happen,' Aldo said, easing the stiletto from his boot.

'Quite so. Still, I expect a handsome reward when I take these satchels to Venice. The Inquisitori di Stato was most irritated at losing a cipher book to a rival city-state.'

'Don't let me stop you leaving.'

'Actually, I was going to offer you the same opportunity. My journey onwards would go easier if I didn't have to look over my shoulder for you the rest of the way. Why don't you leave and I promise to let you go unhindered? No need for more bloodshed.'

'That's a very generous offer.'

'Yet you don't seem in a hurry to accept it.'

'Night will fall soon enough,' Aldo said.

'True.'

'And my pistol put a wound in your shoulder.'

'Actually, it damaged my tunic,' Dandolo replied. 'Your shot only grazed the skin.' Aldo heard a creak below. Was that the church door opening? 'Ahh, I was wondering if you were going to be of any help.'

Someone whispered, but Aldo couldn't make out the voice.

'Well, if you insist,' Dandolo replied.

There were footsteps and the church door opened before closing once more. Aldo risked looking over the side of the bell tower and saw Dandolo strolling away, one hand picking at a tear in the shoulder of his tunic. But who was below in the church?

'You can come down now,' a soft voice called.

Palle!

It couldn't be.

And yet it all made sense . . .

Aldo looked down through the entry hole at the waiting woman.

'Contessa Valentine Coltello,' he said. 'What a pleasure it is to see you.'

'Well, are you coming?' she asked. 'I promise not to hurt you.' Mischief was tugging the corners of her mouth into a smile, and a twinkle danced in those striking eyes.

'Very well.' Aldo swung his legs over the edge of the bell-tower entry hole, careful to keep his uninjured arm looped through the ladder for support. Slowly, carefully, he made his way down to the church below. The contessa smiled, though the warmth had left her eyes.

'That's better,' she said. 'Now, how can I put this best?'

'You wish me to leave?' Aldo asked.

'Not exactly,' Coltello replied.

Her gaze slipped past him.

Aldo turned to see her maggiordomo striding towards him. Pozzo was the voice he had heard inside the stable. But why were they here in Le Casette—

Pozzo's hand came at Aldo's head.

Then all was darkness.

Chapter Thirteen

Monday, February 12th 1539

Aldo does not know if he is dreaming. High walls surround him, their cold bricks rough against his naked back. It is dark, a crescent moon appearing for a moment between clouds before hiding away once more. Footsteps approach, but he cannot tell from where.

'Close your eyes,' a voice whispers, husky with lust and haste.

Aldo does as he is told.

The first hand to touch him is warm, strong.

Fingertips splay on his chest, pressing him into the wall. Thumb and forefinger find a nipple, rubbing over it in tiny circles before clasping him there, pinching, teasing.

He opens his mouth to say a name . . .

. . . and lips silence him.

The fingertips slide down, past the close curls of hair to his—

Aldo jolted awake, gasping in breath. He smelled where he was first: damp, the air thick with mildew, mould and decay. Another scent lingered nearby, one that made his lips dry and his eyes itch. He knew that sharp tang on his tongue. The sea, he must be near the sea, or seawater. The familiarity of that odour made his palle clench.

His eyes had been covered, bindings tied over them to hide where he was taken. His wrists and legs had been bound too, preventing escape. Trussed like a capon for roasting, he had been forced into a trunk on the back of a carriage. Then the journey began . . .

At least one night passed during the interminable hours that followed. He was given no food or drink, no way to relieve himself. When the need to piss became too much, Aldo bellowed for help. The carriage stopped and the trunk was opened, cold night air making him shiver. He was lifted out, his hose pulled down long enough for him to empty his bladder and then were pulled back up again. When he asked for water, rough hands shoved him into the trunk, and the journey began again.

He recalled one other stop. The trunk was lifted, and pushed across an uneven surface – wooden boards, perhaps. The air had been different, less dusty; he heard the cries of seabirds in the distance. Then the trunk was lowered onto something that lurched and shifted beneath it. His last memory was a queasy sickness gripping him . . .

Aldo opened his eyes but it was still dark. His hands were free, as were his legs. He pulled the bindings from his head. Light rushed in, blinding him, forcing both eyes shut. But slowly, slowly he squinted them open, growing accustomed to his surroundings.

The room was murky, thin light seeping past the edges of battered wooden shutters set into one wall. There was no furniture, no adornments to hint at where he might be. Plaster flaked from the walls like dried skin on the shoulders of an aging merchant. Something fast scuttled across the floor on the far side of the room, keeping close to the wall: a rat. It paused to stare at Aldo, before squeezing under the door and scampering away.

He was lying on an uneven straw mattress, without blanket or bedsheets. His toes were cold, limbs stiff and sore. Aldo could make out voices murmuring nearby. In the distance were cries of greeting, sharp calls he had not heard in years. Another noise sipped at the air, close and insistent: the lapping of water.

He couldn't be here. Not again. Not now.

Aldo struggled to his feet, legs protesting from days of riding and worse. He inhaled his own stale sweat mingled with the ripe smell of horse. His tunic and hose were almost stiff with it. The satchel he had brought was missing, probably still in—

Le Casette.

Dandolo.

The contessa and Pozzo.

In a rush it all came back to him.

Aldo marched to the shutters, throwing them open.

A gondola floated by on the canal outside.

His worst fears were confirmed.

He was in Venice.

Armando Dandolo smiled as his boat glided across the lagoon. After so long away – and an arduous ride from Florence – being back on the water was a blessing. Venice truly was the most beautiful of cities, made more so by having to approach it this way. The view never failed to lift his spirits, reminding Dandolo why he loved to call the Serenissima home. The gentle rocking of the boat, the cool water against its sides, the scent of the Adriatic on the air, and the creaking of oars . . . This was what Heaven must be like.

A boat was by far the most elegant way to travel, a truth made more certain by his experiences of late. Unlike most Venetians, Dandolo was confident in a saddle. But that did not mean he had enjoyed riding to Florence and back. If he never saw a horse again it would be too soon, and his feelings about the Tuscan city-state were similar. But the trip had been a triumph, achieving what his master demanded and so much more.

A brisk examination of what he'd taken from inside Palazzo Medici had revealed much to interest Signor Bragadin and the Inquisitori di Stato. One particular volume caught Dandolo's eye. Its exterior was unremarkable, a plain red binding with a small black letter C stamped in the top-left corner. But two things inside had made Dandolo's blood quicken. First, the hand in which it was written. Comparing it with the other letters and documents, he believed this to be the hand of Duke Cosimo de' Medici. That proved the journal was important; most of the papers were by another hand, perhaps a private segretario. Second, the text was written in code, probably one of the duke's own devising.

For Cosimo to have used such measures meant this journal must be important. Given enough time, Dandolo could have unlocked its secrets himself. But there were codebreakers within the Doge's palazzo, men employed by the Inquisitori di Stato to decrypt such things. Once they had done so, the fact that he had gone beyond his authority as an assistant to the Inquisitori di Stato and beyond the task given him by Signor Bragadin would be forgotten. Once the true value of what he had brought back had been confirmed, he would be just as celebrated as his brothers and others within the esteemed famiglia Dandolo.

Soon, he would have the respect his talents deserved.

Up ahead the magnificent bell tower of San Marco rose from the heart of Venice. To its right were the Byzantine domes of the basilica where Dandolo went to Mass and, closer to the lagoon, the majestic palazzo of the Doge. People crammed the piazzetta in front of it, Carnival making that area even busier than usual.

The piazzetta was known as the broglio, a place where patricians gossiped, debated politics and sought each other's vote.

Dandolo rose to his feet as the boat approached a wooden jetty jutting out into the lagoon. He slung two well-laden satchels over his right shoulder, keeping a firm grip on both. Losing them to the waters would be a tragedy after all he'd done to acquire their contents. But Dandolo was a son of the salt water, as comfortable there as on dry land. He stepped nimbly from the boat to the jetty without difficulty.

Now to seek his master . . .

Girolamo Bragadin was one of the youngest patricians ever to be made a senator, yet his ambition had only grown since that day. Rivals whispered that the blood of Bragadin's enemies stained the cell walls within the Doge's palazzo. It was not true – at least, Dandolo had seen no proof of that – but the rumours still lingered. Bragadin gloried in his reputation, using it to secure a position he had long coveted: that of a red-robed advisor to the Doge.

When the new Inquisitori di Stato was being formed, Bragadin had his assistants ensure his name was foremost on the lips of those selecting its first incumbents. Two Council of Ten members were chosen, along with one of the Doge's advisors. The term of office was a single year, and the work without salary, yet Bragadin had made no effort to mask his belief that it was another step towards his ultimate goal: becoming Doge.

Dandolo's task in Florence was delivering Bragadin's letter to Contessa Coltello, summoning her back to Venice for an audience with the tribunal. The recovery of a stolen cipher book had been mentioned in passing by Bragadin, yet how that might be obtained went unspecified. Goading five exiles into a foolhardy attack on the Medici leader as a diversione while stealing papers from the ducal residence was almost certainly not what Bragadin had in mind. Nonetheless, the satchels' contents would soon assuage his inevitable anger.

Dandolo moved through the broglio, going from one group of patricians to the next, listening to their whispers about what had occurred while he was away. The usual boasting and gossip continued, as did frequent worries about what the Turks might do next in their quest to claim dominion over Venetian territories in the Adriatic.

A flash of red caught Dandolo's attention.

Girolamo Bragadin was coming.

Footsteps approached the room where Aldo was being kept. He reached for the stiletto in his left boot, but found nothing there except his leg. No matter. He could defend himself with fists, if need be. A key turned in the lock and Coltello's maggiordomo pushed the door open.

'The contessa wishes to see you,' Pozzo said, covering his nose and mouth with a cloth. 'But I strongly suggest you should bathe first, for the good of everyone.'

'No,' Aldo replied.

'No?'

'It's your fault I stink this bad. You tied me up, kept me in a trunk for days—'

'One night,' Pozzo cut in. 'You were in there for only one night.'

'This is her Venetian palazzo, yes?'

Pozzo nodded.

'Then you can take me to see her as I am.'

'So be it.' The maggiordomo gestured to his left.

'No. You lead.'

Pozzo rolled his eyes before stalking away.

Aldo followed, keeping a few paces back to take in his surroundings. The more he knew about this palazzo, the better his chances of finding a way out.

The contessa listened to a litany of problems until she could stand Amaro's voice no longer. She raised a hand to silence her Venetian maggiordomo, enjoying his frustration at being interrupted. Amaro had been in charge of the crumbling palazzo during her long absence, and now seemed to think of it as his own property. Would that this were true! Alas, the tiresome responsibility for protecting it from the lagoon was entirely hers.

'In summary,' she said, 'the lowest level of this building has become a mouldy collection of decaying chambers. The roof is near collapse, with rain leaking into the servants' quarters whenever the weather wishes. And the two levels in between – where I might expect to reside and receive visitors – will soon be just as vulnerable unless extensive and expensive restoration work is undertaken immediately. In other words, this entire palazzo best resembles a woman working at a bordello after an army has visited.'

Amaro frowned, confusion creasing his supercilious face. 'Contessa?'

'It's completely fucked,' she replied with relish. It was not often she got to speak so coarsely but sometimes this was necessary. On such occasions, it was also rather enjoyable.

The maggiordomo drew back, shock making his eyes bulge. 'Such language! Forgive me saying so, Contessa, but if your late husband was still with us—'

'But my husband is no longer with us,' the contessa said, 'as you so helpfully note. I was aware of that, but being reminded of his death always improves my mood. Grazie mille.'

Amaro spluttered, apparently uncertain of her sincerity. He was a tiresome, self-righteous individual. Amaro was at least fifty, flabby of face and belly, yet unyielding in the stiffness of his beliefs. He was the sort of fool who kept wearing an unsightly wig years after it had gone out of style simply because he believed it the right thing to do.

The Venetian hated her, of that the contessa was certain. He had hated her from the day when the count first brought his betrothed to view the palazzo. Amaro hated her more when she had arrived for her wedding night and dismissed him for the evening rather than suffer his judgemental presence a moment longer. And he hated her most of all for suggesting the count move to Florence rather than reside in this crumbling residence, where the sound of dripping and scent of damp were ever present.

'Forgive me, Contessa,' Amaro said. 'I did not mean to suggest—'

'Enough,' she snapped. 'Why don't you go and see what meal your delightful wife proposes to present this evening?' The maggiordomo's wife was also the palazzo cook. She was anything but delightful, with a face to rival any hatchet in her cucina. Being married to a man like Amaro would do that to any woman, let alone having to share his bed.

'Of course,' he replied, giving the smallest of bows on his way out.

The sooner she was rid of both Amaro and this palazzo, the better. It was a pity the building had fallen into such disrepair. The high vaulted ceilings were impressive, while the arched lancet openings looking out over two adjoining canals were quite elegant. The residence had a most appealing location, too, just a few minutes' walk north-east of the Doge's palazzo, yet far enough from the more crowded parts of Venice to know peace. But what she found most appealing about it was the bridge immediately outside: Ponte del Diavolo.

Pozzo stumbled into the salone, a hand clutched to his head.

'Where is Aldo?' the contessa asked. 'You were supposed to bring him here.'

'I was,' Pozzo replied, wincing. 'But as we passed the main entrance Aldo attacked me from behind. He struck my head against a wall, and fled. He could be anywhere by now.'

'Perhaps, but I'm told that Aldo has not been in Venice for twenty years.' Coltello smiled. 'I suspect the only place he will be by now is lost.'

Signor Girolamo Bragadin was not fond of patience. It had taken him decades to become an advisor to the Doge, and Bragadin knew any chance of wearing the golden robes reserved for the Doge was still years away. It would not come with the inevitable passing of Pietro Lando, the present incumbent, but perhaps after the death of his successor. Until then, being part of the Inquisitori di Stato was helpful for putting in place those Bragadin would need.

The tribunal was responsible for Venetian state security, including the supervision of its many spies. The Serenissima had informants across the city and far beyond. These all needed managing and their reports filtering, otherwise the Inquisitori di Stato would be awash with gossip of little value. That, in turn, required spymasters in territories outside Venice.

Bragadin had not wished to make his witless nephew the tribunal's spymaster in Florence; it was a post for which Grossolano was utterly ill-suited. But his doting mother – Bragadin's only sister – demanded her son be appointed. The murder of Grossolano less than a day after arriving in Florence had proven the folly of that decision.

News of the killing came from Grossolano's predecessor as spymaster in Florence, Contessa Coltello. She was a woman notorious for having more cunning than the serpent in the Garden of Eden. Her letter was full of heartfelt sympathy, which aroused Bragadin's suspicions further – but suspicions were not proof. Coltello suggested his nephew had been killed by a murderer stalking the city, yet word soon reached Bragadin that one of the tribunal's own men, Gonzalo Zilio, had been convicted in absentia by a criminal court of the murder. That meant Zilio could no longer enter Florence, forcing the tribunal to retain Coltello as its spymaster there. It had taken several visits by Dandolo to uncover at least some of the truth.

To be certain the contessa was responsible for his nephew's murder, Bragadin needed evidence – and there was no easy way of getting that, not while the contessa remained in Florence. Yet whenever Bragadin met his grief-stricken sister, she begged for answers. Who murdered Tito? Why were they not being brought to justice? What was the point of the Inquisitori di Stato if it could not uncover the killing of one of Venice's own spymasters? Why was her brother Girolamo always so weak, so . . . impotent?

Bragadin lost what patience he possessed and sent Dandolo with a letter summoning the contessa back to Venice so she could answer to the tribunal. It was another assistant, Culmine, who brought word of Dandolo's return. He had been spied on the broglio. Dandolo was not hard to notice; few Venetian men wore hair down to their shoulders, and he possessed a quite unmistakeably large nose.

Bragadin marched across the piazzetta. Patricians parted as he strode towards them, clearing a path; a fearsome reputation had its uses. Dandolo bowed as Bragadin approached.

'Where is she?' Bragadin looked past Dandolo but could not see Coltello. 'Well?'

'The contessa came ahead of me,' the assistant replied. 'I thought it best—'

'You thought?'

'Yes, I—'

'You thought?'

Dandolo nodded, his eyes cast down.

Bragadin stalked back towards the Doge's palazzo. 'My ufficio,' he snarled. 'Now!' By the time Bragadin reached the main entrance, Dandolo was hurrying alongside him, clutching the satchels. 'Make your report,' Bragadin demanded. 'Be brisk.'

Dandolo spoke as they strode across the wide internal courtyard, and up an inner staircase. By the time Bragadin reached his small, wood-panelled ufficio he'd heard enough. 'I sent you to Florence with the simplest of tasks: hand a letter to Contessa Coltello that called her back here to appear before the Inquisitori di Stato. Instead, you took it upon yourself to dupe five exiles into attacking the Duke of Florence so you could get inside his residence and pilfer his papers. When the duke sent his head of security to hunt you down, you killed the man with a crossbow. And, as if that was not enough, you let the contessa make her own way to Venice. Was it not clear that you should accompany her?'

'Signor, you never said that I should—' Dandolo began.

'I shouldn't need to tell you,' Bragadin cut in. 'You should know.'

The spluttering assistant pulled two books from his satchels. 'Please, you need to see what I have brought back from Palazzo Medici.' He opened one of the books on Bragadin's table, gesturing at its contents. 'These are the stolen ciphers I brought back from

Florence. And this –' he held out the other book – 'I believe this is Duke Cosimo's private journal. Here, on this page, he writes the name Coltello. Again here, and on the next page.'

Bragadin snatched the journal from Dandolo and gave it a cursory glance. 'I see the contessa's name, but the rest is in some kind of code. If this is the duke's own journal – and that is far from certain – we do not know what he has written about Coltello.'

'Venice has the best code breakers in Europe,' Dandolo said. 'They can—'

'Silence!' Bragadin snapped the journal shut. 'I shall give this to Culmine. He will see if any sense can be made of it.'

'Culmine? But I brought the journal to you. I risked everything—'

'Precisely.' Bragadin loomed over Dandolo. 'You risked everything, including my reputation, with this foolhardy misadventure of yours. Yet you expect me, a senior advisor to the Doge, to applaud that same behaviour? Very well, I shall.' Bragadin clapped his hands together. 'Bravo, Signor Dandolo. Bravo indeed!'

The assistant's chin dropped to his chest. 'Forgive me, signor.'

'Get out of my ufficio,' Bragadin hissed. 'If this journal proves to be of any value, I shall summon you back. If not, you can consider your time in my service at an end. Go!'

Dandolo stumbled away, his shoulders slumped.

Good. He was far too ambitious.

There was only room for one ascending star in this palazzo.

Chapter Fourteen

Aldo feared he was lost. After attacking Pozzo and escaping the contessa's palazzo, he had dashed over the nearest bridge, the words Ponte del Diavolo carved into nearby stonework. Trust Coltello to have a home by the Devil's Bridge. He hurried along a narrow path beside a canal, glancing back for any pursuers. Once out of sight from the palazzo he cut a ragged path, turning right and right again, determined to elude anyone who might be following him. He crossed bridge after bridge, hurrying along narrow calle, searching his surroundings for landmarks . . . but nothing looked familiar.

It was years since he had left this city, vowing to forget everything about it. Now he wished those long-buried memories would return. Venice was not one island, that he did recall; instead, it was a city sprawling over dozens and dozens of islands, linked by numerous bridges, most made from wood. Where Florence gave its visitors an occasional glimpse of the Duomo between buildings as a way to navigate the city, Venice offered no such help. Palazzi here stood tall with four levels rather than three. Unless one was familiar with the city, within sight of the grand canal or by the lagoon, it was impossible to navigate this water-locked maze.

Eventually Aldo stumbled to a halt.

There was no denying it.

He was lost.

Setting pride aside, Aldo approached a woman coming in the opposite direction. She was small and round, clad in the black of a widow, with a weary face and kind eyes. But when Aldo spoke, she stared as if he were a diavolo in human form. The woman babbled as she scuttled away, her voice sibilant and words strange to his ears. It took a moment to realize she was speaking in the Venetian dialect. His Tuscan tongue must sound equally unnerving to her. Aldo tried again with another woman, and then an old man. Both backed away, shaking their heads as they retreated from him.

Why were they all so afraid?

Aldo glanced down. Out here in daylight his clothes looked even worse. The tunic was stiff with dirt and sweat while his hose stank of horse, piss and merda. He had not shaved in days, and his hair was greasy and knotted when he ran a hand through it. Aldo leaned over a stone parapet to see himself in the canal below. He looked like a beggar, and stank worse.

He lurched on a while, crossing more bridges, stumbling along calle.

But it was hopeless.

Hunger gnawed at his belly and his head was throbbing. When was the last time he ate or drank? Finally, he sank down on a small bridge, unable to go any further.

He was exhausted, lost in a city he despised.

He had no allies here, no way of leaving.

He had no coin. Even if he did, there could be no return to Florence, not without the duke's private journal or proof that it had been destroyed.

Effectively, he was banished.

Never again would he see Saul's warm hazel eyes.

Never again would he feel the softness and the strength of Saul's touch.

Wintry rain began to fall, spattering the wooden bridge.

Even the weather seemed to be mocking him.

Aldo got to his feet, retreating to a narrow path that went beneath a building. The Venetians had a particular word for these kind of passages – sotoportego, that was it.

A name carved in the stonework outside the sotoportego caught his eye: Ponte del Diavolo. The Devil's Bridge. That meant he had run and stumbled and turned and twisted in search of escape, and all that had done was bring him back where he'd started. He was standing outside Contessa Coltello's palazzo.

Pietro Aretino never tired of watching the Grand Canal from his lodgings in Palazzo Bollani. It was a sight of divine beauty and a delight every day, whatever the weather. His residence might be less grand than the other palazzi nearby, but that did not matter. He had the most beautiful view in the world, of that Aretino was certain.

Being opposite the Rialto ensured there was always something to see and people to watch. Rich merchants arguing over prices for their wares; the stands at the fish and meat markets, their different aromas mingling with the salt water of the lagoon and the hint of spices on the air from other stalls. Barges floating on the water, each laden with the season's produce, the craft lashed together so traders could run back and forth across them.

When beautiful ladies glided by in their gondole, Aretino observed the fineries each woman wore, how they shimmered with jewels, silks and gold. He enjoyed entertaining his guests with tales of those who passed his lodgings. He also noted any particularly rude or witty comments bellowed by the boatmen. Their words were crude yet they still deserved to be captured for an appreciative audience. Just as a painter finds his models in truth and life, so does a writer find their own truth in the words and speeches of others.

A cold winter breeze rattled the shutters, persuading Aretino to retreat inside. He pulled the heavy woollen cloak closer around his shoulders, before smoothing his long brown beard over it. Strands of grey and silver glinted in the light of a lantern but, unlike the gold and jewels of the passing ladies, they offered no promises beyond old age and infirmity. Aretino wondered how many of those fine women would grace his residence later? Too few, too few. His reputation made an invitation to Palazzo Bollani scandalous for some, despite the fact that he lived in a building owned by Bishop Domenico Bollani.

It did not seem to matter how many pious religious works Aretino wrote, nor how well those sold. His recent *Life of the Virgin Mary* had been much acclaimed, and he was certain the *Life of Saint Catherine*, to which many hours had already been devoted, would be equally successful. Nor did people appreciate how his arguments and writings had saved great artists from prison or worse. No, it was the fact that years ago he wrote sixteen sonnets describing the positions depicted in a series of erotic drawings which people always recalled. That, and the fact that he had to flee Rome soon after to escape the Pope's wrath . . .

No matter. Let those who would come to his home, come. He kept an open house, welcome to all willing to set foot inside. Those fearful of being tainted by his supposedly wicked, wanton ways could stay in their own palazzi and continue living lives of tiresome sanctimony. Such self-righteous souls deserved no joy from him, none at all.

Aretino settled down at a table to write a letter. To whom it would be addressed, he was not certain; in truth it might never be sent. But he found composing his thoughts in such a manner helped create the mood for other writings. And, having published one volume of his letters to quite astonishing success, it was wise to gather more missives for potential inclusion in a new collection of his celebrated correspondence.

But no sooner had he settled on a topic – the seasonal delights of nature – than one of his servants bustled into the room, a sly smile on her face. Cisti was a maid with a talent for gathering gossip, something which he valued highly.

'She has returned,' Cisti gushed.

Aretino set his pen aside. 'Who has returned?'

'Contessa Coltello. I'm told she arrived late last night, or early this morning.'

'Has she now? How wonderful . . .' Aretino's testiness at being interrupted vanished. It was far too long since he had seen that delightful, devious creature. Aretino feared she might not return to Venice, especially after the unfortunate death of her dreary husband in Florence. But if Cisti was correct – and the maid was almost never wrong – then it seemed something or someone had lured the contessa back to the Serenissima.

'Do we know why she has returned now?'

Cisti came closer, lowering her voice to a whisper. 'It seems the contessa has been summoned to stand before the Inquisitori di Stato.'

Naturally, Aretino knew about this new tribunal. Whispers from the broglio often reached him, and were a frequent inspiration for his more provocative letters. The Inquisitori di Stato had been active only a few months, yet it was already much feared. It was said the tribunal interrogated suspects and witnesses with the strappado, where the wrists were bound behind the back and the subject suspended by a rope attached to their arms. The mere thought of how agonizing that must be made Aretino wince. Some even claimed the Inquisitori di Stato sat long into the night and, if a suspect was found guilty of a capital crime, had the culprit drowned before dawn as a punishment.

For the contessa to be brought before this tribunal . . . That did not bode well. Aretino needed to know more, and the contessa was the best source for that. Dismissing Cisti, he bent back over his paper and ink. The question of who should receive his letter was resolved, but inconsequential musings about the seasons of nature were long forgotten now. No, if he was going to lure Coltello to his home later, it required a temptation even she could not resist . . .

Coltello arched an eyebrow when Pozzo brought Aldo into her salone. The maggiordomo, his face full of anger and disdain, announced that Aldo had returned of his own volition. As for the man beside him . . . Aldo's clothes were a disgrace, while that tired face showed all of his forty-two years, bearing more creases than her bed linen after a particularly torrid night.

But the smell which Aldo brought with him was by far the most shocking thing – oh, the smell! Ripe and repulsive were the kindest words to describe it, though the contessa knew several far more accurate terms, most of them more appropriate to a latrina. She leaned back, lifting a delicate hand over her mouth and nostrils to shield them from his offensive odour.

'My dear Cesare, I would say it is a pleasure to see you again, but that would be a lie. Pozzo, did you not offer my guest a chance to wash before bringing him before me?'

'He refused my first suggestion,' the maggiordomo replied. 'I offered him another chance on his return, but he insisted on speaking with you first.'

'Much as I appreciate your enthusiasm to see me, Cesare, washing first would have been a wise choice. Very well, Pozzo, you may go. I'll call if I need you.'

'Very good, Contessa.' Pozzo bowed on his way out.

'Welcome to Palazzo Coltello,' she said, gesturing at their surroundings. 'Not the equal of my home in Florence, yet this floor has its charms, despite the rather ornate tapestries on its walls. The count insisted on keeping them as a reminder of his dear mama. I spend so little time here that there seemed no point in replacing them.'

'Why have you brought me to Venice?' Aldo's voice was a rasp of anger.

She rose from her chair, strolling towards the shutters set into the salone's south wall. 'I was told by my new dressmaker Patricio that you swore long ago never to return to this city. If that is true, your dismay at being here is understandable. But you might as well enjoy the experience. Venice can be a very lively city, especially now during Carnival.

'Then there is the fact that you chose to return to my palazzo after slamming poor Pozzo's head into a wall and fleeing the building,' she continued. 'Clearly, you believe we can be of assistance to one another, otherwise you would not have come back. And yet you expect me to give answers simply because you demand them . . .' Coltello shook her head, tutting loudly. 'My dear Cesare, it seems you do not know me at all.'

He did not reply immediately. Good. Hopefully that meant he was recognizing the folly of such a blunt approach. 'You are correct,' Aldo said, his voice now a respectful murmur of contrition. 'Please, forgive my trespasses. It has been . . . a difficult few days.'

She was minded to refuse the apology. Pozzo was going to be in a foul mood after what had happened, and getting him to work with Aldo would require all her persuasion. Coltello suppressed a sigh. It was a source of ongoing frustration that men pouted and whined like children when facing a reversal of fortune. Women had to cope with far worse yet were expected to offer their sympathies for every bruise a man suffered to his body or sense of self.

It was quite exhausting.

But Aldo did bring with him the potential to be of considerable assistance, if he could be tamed. 'Very well,' she said. 'But do not try my patience again. Should you do so, the consequences will be tiresome for me – and might well be fatal for you.' She turned and smiled, letting no warmth into her eyes so he knew the threat was truthful.

'I understand,' Aldo replied.

'Very well. In the spirit of forgiveness, I propose that we take it in turns to ask each other a question. That way you will have the answers you seek, assuming they are in my power to give, and I can determine how best to make use of you here in Venice.'

'Make use of me?'

Coltello waggled an admonishing finger. 'First, do me the courtesy of washing. Pozzo will provide you with water and fresh clothes. I am fond of you, Aldo, but not nearly enough to stomach your stench any longer. Wash now, questions after.'

Dandolo waited in the vast courtyard of the Doge's palazzo, shivering in the cold breeze that often blew through it during winter and early spring. He wasn't sure what to do with himself. Going home to questions from the famiglia Dandolo was not appealing, though they must be faced eventually. He had set off to Florence with such hopes, so confident of winning the respect of his famiglia at last. Was that why he had so boldly exceeded Bragadin's orders? Perhaps. But he was tired of doing as he was told, waiting for others to see his talents. Better to reach high and fail than scuttle about at Bragadin's bidding, as Culmine always did.

No sooner had Dandolo thought of his rival than Culmine was hurrying across the courtyard. He was at least ten summers older than Dandolo, yet little sign of that showed in his square shoulders and firm jaw. There was grey creeping into his hair, and a few lines at the corners of his eyes, but that was all. Culmine surviving for so long in service to Bragadin proved he was a skilled administrator and also no threat to their shared master.

There was something in Culmine's grasp: a red journal.

Dandolo strode out to intercept him. 'Going to the cipher deputies?'

Culmine kept his pace, making Dandolo hurry alongside him. 'I can't be seen talking to you, Armando. Not after what happened in Florence.'

'After what I did?'

Culmine paused, glancing around to see if anyone was close enough to hear them. 'Bragadin is furioso with you, and everyone knows it.' He rested a gentle hand on Dandolo's shoulder. 'You should go home before he discovers you're still here. That would only make matters worse.' Culmine gave a weak smile before hurrying away.

But Dandolo was not ready to be dismissed. 'We are of equal rank in Bragadin's ufficio,' he said, following Culmine. 'You need not warn me about his moods. Besides, you didn't answer my question. Are you taking that journal to the deputies?'

They were the men responsible for deciphering all coded despatches and letters from Venetian ambassadors and agents beyond the Serenissima. A plain text document was made and attached to the coded original so the Doge could easily read its contents.

'I am,' Culmine replied. 'Bragadin wants the first page deciphered, but no more. After that it is going into the secret archive.'

Dandolo could not believe what he was hearing. 'But if the deputies only decipher the first page, nobody will know what is written in the rest of the journal. How am I to be vindicated, unless . . .' Dandolo's words died on his lips. Bragadin had no intention of allowing any vindication. This was deliberate.

Culmine gave a weak smile. 'I'm sorry, Armando. Truly.' He strode away.

Dandolo was left alone in the courtyard. All had seemed so promising as he arrived back in Venice. Now he was in danger of being dismissed from the Doge's palazzo. He had gambled, and lost. The true cost of that still remained to be seen.

Aldo hated to admit it, but the contessa had been correct: washing away the sweat and grime and merda of the past few days was restorative. Putting on another man's clothes – fine blue woollen hose and a shimmering tunic of cerulean silk, along with a pair of supple boots – was less welcome, but necessary. His own garments were fit only for burning, and the boots he'd worn from Florence were beyond repair. Still, he would miss them.

Once he was ready, Aldo let himself be ushered back to Coltello in her salone. Pozzo kept two steps behind, but Aldo had no attention of fleeing this time, not when there were answers to be had. The contessa smiled, thanking Pozzo before dismissing him.

'My dear Cesare,' she said, 'you look better than my husband ever did in his clothes.' Coltello sniffed the air. 'And you smell better than before, too. Good.' She patted the chair beside her. 'We've much to discuss.'

Aldo perched on the well-padded seat, cautious and ready to respond if a threat should approach. The contessa was showing her most welcoming face, but she was capable of wearing many masks. 'You suggested we take turns asking each other questions,' he began.

Mischief twinkled in her bewitching emerald eyes. 'Is that your first question?'

'No, simply a statement of fact. But that was your first, so now it's my turn.'

'Very good. Well, then, ask me whatever you wish.'

Aldo had been deciding what were the most urgent questions to resolve while washing, so his first was easy. 'Where is Dandolo?'

'The Dandolos are a famiglia of some importance here in Venice, with many bearing that name. You need to be more specific with your questions, Cesare. I should have thought all those years investigating for the Otto would have taught you better.'

'Perhaps I am out of practice.'

'Nevertheless, I get the next question. Why were you and that other man pursuing Armando so relentlessly? I could understand hunting him as far as Scarperia, perhaps even to Bologna. But all the way to Le Casette . . .'

'The other man is – or was – Ottone, Duke Cosimo's head of security.'

'Ahh, so it was Ottone. That explains why he had a pistol aimed at you. I doubt you would have left that village alive if not for Dandolo's surprising skill with a crossbow. But you still haven't answered my question. Why pursue him all the way to Le Casette?'

'To reclaim what he stole,' Aldo replied. 'Now, where is Armando Dandolo?'

'I don't know.'

Aldo arched an eyebrow at the contessa, making his disbelief evident.

'Truly, my dear Cesare, I do not know. The last I saw him was at Le Casette as my carriage was leaving with you in a trunk strapped to the back. I offered him a seat beside me, but he declined. Dandolo insisted we must enter Venice by different means on different days. My maggiordomo here, a rather tiresome man called Amaro, tells me Dandolo is due to arrive tomorrow. How accurate that report is remains to be seen.' She leaned closer. 'Now, what did Dandolo steal from Palazzo Medici? And please do not insult my intelligence with another half-answer. I would not wish to think less of you.'

Aldo hesitated. Much as he enjoyed jousting with the contessa, there was little to lose and more to gain by being candid. 'Thanks to your intervention, and the help of his foolish cousin, Armando Dandolo stole a book of Venetian ciphers from inside the ducal residence. He also filled two satchels with papers and correspondence belonging to Cosimo de' Medici, including a journal written in code by the duke.'

Coltello's eyes lit up. 'I imagine such a journal must contain important private thoughts and musings, otherwise he would not bother using a code.'

'It holds Cosimo's opinion of his patron, the Holy Roman Emperor, and what he thinks of His Holiness the Pope, amongst other things. Should the journal fall into the hands of those capable of deciphering it—'

'A skill at which Venetians are among the best in the world.'

'– the consequences could be Cosimo's undoing.'

'It is no wonder you went to such lengths to reclaim this journal.'

Aldo nodded. Having told her so much truth, it was the right moment to build upon that trust. 'But you see, Cosimo is not the only one threatened by it. The duke also wrote of his belief that you were responsible for the murder of Tito Grossolano in Florence. I'm told Grossolano's uncle is a man of great importance with the Inquisitori di Stato. If that journal should reach the tribunal, it could be your undoing, Contessa.'

Chapter Fifteen

❦

Coltello wanted to believe Aldo was lying. His words had the temptation of a snare, perfectly crafted to draw her in. But the possibility of such writings was credible, and if these could implicate her in the murder of Bragadin's nephew . . . That left her no choice. She must use whatever means were necessary to destroy that journal.

She licked her lips, savouring the fear and excitement which was making her blood race and her breath quicken. It was too long since she had faced a true threat to her position, let alone to her life. Wordplay and teasing were all very well, but rare were the occasions when they brought any meaningful danger – for her, at least. Yet this trip to Venice was fast becoming more than an adventure with each passing hour.

How delightful.

'My dear Cesare, I am so glad you have brought this to my attention.' Coltello rested her fingertips on Aldo's thigh, appreciating the taut muscles beneath his hose, the tremor of response that touch brought despite his preferences. Most people had an idle curiosity about the boundaries of their sex and the fidelity of those boundaries, in her experience. But few had the courage or wit to act on such curiosity, letting themselves be constrained by habits or their beliefs. If she and Aldo survived the next few days, she might invite him to test those boundaries with her. 'Now, I believe it is your turn to ask a question.'

'Grazie,' he replied, a pleasant smile hiding whatever he was thinking. 'Was it your idea to bring me to Venice, or did Dandolo suggest it?'

'That was my notion. Dandolo would have killed you in the church at Le Casette if I had not persuaded him to let me decide your fate.'

'Grazie mille,' Aldo said. 'Your turn.'

Coltello sat back in her chair. 'You owe me a debt. Are you willing to repay it here?'

'A debt?'

'Answering a question with another question is no answer at all, as we both know. Three months ago, you pleaded with me to intercede against a troublesome priest on your behalf. Father Pagolo Zati, I believe his name was.'

'Zati was far more than troublesome. He murdered two men in Florence, attacked another priest, and was suspected of killing many of his elderly parishioners. I've met others who developed a taste for killing, and they were dangerous. Zati was something far worse, a predator in priest's clothing. Only his own death will stop him killing again.'

'Yes, yes,' she said, not bothering to hide her impatience at this recitation. 'You told me Zati was being banished by the diocese and it seemed likely he might find a way here to Venice. You asked me to ensure he could take no more lives. I have done this.'

'Zati's dead?'

'Again, that is another question. Like most men, Cesare, you struggle to remember when it is the woman's turn to be gratified. I shall forgive that, as I suppose you have less experience in such matters. To answer your question, yes, Zati is dead. He drowned in a canal. Venice can be a treacherous place for visitors and inexperienced swimmers.'

Aldo opened his mouth, but stopped himself from speaking.

'Very good,' Coltello said. 'Now you can reply to my previous question. Are you willing to repay the debt you owe me here in Venice?'

'Yes.'

That was too easy an answer but she would have to accept it. 'Very well.'

'Was Zati's body recovered from the canal?'

'No. He . . . fell into the water during the last acqua alta and was swept away, making it impossible to reclaim his corpse. Trust me, anyone who drowns in the lagoon stays drowned. Father Pagolo Zati is quite dead.'

'Good,' Aldo said. 'Grazie.'

'Prego.' She paused. There was another question that needed asking, but it seemed unlikely any answer Aldo gave to it would be truthful. Besides, she had a plan for testing if her information was correct which was likely to be far more reliable.

Amaro appeared in the salone doorway, clearing his throat to get her attention. 'A message has come for you, Contessa.' He brandished a letter sealed with blue wax.

'Bring it here,' Coltello said, beckoning him forwards. She gestured at Aldo. 'Amaro, this is my guest, Cesare Aldo. He will be staying in the lavender room.'

'As you think best,' Amaro said, handing her the letter.

His apparent civility did not hide the insult behind his words. She made a note to see such behaviour found a suitable punishment before she left the city. 'Aldo, this is Amaro, who was my late husband's faithful maggiordomo here in Venice.'

The implicit threat in her words – that if she stayed on in the city, Amaro would not remain long as maggiordomo – brought a flash of anger to his supercilious face.

Good. Let him seethe.

Coltello took the letter, dismissing the maggiordomo with a flick of her fingers. Only when Amaro was gone did she break the seal and read what was within. 'How wonderful! An old acquaintance heard I am back and has invited us to a Bacchanal at his palazzo.'

'Us?' Aldo asked.

She gave him a playful glare. 'Another question? You really must learn some self-restraint, Cesare. If you don't, I shall be obliged to teach you. No, my friend does not know about you or your presence here in Venice. But I'm sure he would not object to my bringing an acquaintance. When it comes to a Bacchanal during Carnival, the more the merrier. Besides, I need someone to lean on when I wear my accursed zoccoli later.'

Aldo opened his mouth but stopped himself asking another question, a smile playing on his lips. The contessa was pleased he was such a quick study. Aldo would make a droll companion for her. That was as well, considering what she had planned for him . . .

Coltello rose to her feet, eager to start preparing. After so many months away, it was important to look both ravishing and unobtainable for her first public engagement.

Aldo joined her as she strolled across the salone. 'I have one more question,' he said.

'Make it brisk.'

'What happened to my stiletto? It was in my left boot, but now . . .'

'Pozzo has that. He will return the blade to you once matters here are at an end.'

Aldo nodded, but his discomfort at being in her service was still apparent.

Coltello stopped at the salone door, smirking at him. 'Don't look so concerned, Cesare. I believe you can be of assistance to me. Who knows? You might even find the experience pleasurable. One must always be open to new sensations, yes?'

Several hours later, Aldo was hesitating. He prided himself on being able to stand tall in almost any situation, to stay resolute no matter the threat or danger. Yes, he knew fear; all men did, no matter what face they presented to the world and what lies they told themselves. Without fear, courage and bravery were simply foolishness dressed in a noble cloak. Those without the sense to see peril in front of them had no reason to be afraid. As a wise woman once said, the world was made for those who were not cursed with self-awareness.

Aldo had faced men far more powerful than himself, had stood his ground without weapons while confronting multiple attackers. There were more times than Aldo could recall when he had expected to die, when he should not have survived. The years spent on the streets of Florence after Lucrezia banished him from Palazzo Fioravanti. The battles fought as a mercenary alongside Giovanni delle Bande Nere while outnumbered and outflanked. Those crimes investigated for the Otto that brought him face to face with madmen and murderers.

But nothing made his bowels so weak as this.

'Why you waiting?' the contessa asked with a huff of impatience. 'Get in.'

That was easy for her to say. She was used to doing this, she did it without thinking.

But Aldo had never been comfortable in a boat or on water.

The sea, the lagoon, canals . . . none of them could be trusted. One moment the surface appeared placid, benign, little threat to anyone or anything. The next it could shift and swirl, move unexpectedly, jolt and jerk. Water was akin to a wild beast, but one too large ever to be tamed, a vast animal full of invisible currents and coldness.

'Get in,' Coltello repeated.

Aldo willed himself to step from the short platform outside Palazzo Coltello to the gondola floating on the canal. But the wooden craft kept moving, never staying still atop the water. The contessa had made this look so easy, so simple.

'Now,' she said, steel in her voice.

Aldo stretched out a leg – and the gondola shifted away from him, the gap between it and the platform widening, expanding. Palle, he was going to fall into the water –

– but the gondola bobbed back, his boot met wood and he was across.

'At last!' Coltello rolled her eyes. 'Now sit down before you tip us over.'

Aldo did as she bid, lowering himself onto the seat beside her. The gondola was wide enough to fit two easily, but the padded cushions on either side pushed Aldo and the contessa together so they were hip to hip, thigh against thigh. She seemed to radiate warmth and this close her scent of jasmine and musk was intoxicating. Coltello rested a hand on his leg.

'You're trembling,' she said, stroking his hose-clad thigh.

'I prefer travelling on foot or by horse.'

The contessa gestured for her gondolier to proceed. He pushed them away from Palazzo Coltello, the craft wobbling a little. Aldo grabbed the side nearest to him, fingers clenching tight. Then they were gliding forwards, the movement far more gentle and graceful than Aldo expected. His fingers loosened their grip a little.

'Are you afraid of boats?' Coltello asked, amusement in her voice.

'No,' Aldo insisted. 'A boat is a boat, nothing more.'

'Don't say that too loudly. People here live and die by boat. Venetians respond poorly to any outsider who sneers at the fact that this city was built out of marshes and mud.' She smiled. 'If the gondola is not your enemy . . . my dear Cesare, are you afraid of water?'

He did not reply. Silence could speak for him.

Coltello laughed. 'I never imagined a man like you could be made so timid. Have you never learned to swim, is that the problem?'

Knowing she would not let this go without an answer, Aldo cleared his throat. 'I've never had the need. Only a fool swims in the Arno, not when you know what goes into it from the tanneries and fabric-dye workshops upriver.'

'Yes, that makes sense, but still –' she patted his leg before letting go – 'the more I learn about you, the more I discover there is to learn. It is most enjoyable.'

Aldo feigned a smile but was more interested in observing landmarks as the gondola made its way along the canals. The sooner he could commit the city to memory, the less he would have to rely on the contessa. Coltello was happy to play host, but she had brought him to Venice for a specific reason. Whatever that might be, it was likely to be dangerous. Better to have a way out he could follow alone, if necessary.

Travelling in a gondola was initially unnerving. The craft sat so low in the water that the buildings on either side looked like towers, stretching up into the cloudy sky. Yet where the palazzi met the canal, their stonework was stained green. Was that moss growing where water lapped at the buildings? In some places structures had sunk down into the canal, the bottoms of exposed wooden doors and shutters rotting.

'I'm not surprised you chose to stay away from Venice so long,' Coltello said. 'A man as uncomfortable around water as you would struggle here. But, perhaps, there was another reason why you fled the Serenissima . . .'

Aldo stayed silent, refusing to give her any satisfaction in this. The contessa could share what she knew or believed without his assistance.

'Do you like my gown?' she asked, smoothing down its emerald silk. 'I must say your friend Renato Patricio is quite an artist with a needle and thread. This is one of his creations.'

'Very fine,' Aldo agreed.

'In truth, I only employed him to discover what gossip about your past he might be willing to share. That he proved such an able dressmaker – well, it was a pleasant surprise.'

Aldo nodded. The contessa had been teasing him about Patricio for days. It would not have taken much effort by Coltello to coax the dressmaker into revealing what he knew about Aldo's past. Patricio loved hearing and sharing the things others did not wish known. A little praise about his skills with a gown, a glass or two of good wine, and Patricio would tell all.

'But it was what he said about you, Cesare, which intrigued me most. I didn't believe all of it – your friend embroiders his stories even more than his dresses – but he seemed quite truthful while telling me why it was you swore never to come back here.'

'Indeed?'

'Yes. According to Patricio, you had your heart broken in Venice. Is that true?'

'It's so long ago,' Aldo replied. 'I don't recall.'

Coltello gave a giggle of delight. 'How delightful!' She raised a hand in the air, gesturing to the gondolier behind her. 'Luigi, go left up ahead.'

'Of course, Contessa, but that will—'

'Yes, I know. That will take us away from the Grand Canal, not towards it. But there is someone we need to call upon before arriving at Palazzo Bollani.'

'Very good, Contessa.'

The gondolier followed her instructions, turning left at the next opening on that side. Despite his efforts to commit the journey to memory, Aldo had lost all sense of whether they were moving north, east, west or south. The lack of sunshine meant any shadows were muted, denying him an easy way to determine their direction.

When the contessa spoke next, he struggled to grasp the meaning of her words. Most were familiar to him, but some were in the Venetian dialect. Aldo guessed at a reply.

Coltello laughed. 'You did not understand what I just said, did you?'

'No,' he admitted. 'Not all of it.'

'Ask me a question as if we were both Venetian.'

Aldo did his best, scratching at his memories from long ago, but the words would not come briskly or with any conviction. The contessa shook her head. 'No, no, that won't do, not for the gathering to which we've been invited. You may be able to follow much of what people say, but you certainly won't be capable of holding a conversation.' She tapped an elegant finger against her lips. 'Very well. I shall tell everyone that you are a mute, born without the power of speech, and nor are you capable of reading or writing, you poor thing.'

'Is that necessary?' He could understand the stratagemma of

saying he was mute; it meant he could not betray himself as a son of Tuscany by speaking. But Coltello announcing he also did not have his letters seemed a needless and petty humiliation.

'Perhaps not for tonight. But there are places in Venice where only men incapable of reading and writing are allowed to go because they can be no threat to what is kept there.' She was alluding to the secret archive. Aldo had heard whispers of this place, but knew little more beyond its location being deep inside the Doge's palazzo. 'Perhaps I should also say you are unable to hear?' Coltello went on. 'That would enable you to listen in to all kinds of conversations.'

'Pretending to be a mute is easy enough. Having no hearing is far harder a task at which to convince; responding to the slightest noise would give me away. Besides, many people wrongly presume those who cannot speak also cannot hear.'

'Very well,' the contessa agreed. 'Mute and illiterate it is. But there is one more thing we need to do before reaching our first destination.' She pulled aside the corner of her cloak to reveal a black mask with silver details, and red silk ribbons dangling from it. 'Put this on. It will conceal your face from the nose upwards.'

'Why do I need to wear a mask?' Aldo protested. 'I am not known in Venice.'

'And this will help you remain unknown.' Coltello pressed it into his hands. 'For you to assist me in the coming days, it may be important that few see your face tonight.'

Her answer was full of evasions, as usual. She had another reason for hiding his face but was not going to share that. Not yet, at least.

Aldo put on the mask, tying the ribbons in a double-bow behind his head. It was more comfortable than he had expected, and he could see clearly through the eyeholes. 'Good enough?'

The contessa regarded him. 'Very good indeed. Ahh, Luigi, slow us down. I'm told that the master of that palazzo up ahead takes a glass of wine on this balcony most days as sunset approaches. Let us see if my information is correct . . .'

Culmine found regularity reassuring. So much of his day was devoted to the needs of others that where he could make his own choice, Culmine took comfort in the familiarity of habits. He woke at the same time every morning, no matter if it was summer, autumn or Carnival. He kissed his wife Livia and two daughters three times before leaving their modest home. He always followed the same path to the Doge's palazzo, careful to arrive at the ufficio of Signor Bragadin in good time. It was important to be dependable, to do the best he could.

That helped him to have some small measure of control.

Once Bragadin reached the ufficio, there was no knowing what demands he would make. Preparing for meetings of the Inquisitori di Stato had a certain shape, but the Doge's advisor was a man driven by his humours. Often Bragadin was a thunderstorm full of fury and deafening bursts of noise, his rage striking unexpected targets. When his humours were more melancholic, Bragadin sank to dark depths where no tide could raise his spirits. Working for him was a daily terror, bringing a fear that could empty any man's bowels. None in Bragadin's service knew what he would be from one day to the next.

It was exhausting.

When Bragadin was selected for the Inquisitori di Stato, Culmine had hoped to be left behind. Surely the Doge's advisor would want different men to assist him in such an important role? Culmine had been happiest when his principal role was safeguarding the secret archive. Instead, Bragadin chose to keep the assistants he already had – better the diavolo known, he said – but they also had to maintain their previous roles as well.

The tribunal met during the day but, at Bragadin's suggestion, the three inquisitors now often also held sessions at night. Suspects and witnesses were more likely to talk when nobody else was close enough to hear their screams, Bragadin had said with a smile. It was unclear if that was jest or threat. Either way, Culmine had to be there in attendance.

He went home each evening to eat with Livia and the girls before returning to the Doge's palazzo for night sessions. Ahead of meals he took a cup of wine out onto their small, low balcony and watched the waters of the canal. Livia had taught the girls not to trouble him then, that their papa needed his time alone so he could have peace . . .

'Signor Culmine!'

But not everyone understood that.

'Signor Culmine!'

The voice was that of a woman, calling from a gondola as it floated along the canal, approaching the balcony. It was close to dusk, but Culmine could see she had a handsome face and was wearing a vibrant emerald gown. There was a man sitting beside her, dressed in rich but more understated clothes, his upper face hidden behind a Carnival mask.

'Buona sera,' Culmine replied as the gondola glided to a halt beside the balcony. 'Forgive me, signora, but I do not recognize you.'

She smiled, her green eyes sparkling at him. 'I would not expect you to, signor, as I've only just returned to Venice. But I must congratulate you on such an impressive rise amid the ranks of those at the Doge's palazzo. To become the most noted assistant of Signor Bragadin and the Inquisitori di Stato – well, more than once have I heard your name mentioned with great respect and appreciation. Bravo, signor. Bravo.'

'I . . .' Culmine was at a loss for words. 'Grazie. Grazie mille.'

'Prego,' she replied, bowing her head a little. The man beside her muttered a word. 'You must forgive my companion. He's eager to see Carnival in all its splendour.'

'Of course.' Culmine looked again at the man by her. There was something familiar about him, despite the mask covering much of his face. The set of his shoulders, the strength of those hands, the way he held himself . . .

'Papa, Papa!' Culmine's youngest daughter called from the doorway behind him. 'Mama says to tell you to come in. I'm hungry and cena is ready.'

'I'll be right there,' Culmine replied.

'We will leave you to eat with your famiglia,' the woman in the gondola said, waving a hand in the air. The craft moved away from the balcony, easing out into the canal. 'Buona sera, Signor Culmine!' she called. 'I'm sure we shall meet again soon.'

'I still do not know your name,' he shouted after her.

'Coltello,' she replied. 'Contessa Coltello. Enjoy your evening, Vincenzo!'

Chapter Sixteen

Vincenzo. The moment Aldo saw him it was as if clouds that had been blocking the sky for days beyond number suddenly parted; in that moment, the sun shone down on them, turning the canal a sparkling blue, full of light and life and long-forgotten joy. Everything else fell away – the gondola on the water, the contessa beside him – and all he saw was Vincenzo. That face so familiar, the yearning for him so powerful Aldo was made dizzy by it.

Pain brought him back. Aldo had unclenched his fists to find red crescents where his nails were pressed into both palms. Beside him the contessa was talking, but Aldo didn't listen. It took all his strength not to stare at the figure on the balcony. Instead, he feigned disinterest, hoping the mask would conceal his gaze.

Vincenzo looked much the same as he had so long ago. Yes, he was older, with grey hair at his temples and lines at the corners of both eyes. But he still had that firm jaw, those square shoulders. He still stood tall, and was lean of body. Age and the years had not stolen away the narrowness of his hips, the strength in those legs. Above his tunic, something in the hairs on Vincenzo's chest caught the sun: a small ornate key on a cord hung round his neck. That was new, he never wore jewellery before. Aldo squinted to see the key better but the setting sun kept glinting off it, bringing a curse to his lips.

Coltello spoke again and the gondola moved on, away from the balcony. Vincenzo called to the contessa and she replied with her name. 'Enjoy your evening, Vincenzo!'

Then he was gone, all sight of Vincenzo lost.

Aldo sank back in the gondola seat.

Coltello smirked at him.

She knew.

She knew about him and Vincenzo, what they had meant to each other.

How did she . . . ?

Patricio.

Aldo's thoughts raced back across all that Coltello had said, her little hints and teases. This must be why she had brought him to Venice, because of his history with Vincenzo. She had seen an opportunity to use it as a weapon or a snare. She believed using him would help to secure Vincenzo's help. If so, Patricio had not told her everything. The dressmaker had not told Coltello how things ended with Vincenzo, otherwise she might have devised a different stratagemma. But Patricio could not tell her because he did not know the whole story.

The contessa's cold, calculating methods were no surprise. She was quite willing to use anything and anyone. Everything was in service of her needs. Aldo's encounters with her in the past had been playful, with far less at stake. Now he was realizing what it was to be on the wrong end of her attentions.

But how far would Coltello go to achieve her ends? Aldo already knew the answer to that question. Grossolano had been killed on her command in Florence. The contessa did not get blood on her own hands, of course, but she showed no hesitation in having others murder for her. Those who were still useful remained alive; those who outlasted their helpfulness did not.

So long as he stood by her side, Aldo suspected he would be safe enough.

But any hint of betrayal, any disappointment . . .

. . . that would be fatal.

How did she intend to use his past with Vincenzo? The answer to that was what he needed, but asking directly would bring no answer and no satisfaction. Patience was required to get any truth from her. Better to go along with those games and tricks, to smile and nod. If he performed well, she might reward that with a glimpse of what lay ahead.

Aldo let the corners of his mouth turn up for Coltello to see.

'Is that a hint of a smile?' she asked, using the Tuscan tongue rather than the Venetian she had spoken with Vincenzo. 'I worried that presenting you with a past lover might cause a different response. Not everyone appreciates my taste for intrigue.'

'Then they do not know you well,' he replied. 'We are all of us floating from birth to death. Those who cannot enjoy the journey make for dull companions.'

'Indeed. So, my dear Cesare, how was it?'

'Meeting Vincenzo again?'

She nodded, her gaze fixed on him.

What to tell her? Seeing Vincenzo was akin to having an old wound ripped open. No, the sensation was closer to an insetti bite, one that brought a delicious need to be scratched, a craving to claw at his own skin until it was red and raw. Vincenzo had been a compulsion for Aldo, one he had repressed and even forgotten for a while, but which never truly went away. The need, the wanting, the craving was always there, below the water. Nothing could drown that, not for ever. Like an inconvenient corpse, it always found a way back to the surface.

Seeing Vincenzo had caused a quickening in Aldo's chest, his heart galloping faster than any horse. He had hoped that had long since passed. But nothing could be further from the truth. Gone for years, back within moments. It was dizzying to stand on the edge, to look down at an abyss and know that diving in would bring nothing but pain and anguish. Yet the temptation was still so strong. This was not love, Aldo knew that now.

This was lust; pure, animal lust.

'It was . . . unexpected,' Aldo said.

'I should hope so,' she replied. 'I went to considerable lengths to ensure you did not know where we were going, nor whom we would encounter. I feared my comment about a broken heart was too much, yet you seemed surprised when we met Signor Culmine.'

'I was. Bravo.'

'It is Amaro who deserves your praise. Once Patricio told me some weeks ago about your time in Venice, I had my maggiordomo here investigate Vincenzo Culmine. Imagine my delight on hearing he works within the Doge's palazzo, let alone that he was among those assisting the Inquisitori di Stato! I am no great believer in fate, my dear Cesare, but I cannot help laughing sometimes at how often fortune favours the fearless.'

The gondola floated on, the canal growing wider. Dusk was settling over Venice, yet the bridges they passed beneath were thronged with men and women in masks and elaborate clothes, carrying lanterns to light their way. In Florence this would be forbidden by curfew, but it seemed such laws were ignored by many Venetians during Carnival.

Aldo had been too distracted to note much of what passed between Vincenzo and Coltello, but some of their words had lingered. Forgotten phrases in the Venetian dialect were returning to him. 'You were congratulating Vincenzo on his position at the Doge's palazzo.'

Mischief danced in the contessa's green eyes. 'You are recalling more of this city's speech? Good. You will need all of that and more.'

'Vincenzo works for Bragadin at the tribunal.'

'Indeed.'

Aldo was starting to suspect what she wanted him to do next. It was even more dangerous than he had feared.

Pietro Aretino was perplexed. 'My dear Evelina, you want me to lift up your skirts? Here? In front of everyone?' Pretending to be scandalized, he looked around at all those gathered in his salone: friends, fellow writers, artistic collaborators, mistresses, servants and those patricians brave enough to attend his Bacchanal. 'Whatever should I do?'

'Lift them!' called out the sculptor and architect Sansovino.

'Lift them up!' shouted Aretino's business partner, Marcolini.

Soon everyone was joining in, chanting 'Lift them up' in a single voice.

'Well, if you insist . . .' Aretino replied, reaching down to grasp the courtesan's skirts. Evelina was wearing an elaborate gown of brocade and silk, a tight corset enclosing her petite bosom before the fabric flared out at the hips.

Aretino wafted the skirts a few times to tease those watching, before he lifted the fabric high into the air . . . revealing Evelina's legs, encased in breeches and hose! The room roared its approval, cheering Evelina for dressing as a man beneath her gown. Such garb was forbidden for women. The authorities feared it would stimulate men's lust for other men – which was against the law – or promote sodomy with women against the law of God.

The prohibition had failed, of course. There were thousands of courtesans in Venice, and preventing them all from dressing as men was impractical, if not impossible. Aretino considered any attempt to control what they wore pure folly, just as the Council of Ten forbidding men from dressing as women was equally futile. It was Carnival, a time when so many in Venice proudly wore masks and pretence.

Aretino let Evelina's skirts drop. 'As ever, you are a thing of wonder and surprise,' he said, kissing her on the cheek. 'Were I not already involved elsewhere, I would happily take you to my bed here and now!' That brought another roar of approval, as Aretino knew it would. He had a reputation to maintain, after all.

A servant in a nearby doorway was gesturing to him. 'Now, you must forgive me, but I have other guests to attend to!' he announced to booing and groans. 'Much as I love you all, there is only so much Pietro to go around.' Aretino waved to Cisti. 'More wine!' he told the maid. 'Let no man, no woman, no diavolo go thirsty in my home.' That seemed to satisfy those nearby; the gathered throng let him stroll from the salone unhindered.

'Forgive me for interrupting, signor,' the servant said. 'A woman has arrived whom I do not know. She claims that you invited her, but did not bring this supposed invitation.'

Could it be the contessa? Aretino had received no reply to his invitation, and she had always been most fastidious in such matters. That outward appearance of prim propriety made her behaviour behind closed doors all the more surprising to those who did not truly know her and, therefore, all the more enjoyable. Perhaps she had been too busy to reply? His invitation had been sent late in the day, giving her little notice.

'Take me to her,' Aretino said, and he followed his servant to a door leading out on to the Grand Canal. There a gondola waited with an impatient woman in a gorgeous gown of emerald silk, accompanied by a masked man. 'My dear contessa, please forgive my servant,' Aretino said, bowing low. 'He has only been with me a few months, and it is some time since you last graced my humble residence with your delicious presence.'

Coltello gave a small nod. 'There's nothing to forgive,' she replied, stretching out a delicate hand for Aretino to help her from the gondola. The masked man held her other hand as she stepped into the palazzo, her balance a little uncertain. 'It is some time since I have worn zoccoli,' the contessa said, lifting the hem of her gown to reveal two tall platforms on which she was standing, her slipper-clad feet tied into the overshoes that topped the zoccoli.

The platforms were at least a hand in height to Aretino's eye. What had been invented as a practical solution to a common problem – Venice was forever damp, its calle awash with mud and worse – soon became a statement of both style and prestige. The taller the zoccoli, the higher the status of their wearer. Aretino had sometimes considered writing about this, but concluded that not everything needed his commentary. Far too many men could not resist the urge to pass judgement on the ways of women.

'Zoccoli are neither necessary nor common in Florence,' Coltello added, 'for which I am grateful. But, when in Venice, one must do as everyone does.'

'Perhaps,' Aretino said, 'but I have never known you to be enslaved by the whims or expectations of others.' That brought a smile of appreciation from the contessa. She gestured at the companion who had followed her into the palazzo, staying close by the contessa's side. Was this her new lover? He had a lean and lithe figure with an upright stature, yet did not seem quite comfortable in his fine clothes. Judging from what was visible beneath the mask, Aretino guessed the newcomer must be closer to forty than thirty.

'This is my new servant, Cesare.' Coltello leaned closer. 'He's Florentine, but don't hold that against him.'

'I would never judge another man by his origins,' Aretino replied before slipping into the Tuscan tongue to address her companion. 'My famiglia home was in Arezzo, so I know how overwhelming the Serenissima can be to a visitor. Take comfort that there are few present tonight who can truly claim to be born in the salty water. You are very welcome.' Aretino waited but got no reply. The servant looked at the contessa instead.

'You must forgive Cesare,' she said. 'The poor fellow is a mute. Quite unable to utter a word since he was a child, apparently. I'm told some terrible accident stole away his ability to speak. Most unfortunate. I pray for the day when his mouth finds its true use.'

'How regrettable,' Aretino agreed, reverting to Venetian.

Coltello rested a hand on her companion's shoulder. 'Cesare, this is Pietro Aretino. Writer, correspondent, observer, wit and all-round scoundrel. I would tell you to be careful what you say around him in case it might end up in one of his infamous letters but, as you can neither speak nor read, I doubt that will be a concern.' She smiled at Aretino. 'Now, where are these distinguished signori you wished me to meet?'

'This way, this way,' he replied, ushering her along a corridor. Cesare came with the contessa, her hand on his shoulder for support. They passed the throng still being entertained by Evelina in the salone, and continued on towards a smaller, far more peaceful room. One of Aretino's closest friends stepped into their path, his piercing eyes fixed on Coltello.

'Pietro,' Tiziano said, 'who is this ravishing beauty that stands before me?'

Aretino introduced the contessa. 'You must excuse my friend,' he warned, 'but Tiziano is a painter and always in need of fresh faces to inspire him – or fresh bodies.'

Tiziano tutted. 'You do me a disservice! I am not some fiend using his work to seduce anyone who poses for him.' His gaze returned to the contessa. 'But it would be a great honour if you were to model for me. I am starting a new painting soon inspired by the writings of Ovid, a scene featuring Jupiter and Antiope. You would look most ravishing if captured on such a canvas. Or perhaps you prefer to be painted as Venus? I can see that suiting you equally well—'

'Enough,' Aretino said. 'I brought the contessa here to meet someone else, Tiziano. If there is time later, you can charm her with your words then, yes?'

The painter pouted a little before he stepped aside, bowing to Coltello. 'Should you set some time aside for me, Contessa, it would be a great pleasure . . .'

Aretino led Coltello and her companion past Tiziano to the small side room. There three men were playing cards at a table while arguing about the Doge. 'Lando is an old fool who lets the glory of Venice sink into the lagoon while the Turks humiliate him,' a scowling man complained, slapping a card down. Afani Mastello was a senator known for the strength of his views about the way wars were waged despite never having spent a moment near a battle. In Aretino's experience, Mastello was never happy unless he was angry.

'The Doge may be an old man,' the jovial fellow by Mastello said, 'but then we are all old in the Senate, are we not?' Filippo Salvadori was round of face and belly, a man fonder of food than anything else. 'We pay others to fight, and wonder why they surrender so easily.'

'This is true,' the last of the three agreed, 'but our doge wastes his time on laws that will never endure. I mean, his notion of purifying Venice by forbidding all the courtesans from wearing jewellery or silk clothes? Utter nonsense!' Jacopo Alberto had a hawkish face, and long fingers that jealously guarded his cards. Like the others he was close to sixty, yet age had not diminished his passion. 'We all know what happens to such rules in this city.'

'A Venetian law lasts but a week,' Mastello and Salvadori chorused in reply.

'Exactly.' Alberto placed his cards face up on the table, causing howls of protest. 'I win again. Get out your purses, both of you. I want coin and I want it now!'

'You can forget that invitation I sent for my masked ball tomorrow night,' Mastello sighed, reaching for his pouch. 'Take any more coin and I'll have to cancel it altogether.'

'Signori,' Aretino said, loud enough so his words would be heard over their bickering. He introduced all three men by name. 'This is a good friend of mine. Her name is—'

'Call me Valentine,' the contessa announced. She bowed, letting the trio savour the valley between her breasts. Aretino suppressed a smirk; Coltello was quite shameless when it was needed – and often when it was not. 'If Pietro reveals any more, I fear it may frighten you.'

'That sounds like a challenge,' Mastello roared, banging a fist on the table.

'More like a warning,' Salvadori said, but his interest was plain to see.

'Come, sit.' Alberto gestured to an empty chair between him and Salvadori.

'How kind,' Coltello replied, her masked companion helping her to the seat. She whispered something in his ear before sinking into the chair. 'Now, what game are we playing, signori, and who shall be most in my debt when I win?'

That brought laughter and bellows of approval from all three. The contessa nodded her thanks to Aretino. He withdrew, Cesare following him out of the room. 'Are you hungry?' Aretino asked in the Tuscan tongue. 'There is food and good wine, if you wish.'

Cesare shook his head.

'Very well. You may go where you desire while here. I shall explain to my other guests that you cannot speak. Do not worry, they will talk enough for you and themselves.'

Cesare nodded.

Satisfied, Aretino strolled towards the salone before pausing in the doorway. 'One last thing . . . You need not wear a mask while at this palazzo. Whatever happens within these walls remains here. It would not be a Bacchanal without some scandalous behaviour, but none of my guests would ever betray me by speaking of that.'

Cesare gave no reply.

'Well, do as you wish,' Aretino concluded. 'I know I shall.'

Bragadin stayed late in his ufficio to review evidence coming before the tribunal. There were too many distractions during the day, too many patricians wanting his time or his vote. Only at night did the Doge's palazzo fall quiet enough to perform duties properly. Culmine appearing was, therefore, far from welcome. The diligent assistant usually knew better than to intrude. Ignoring an unwanted visitor often persuaded them to leave – but not tonight.

'What?' Bragadin eventually snapped.

'Scusi, signor, but there's something I must share with you.'

'What is it?'

'This may be nothing, but I believed—'

'Say what you must, before I lose patience.'

'Forgive me. It's just . . . I have been approached by Contessa Coltello.'

Bragadin set aside his papers. 'She came to you?'

'Yes, signor.'

'Where? When?'

'Outside my residence, at twilight. She was in a gondola which paused by my balcony so she could speak with me. I did not realize who she was, and Coltello did not tell me her name until she was leaving.'

'I see.' Bragadin brought both hands together in front of his face, forming the fingers into a steeple. 'And what did the contessa ask of you?'

'Nothing. She praised me for becoming an assistant to the tribunal, and said she had heard others speak highly of me. Those are her words, signor, not mine. Then she left.'

'Was there anyone with her in the gondola?'

'A man sat beside her, wearing a Carnival mask.' Culmine hesitated a moment, as if weighing his words. 'I couldn't see his face, and she did not mention his name.'

'Did you observe anything else?'

'No, signor.'

Bragadin glared but Culmine neither flinched nor looked away. For the most part the assistant kept himself cloistered from the likes of Dandolo, which made Bragadin wonder what Culmine was concealing. Every man had a secret, a part of himself he hid away. In most cases it was of no importance; for some, it was enough to destroy a man's reputation. Yet no deceit or omission was apparent in Culmine's face. 'You were right to bring this to me.'

'Grazie, signor.'

'You may go, for now. But should the contessa approach you again, in person or through an intermediary, you will inform me immediately.'

'Of course, signor. Buona sera.'

'Buona sera.' Bragadin sank back in his wooden chair once Culmine had gone. The contessa was no fool, far from it. She must know this encounter would be reported. Going to Culmine at his residence . . . it was a bold choice, considering the peril she faced from the tribunal. Some might call announcing her presence in such a manner folly.

Bragadin knew better.

The contessa was taunting him. She intended to humiliate the Inquisitori di Stato. She had ordered the killing of his nephew, Bragadin was certain of that, so there was no doubt about how calculating and dangerous Coltello could be.

But she was in Venice now. This was his city.

Bragadin smiled. He was going to enjoy humiliating the contessa.

Chapter Seventeen

Aldo waited until he was alone at Palazzo Bollani before lifting the mask from his face. He had not recognized Aretino at first, but it was more than ten years since they met on the night Giovanni delle Bande Nere died. Aretino had seemed an unlikely ally for the condottiere, yet he rushed to Mantua to comfort the dying Giovanni. It was Aretino to whom Cosimo had written a letter of introduction for Aldo in case his pursuit of Armando Dandolo led all the way to Venice. The letter had been lost, left behind in Le Casette, but Aretino did not seem a man who would require such an introduction.

The gathering in the salone was becoming ever more raucous, full of laughter and passion, with men shouting over one another to be heard. Amid the tumult Aldo heard a woman mention a name he knew. 'Yes, yes, Armando's back!' she announced. 'I heard he was only on the broglio a moment before Bragadin dragged him inside!'

Aldo realized his ear for the Venetian dialect was returning faster than he might have expected. He would still struggle to speak it himself, but could follow what was being said. Slipping the mask back over his face, Aldo strolled into the salone. Lanterns and candles at the edges of the room gave it a warm, welcoming glow, but some areas remained in shadow. Tiziano was arguing with two other men, while a pair of women were kissing in a corner, their hands hidden beneath each other's skirts. A courtesan in a man's breeches and hose swayed atop a table. Her small breasts were exposed, yet nobody was looking. Carnival seemed to give those with wealth or powerful friends permission to be as debauched as they wished. Aldo doubted Venice's working women and men enjoyed such indulgences.

The woman who had spoken about Armando was gossiping with Aretino. They stood by tall, open shutters which led to a balcony overlooking the Grand Canal. Neither paid any attention to what was outside, too absorbed in their conversation. The woman had the sibilant voice of a true Venetian. Her black hair cascaded over a striking gown of scarlet silk. She stood half a head higher than Aretino, suggesting she – like Coltello – must be wearing zoccoli. 'Armando was sent from the Doge's palazzo in disgrace, but nobody knows why.'

'Nobody?' Aretino asked.

'Well, nobody who's willing to talk,' the woman smirked.

Aldo moved closer, intending to join the conversation. Before he could speak, Aretino smiled at him. 'Ahh, Cesare! Sofia, this is Cesare. He might be the perfect man for you.'

Sofia regarded Aldo with an inquisitive eye. 'And why is that?'

'Because he is a mute, so he would never interrupt you.'

Sofia gasped as if insulted before smacking Aretino's arm. 'You diavolo!'

It was as well Aretino had spoken before Aldo could; in his eagerness to hear where Dandolo was, Aldo had forgotten he was meant to be a mute. Coltello's stratagemma did hide his inability to speak as a Venetian, but also prevented him asking any questions.

How was he to find out what Sofia knew without speaking?

She had taken a step back to study him, her gaze lingering on the contents of his hose. 'You work for Coltello?' He nodded. 'I hear she's a widow now. You must be very busy.'

'Unlike you,' Aretino said, 'not everyone uses servants for their own pleasure.'

'Then they must lack my imagination,' Sofia replied, before moving close enough to whisper in Aldo's ear. 'I can be very imaginative, when the mood takes me.' One of her hands found Aldo's buttocks, exploring them through his hose. 'Perhaps the contessa would be willing to share you?'

'Leave the poor man alone,' Aretino laughed. 'Are you quite insatiable?'

'Yes, often,' Sofia said, giving Aldo a final squeeze before releasing him. 'Especially in the right company. Now, what were we talking about, Pietro?'

'Your friend Armando being banished from the Doge's palazzo.'

'Signor Dandolo is no friend to anyone but his own ambition,' she said. 'He always exceeds any authority given to him. I've long thought that will get him killed one day . . .'

'Or elected as Doge,' Aretino suggested before laughing.

Aldo bowed to both of them before leaving the salone. Sofia called to him, making several salacious suggestions, but Aldo ignored them. He needed to warn Coltello that Dandolo had returned early. They had to find him and reclaim Cosimo's private journal before it reached the Inquisitori di Stato.

But if what Sofia said was true, they might already be too late . . .

Coltello feigned a look of innocent bewilderment. 'Signori, I must apologize. It seems I have beaten you again.' She lay down her cards, eliciting groans from the patricians around the table. 'I have never known fortune to favour me so,' she added with a disingenuous smile.

That Salvadori, Mastello and Alberto had consumed several bottles of wine while she sipped demurely at a single cup was not inconsequential to this outcome. Nor was the unwise boldness of their play as each man strove ever harder to impress her. The contessa slipping several useful cards unnoticed into the left sleeve of her gown would also have been part of her success but, as it transpired, she had not needed them to win.

Coltello rested a warm hand on the thigh of Salvadori at her right, letting the nails graze up and down his leg. The cherubic fool had been especially attentive since she joined them, his hungry gaze never straying far from the swell of her breasts. It was comical how simple some men were, how easily their lusts were excited and their attention distracted from what was happening. Mastello had suggested playing for more and more coin, but Salvadori had been the most enthusiastic with his wagers. Whenever he did so Coltello had licked her lips, encouraging him further. Now he owed her a considerable sum of coin.

Good. All was unfolding as she had hoped.

Aldo appeared in the doorway, still wearing that ridiculous mask she'd given him. He made a discreet gesture, beckoning her from the game. 'Signori, it seems my presence may be required elsewhere,' Coltello said. 'Can you ever forgive me?'

The three of them all agreed, perhaps eager to avoid losing any more.

'That is most understanding,' she said. Coltello rose, the zoccoli on her feet causing no end of pain and instability. 'Now, how much does each of you owe me? Jacopo, I believe you were the one keeping a note of losses, yes?'

The hawk-faced Alberto nodded. 'I consider myself fortunate to owe only this much,' he said, showing her a number written on a scrap of paper. 'Mastello has a similar amount to pay, but poor Salvadori . . .' Alberto shook his head. 'I fear our friend is much in your debt.'

Salvadori's face fell when he saw the total against his name. 'Can that be correct?' The ruddiness left his fulsome cheeks, replaced by a ghastly pallor that did not suit him.

'I fear so,' Coltello replied. She stepped away from the table, reaching out a hand for him to take. 'Perhaps you could help me to my gondola, and we can discuss a solution? After all, you would not wish it known that one of the Inquisitori di Stato's members did not or could not pay his debts . . .' She let her words trail away, the threat behind them all too clear.

Salvadori accompanied her from the room, meek as a fearful child. She waited until they were in the passage and well beyond the hearing of Martello and Alberto before speaking. 'My dearest Filippo, I'm delighted to say I will forgive your debt entirely.'

'Y-you will?' he spluttered, hope returning to his bulging eyes.

'Yes. In return, you shall owe me a favour.'

'A favour?'

Why did this fool keep repeating everything she said? It was an annoying and rather tiresome habit, almost as unwelcome as the sour stench of too much red wine on his breath. Both made her consider withdrawing the offer, but that would not help her attain what she needed. 'Yes, a favour. Do try to keep up, signor.'

'Forgive me, I . . .' Salvadori's brow furrowed. 'What kind of favour?'

'I do not know,' the contessa lied. 'Whatever I might ask of you, it is unlikely to be anything illegal or illicit. Almost certainly not.'

'I see . . .'

No, he didn't, but that was of no consequence. Further along the hallway, Aldo was striving to get her attention. Coltello ignored him. This was far more important. 'It might be days, weeks or even years before I have need to ask for my favour's repayment, Filippo. But I am certain that when I do, you will not fail to satisfy me, yes?' She leaned closer to him, one hand brushing across the front of his hose. 'Yes?'

'Y-y-yes,' he replied.

Coltello let a smile spread across her face, so Salvadori could bathe in the warmth of her apparent affection. 'How wonderful! I knew I could rely on a man of your splendour. Now, you must excuse me. My servant had an urgent matter for my attention.'

'Of course.'

The contessa strolled away, doing her best to disguise the unsteadiness of each step atop her zoccoli. Truly, these platform shoes were the handiwork of a diavolo.

'But there is one thing I need to know,' Salvadori said, hurrying after her.

'Indeed?'

'Your name. Should you come to my residence or seek me out at the Doge's palazzo, I would not wish you to be turned away because I did not know your name.'

She smiled at him. 'I am Contessa Valentine Coltello.'

'Grazie. I am most—' Salvadori's thanks died on his lips, a sudden fear in his eyes. 'Did you say Coltello?'

'Yes.'

'The same Coltello that Signor Bragadin is bringing before the tribunal?'

The contessa nodded, enjoying Salvadori's rising discomfort.

'But if I had known that, I would not have –' He swallowed hard. 'Dio in paradiso.'

'I shall see you again soon, signor,' Coltello said before strolling on. She reached out a hand to Aldo, using his strength for balance.

'Is my new friend still standing in the hallway?' she asked, not wishing to turn round. 'Does he appear broken?'

Aldo nodded.

'Good. Now, what is so important?' When the contessa heard what Aldo had learned, she understood at once. 'Help me into the gondola, then fetch Aretino so I can thank him.'

'Do we have time for that?' Aldo asked.

'Don't question my judgement,' Coltello warned. 'Aretino's invitation may have saved both our lives. Now, do as I say.' She was settled in the gondola by the time Aldo returned with their host. Aretino was crestfallen the contessa was leaving so soon.

'Grazie for bringing me here,' she told him. 'Grazie mille.'

'It was my pleasure,' he replied. 'May I ask, what happened to Signor Salvadori? The poor man looks more unwell than my mama on her deathbed.'

'He will recover,' Coltello said as Aldo gingerly climbed aboard. 'Buona sera, Pietro.' Soon the craft was gliding along the Grand Canal, heading towards the lagoon. The water was black as ink, except where lights from lamps at its edge danced across the surface.

'Back to Ponte del Diavolo?' the gondolier asked.

'No. Take us to Palazzo Dandolo first. We have another friend to visit.'

Aldo lifted the mask from his face. 'Dandolo is no friend of mine.'

'Nor of mine,' Coltello said. 'He lied to my face, insisting he would not be back in Venice until tomorrow. Worse still, I believed him. That shall not happen again.' She arched an eyebrow. 'You'd best keep that mask on. You will be needing it.'

* * *

It took longer than Aldo expected to reach Palazzo Dandolo, the contessa's gondola wending a slow path east. From what she told him about the famiglia, he had assumed the residence would be far closer to the Doge's palazzo. The further east the gondola went on, the quieter their surroundings became. Where the Grand Canal had been alive with craft on the water and Carnival revellers on its banks, the Castello district was silent as a crypt, with lapping water providing the only sound.

The streets alongside the small internal canals – Venetians called them fondamenta, Aldo recalled – were deserted. No laughing men or women in masks, no lanterns to guide the way. Even the shutters that overlooked these waterways were closed, light seeping out from few of them. In this part of the city, it seemed most people went early to their beds.

When the gondola approached a grand, five-level residence the contessa had the craft stop long enough for Aldo to clamber out. 'Go to the door and ask for Armando. Say I wish to see him, and it's a matter of great urgency,' she commanded. 'I will wait further along where we are less likely to be observed. Bring Dandolo to me, but do not reveal yourself.'

'Won't he recognize me?'

'Not in those clothes, and not while you wear that mask,' she said. 'He will think you are one of my servants, and beneath his attention. Such men always believe that.'

'Perhaps, but surely Dandolo's servants will—'

'This is Venice during Carnival, my dear Cesare. A masked man is commonplace.'

Coltello was correct. When Aldo presented himself at the palazzo's main entrance, the gaunt maggiordomo who answered did not appear surprised. In Florence, any man calling at a palazzo after curfew would provoke suspicion and fear – but not here.

When Dandolo emerged, he paid no attention to Aldo, asking only where to find the contessa. Aldo gestured along the canal before following Dandolo to her. She had stopped in a dark part of the waterway, the lantern suspended on the gondola the only light.

'Why are you here?' Dandolo demanded. 'We agreed to have no contact in Venice.'

'True,' she said. 'But you also told me you were arriving tomorrow.'

'I made better time than I expected.'

'You lied.'

Dandolo shrugged. 'What if I did?'

'I expect to be deceived by men,' Coltello replied. 'They are faithless creatures who care only about their own pleasure, their own importance, their own ambitions. But on most occasions, I can sift the lies from the truth. With you, I could not.'

'That is your concern, not mine.'

'Perhaps so.' The contessa smiled, but the cold glint in her eyes sent a shiver through Aldo. Dandolo did not seem to realize how close to danger he was. 'I am not the only one with concerns here,' Coltello went on. 'I'm told Signor Bragadin banished you from the Doge's palazzo today. Did you exceed your authority with that misadventure in Florence?'

Dandolo bristled at the accusation. 'I have not been banished. Signor Bragadin is simply reviewing the trove of material I brought back. Once he sees the wealth of secrets in those papers, he shall be commending me for my initiative.'

'Even my gondolier knew that was a lie,' Coltello said. 'So, you have already given Bragadin all that you took from Palazzo Medici?' Her gaze shifted to Aldo for a moment, and she gave the smallest of nods. He removed his mask.

'This is no concern of yours,' Dandolo said, still ignoring everything except Coltello.

'It concerns us all,' Aldo said, moving to block the path back to Palazzo Dandolo.

'You're a servant, what would—' Dandolo stopped, staring at Aldo. 'But . . . you're supposed to be dead. The contessa told me she—'

'I can lie too,' Coltello said. 'It is one of my finer skills, though I've many others.'

'Where is the duke's private journal?' Aldo asked, advancing on Dandolo.

'What journal are you talking about?'

'Don't try our patience with evasions,' the contessa said. 'You took it from a locked cabinet inside Palazzo Medici, along with a book of Venetian ciphers and many papers.'

'Did I? Sorry, but I don't recall—'

'The journal has a plain red binding,' Aldo cut in, moving nearer. 'There is a small letter C stamped in black ink on the top-left corner.'

'I don't understand what you're saying,' Dandolo replied, taking a step back, closer to the gondola. 'The Tuscan tongue, you see, it's so difficult to follow.'

'You had no such problems in Florence,' Coltello observed.

'The journal,' Aldo hissed, putting steel into his voice. 'Where is it?'

'I don't know.' The words trembled from Dandolo's lips, betraying his fear. He took another step away from Aldo, glancing back to make sure he would not fall into the canal. 'I swear to you, I don't know.'

Aldo nodded to the gondolier.

Dandolo twisted to see where Aldo was looking . . .

. . . and was struck full in the face by a long wooden paddle.

Dandolo staggered before folding forwards, cursing and clutching a hand to his head. Blood streamed through his fingers, running down his face. 'You hit me!'

'We'll do worse, if we have to,' the contessa sighed.

Aldo loomed over Dandolo. 'Where is it?'

'I've already said, I don't know.'

Aldo grabbed Dandolo's tunic, pulling him upright. 'Where?'

'I don't know. I swear!'

'Perhaps he doesn't,' Coltello said.

'No,' Aldo replied, glancing at her. 'This is—'

His next words were stolen by a knee smashing into his palle. Pain shot through Aldo, stealing his strength. Dandolo tore himself free and dashed away into the dark.

Aldo gasped in air, hands clutching his groin, both legs trembling.

'Well?' the contessa asked. 'What are you waiting for?'

Aldo glared at her, shaking his head.

'Go on,' she urged. 'Get after him.'

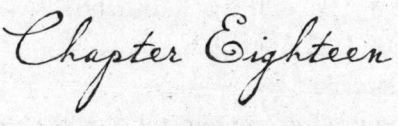

Dandolo staggered along a dark calle, struggling to see through the blood dripping into his eyes and the dizziness blurring his vision. There were two – no, three – of everything ahead. The walls on either side seemed to dance across his gaze. He closed his eyes and stretched out both arms, using fingertips to feel the brick and plaster. Yes, that was better. He could not trust to see, but his touch was still true.

Dandolo stumbled on.

He should never have stepped outside; that was foolish. But he had believed himself safe. The contessa must be desperate to come to his home demanding the journal. This was his city. He was the one born in its salty water, not her. He was the one working inside the Doge's palazzo, not her. He was the one who bore the noble name of Dandolo.

Ughh, that blow to his head . . .

This must be what it was like for a bell inside a tower.

The pain of being struck did not leave. If anything, it was getting worse.

As if someone was bellowing in his head, the noise getting louder and louder.

As if he was an anvil and a hammer kept pounding inside his skull.

As if he was a servant to be beaten and punished.

No. It must not be so. It was intolerable.

He was a Dandolo, after all.

He was a Dandolo.

His boots stumbled against something on the neglected calle – a stone, or an uneven slab – and he almost fell. Dandolo staggered, hands sliding along the walls, searching for a grip. His fingers caught on a metal ring, taking hold, clasping, grasping.

There. Stop there.

Just for a moment, for a breath or two or more.

Let the spinning in his head cease.

Let it settle.

As the worst passed, he recalled a glint in Coltello's eye. He had thought it bravado, or the light from a lantern catching her gaze. But it had been the look of a predator, knowing their prey is near. She was wrong. He would find a way out. If he could reach Bragadin . . .

The Doge's advisor habitually worked into the night. Get to him, and Coltello would be the one trapped. Dandolo knew he'd been right about that journal; the contessa's behaviour proved that . . .

Dandolo pressed a hand to his head. It came away wet, blood glistening blackly in the near dark. He wanted to lie down, to rest. If he could sleep, the pain would pass. Let the darkness claim him for a while –

No.

They must be hunting him, the contessa and her Florentine ally.

Dandolo heard a noise nearby, boots trudging towards him.

Aldo, that was the name of Coltello's man. He had come all the way from Florence for that journal. He would not stop, not until he was dead. No. Not unless he was dead. Dandolo smiled through the pain. Yes, that was the answer.

Kill Cesare Aldo.

All he needed was a stone or a brick.

Aldo grimaced. The pain in his palle was receding, the queasiness abating. Experience showed he would soon recover, but it never failed to shock how one simple, quick blow could unman him so easily.

The calle ahead was dark. Aldo could hear water lapping at stone, so he must be near a canal – but that was true of most places in Venice. The buildings on either side were silhouettes in the meagre light, reaching up towards clouds illuminated a little by the moon. Ropes criss-crossed high up between the buildings, bemusing Aldo. No, not ropes; those were cords. Lines for washing to dry on. In a city so crowded and damp, even the sky had to give way to the needs of people living here . . .

Dandolo. He had to find Dandolo.

The Venetian was cunning, yes, but also arrogant and bold, believing himself superior to almost everyone he met. The way he sacrificed the five exiles in Florence, how he used his own cousin as a false lure: all were proof of how far Dandolo would go to achieve his aims. Yet it seemed he had over-reached himself, if the gossip at Aretino's palazzo was true.

There might still be hope of recovering the journal.

But to do that required finding him.

The blow to Dandolo's head had been well struck. Not enough to kill, but the effects would not pass so easily as a knee to the palle. Aldo had seen men on the battlefield staggering for days after being hit on the head, even when no blood was drawn.

And Dandolo had been left bleeding.

Blood. That was the answer.

Aldo looked down.

The stones beneath his boots were hard to see in this darkness.

But if he moved his head to one side . . .

The clouds parted for a moment, and he caught a glimpse of the moon in two black circles on the slabs. No, they only looked black in this light. Aldo dipped a finger into one of them, held it to his nose, inhaling: the coppery scent of blood.

The drops were fresh. They might not be from Dandolo . . .

. . . but there was nobody else around to shed them.

Squinting, Aldo studied the way ahead.

There were more black circles.

Leading to the next corner.

Dandolo gripped a broken brick in both hands, having prised it from the wall behind him. He strained to hear, but the approaching footsteps were gone.

'Looking for me?'

The voice came from behind Dandolo, that superior Florentine tone mocking him.

He twisted round, swinging the broken brick through the air.

It missed Aldo by a hair's width –

– and hit the wall, jolting from Dandolo's grasp.

A fist came at him, striking his nose with a fierce crack.

White dots danced before his eyes, and the taste of blood made him gag. He touched his face; his proud and mighty nose was twisted to one side, making it hard to breathe.

'You broke my nose,' Dandolo rasped.

Aldo stepped closer. 'That's not all I'll break.'

Something slammed into Dandolo's palle. He staggered back, hands clutching at his groin, unable to speak or think –

– then there was nothing beneath one boot . . .

Aldo was enjoying Dandolo's pain and disbelief until the fool stumbled towards the canal.

'Don't, you'll—'

Dandolo toppled into the murky water, sending up a great splash.

Aldo rushed to the canal, almost falling in himself before grabbing at a mooring post. If Dandolo drowned, their only lead to getting back the duke's journal would also be lost. Aldo dropped to one knee, eyes scouring the water for Dandolo.

Nothing. There was nothing.

Aldo lay full length on the damp stones to reach down into the canal. The water was cold and heavy against his arms, soaking both tunic sleeves. The idiota had not fallen far from the edge, but there was no trace of him in the water . . .

A face burst from the canal: Dandolo.

'Help me!' he cried out. 'Help—'

He sank back into the waters, but his flailing arms were still visible.

Aldo grabbed one of the hands, grasping it.

He pulled the arm closer, up from the water.

Dandolo's face broke the surface again.

'I've got you,' Aldo said. Dandolo spat out water and blood. Aldo pulled him closer, getting a tight grip on Dandolo's tunic below the neck.

'Please, help me climb out,' Dandolo whimpering.

'I will in a moment,' Aldo replied.

'Grazie—'

'Once you tell me what I want to know.'

Dandolo was cold to his bones, everything except his head and hands immersed in the freezing canal. He slapped at Aldo's grip but found his shivering hands had no strength. He clawed at the Florentine bastardo, but Aldo pushed him back under the water and held him there. When he cried out for help, his mouth filled with water.

Those clutching hands pulled him back up, back into the air.

'Enough!' Dandolo spat between mouthfuls of water. 'I'll talk.'

To succumb to this foreigner, this outsider . . .

It was humiliating.

But necessary.

For now.

'Where is the duke's journal?' Aldo asked.

'I don't—' Dandolo began.

'I want answers,' Aldo warned, 'not denials.'

Dandolo searched the Florentine's face. There was no hesitation there. This man showed no reluctance to kill, if required.

'I was telling the truth,' Dandolo said. 'Bragadin took the journal from me. But I can say where it will be soon, if it's not there already.'

Aldo glowered at him. 'Where?'

'Bragadin gave the journal to another assistant, ordered him to have the first page decoded. If that doesn't uncover anything that helps Bragadin, he will lock it away with all the other papers I took from Palazzo Medici.' Dandolo heard a familiar sound: the gliding movement of a gondola approaching. He was going to call for help when a familiar face peered from it: Coltello.

'Where?' Aldo demanded. 'Where will Bragadin put the journal?'

'The secret archive,' Dandolo said, 'inside the Doge's palazzo. That's where all valuable documents are kept, safe from foreign agents and enemies of the Serenissima. But there are guards standing sentry outside the only door into the secret archive all day, and no outsider can enter the Doge's palazzo after dark without permission.'

By now the gondola was close, yet it did not slow down.

'Who has access to this secret archive?'

'You need two keys.' Dandolo replied, his teeth chattering together. 'One is held by a member of the Inquisitori di Stato, the other by an assistant to the tribunal.'

'What are their names?' Aldo glanced at the oncoming craft. 'Give me their names before the contessa's gondola hits you.'

'Afani Mastello is the tribunal member.'

'And the assistant?'

Dandolo could feel water being pushed at him by the gondola. 'Please, pull me out!'

'Who is the assistant with a key to the archive?' Aldo demanded.

'Culmine!' Dandolo shouted. 'Vincenzo Culmine! Now quick, pull me—'

Aldo let go. Something heavy struck Dandolo's head.

Then he was sinking, down and down.

Darkness took him.

Coltello signalled at her gondolier to stop after the wooden craft had hit Dandolo. 'Make sure he doesn't come back up,' she called as the craft slowed to a halt. 'Well? What did Armando say before his unfortunate accident?'

Aldo gave a brisk summary, yet it offered little comfort. Coltello already knew of the secret archive; it was where her reports from Florence were stored. But she had not realized getting inside would require two keys. That was going to complicate matters.

'Did you know?' Aldo asked, a sulky tone to his words. 'That Vincenzo was responsible for safeguarding this archive? Is that why you brought me to Venice?'

'I had my suspicions,' she conceded. 'But I did not know about the duke's private journal until you told me Dandolo had stolen it. No, I had another purpose in mind for you and the charming Vincenzo. Now it seems you and he can both help with both matters.'

'He wore a key.' Aldo touched a hand to the notch below his neck. 'Here.'

'I saw that too,' Coltello agreed. She glanced back at the gondolier; Luigi shook his head. 'It seems poor Armando will not be resurfacing. You'd best get into the gondola, Aldo. Accidental drownings do happen, but that will not be credible if we're seen lingering here.'

Chapter Nineteen

Tuesday, February 13th 1539

Aldo rolls over, and a familiar arm embraces him from behind. A body presses into his back and legs: strong, muscular thighs, a lean chest, and hard warmth. He inhales their scent, all sweat and sunshine, musky and masculine. A hand slides across his skin and through tight curls of hair to find his cazzo, a murmur of appreciation as its readiness.

'Not now,' Aldo whispers. 'Need to sleep. Soon, Vincenzo. Soon . . .'

The person behind him sits up. 'Who's Vincenzo?'

Aldo knows that voice: Saul.

He twists round.

Sees the hurt in those warm, hazel eyes.

'Saul, I didn't mean . . . I would never . . . I . . .'

Aldo jerked awake, panting and gasping for breath. It was a fantasia, nothing more. He hadn't betrayed Saul, not with Vincenzo nor anyone else. The disbelief fell away, leaving sweat on his brow and under both arms. Yet he was still guilty – why? It had been a wandering of his thoughts while sleeping. The mind played its tricks at night, sending him on strange odysseys which could never be true, never come true.

But the guilt lingered.

Seeing Vincenzo had been so bewitching, Aldo realized he had not thought of Saul since the previous morning; Just thinking about Vincenzo had his cazzo hardening . . .

Enough. Enough!

Aldo threw back the covers and swung his legs out of bed. The contessa was right to call this lavish bedchamber the lavender room. Every surface bore the colour – walls, ceiling, even the furniture had been painted that hue. The aroma of lavender lingered in the air too, thanks to dried flowers in bowls around the room.

The scent transported Aldo to a memory: the convent at Santa Maria Magdalena in Florence. The courtyard was filled with early blooming lavender, its scent suffusing the senses. Now, whenever Aldo smelled lavender, it took him back to those desperate days. Was his time in Venice to be the same? Hopefully not.

He rose, emptying his bladder into a pot for that purpose before washing with cold, crisp water from a bowl. The rich man's clothes from the previous day were gone, much simpler garb in their place: a port-coloured tunic, dark woollen hose, and boots of supple leather. A servant must have brought them in while he slept. It unnerved Aldo that people could come and go without waking him, but that skill was part of their job. A servant who drew the eye was soon dismissed, unless they were a maggiordomo or a lady's private maid. Aldo grimaced; nobody had waited on him since his boyhood at Palazzo Fioravanti, and he had not missed it. A man unable to take responsibility for himself, for his own clothes and appearance, was not a man to trust.

That word had many meanings, especially for a guest of Contessa Coltello. Aldo trusted her welcome would remain while he was still useful. He could trust Coltello to play games and enjoy the intrigues she created. But he could also trust her to be entirely ruthless when a moment required, as Armando Dandolo had discovered the previous night. How long before he was found? Experience of bodies found after drowning in the Arno suggested the corpse would not resurface for two or three days, but sometimes they were found sooner. Aldo grimaced. Whatever the contessa was planning, it had best be complete before then.

There was one task that mattered now: retrieving or destroying Cosimo's private journal. Otherwise, banishment from Florence was awaiting. Aldo had already spent too long away from the city, first while riding as a mercenary, and later when exiled to the countryside as a constable of the Otto. He would not let himself be cast out again, whether by ill chance or choice. Whatever was necessary to get that journal, he would do.

A sharp knock at the door demanded his attention.

'What?'

'The contessa wishes to meet,' Pozzo called. 'She says there is much to discuss.'

'Where, in the salone?'

'At this time of morning?' The maggiordomo laughed. 'No, in the sala, of course.'

'Of course,' Aldo agreed. 'How could I be so foolish.'

'She expects you there imminently.'

'Then I shall not disappoint.'

'That would be wise,' Pozzo replied before stamping away.

It seemed the maggiordomo remained angry, but his mood was of no concern. It was the contessa's plan that mattered. She had not spoken after returning from Palazzo Dandolo, so there was much to be discussed. Aldo wished that, for once, Coltello might choose to speak plain and true, without games.

But that seemed far from likely.

* * *

The contessa had little use for food in the morning. When it was necessary to eat before the sun was at its highest, whatever was brought to her always disappointed. Bread, preserves, fruit? That was not a meal, no matter how colourful the ceramics on which they were presented. No, it was closer to an insult, or at least an acknowledgement that those responsible for preparing her food had made the smallest possible effort.

But eat she must.

There was no way of knowing how this day would reveal itself once the mask of politeness was removed. The initial letter from Bragadin and his Inquisitori di Stato had invited her to appear before the tribunal at her earliest possible convenience. Their words were a feint, of course, a ruse intended to suggest she was in no danger. Coltello saw this invitation for what it was: not a loop of delicate silk, but a hanging noose of coarse rope.

Now a new letter had been delivered, welcoming her back to Venice and asking that she present herself that morning. No, not asking – demanding. The words were polite, but the underlying threat was as evident as the ink with which they were written. Coltello had not seen the cells of the Doge's palazzo, yet knew enough to be sure they were best avoided.

If all went well with the tribunal, she might be free for a proper meal later. Far more likely was a long, wearying day of intrusive enquiries, each one a snare designed to trap her in some unwanted admission. If she survived, it could be hours before food was in front of her again. So, eat she must – even if the plates in her sala offered nothing more than bread, preserves and fruit. How very tiresome.

Equally tiresome was the absence of her maid. According to Amaro, Agnese – who had been born in Venice, but went with the count and contessa to Florence – had left the previous day to visit famiglia and was yet to return. Coltello had been forced to rely on one of the palazzo maids to help her wash and dress; the hapless girl was as adept as a nun handling a hard cazzo.

Aldo's arrival at least offered someone capable of conversation. 'Buon giorno,' he said.

She gestured for him to sit. 'You look rested.'

'I slept better than I have in several days,' Aldo replied.

'Eat, eat,' she said, waving at the food. 'It's not much, but will have to do.' Coltello watched him gorge on the meagre offerings while she described the tribunal's message.

'It's a trap, of course,' Aldo said. 'Bragadin blames you for his nephew's murder and believes he can establish your guilt through trickery or fear.'

'Now that I have introduced myself to one of his assistants – your friend Vincenzo Culmine – Bragadin knows I too am willing to play games with my opponents. So, I expect him to threaten me in the hope that I will crumple before the force of his will and his mighty tribunal.'

Aldo laughed. 'Clearly, the man is a fool.'

'Why do you say that?'

'If he believes you responsible for his nephew's murder, Bragadin should grasp how dangerous you are. Grossolano arrived in Florence to replace you and was dead before the next dawn. Only a fool underestimates someone they believe ruthless enough to act in such a swift, decisive manner.'

Coltello suppressed a smile. 'Is that all?'

'No. Whoever had Grossolano killed ensured it was impossible to bring those responsible to justice. If the most powerful criminal court in Florence could not prove you were behind that murder, how can Bragadin expect to do so several months later, here in Venice? The truth will not be your destruction, Contessa. That will require lies or deception.'

'Quite.' She sipped at a cup of sweet wine, but the taste was sour on her tongue. 'I'm told the tribunal can only convict if all three inquisitors agree on a verdict. I have a way to prevent that, if required, but there remains our other, mutual problem to resolve.'

'Cosimo's journal,' Aldo said.

'That is where you can make yourself useful while I keep the tribunal occupied.'

Aldo and Coltello set off for the Doge's palazzo after she changed from her usual vibrant clothing to the dowdy, drab garb of a widow. The contessa also dispensed with her zoccoli, announcing they were both painful and impractical. 'A grieving woman should not seem interested in clothes or shoes,' she said.

The journey was uneventful until the gondola emerged from a small canal onto the expanse of the lagoon. There the water became choppier, their progress less certain. Gripping the side of the boat, Aldo glanced at the gondolier. Luigi's place at the back of the boat had been usurped by a muscular figure with a swarthy face and dour expression.

'That's Marco,' the contessa said. 'Luigi has gone to visit his famiglia on one of the outer islands, with a generous pouch of coin to help him stay there. Better he is not around to answer any unwanted questions about last night's . . . accident.'

Aldo nodded. The best way to avoid an enemy attack was not to be there when it came. The contessa was doing all she could to escape such difficulties.

Ahead of them an imposing stone building on the shoreline announced its presence with authority. An arcade stretched along the ground level, supported by ornate pillars. Above that was an elaborate loggia, and then two further levels of patterned brickwork and tall, arched openings. The stark majesty of the building and its central position meant this must be the Doge's palazzo, seat of the Venetian republic.

When the gondola reached the palazzo Aldo clambered out first before helping Coltello from the craft. She straightened up, regarding the structure that loomed ahead. 'I suspect buildings would look very different if women designed them.'

He followed her gaze, taking in the sharp edges and brooding shape. 'Less brutal?'

She nodded. 'More curves, I would hope, a more welcoming silhouette. Something that works in harmony with the world, rather than stamping a boot on its surroundings.' The contessa sighed before gesturing at the piazzetta between them and the palazzo. 'This area is the broglio. It's still early, but patricians will soon crowd this place with gossiping and arguing. Wait for me here once your task is complete.'

Aldo followed her to the entrance, remaining two steps behind like a dutiful servant. Coltello announced herself to those on guard and was ushered inside. She was led along a dark corridor, Aldo close behind.

When they emerged into the light, he could not help but gasp.

The inner courtyard of the Doge's palazzo was vast, so long and wide two Florentine palazzi could have been built within it and still leave room enough to stroll around them. At the far end the domes of a basilica stood near to the Doge's palazzo, suggesting the republic had a comfortable relationship with the church; in Tuscany, places of worship were never so close to the uffici of power. But it was the sheer scale of what encompassed the courtyard that commanded Aldo's awe.

The top two levels of the palazzo were magnificent in their stonework, with tall and elegant openings observing the courtyard from above. The next level down was an elaborate loggia spanning three sides, while long arcades stretched beneath them at ground level. Aside from a few men with the look of assistants striding about, the courtyard was quiet, both impressive and oppressive.

'Close your mouth,' Coltello said, 'or you will catch flies.'

Aldo did so, reclaiming his composure.

'You have the message?' she asked. He patted the document in his tunic. Aldo noticed her hands were trembling. She clasped them together, forcing a smile. 'It's a while since I've had to argue for my life. I'd forgotten how exhilarating this can be.'

But Aldo could see fear, not excitement, in her eyes.

Coltello took a breath. 'Let battle commence.'

Bragadin watched from his ufficio as Coltello strolled across the courtyard. A servant had hurried in to announce the contessa's presence, having spent the morning outside waiting for her. Bragadin squinted to see Coltello better. Was she wearing the clothes of a widow? Yes, she was! He laughed. Perhaps the strega hoped this might win her sympathy. It was a false hope. They all knew the count had been dead more than a year.

But it showed Coltello would turn anything to her advantage.

The contessa paused for a moment in the courtyard, staring up at the shutters where he was standing. Did she know this was his ufficio? Was she watching him as he was her? To his knowledge, she had been inside the Doge's palazzo only once before, accompanying her husband when he was appointed the Serenissima's spymaster in Florence. Even that was unusual, yet Coltello had insisted. The contessa had been behind that, Bragadin suspected.

He had met her before, at Coltello's wedding. It was a large and elaborate ceremony with numerous guests, yet Bragadin could not help noticing the bride was in charge of everything that took place. The count was a genial host and clearly besotted with his much younger wife, but she had a steely glint to her gaze. There was no doubt who had been on top in their marriage bed.

For a moment Bragadin could not help imagining himself in bed with the contessa astride him, moving up and down, clenching herself around his cazzo, biting her bottom lip as he thrust up from his hips, making her call out his—

'Signor, should I notify the other tribunal members?' the servant asked.

Bragadin had forgotten the fool was still standing there, awaiting instructions. 'Yes, yes,' he snapped. 'I'm calling the Inquisitori di Stato into session immediately.'

'Very good,' the servant said, bowing before they left the ufficio.

Bragadin glanced down at the courtyard but the contessa was gone. Soon she would stand before him and he would strip her bare of every lie until she was begging for mercy. Coltello could use every stratagemma she knew but they were no protection from the might of his tribunal. Bragadin smirked. Yes, she would beg him for mercy.

Coltello let herself be escorted through the Doge's palazzo, up flights of stairs and along several wood-lined corridors until she was told to wait outside a sturdy door. Aldo had slipped away at the top of the first staircase, adopting the guise of a humble messenger so he would attract little attention. He had his own task to perform while she stood before the tribunal, one as important as her own.

Could she trust him to fulfil it? Yes – and there were few men of whom this was true. It was not that she trusted him to do everything she asked, and certainly not in the way she suggested; better to let a man such as Aldo choose his own path, rather than stifle his natural talents. Perhaps trust was the wrong word. She believed him capable of doing what was necessary, because his ruthlessness was almost the equal of her own. There could be no higher praise than that.

Men's voices echoed through the door beside her. One was laughing, almost friendly, while the second was stern but still warm. A third joined them – curt, cold, dismissive. That would be Bragadin, asserting himself over the others. Being a doge's advisor gave him access and importance. The tribunal was intended as a trio of equals, but it was clear who considered himself in charge.

The door swung open and a cold-faced assistant glared at her. 'Contessa Valentine Coltello?' he asked, though it was more a demand than a question.

She nodded, eyes cast down, a kerchief clutched in one hand.

'Follow me.' The assistant strode across a marble floor of angular tiles, their pattern creating a dizzying effect on the eyes. No doubt this was intended to make those brought here unsteady and uncertain. Coltello followed the assistant to a short, narrow set of steps leading to another, smaller room. There three men sat behind a long table, two dressed in black and Bragadin in red.

The assistant gestured for Coltello to go up. 'The tribunal is waiting.'

'Grazie.' Lifting her hem to see the steps, she ascended into the chamber. The walls were panelled with dark wood, while the ceiling was bordered with gold. Coltello looked around but there was no chair for her, nowhere to sit. The tribunal expected her to stand.

The contessa faced her inquisitors, smiling and nodding at them.

'Signor Mastello, good to see you again,' she said to the man on her left, enjoying his discomfort before turning to the man on her right. 'Signor Salvadori, it seems like only yesterday since last we met!' In fact, it was the previous night that she had bested them both at cards, but Coltello was willing to bet all her winnings that neither had mentioned that to their leader. She smiled at him last. 'And Signor Bragadin, what an honour it is to stand before you. I believe we have met twice before, but not for some time.

'Grazie for coming before this tribunal so promptly,' he replied. 'We have many questions for you to answer, Contessa.'

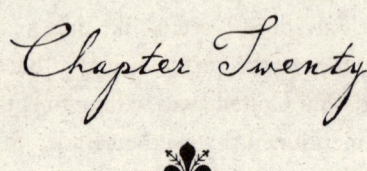

Aldo went unquestioned as he explored the east wing of the Doge's palazzo, thanks to being dressed as a servant. There seemed to be no women here; much like the Senate in Florence, Venice's place of power was an all-male enclave. When he was stopped, Aldo showed the sealed message Coltello had given him and looked helpless. He got instructions about how to find the intended recipient, sending Aldo deeper into the palazzo.

Eventually he reached a corridor that ended in a heavy wooden door with two sentries outside it, their hands resting on the hilts of short swords. The door behind them had none of the golden adornment or decoration he had seen in other parts of the palazzo. Instead, it was plain and solid, with two keyholes. This must be the entrance to the secret archive. Aldo approached the sentries, the message held out in front of him. 'We can't read,' one of them said when Aldo pointed to the name written by the wax seal.

'That's why the Council of Ten has us standing here,' his companion added. 'They know we wouldn't understand anything behind this door.'

Aldo was grateful Coltello had made him practise speaking in Venetian dialect before they left her palazzo. Mustering his courage, he asked for the man named on the message.

'Not here,' the first sentry replied. 'Should be back soon—'

'Here he is now,' the other cut in. 'Signor, this servant's got a letter for you.'

'I'm not expecting any correspondence,' a voice replied.

'It's a surprise,' Aldo said, turning to face the approaching figure. 'But I am sure you will want to read what is inside.'

Vincenzo stopped, staring at Aldo in disbelief. 'I—'

'See?' Aldo glanced back at the sentries. 'I said it was a surprise.'

The second one laughed. 'Signor Culmine looks like he's seen a fantasma!'

Aldo approached Vincenzo, holding out the message. 'For you, signor.'

Vincenzo's eyes never left Aldo's face. 'Grazie.'

'Do you wish me to wait for a reply?'

'I . . .'

'Signor Culmine?' one of the sentries asked.

Aldo stared at Vincenzo, willing him to speak, to reply.

Certainty took the place of confusion in Vincenzo's face. He smiled at the sentries. 'Just a message from an old friend I haven't seen in a while.' Vincenzo took hold of Aldo's arm, leading him away. 'Please, come with me.'

Bragadin ignored the contessa while she described her network of informants in Florence, how useful they were to Venice. It was her opening words that occupied his thoughts, the way she spoke to Mastello and Salvadori as if they were old friends . . . He knew of her approach to Culmine, but what else had this strega done since arriving in Venice?

Glancing at Mastello, Bragadin saw no evidence of sympathy there; Salvadori was another matter. Coltello said it seemed like only yesterday since her last encounter with him. Had they met since her return, or was the contessa toying with him? Bragadin tilted his head to study the plump figure at his left. Salvadori never sat still for long, but he appeared especially restive today. His hands would not settle, and he kept wiping both palms against his black robe. A fat bead of sweat emerged from his hairline, trickling down that flabby skin. He was trembling, too. The contessa was clearly the cause.

Hearing Coltello mention the name Grossolano, Bragadin shifted his attention to her. She was expressing sorrow for his nephew's death, a kerchief clutched in one hand as if ready to dab away tears she was holding back.

'Yes, yes,' Bragadin said, cutting short her show of sympathy. A scorpion's tears would be more trustworthy. 'You told us of these deep regrets when you wrote informing the tribunal of Grossolano's death. What we asked you here to explain was the circumstances surrounding his murder.'

'The circumstances?' Coltello's face became a mask of bewilderment.

'Yes.'

'I . . . I do not understand.'

So, she intended to persist with her claims of innocence. Bragadin was almost grateful. It would have been disappointing if the contessa simply admitted her part in the killing. Better the victory be hard-won; better to make her beg for a chance to admit her complicity, to have her pleading for mercy. That would be true satisfaction.

'Contessa, let us not be coy about this,' Bragadin said. 'Everyone present here knows Grossolano is – was – my nephew. In the letter informing us of his murder, you stated that he had indulged in too much wine at your Florentine palazzo. Ignoring warnings, he then went out into the city after dark and was murdered. You suggested this was the work of an individual who had already killed two men in Florence, and my nephew was – how did you put it? – most unfortunate in falling victim to this person's deadly ways.'

'That's correct,' Coltello agreed. Her stance straightened a little. The change was slight but did not escape Bragadin's gaze. She was on her guard.

'Yet it was one of the tribunal's own men, Gonzalo Zilio, who was convicted in his absence by a Florentine court of murdering my nephew. Zilio was our go-between, managing spymasters in rival city-states, such as yourself. He had nothing to do with this killing.'

'I agree,' she replied. 'I hear from my contacts that it was Duke Cosimo who directed the Otto wrongly convict Zilio as a means of effectively banishing him from Florence.'

'And where were you when all of this happened?'

'Where was I?'

'Yes, where were you on the night my nephew was killed?'

'I . . .' The contessa hesitated, as if confused to be asked. 'I was at home, in my Florentine palazzo, as you've already said, Signor Bragadin.'

He switched his point of attack. 'You consider Florence your home? Not Venice?'

'I . . .' Again, she feigned bewilderment.

'Let us try another question,' Bragadin said. 'Did you see my nephew leave?'

'No.'

'Why not? You claim to have known when he left, you did not see him go?'

'I was in my bedchamber.'

'Alone?'

A flash of anger crossed Coltello's eyes. 'Of course.' She gestured at her clothes. 'I am a widow, as you can clearly see.'

'Then you were not entertaining a guest in your bedchamber when my nephew – drunk, according to you, and a stranger in your city – stumbled out into the night?'

'No, signor, I was not.'

'Why did you leave him alone?' Mastello asked, leaning forwards in his chair. 'He had been in Florence but a few hours and was your guest.'

It was a strong question. Clearly, Mastello was no ally of the contessa.

'I was unwell,' she replied. 'Ask my maggiordomo, Pozzo. I brought him with me to Venice. He can tell you what happened on that unfortunate evening.'

Mastello snorted. 'Is your maggiordomo a loyal servant?'

'Of course.'

'Then he is likely to tell us exactly what you would wish, isn't he?'

'Well . . .' The contessa could not deny the truth of that so was delaying her answer, no doubt searching for a way out of the trap Mastello was laying. She didn't realize stepping away from one snare only led her towards another . . .

'Perhaps you are right, Signor Mastello,' Bragadin said, as if interceding on the contessa's behalf. He enjoyed the frown that brought to her face for a moment. 'But, of course, not all servants are so loyal.'

Coltello shook her head. 'Forgive me, signori, but I do not understand what it is you wish to hear. I've said all I know about the death of Signor Grossolano, and offered my regrets for what happened. It is a sad loss for his famiglia and for all of Venice. Who knows what he might have achieved on behalf of this tribunal if not for the actions of a killer. But your letter asked me to share what I know, and I have done so. Yes, I feel some responsibility for his death. If I had not become ill, if I had not left him alone, your nephew might still be alive. But that is not what happened, and I shall have to live with the guilt of that. Now, unless there is something else with which I can assist you—'

'There is,' Bragadin replied, before raising his voice. 'Send her in!'

The door behind Coltello opened and a young woman in a maid's clothes entered, her face ashen. She stopped by the contessa, whispering something Bragadin could not hear.

'What did you just say?' he demanded.

The maid hesitated. 'I told the contessa I was sorry.'

'You and I have already spoken, have we not?' Bragadin asked.

'Yes, signor.'

'But my fellow inquisitors have not met you before, so please tell them who you are and how it is that you know the contessa.'

'M-my name is Agnese. I am Contessa Coltello's private maid in Florence.'

'And you will tell us the truth about what happened the night Signor Tito Grossolano died? Lying to this tribunal is punishable by imprisonment. You have already spent one night in the cells here. You would not wish to end your days there, would you?'

'N-no, signor.'

Bragadin stared at Coltello, letting a broad smirk spread across his face. 'Good. Because it is past time we got to the truth of this matter.'

Vincenzo marched Cesare to an empty ufficio, closing the door behind them. He leaned his forehead against the woodwork, struggling to make sense of the questions whirling through him. Of all the people from his past, why Cesare? Why now? It was – no, there was no use trying to make sense of this. Better to let Cesare answer – if he would.

Turning, Vincenzo looked at Cesare properly for the first time since . . . How long since their last meeting, since the night that Aldo vanished during Carnival? Twenty years? More? He appeared much the same. Older, of course. But his eyes were the same, their unflinching gaze just as it was. Those lips, still asking to be—

No, he would not think about that. It had taken too long to stifle those wants, to learn how to keep them locked away. He was a married man, a papa. The past was the past. He had been different then, a young fool guilty of sinful mistakes, of giving in to forbidden desires.

Vincenzo straightened up, lifting his chin. 'Why are you here?'

Cesare smiled, warmth filling his face. 'I brought you this message.' He held up the sealed document, but Vincenzo did not take it. There was no way of knowing what was lurking inside, hidden behind that wax seal.

'Who asked you to deliver it?'

The smile faded. 'Contessa Valentine Coltello.'

Of course. The confusion was receding now, parting as mist did before the sun on a spring morning. What were Cesare and the contessa to each other? Allies? Lovers? Vincenzo could not imagine Cesare finding satisfaction with a woman; in that, they had never been the same. 'It was you behind the mask in her gondola last night.'

'Yes. She needs your help with the Inquisitori di Stato.' Cesare stepped closer until Vincenzo could smell his scent; manly, musky. 'We both do.'

'Signor Bragadin suspects her of murdering his nephew, Tito Grossolano.'

'Coltello has never murdered anyone.'

'How can you be so certain?'

Cesare pursed his lips. 'I've met enough killers to know one.'

Vincenzo chose not to ask how or where Aldo had gained this knowledge. There were more urgent questions that needed answering. 'So, she gets others to kill for her, just as she got you to come here and ask for my help.'

'What makes you think that?'

'Signor Bragadin says—'

'Bragadin says,' Cesare cut in, 'and you believe it, without question or reason?'

'He is an important man, an advisor to the Doge.'

'That doesn't make him right,' Aldo insisted. 'You have your own mind, Vincenzo. You used to believe in what you could see and taste and feel, not simply what others told you. When did that change? When did you become . . . this?'

'I grew up. Accepted my responsibilities.'

'That doesn't mean denying who you are, or who you love.'

'I know who I am,' Vincenzo insisted, keeping his voice to a murmur so it would not be heard outside the ufficio. 'Why are you really here?'

Cesare's gaze slid down to Vincenzo's chest. 'Since when did you wear jewellery?'

Vincenzo put a hand to the key on a cord round his neck. 'This isn't jewellery.'

'Must be important for you to keep it so close. I saw that glinting in the hairs on your chest last night.' Cesare put his hand over Vincenzo's, their fingers touching, intermingling . . .

Vincenzo pushed Cesare back. 'What do you want?'

'You know what I want . . . what we both want.'

Vincenzo forced himself to hold Cesare's gaze. 'No.'

'You used to say yes to me.'

'That was twenty years ago. I was young, and a fool.'

'You knew exactly who you were, and what you wanted. We both did.'

'What we did was wrong.'

'No, what you did to me was wrong, but I will forget that if you help me now.'

'I don't understand. What do you think I did? You're the one who vanished, not me.'

Cesare's laugh was full of bitterness. 'Don't lie to me. You can dupe yourself all you want, deny who you truly are, but don't try to deceive me.'

Vincenzo was baffled by these accusations and said so. 'Truly, I do not know what you are talking about. I swear it on the life of my bambini.'

Cesare stepped back, shaking his head. 'You remember the last time we met?'

'Yes, of course.'

'It was Carnival then, too. You told me to meet you at curfew in that alley, the place where we first—'

'I know the place,' Vincenzo cut in, not wanting to recall what they'd done there.

'You promised to run away with me, that we would be together. Just us against the world, that's what you promised me.'

'*Contra mundi*,' Vincenzo whispered, remembering their secret words.

'*Contra mundi*,' Cesare said. 'But you never came. I waited and waited, ready to leave with you that night, but you never arrived. Instead, you sent four men to do what you could not. They beat me black and blue. I was fortunate to escape with my life. I left Venice that same night and swore never to return, and it took months for me to heal.'

Vincenzo stared at Cesare, searching for any sign this was a lie, a stratagemma. But the quiver in his voice, the tears brimming in his eyes . . . those were all true.

'You know what they said before the blows started? Vincenzo sent us.'

'I didn't.' Vincenzo shook his head. 'I swear, I would never . . .'

'Then who did?' Cesare demanded, stalking towards him. 'Tell me that.'

'I don't know.' But that was a lie. Now Vincenzo had heard what happened to Cesare that night, he could see what had been hidden in plain sight all these years. He had gone to his younger brother Battista for help, confided in him. Battista vowed to keep their secret. But when Cesare disappeared and Vincenzo was distraught, Battista had said it was for the best. Vincenzo remembered the red marks on his little brother's knuckles that day. A scuffle on a bridge with a rival famiglia, Battista had claimed, but he could not meet Vincenzo's gaze.

'Tell me the truth,' Cesare insisted.

'It doesn't matter. The one who probably did that to you . . . they died four years ago.'

'Swear it on the life of your bambini.'

Vincenzo stared into Cesare's eyes. 'I swear it—'

Then Cesare was kissing him, one hand in Vincenzo's hair, the other holding him close, their bodies pressing together, their heat finding each other—

Vincenzo shoved him away. 'No. No! I'm a papa, a husband—'

'Then why is your breathing so fast?' Cesare asked, a smirk spreading across his face before he nodded downwards. 'Why are your hose telling me how excited you are?'

Vincenzo had willed his cazzo not to respond. 'That's—'

'Nothing?' Cesare pushed him back against the door, one

hand reaching down between them. 'Doesn't feel like nothing to me.'

'Enough!' Vincenzo pushed past him, putting as much distance as he could between them in the small ufficio. He would not give in to temptation. 'What do you want of me?'

'You have access to—'

The door pushed into Cesare, startling him. 'Somebody in there?' a voice outside demanded. 'Why won't this door open?'

'Give me a moment,' Vincenzo called back. He rearranged his hose, pulling down his tunic to better cover the crotch. 'You must go. You can't be seen here.'

'Only if you promise to meet me later.'

'No, I have to—'

Cesare put his hand to Vincenzo's face. The warmth of his skin, the tenderness and strength, was intoxicating. 'You owe me this after what happened. Promise me you will come – and keep your promise this time.'

Vincenzo wanted to say no, but another word escaped him. 'Where?'

'Do you know Ponte del Diavolo?'

'Yes.'

'Be there at dusk tonight.'

A fist hammered at the door. 'Open up!'

Vincenzo opened the door, nodding to the impatient assistant outside before ushering Cesare from the ufficio. They strode away, Vincenzo leading Cesare to the nearest staircase. 'Grazie for bringing me this,' Vincenzo said, taking the sealed message.

'Prego,' Cesare replied, leaning closer to murmur in his ear. 'Remember, Ponte del Diavolo at dusk. Come alone.'

Chapter Twenty-one

The contessa listened to Bragadin and Mastello interrogating Agnese. The presence of her maid answered Coltello's own question about where Agnese had been since the previous evening. Bragadin must have had her brought to the Doge's palazzo for questioning and, believing her a useful witness, kept Agnese there. She looked exhausted and fearful, but her testimony was frustrating the tribunal.

'You must be able to recall that particular night,' Mastello demanded. 'Or do guests often leave the contessa's palazzo and get murdered?'

'I do not understand, signor,' Agnese replied. 'Does that happen in Venice?'

'No, of course not!'

'Then why should it happen in Florence?'

'But it did happen in Florence,' Mastello insisted. 'Signor Grossolano left Palazzo Coltello that night and was killed, yes?'

'So I have been told, signor. I did not see him being killed.'

'No, I didn't say you had—'

'Perhaps we should ask a different question,' Bragadin cut in. 'Signorina Agnese, do you recall Signor Grossolano arriving at the contessa's palazzo?'

'Yes, signor. He stepped in horse merda getting out of his carriage and left a trail of it behind him wherever he went.'

'That's true,' Coltello said, nodding.

'We are questioning your maid,' Bragadin warned her. 'Not you.'

Coltello held up a hand to acknowledge he was correct, knowing it would infuriate Bragadin further. An angry man was dangerous, but less likely to think clearly. 'Please, go ahead,' she said, smiling at him.

Bragadin pressed his lips together so hard they became white before he shifted his gaze back to Agnese. 'Signor Grossolano had a meal at the palazzo?'

'Yes, signor,' she confirmed. 'But he drank far too much wine and ate too little of his food. Perhaps that is why he put his hand up one of the maids' skirts.'

'He did what?' Mastello asked.

'That is of no importance,' Bragadin insisted. 'Signorina Agnese, please keep your answers to yes or no. Do you understand?'

'Yes. But should I not call you signor, signor?'

Coltello struggled not to laugh as rage flushed Bragadin's face crimson.

'Yes,' he eventually replied. 'Please call each member of the tribunal signor.'

Agnese nodded. 'Yes, signor.'

'Did Signor Grossolano leave the palazzo after his meal?' Mastello asked.

'Yes, signor.'

'And he never returned?'

'No, signor.'

Bragadin leaned forwards, his eyes narrowing. 'Was the contessa in her bedchamber when Signor Grossolano left?'

'Yes, signor,' Agnese replied.

'And was she alone in her bedchamber?'

The maid hesitated, glancing at Coltello.

'Don't look to the contessa for the correct answer,' Bragadin snarled. 'Tell us the truth! Was she alone in her bedchamber when Signor Grossolano left the palazzo?'

'I . . .' Agnese lowered her head, unable to hold Bragadin's glare.

'Answer the question, or you shall spend another night in the cells! Was the contessa alone in her bedchamber when my nephew left her palazzo?'

'No, signor,' the maid confessed.

'There we have it,' Bragadin roared, turning to Mastello and then Salvadori for their agreement. 'Proof that the contessa has been lying to this tribunal. In her own testimony, Coltello claimed she was alone in her bedchamber on the night of the murder. But now her own maid admits there was somebody else with the contessa.'

Coltello waited until Bragadin was looking at her again before speaking. 'Signor, if I may, there is one question you have not asked my maid.'

He sneered at her. 'And what is that?'

'Who was with me in my bedchamber,' Coltello replied.

Bragadin dismissed that with a wave of his hand. 'This tribunal has no interest in who a self-proclaimed woman of supposed virtue takes to her bed. All that matters is the fact you lied, Contessa. You lied and that shall be punished.'

Aldo waited for Coltello in the vast courtyard of the Doge's palazzo, but his thoughts were all on Vincenzo. After so many years of dwelling on their time together, the reckless passion they'd known, after blaming Vincenzo for so long for what had happened . . . now it seemed he had been wrong.

Did he believe Vincenzo's denial? Yes, he probably did. And

believing that meant everything looked different now. He had not been cast aside. Vincenzo had not betrayed him – not intentionally, at least. The possibility of a passionate, dangerous life together . . . well, it probably would never have lasted.

Aldo had seen the fear in Vincenzo's eyes today, and how that unmanned him. Vincenzo was afraid of who he truly was, afraid of being his honest self. He'd denied it, denied he was living a life half lived, one without what had been and what could have been.

Aldo was sorry for Vincenzo – and yet a little envious. How much easier his own life might have been if he could pretend, if he could hide his truth from everyone, especially himself. But Aldo had long since accepted his heart wanted what it did, his body needed what it did, and denying that was beyond him. It had been a lonelier life at times, but an honest one too.

Aldo did not believe in purgatory as the Church described it. But the life Vincenzo was living? That must be a—

'Aldo, is that you?'

Most voices were lost in the wide expanse of the courtyard – but not this one. It sent birds flying up into the air and had patricians looking to see who had spoken so loudly. A burly figure with red hair and a bushy beard strode towards Aldo: John of Scotland.

'I thought you were only going to Le Casette?' John asked as he slapped Aldo on the back. 'If I'd known you were coming here, I could have accompanied you.'

'My plans changed,' Aldo replied.

'Where's your man Dandolo?'

'Dandolo?'

'Aye, the one you were with in Bologna.'

Aldo remembered introducing Ottone as Federico Dandolo. So

much had happened since, it seemed a lifetime ago. 'He stayed in Le Casette.'

John laughed. 'Best place for him. That cazzo was no fun at all.'

Aldo nodded. 'How long have you been here?'

'Arrived yesterday and already busy. Had to bring some contessa's maid for questioning by Bragadin's tribunal.' John held up a bandaged hand. 'She bit me!'

'You always did have a way with women.'

'And what are you up to here? Working for the Doge now?'

'Not exactly,' Aldo replied. Coltello had complained earlier about her maid Agnese missing work. It seemed John had been the cause of that.

Coltello gazed at the floor of the tribunal chamber while Bragadin celebrated his victory, waiting for him to draw breath. When he did, she fixed Salvadori with a cold stare and nodded. He had not spoken until now, but chose this moment to make himself heard.

'If I may, Signor Bragadin, an answer to the question of who was with the contessa in her bedchamber the night Grossolano died may be helpful. This individual could offer testimony about what happened to your nephew, yes?'

Coltello suppressed a smile as the triumph faded from Bragadin's vainglorious face. He twisted towards Mastello, who nodded his agreement with the suggestion.

'Very well,' Bragadin said. 'Since my fellow inquisitors deem it to be of interest . . . Signorina Agnese, please tell us who was in bed with the contessa that evening?'

'Nobody was in her bed, signor,' the maid replied.

'But you said—'

'She said I was not alone in my bedchamber,' Coltello cut in. 'Agnese never suggested someone was in bed with me, signor. That was your assumption. For a member of this tribunal, an advisor to the Doge, to leap to such an immoral and unseemly conclusion without proof . . . It reflects poorly on you, signor.'

'I . . .' Bragadin stumbled on his own words.

'The contessa is correct,' Salvadori said.

'Perhaps so,' Bragadin replied, recovering a little. 'Then please tell us, Signorina Agnese, who was in the bedchamber with the contessa?'

'I was,' she said. 'The contessa became unwell during the meal she shared with Signor Grossolano, and retired early to bed with the illness that afflicts women each month. I was tending to her needs when Signor Grossolano left the palazzo.'

Bragadin's mouth opened and closed, no words emerging.

'Of course,' Coltello said, letting realization blossom across her face. 'I had quite forgotten how helpful Agnese was that evening. Please forgive my earlier omission. When you have a servant as invaluable as her, you sometimes fail to remember how much you depend on them every day.' She clasped Agnese's left hand and kissed it. 'Grazie, Agnese.'

Bragadin remained speechless. Instead, Salvadori spoke. 'When asked about the night Signor Grossolano died, why did you forget your maid's presence in the bedchamber?'

'As Agnese told you, I had my menses and this clouded my recollection.'

'I often forget my maggiordomo is at my side,' Salvadori volunteered.

'Alas, because Agnese was tending to my needs,' Coltello went on, 'she can offer nothing further on what happened to Signor Grossolano. Isn't that right, Agnese?'

'Yes, Contessa.'

Bragadin stayed silent, his face flushed crimson, so Mastello took charge.

'That being the case,' he said, 'I believe the matter can be brought to an end. Of course, if fresh evidence should reach us, this investigation would be reopened. Nonetheless, grazie, Contessa, for assisting us. The tribunal is most grateful.'

'Prego, signori,' Coltello replied, bowing to each of them in turn.

'In recognition of your help,' Salvadori said, 'might I suggest that the contessa should remain as our spymaster in Florence?'

'What?' Bragadin spluttered.

'The quality of recent reports has been excellent,' Mastello said. 'I can see no reason now not to make her position permanent. That is, if you wish to continue, Contessa?'

Coltello was struggling to keep from laughing. 'I am humbled by your confidence, signori, and would be honoured to accept.'

'Then we are agreed?' Mastello asked, glancing at Bragadin.

The Doge's advisor did not reply, but his face . . . Never before had the contessa seen a man suffering such an equal measure of anger and anguish. It was quite delicious.

'Yes, it seems we are,' Salvadori replied. 'Congratulations, Contessa.'

'Grazie mille, signori,' she said. 'Now, I will take my maid to get some rest. A night spent in the cells of the Doge's palazzo would exhaust anyone, be they witness or accused.' Coltello nodded to Mastello before leaving the tribunal chamber. He returned the gesture and, as he did so, she glimpsed a key on a cord around his neck.

Mastello rose from his chair, as did Salvadori. Bragadin remained seated, red-faced and scowling. Coltello smiled at him before leading Agnese to the door. Thankfully, the long carriage journey from Florence had given her and the maid ample time to prepare their testimonies in case the tribunal brought Agnese before it for questioning.

Coltello swept from the chamber, allowing herself a small smirk. The tribunal's summons was as dead as Bragadin's tiresome *idiota* of a nephew. Better still, she had won a permanent post in Florence, far from the anger of Bragadin. There still remained the matter of retrieving Cosimo's private journal from the secret archive, of course. Hopefully Aldo had—

'Contessa!' Bragadin roared behind her.

The contessa sent Agnese ahead as Bragadin stalked closer, fists clenched at his sides, spittle flecking his lips. Looking at Bragadin now, Coltello could see the resemblance to his boorish nephew. What a pity she couldn't arrange for Tito's uncle to meet a similar end.

'Yes, signor?' she asked, arching an eyebrow.

He stamped to a halt in front of her, huffing and puffing. 'You may have duped my fellow inquisitors, but I know the truth,' he raged.

'You should lower your voice, signor. Shouting at a woman in this palazzo . . . is that the mark of a man who hopes one day to become Doge?' Coltello leaned closer. 'Know when you are beaten, signor, and accept defeat gracefully.'

'I will see you in chains, you vicious *fica*—'

'Tut, tut!' The contessa shook her head. 'What a foul mouth you have. Almost as repugnant as your boorish nephew. I'm surprised he wasn't killed sooner. Let us hope the same fate does not befall anyone else close to him.'

'How dare you threaten my *famiglia*,' Bragadin thundered.

'There was no threat in my words,' she said. 'I merely expressed my hopes for your happiness. What could be more kind? Now, if you don't mind—'

Bragadin grabbed her by the arm. 'Nobody walks away from me, strega. I will bring you down, mark my words. This is not over.'

Coltello stared into his eyes, showing him every part of her anger. 'So be it. But remember that I gave you a chance to withdraw. What happens next is your own fault.'

She pulled her arm free and strode away.

Aldo was listening to one of John's enthusiastic tales when he spied the contessa striding across the courtyard, headed out of the palazzo. Fortunately, she was well behind the burly mercenary, who did not see her. 'Scusi, John. Maybe we'll see each other again soon.'

'I hope so – you still owe me a drink!'

Aldo followed Coltello out but kept his distance until they were beyond the palazzo. John was working for Bragadin, which limited how much he could be trusted. The Scotsman had once been an ally, yet was overly fond of coin. Better not to test his loyalties. When Aldo did approach Coltello, she was comforting a tired young woman in crumpled maid's clothes.

'Is it true you bit the man that brought you here?' Aldo asked.

Agnese nodded, her face sour. 'I'd have done worse, but he was bigger than me.'

Coltello frowned at Aldo. 'You can explain how you knew that once we are away from these curious ears.' The broglio was busy now, patricians crowding the piazzetta. Aldo helped Agnese and the contessa onto her gondola before climbing aboard himself. Agnese perched on a cushion in front of them so that Aldo could share the seat with Coltello.

The contessa called over a shoulder to her gondolier. 'Marco, take us along the Grand Canal towards Rialto. We need to call on a friend.' The craft eased away from the piazzetta, moving out into the choppy waters of the lagoon.

'You're going back to see Aretino?' Aldo asked.

'We both are. Marco can leave us there before taking Agnese on to my palazzo.' Coltello leaned closer to whisper in his ear. 'Just as the broglio is the last place one should discuss matters of importance, the same is true of my own palazzo. After what happened with the tribunal, I suspect someone among my Venetian servants is more loyal to Bragadin than me. Aretino will provide us with privacy, and he has friends whose help we may need. Now, tell me, how did you know Agnese bit the man who took her?'

Aldo explained his occasional friendship with John, how they were reunited in Bologna, and his encounter with the burly Scotsman in the palazzo courtyard.

'Where do you believe John's loyalties lie?' Coltello asked.

'He is a true mercenary. Pay him enough coin, and he will do whatever you wish.'

The contessa nodded.

'What happened with the tribunal?' Aldo asked.

Coltello pressed a finger to his lips. 'We can discuss all of that soon enough.' Her eyes darted back towards Marco for a moment, the meaning clear: the gondolier could be trusted to transport them, but no further. Not every enemy hid behind a mask.

Chapter Twenty-two

Aretino resented interruptions when he was writing, but welcomed them when the work was not going well. Some days words flowed like ink from a bottle; others, it would be easier to find a virgin at a Carnival orgy than to write prose worthy of the name. Alas, it was one of the latter days, with little of note reaching the page despite hours of scrawling. Thus the appearance of his maid Cisti with word of an unexpected arrival at Palazzo Bollani brought a smile to Aretino's face.

'My dearest contessa!' he said while helping Coltello from her gondola. 'You have no idea how happy I am to see you again, and so soon.'

'Most kind,' she replied, stepping into his residence. 'You recall Cesare?'

'Of course. It is not often one encounters a mute in Venice.' Aretino bowed his head to her servant. Cesare was not wearing a mask this time, but still hid his thoughts behind a watchful and guarded face. 'Most Venetians and many visitors cannot seem to stop themselves from talking. A man of silence is a welcome change.'

'Actually, Cesare is neither a mute nor illiterate,' Coltello said, mischief dancing in those delightful green eyes of hers. 'I hope you will forgive our small deception last night.'

'Well, I'm sure you had your reasons . . .'

'Indeed.' The contessa sent the gondola onwards to her residence with a weary maid inside it, but instructed the gondolier to come straight back. 'Now, Pietro, is there somewhere we might talk without being disturbed?'

'I would suggest the room where I write, but that is awash with the evidence of my failings today. Let us go to my sala instead. Have either of you eaten? There was far too much food left over last night. It will go to waste unless you can help me.'

'How generous,' Coltello said. 'I've had a tiresome morning and am in need of a meal to sustain me.' She let Aretino guide her, Cesare following close behind.

Once they were seated around a table laden with spiced meats, fruits and cheeses, Aretino asked a question that had been nagging at him. He had always believed it best never to question the choices of a woman, but Coltello's current garb was . . . unexpected. 'Contessa, may I ask, what are you wearing?'

She laughed, much to his relief. 'Oh, this dreadful gown! I had quite forgotten it. These, my dear Pietro, are my widow's clothes.'

'I can see that, but why? The count died more than a year ago.'

Coltello exchanged a look with Cesare. 'I see we shall have to tell you everything. But first, regrettably, you must swear never to repeat or write a word of what we say.'

Aretino pressed a hand against his chest. 'I swear.'

It took an hour, much food and plentiful wine for the contessa to share all she had endured that morning. By the end of her tale, Aretino was regretting his vow not to share what he had heard; this would have made quite a story, assuming anyone could believe it.

'What do you think?' Coltello asked him when she'd finished speaking.

'I agree your trouble with the Inquisitori di Stato may be at an end,' Aretino began, 'but you have made a more dangerous foe in Bragadin. Be wary, Contessa. You outwitted him in front of the other tribunal members; Bragadin will see that as a humiliation, one that must be avenged. From what I've heard, he values his esteem in the eyes of others above all else. He shall not rest until you are defeated – or dead.'

Coltello frowned. 'Bragadin strikes me as a man who is compensating for some personal inadequacy. A small cazzo, perhaps, or one that does not rise to the occasion when needed. He seeks satisfaction by humiliating others instead.'

Aretino turned his attention to Cesare, who had remained silent through all of this. 'And what were you doing while the contessa was making an enemy?'

Cesare opened his mouth, but Coltello spoke first. 'That is something which Cesare and I must discuss by ourselves – for now, at least. I know it is a dreadful imposition, Pietro, especially when you have been so welcoming, but perhaps . . . ?'

'You wish me to leave?'

The contessa shrugged and smiled at him, somehow making that seem charming.

'Very well,' Aretino sighed. 'Call for Cisti if you need anything.' He rose and left the sala, closing the door behind himself. Considering what the contessa had already revealed, what must she and Cesare have to discuss that they could not share with him?

The contessa listened while Aldo described his meeting with Culmine. She studied Aldo's face as he spoke, the way his hands inscribed the air. The facts were simple enough: Aldo had secured another meeting with Culmine, away from his famiglia or the

Doge's palazzo. However, there was more involved than that, judging by Aldo's attitude.

'Do you believe Culmine will come?' she asked.

'Fear might keep him away.'

'Is that what happened before?'

Aldo did not reply.

Coltello could see his discomfort discussing Culmine, what they'd meant to each other.

'My dear Cesare, do you love him?'

Aldo did not answer.

'I need to know the truth. There still remains Cosimo's private journal to obtain, which is now locked inside the Serenissima's secret archive. Unless we can retrieve or destroy that book—'

'I'm quite aware of the danger it represents.'

'Good. But if you are unable to face Culmine, I must find someone else—'

Aldo shook his head.

This was the first time the contessa had seen Aldo without pretence. 'When I was a much younger woman,' she said, 'a wise person once told me something I have never forgotten: "Hide your true self behind a mask long enough, and you become that mask." Culmine has a wife, a famiglia. Perhaps he stopped being the man you knew years ago.'

'When you want someone,' Aldo replied, 'it does not stop. That need does not go away, no matter how many lies you believe.'

'Are you speaking about Culmine . . . or yourself?'

Aldo glared at her, bristling with anger.

She held up a hand in apology. 'Perhaps I go too far. But none of us is always the same. You know what kind of person excites you, you have absolute certainty in that, yes?'

He gave a grudging nod.

'Yet, when we first met, I was able to have an effect on you – and I am not a man.'

Aldo arched an eyebrow. 'I imagine you are able to excite almost anyone, if needed.'

'I shall take that as a compliment,' Coltello said. 'It's not quite true, but I have certain talents. My point, dear Cesare, is this: we all believe we know ourselves, who we are, what we want and need. But we each have a gap in our armour. The right person can pierce that, intentionally or otherwise. We cannot control our love or our lusts.'

'You're suggesting that I was, what, an aberration for him? That Vincenzo is a good, honest man to his wife and famiglia who once strayed from his true path because of me?'

'It is a possibility.' The contessa smirked. 'I've known women who found certain . . . needs and pleasures beyond their marriage bed because they were with me. It does not mean they do not return to their usual ways afterwards. I simply show them another path. It is up to them to determine whether it is a path they wish to pursue.'

Aldo kept his silence, but she could see him considering her words.

'Let me put it differently. Perhaps you were not an aberration, nor a mistake. Perhaps you were the exception for Culmine, the one man capable of unlocking that part of him. He might never have known this without you. For some, finding that truth brings fear instead of joy. It goes against all they have been taught to believe.'

Aldo rose from his chair to open the sala shutters, letting more light into the room. He stayed there, looking out at the Grand Canal. 'I will get a copy of the key that Vincenzo carries, one way or another. But what about the second key? I saw the door to the secret archive. Dandolo was not lying; we will need two keys to open it and retrieve the journal.'

'The solution to that is part of the reason I brought you here.'

Coltello went to the door. 'Pietro, we need you!' By the time she was back in her seat, Aretino had returned.

'You called?'

'Last night, just before you introduced me to the three signori, I heard one of them mention a masked ball tonight. Do you know where it is?'

'Yes, Mastello is hosting it at his palazzo. He has one every Carnival.'

Coltello smiled at Aldo. 'See? Pietro knows everyone and anything worth knowing.'

'What can you tell us about Palazzo Mastello and its owner?' Aldo asked Aretino.

'I know Signor Mastello well enough to have him play cards with his allies here, but the expert on that man and his palazzo is a friend of mine, the architect Jacopo Sansovino. He spends most of his days working on the biblioteca opposite the Doge's palazzo, but before that Sansovino had the ill fortune of overseeing renovations for Palazzo Mastello. What Jacopo doesn't know about the inside of that building isn't worth knowing.'

'Delightful,' Coltello said, clapping her hands together. 'And if you were to send Sansovino a message, how soon do you think he could be here to share this knowledge?'

'It depends how soundly he slumbers,' Aretino replied. 'Jacopo is upstairs in one of my guest bedchambers, still sleeping off his excesses from last night.'

Aldo and the contessa left Aretino's residence after meeting with Sansovino. He was scathing about Mastello, his bitterness born of disagreements that arose during the renovation. The architect claimed he was still owed part of his fee, and said Mastello frequently complained about the work in public. 'That man has carried my name in his mouth for three years,' Sansovino sneered, 'and spits it out whenever anyone asks how he is. Bastardo!'

As a consequence, the architect was eager to share all he knew about the palazzo, its strengths and vulnerabilities. 'Mastello demanded I build him an inner sanctum, a chamber on the highest level where he could keep all he deemed to be of importance: his Bible, his gold, his famiglia crest, vital papers, and all his keys. The rich often have such affectations in their homes, as if believing their tawdry possessions are worth more than any other citizen. A true Venetian would value books and learning over such baubles!'

The chamber was guarded night and day by two men, according to Sansovino, so if one of them fell ill or had to step away there was always still a sentry outside the door. Aldo asked if the sanctum had a balcony. 'No, but there is a tall set of shutters,' the architect replied. 'A narrow ledge runs beneath those shutters, but it is little wider than my thumb. That was one of the things I argued about with Mastello. The levels below had wider ledges, but he would not grasp the need for symmetry and . . .'

Sansovino ranted on for a while after that, but offered little more of value. Aldo and the contessa thanked him profusely before leaving. Coltello's gondola was waiting for them on the Grand Canal. When Marco asked if the contessa wished to be taken home, she suggested taking a less direct journey past Palazzo Mastello.

'I'm going to a masked ball there tonight. I should like to see the entrance in daylight. Too many wealthy Venetians fail to keep the moss away from the steps into their palazzi. Good, honest citizens know how dangerous that can be. I should hate to slip or fall tonight.'

Marco nodded his agreement, pushing the gondola out into

the waters. It headed away from Ponte di Rialto, passing the last of the markets before turning off the Grand Canal. 'This is Cannaregio,' the contessa murmured to Aldo. 'Most of those who live here are workers, not patricians, so Mastello's palazzo will be obvious when we get closer.'

The gondola navigated its way through the maze of canals, Marco calling out before turning each sharp corner. 'This must be it,' Coltello murmured as an impressive palazzo loomed up ahead. The buildings on either side had the same number of levels yet Mastello's residence stood taller than them. It was clad with grey stucco and pale stone ornamentations. Elaborate openings with grand shutters behind them showed the palazzo was owned by a man of substance and significance. On the middle level the openings were all rounded arches, but those above them were far more decorative, stonework gleaming in the weak wintry sun.

Aldo studied the palazzo, searching for signs of the chamber Sansovino described. All the openings on the highest level facing the canal opened on to balconies. But as the gondola got closer Aldo spied a narrow waterway along the side of the palazzo, separating it from adjacent buildings. One set of shutters were open on the top level, but had no balcony. Squinting, Aldo could see a thin ledge along the length of the palazzo. Sansovino had not been jesting when he said it was little wider than his thumb. The prospect of using that to reach Mastello's sanctum was daunting.

Coltello made a show of examining the water-level entrance to the palazzo as they floated by. 'That doesn't look too bad,' she announced. 'I need not have worried.' The contessa gestured for Marco to take them on before whispering to Aldo. 'Well?'

He scowled. 'Let us hope there is another way into this sanctum.'

* * *

Staying busy kept Vincenzo from dwelling on what happened earlier with Cesare. Signor Bragadin had stalked out after the tribunal session, leaving no word as to when he would return. This left time for Vincenzo to tackle the dozen different tasks for which there was never normally a moment, such as dealing with the teetering pile of papers in the cramped ufficio shared by assistants to the Inquisitori di Stato.

Vincenzo went to the cipher deputies and retrieved the red-bound journal he had taken there the previous day. A single sheet fixed to it offered a decoded copy of the journal's opening page. There was nothing of note within the text, and certainly no mention of Contessa Coltello. After detaching the copy and placing it in Bragadin's ufficio, Vincenzo took the journal to the secret archive. Signor Mastello was using his key to secure one of locks in the door for the day, and took some persuading to reopen it.

'I have a Carnival celebration at my palazzo tonight,' he huffed. 'My famiglia will not be pleased if I am late for my own masked ball.'

Vincenzo feigned sympathy. 'I appreciate you taking the time.' Once the door was unlocked, Vincenzo slipped inside and placed the journal atop a stack of reports waiting to be stored on the plain wooden shelves lining the walls.

Task complete, he and Mastello locked the archive door with their respective keys before the tribunal member strode away. Vincenzo left the palazzo soon after for his habitual journey home. It was a relief not to be coming back later, so he could spend the evening—

Vincenzo stopped halfway across a narrow wooden bridge. Cesare, he had agreed to meet Cesare at dusk. A glance at the sky confirmed what Vincenzo knew. If he was going to fulfil his promise, it meant turning around now.

He stared at the canal below, weeds swirling beneath the water's surface.

Should he go to Cesare, or go home? What would happen if he broke this promise? Cesare had not made any threats, yet the simple fact that he had come to the Doge's palazzo was threat enough. What else might Cesare be willing to do?

Vincenzo knew too many men whose reputations had been destroyed with a careless word in the wrong ear or by the briefest of written denunzia. There were numerous places in the Doge's palazzo where anyone could deposit an anonymous complaint; grotesque stone masks with openings called lions' mouths set into the walls. If Cesare put a denunzia in one of those, it would be passed on to the Inquisitori di Stato. Even if the complaint was dismissed, the taint would linger. Worse still would be how it would hurt Vincenzo's famiglia . . .

No, he could not allow that.

He was faithful to his vows, no matter the temptation to do otherwise. No matter what he felt, when he desired . . . He would be faithful. He would be true.

He must. He must.

Chapter Twenty-three

Aldo waited in the shadows outside Palazzo Coltello, his gaze fixed on Ponte del Diavolo. An occasional gondola passed beneath the bridge, but the narrow pathways on either side of the canal were empty as dusk settled over Venice. Workers had long since returned home, and Aldo presumed those with wealth were busy preparing themselves for a night savouring the delights of Carnival, as the contessa was doing.

Approaching footsteps brought Aldo forwards to see who was coming. But it wasn't Vincenzo, merely a male servant hurrying on an errand for his employer. He passed the other side of the bridge, too intent on his task to notice Aldo. The footsteps faded and were soon gone, leaving only the sound of water lapping against stone.

Perhaps Vincenzo would not come? When they spoke earlier, it seemed there was an understanding between them, an agreement. Yet the sun had long since disappeared from view and the twilight air was getting colder by the moment. If Vincenzo did not come, Aldo would have to confront him at home or on his way to the Doge's palazzo. That was dangerous, but they needed his help, willing or otherwise.

Hurried footfalls announced another arrival.

It was Vincenzo.

In this waning light, he looked as he had years ago. Dusk hid the lines on his face, the silver in his hair. Breath caught in Aldo's chest. He still wanted Vincenzo, even now.

Vincenzo slowed as he reached Ponte del Diavolo, looking around.

Aldo stepped from the shadows.

'I cannot stay,' Vincenzo said. 'I'm expected at home.'

'This won't take long,' Aldo replied, beckoning him across the bridge. Vincenzo ventured over, glancing around. 'Don't worry, nobody is watching.' Aldo pushed open the door to Palazzo Coltello, light spilling from inside. 'We can talk in here.'

Vincenzo stopped, fear on his face.

Aldo took him by the hand, leading Vincenzo into the palazzo and closing the door behind them. Inside, lanterns and candles warmed the entrance hall. In here Vincenzo looked like the worried, careworn man Aldo had found at the Doge's palazzo.

That didn't stop Aldo kissing him.

He pushed Vincenzo back against the door, one hand sliding behind Vincenzo's back, the other into his hair, pulling him close, their mouths meeting. At first Vincenzo did not respond . . . and then his hands were on Aldo, holding him as their kisses deepened.

Thought and sense and guilt left Aldo.

All that remained was lust.

The contessa let the two men savour each other a while before striding into the entrance hall. 'Oh my!' Coltello gasped, doing her best to appear shocked, even horrified. 'Cesare, what are you— Who is this man? Why is he kissing you?'

Aldo stepped back, and Culmine wiped a hand across his mouth, eyes wide with fear. 'Cesare kissed me,' Culmine protested. 'He kissed me!'

'Really?' The contessa arched an eyebrow. 'It looked like you were both kissing each other. And as for what your hands were doing . . .' She resisted the urge to tut. Better Vincenzo believed her appalled by what she'd seen; it would make him more compliant. 'If I sent a denunzia to your masters at the Inquisitori di Stato, would they worry who was kissing who? Or would they be more concerned that one of their assistants, a man much esteemed at the Doge's palazzo, was seen being . . . passionate . . . with another man?'

'You can't.' Culmine's blush was fading, the colour draining from his face. 'Please, you mustn't.'

Coltello sighed. 'You are in no position to tell me what I should or shouldn't do. Not when I can truthfully tell the tribunal I have witnessed you indulging your lusts with this Florentine scoundrel.'

'Dio, no . . .' Culmine crumpled forwards, hands to his face.

The contessa smirked at Aldo. But instead of triumph, he looked stricken – whether by guilt or pity was unclear. How disappointing. Lust and revenge were two of her favourites.

Culmine sank to his knees, weeping and shaking his head.

The contessa felt no pity for him. As a man, Culmine had the luxury of doing whatever he wished while facing few consequences of those choices; as a woman, she had to fight to make almost any decision about her own life. Men like him were given power by virtue of their sex, whereas women had to battle for any influence.

Now Culmine knew what it was to be vulnerable.

Now he knew what it was to be afraid.

'Give me a reason why I shouldn't tell the tribunal about you?' Coltello asked.

Culmine didn't reply, his body wracked by sobs.

'Have you nothing to say?' She gestured at Aldo. 'Make this fool understand.'

It took some time. Aldo crouched beside Culmine, whispering to him. Eventually, Culmine nodded, seeming to understand the truth of his situation. He stood, wiping the tears from his blotchy face. 'What do you want from me?'

Aldo rubbed a hand across his greying stubble. 'Your key.'

'My key?' Culmine frowned. 'For the secret archive?'

'Just so.' Coltello held out a hand. 'Give it to me, and I can have a copy made. Once that is done, you can go home and what happened here need never be mentioned again.'

'But it will do you no good, not unless you have the second key.'

'Then it makes no difference if you help us, does it?'

'What do you seek from the archive?'

'It is better you do not know,' Aldo replied. 'Then you can deny any foreknowledge of our plans, and it will be the truth.'

'The key, please,' Coltello said.

'I can't give it to you.'

'Now, signor, before I lose what patience I have left.'

'I cannot give you what I do not have,' Culmine insisted.

She snapped her fingers at Aldo. He reached forwards, ripping open Culmine's tunic. But there was no cord round his neck, and no key.

'I left my key at the Doge's palazzo,' Culmine said. 'I only take it home when the tribunal has a night session and I have to go back. But the inquisitors aren't meeting tonight.'

'Because Signor Mastello is having a masked ball,' the contessa said. 'Very well. You must take Aldo to the Doge's palazzo now. He can make an impression of the key. After that you will not see or hear from us again.'

'I can't,' Culmine replied. 'The guards only allow me in after dark if I have my key.'

Coltello resisted the urge to curse; it would do no good. 'Then you must take Aldo into the palazzo tomorrow. He will meet you at the broglio soon after dawn, yes?'

Culmine gave a quick nod, one hand clasping his tunic together.

'You may go,' the contessa told Aldo. He frowned, but did as he was told. Once Aldo had left them, Coltello beckoned Vincenzo closer and whispered in his left ear, giving him clear and explicit instructions. 'Do you understand?' she asked. He nodded, but there was confusion in his eyes. 'Do not worry yourself about what I am asking you. Do as I bid, and you will emerge unscathed. Now, you may leave. But do not tell anyone about this, not even Aldo. You know what will happen if Bragadin learns of your complicity...'

Bragadin spent the afternoon at his palazzo going over what had happened at the tribunal. He had been so certain Coltello would succumb, so sure the contessa would get herself caught in a lie or an evasion. For one glorious moment she seemed to stumble into his trap. Yet it had all been for nothing.

Worse still, those fools Mastello and Salvadori dismissed her of any suspicion. They even made her post as Venice's spymaster in Florence permanent! It was beyond his grasp how this had happened, no matter how many times he recalled what was said and done...

Had one of the other inquisitors been in league with Coltello? She presented herself to the tribunal with such ease, as if certain it posed no threat to her. What was it she had said? 'Signor Mastello, so good to see you again,' and 'Signor Salvadori, it seems like only yesterday since our last meeting!'

It was Salvadori who'd intervened on Coltello's behalf. It was Salvadori who'd let the maid say she had been with Coltello when

Tito was killed, turning the contessa's lie into a mere oversight. And it was Salvadori who'd proposed her position as spymaster be permanent.

It was an outrage, a blatant degradation of justice.

And there was nothing Bragadin could do.

Salvadori must be made to pay for this.

But how? How?

Bragadin's maggiordomo ventured into the room, clearing his throat.

'What?' Bragadin hissed. 'I gave explicit instructions I was not to be disturbed.'

'Yes, signor, but an urgent message arrived.' The maggiordomo held it out, the wax seal already broken. 'I read it first to ensure the matter could not wait.'

Bragadin snatched the document from him and read what was inside.

A slow smile spread across his face.

'You were right bringing this to my attention,' he said. 'Grazie.'

'Prego, signor. May I be of any further assistance?'

'Did Signor Mastello send an invitation to his masked ball?'

The maggiordomo nodded. 'I set it aside, knowing you've little time for such events.'

'That is almost always true – but not tonight. I shall need suitable clothes for a ball. And a Carnival mask as well.'

'Very good, signor.' The maggiordomo withdrew, leaving Bragadin alone. This was as good a time as any to test Mastello's loyalties. Bragadin reread the message. A body had been found in a canal by workmen making repairs to a jetty. All the evidence suggested murder, and a witness had named one person in connection with this . . .

Contessa Valentine Coltello.

Chapter Twenty-four

Aldo remained silent as the contessa's gondola made its way north and west through Venice. Coltello lounged beside him, occasionally rearranging the folds of her elegant blue gown or adjusting the silk ribbon that held her Carnival mask in place. She had chosen a full-face covering, the left side painted to match her gown, the other side a rich coppery hue. The contessa had insisted Aldo change into a fresh servant's tunic and hose, along with a new half-mask of pure white to hide most of his face.

As the gondola floated on, Aldo could not keep his thoughts from what had happened with Vincenzo. It had given birth to a squirming serpent of guilt in Aldo's gut, threatening to consume him from within. He was angry at the contessa for the way she had used Vincenzo.

But angrier at himself for helping her.

He knew what it was to be bullied.

To be threatened.

It was not something he would wish on his enemies, yet he had helped Coltello inflict that on Vincenzo. Yes, he had sworn to do whatever was necessary to retrieve Cosimo's journal; without it he could not return to Florence. Without it, he might never see Saul again.

But was destroying Vincenzo a price worth paying to achieve that?

Bad enough to be kissing another man and offering the promise of more.

What would Saul say if he knew what Aldo was doing to ensure that they were reunited?

'You're angry,' the contessa said as the gondola rounded a corner.

'Yes,' he replied. There was no point denying it.

'Perhaps guilty as well?'

Aldo ignored the question, knowing Coltello did not expect an answer.

'You took no pleasure from betrayal, but sometimes it is necessary.'

He remained silent, refusing to succumb to her provocations.

'Well, I say you took no pleasure . . .' She stroked a finger along his hose. 'But perhaps I wasn't looking closely enough. How did it feel, kissing him again after so long?'

Aldo pushed her hand away. 'I'm not one of your playthings, Contessa. We are equals in this, for better or worse.'

'For better or worse? My dear Cesare, are you proposing marriage?'

'Considering what happened to your last husband, that would not be wise.'

Coltello shifted on the seat. 'The count died in a hunting accident.'

'How inconvenient for him . . .' Aldo said.

'It was.'

'. . . and helpful for you. A suspicious mind might question how he died. Most men who fall from a horse suffer bruises, perhaps a broken bone. Tumbling head-first onto a heavy stone and bleeding to death afterwards? That really is most unfortunate.'

'These things happen.'

'Indeed. But I'm sure you took no pleasure from it.'

'Be very sure of that,' she replied, steel sliding into her voice like a blade.

'Palazzo Mastello,' her gondolier Marco announced.

The residence loomed ahead of them, lanterns suspended outside the entrance to welcome guests. Aldo peered up at the sanctum shutters on the top level. They were dark where almost every other opening in the palazzo was ablaze with light.

'Just in time,' Coltello said. 'We wouldn't wish to start the evening on a sour note.'

Aldo followed the contessa into Palazzo Mastello, but they parted at the ballroom entrance. Her task was to find their host and, if needed, keep him occupied while Aldo sought a way into Mastello's sanctum. After delivering Coltello to her hunting ground, Aldo stepped aside to watch what other servants did. The maids withdrew to a smaller chamber adjoining the ballroom, while male servants disappeared along a dark corridor.

Aldo followed the men.

Those ahead of him disappeared down a staircase. Laughter billowed up from below, jokes told by quick Venetian tongues. There was another staircase nearby leading upwards . . .

Just where Sansovino had said it would be.

Aldo took the second staircase.

The higher he went, the quieter Palazzo Mastello became. One level up he could still hear music and laughter from the ballroom. Soon, the sounds were distant, no more than murmurs. When Aldo reached the top level, no sounds drifted up from below.

But he could hear the guards outside Mastello's sanctum.

Aldo crept along a dark, empty hallway to peer around a corner. Two men stood either side of a sturdy wooden door. Both were broad of chest, with thick muscular arms and brooding faces. Candles burning in brackets on the wall lit the men, but little more. They muttered to each other, sharing grievances about the masked ball and how long it meant they would have to stand sentry. Their replacements were busy at the palazzo entrance, stopping uninvited guests. Aldo smiled; their counterparts were doing a poor job. Nobody had challenged the contessa's arrival.

He had hoped Sansovino might be wrong about the guards. But it made sense to have two sentries, especially while the palazzo was full of guests. Even if one could be lured away and silenced, the other would still be at his post. Aldo cursed the contessa for withholding his stiletto.

He would have to clamber along the narrow outside ledge to reach the sanctum. If he reached it, he should be able to get inside and search for Mastello's key to the secret archive. Assuming the shutters were not locked or bolted, of course.

Of all the foolish things he had done, this might be the worst.

Aldo went to an empty bedchamber at the rear of the palazzo. Inside it tall shutters stood ajar, a cold wind making them creak. Stepping out onto the balcony, Aldo studied his surroundings. The back of another palazzo faced him, but no lights were visible behind its shutters, while the canal between was narrow and empty. Aldo leaned over the balcony. Yes, the narrow ledge stretched round the building, but offered little more than a toe-hold.

He glanced up. There was a corresponding ledge above at head height. He could hold on to that while edging his boots along – but it was still madness. Falling four levels was not a welcome thought, even with a canal below. He had no idea how deep it was, and nor could he swim. The water might break his fall, but drown him soon after.

Aldo remembered the terror in Dandolo's face, and shivered.

Best not to fall.

He clambered over the side of the balcony, putting one boot and then the other onto the ledge, his fingers reaching up for a handhold. Aldo considered making the sign of the cross, but keeping a firm grip was more important.

Balancing on his toes, his face pressed against the stone wall, Aldo let go of the balcony. He reached that hand to the upper ledge. There. Now just the small task of making his way along the wall, around a corner and along another wall. All without falling, dying or drawing attention to himself. What could be simpler?

Vincenzo stood on the balcony of his residence, a cup of wine trembling in his grasp. He had lied to his wife, told her that thieves had accosted him in the street, tearing his tunic before they fled empty-handed. She was horrified, of course. Did nobody see, nobody come to his aid? Had he seen the thieves' faces, could he describe them? That an assistant to the Inquisitori di Stato could be attacked . . .

He promised he would report the incident, that he had lost nothing except his dignity and his pride. Yet there was nothing proud about lying to her, about what he was doing. She brought his usual cup of wine and sent him out onto the balcony while their daughters helped prepare the table for food.

Vincenzo stared into the canal. How much easier it might be if he disappeared into the water, sinking down until . . . His famiglia would mourn, of course. There would be questions asked about what caused such a terrible accident. There might even be suspicions that he had wanted it to happen . . .

But that was all a fantasia. Even if the world did not know, God would. To sacrifice the most precious of His gifts – life – was a mortal sin. No. Vincenzo knew his flaws were many, but they could still be forgiven by the Almighty.

The notion of leaving his wife to raise their daughters alone, of causing them all so much grief . . . That was unbearable. Even the prospect of never seeing any of them again was too much. No, whatever happened tomorrow, he must face it for them. He must be steadfast, and hold on to the one truth he believed for certain: that he loved his famiglia and would do anything for them. Even if it meant helping the contessa and Cesare.

The contessa was grateful not to have worn zoccoli to the ball. Yes, this meant she was shorter than almost every other woman present, but it avoided excruciating pain and the prospect of stumbling over her own feet. Seeing where she was going was difficult enough in a mask.

Finding the host was not difficult, even at a ball where everyone's face was hidden. Mastello was wearing the most elaborate and highly decorated mask in the room, but he frequently pushed it up onto his greying hair to talk. That made keeping him in sight simple. Coltello let herself enjoy the occasion a little, joining in with gossip and entertaining the attentions of handsome men with strong thighs and firm jaws.

That soon proved dangerous.

The contessa lost sight of Mastello while a particularly comely young man was whispering in her ear. When she looked round, there was so sign of her host. Declining a drink, she slipped between guests to reach the entrance. Mastello was not there, nor had those nearby seen him leave. Where was he? A possible answer gave cause for concern; had Aldo been caught? If so, it might not be long before guards came for her.

Coltello took one last look around the ballroom, and spied a balcony door ajar. Through it she could see Mastello outside. Who was he talking with? She moved closer, and spied two men with Mastello. One was tall and had no mask, but Coltello could not see much of him. However, there was something familiar about the other . . . He slipped off his Carnival mask, revealing Bragadin. The contessa doubted he had much interest in masked balls, suggesting he had come here for another reason. She paused by the balcony door, tilting her head closer to hear them.

'It's one of our men?' Mastello asked.

'Yes.'

'Drownings are not uncommon, Bragadin. Men get drunk, fall into the canals . . .'

'It seems he was attacked before entering the water, judging by the bruises on his body. And he wasn't drunk, not according to the maggiordomo at the famiglia residence.'

'Still, accidents happen. And passing gondole often hit things which have fallen into the canal. That could explain the marks on his body.'

'There's more to it than an accident,' Bragadin insisted before leaning closer to Mastello. The contessa could not hear what passed between them, but the change in Mastello's face was striking.

She could not be certain, but Coltello suspected the body the two men were talking about belonged to Armando Dandolo. If that had been found, she needed to leave.

Immediately.

Chapter Twenty-five

Aldo nearly fell twice as he clambered around the exterior of Palazzo Mastello; once while edging round a corner, and again when his boots slipped on moss coating the narrow ledge. He was sweating through his tunic, every finger aching from clasping the head-height ledge, his calves taut and close to cramping. But finally, blessedly, he reached the shutters of the sanctum. Aldo pressed a hand against them . . .

. . . but they did not move.

He tried again, harder.

Still nothing.

Merda, were they bolted on the inside?

Slamming a fist against them might force the shutters open, but risked alerting the two guards. The prospect of clambering all the way back with nothing was not inviting. Better to make one last attempt. Aldo leaned back, preparing to punch the shutters—

– and his left boot came off the ledge!

One arm came away from the wall, flailing at the air. Both legs wobbled beneath him, the one still on the ledge threatening to give way. Aldo arched his back, and then threw his shoulder into the shutters—

– and they broke open, swinging inwards. Aldo clawed at them with his free arm to steady himself. He stopped, listening, waiting for the guards to burst in. They must have heard him, surely?

But no voices called out, no key turned in the sanctum door. Instead, there was laughter. The guards had been sharing a jest and did not hear him. Aldo stayed where he was to let the thundering in his chest settle. Once that had slowed, he climbed inside. Pale moonlight drifted between the shutters, illuminating the room a little. Aldo stood to one side, listening to the guards in the hallway while his eyes adjusted.

Sansovino had complained that Mastello used the sanctum for what he deemed important rather than things a true Venetian should value, such as books. Aldo could see only one book. Lying atop a lectern in the middle of the sanctum was an illuminated Bible, its pages open at a painting of Eve in the Garden of Eden, being tempted by a serpent.

An ornate table with an inlaid marble top stood facing the lectern, a golden chair behind it. Papers were stacked in three neat piles on the table. One seemed to be documents from the Inquisitori di Stato. The second was correspondence sent to Mastello, while the third was unpaid accounts for renovation work. That explained why Mastello was so eager to gamble. But papers were of no interest; it was a key Aldo sought.

He spied a small casket behind the tallest stack of papers. Inside was the Mastello famiglia seal with wax, candles and a small flint for lighting them, ink and other writing equipment – but no keys. Sansovino had been adamant Mastello kept all his keys here, yet there were none. Had Mastello changed his habits?

Aldo crept round the table on the balls of his feet to soften each step.

Five keys were arranged on pegs hammered into the table, four on a peg to the left of the golden chair, one on the right. That last key hung on a long, circular cord. It was smaller and more ornate. Yes, that resembled the key Vincenzo had worn. The fact that both were on similar loops of cord made Aldo certain: this was the key to the secret archive.

He reached inside his hose and pulled out a small leather pouch tucked on his left hip. Inside the pouch was a lump of red wax already warmed by his exertions. Aldo pressed one side of the key into the wax, then the other. After returning the key to its peg, Aldo slid the wax into the pouch. They could now make a copy of Mastello's key.

The challenge was leaving his palazzo alive . . .

The contessa waited at the entrance hall of Palazzo Mastello for a gondola. It was impractical for visitors to have their own gondola remain outside; the canal would be choked with craft. The result? A long wait while her gondola was summoned, the last thing Coltello wanted.

Mastello marched from the ballroom, followed by Bragadin and the other man. Now she could see him properly, Coltello recognized the taller man as Giovanni degli Scozzesi, the mercenary who had taken Agnese the previous night. He stood half a head taller than the two tribunal members, and had a formidable torso. She glanced away as the men passed, careful to avoid their gaze.

The three men strode towards a staircase leading upwards inside the palazzo. If she was going to stop them – or at least slow them down – now was the moment . . .

'Signora, your gondola is ready,' a sibilant voice said.

Coltello turned to see a servant gesturing towards the canal.

When she looked back, Bragadin and the others were gone.

'Signora?' the servant asked. 'If you do not wish to leave yet . . .'

'I'm quite ready,' Coltello replied. She stepped onto her gondola giving precise instructions about where to go, what to do; better to be too specific in such circumstances.

The craft pushed away from Palazzo Mastello, leaving Aldo to his fate.

Aldo had one leg out on the ledge and one still in the sanctum when he heard a familiar voice. Was that John of Scotland in the hallway? It must be, nobody else in Venice sounded like him, yet that made no sense. He was working for Bragadin, not Mastello.

If John was in the hallway, Bragadin must be close by. He did not seem a man to enjoy masked balls. That meant he had come to see Mastello. But what would bring Bragadin here now?

Aldo swung his left leg back inside and crept over to listen at the door. John was summoning the guards away in his gruff voice, saying they were needed downstairs. But the two sentries refused, not without hearing the request from Mastello's own mouth. The argument was settled by a sharp command from another voice, demanding the guards come now. That must be Mastello, ordering his men downstairs.

Heavy boots stamped away, voices fading in the distance.

Aldo almost laughed. He could not have planned this better.

He reached for the door, and opened it a crack. There was no need to lock a room if two men were always guarding it. Aldo opened the door wider. The hallway was empty. The footsteps had stamped towards the front of the palazzo. There must be another staircase there; no grand residence would have a single way up and down.

Stepping into the hall, Aldo closed the door behind him. He—

'I'll be right there,' a voice called out. Mastello was coming back!

Aldo stood still as a statue. Should he return to the sanctum, or dash for—

Mastello appeared at the end of the hall, surprise stopping him there. 'What are you doing here? Servants wait on the palazzo's lowest level.'

'I . . . I needed a latrina, and got lost.'

Mastello's gaze shifted to the door behind Aldo. 'Have you been in my sanctum?'

'No, I . . .'

'Stay where you are,' Mastello commanded before calling out, 'Guards, get back up here!' Mastello glanced over his shoulder at the staircase—

– and Aldo bolted. He dashed to the rear staircase. There were shouts behind him, voices demanding he stop. Aldo ignored them, vaulting down two and three steps at a time.

One landing, more steps, another landing.

More steps, more haste.

Another level.

Faster, he needed to be faster.

'Stop, damn you!' That voice was louder, nearer.

Aldo threw himself down the final steps, then raced along the corridor. Maids and male servants were coming towards him. 'Move!' Aldo bellowed to clear a path.

He was close to the entrance, but where was the contessa?

A servant grabbed at Aldo, snatching at his tunic.

Fighting to free himself, Aldo got twisted around.

John of Scotland was charging after him.

Getting closer by the moment.

Aldo pulled free, dashing towards the entrance.

Don't look back, he mustn't look back.

'You can't escape!' John shouted.

Aldo ran as fast as he could.
The entrance.
But no gondola was waiting.
And it was far, far too late to stop.
Aldo leapt into the air, legs and arms pumping. His mask came off, falling behind him. For a moment, Aldo believed he might clear the canal, might make it across—
– but the water took him.
He plunged down into darkness.
The coldness of it was the first shock.
He opened his mouth to cry out—
– and water rushed in.
Filling him.
Choking him.
He flailed his arms and legs.
Kicking out, kicking up, kicking—
His face broke the surface.
Aldo spat out, desperate to gasp in air.
But he was sinking again, water dragging him down.
The cold was all around him.
Its embrace so strong, so numbing.
He could give in, could let go—
Aldo kicked again, pulling himself up with both arms.
Light replaced the dark of the canal's depths.
He could breathe again. He could breathe.
He lurched round in the water.
A gondola, coming at him.
He remembered how Dandolo had died.
Aldo flung himself sideways.
Away from the gondola.
It slid between him and Palazzo Mastello.

'Grab the side,' a voice urged him. 'Grab it, you fool!'

The contessa leaned over the gondola.

'I said, grab hold,' she hissed.

Aldo did, and the gondola pulled him along the canal, away from the palazzo.

'You there!' John's voice bellowed through the night air. 'Gondolier! Did you see anyone in the water?'

'What's that?' Marco shouted back.

'In the water! Did you see anyone in the water?'

'Tell him no,' the contessa hissed.

'No, I didn't!' Marco called.

'Are you sure?'

'Yes. Sorry!'

The gondola floated on, disappearing into the darkness.

Coltello waited until they were some distance from Palazzo Mastello before asking Marco to stop. He clambered past her to pull Aldo into the craft. Then they went on, with the contessa in her seat and Aldo shivering in the belly of the boat. 'Well?' she asked. 'Did you get it?'

Aldo stared. 'Did I get it?'

'It's a simple question, Cesare.'

'You were supposed to be keeping watch.'

Coltello shrugged. 'It's not my fault Bragadin arrived.'

Aldo revealed the leather pouch tucked in his hose. 'I got it.'

'Good.' She smiled. 'Well done. Count yourself fortunate those men chasing you out of the palazzo didn't see us collect you as we went by.'

Aldo seemed too busy shivering to care about that.

'Pozzo can make a copy by morning. Tomorrow, you will go with Culmine to make an impression of the second. Once that is copied, we shall have a way to retrieve what we need. The sooner we leave this city, the better.'

Chapter Twenty-six

Wednesday, February 14th 1539

Aldo floats, arms stretching out, legs gently moving to keep him in place. The sky is a blazing *azzurro*, the sun warming his face, not a cloud in sight. This is joy. No responsibilities, no weight. Aldo closes both eyes, letting himself drift . . .

But when he looks again, the sun is gone. Clouds turn the sky a dark bruise. Aldo looks to see, but there is no boat nearby, no land, nothing. He is alone.

Something tugs from below. A gentle pull at first, but becoming more urgent. He reaches down – and something grabs his wrist. Pulling him over, pulling him below—

Aldo gasps in a breath as water covers his face. He sinks, plunging deeper and deeper, getting colder and colder. A voice shouts at him, distant, distorted . . .

He struggles to see in the inky dark. A shape approaches, and he knows their face. Saul smiles but his eyes are full of mourning. He mouths a word: *why?*

Aldo opens his mouth to answer – and water rushes in. It chokes him, fills him.

Another face looms – Dandolo – he laughs, air escaping him – Dandolo lunges forwards—

* * *

Aldo forced himself upright, fighting to escape the bedclothes wrapped around his arms and legs. He was awake. It had been a fantasma. He was awake.

A fist hammered at the lavender-room door.

'The contessa summons you.'

'I'm coming.'

'Now,' the voice commanded before stamping away.

Aldo scrambled from the bed, finding fresh servant's clothes and a bowl of water for washing. A glance out through the shutters showed how early it was, the air still murky and pallid, dawn not yet claiming the sky. Vincenzo was to be waiting on the broglio at dawn.

With his key and the copy made from Mastello's, the secret archive would be accessible. How early did the guards stand sentry in front of that door? It was one of too many questions to which Aldo did not have answers. He had to trust the contessa's plan.

But she was not the one taking all the risks.

Coltello did not enjoy being made to wait, let alone by a man. Yet it seemed the fate of her sex to spend much of their lives being patient with those who had a cazzo between their legs. Men were so accustomed to their privilege, the right to claim so much for themselves while suffering so little pain, that they never considered the cost of those actions. Making others wait was, perhaps, the least of their many sins but this did not stop it being vexing. Men simply assumed the world would wait for them.

The contessa longed for the day when that was not true.

When Aldo finally arrived in her sala, pillow creases still on his face, Coltello thrust a message at him. He briskly read the few sentences. 'Palle,' he muttered.

'Quite,' the contessa agreed.

'This doesn't state whose body has been found.'

'But it must be Dandolo. There is no other reason that the Inquisitori di Stato would request my presence again today, nor send their demand before dawn.' She sighed. 'I had plans to call on Signor Bragadin at the Doge's palazzo this morning to ensure he was busy while you made an impression of the second key, so this may still work to our advantage. But it says much about Dandolo that, even in death, he finds a way to complicate matters.

Aldo grimaced. 'The maggiordomo at Palazzo Dandolo must have told the tribunal's men that a servant came asking for Armando on your behalf.'

'Then it's as well I had you bring Dandolo to me a good distance from the famiglia residence. With Luigi now well away from Venice, there are no witnesses to what happened.'

'Aside from you and me, of course.'

Coltello smiled. 'Don't worry, Cesare. I trust you to keep our secret.' She clapped her hands together, summoning Amaro. 'Does Marco have the gondola ready?'

'I'm . . . not sure, Contessa.'

'Then go and be sure.'

The maggiordomo stalked out, muttering to himself. Coltello did enjoy annoying him, though she knew it was unwise; irritating a servant only stored up trouble for later. But she had no intention of remaining in this palazzo – or the Serenissima, for that matter – a moment longer than was necessary. If all went well, she should be on her way back to Florence before tomorrow's Fat Thursday festivities.

If the hearing went badly, she wouldn't need this palazzo.

Dead women seldom had use for property.

* * *

Vincenzo had expected to be afraid as he waited outside the Doge's palazzo. It was early, low clouds still being coloured by the rising sun. The broglio was empty, a few servants hurrying by on early morning errands but no patricians gathered yet to gossip. The air was fresh with a light tang of salt from the lagoon, a cool breeze cleansing the senses. Instead of fear churning his belly, Vincenzo knew a calm that matched his surroundings. The worst had already happened, yet another day dawned and he was still here to see it. His back was straighter and his gaze was lifted up, not lowered in respect as it always was, not focused on his boots and the next step in front of him. That ended now, once and for all.

He strolled across the broglio as the contessa's gondola approached. 'May I help?' Vincenzo asked, reaching out a hand. 'This wood is slippery early in the day.'

'I'll remain here, for now,' she said. 'My servant shall accompany you.'

Cesare climbed from the gondola, grasping the outstretched hand. His fingers were cold but his grip steady, no trembling or fear evident. Cesare gave a quick nod to the contessa before facing the Doge's palazzo. 'Shall we?'

Vincenzo led him through the entrance, nodding to the guards. Once in the courtyard, Vincenzo explained how they would go to the ufficio where his key was kept. Cesare listened but said nothing until they reached the first internal staircase.

'I'm sorry for what happened last night. The contessa should not have treated you like that, and I should not have let her.'

Vincenzo continued up the marble and stone stairs. 'Would you have been able to stop her? She calls you a servant, and certainly treats you like one.'

Cesare kept pace with him. 'This is not my city, and I have few allies here. But I would never allow Coltello to do what she threatens. You have my word on that.'

The words seemed heartfelt. Had Cesare faced similar threats? If so, he would know how they cut to the bone. Yet he had let Coltello turn truth into a blade, the contessa twisting it to make the wound wider.

At the top of the stairs, Vincenzo led Cesare to the left. 'The ufficio is at the end of this corridor.' They strode on, side by side. The corridor was empty, the Doge's palazzo still yawning itself awake. 'I also owe you an apology,' Vincenzo said.

'Why? You've done nothing wrong since I returned.'

'For our past, for what happened.'

'We were both much younger . . .'

'I'm still sorry.' Vincenzo stopped. 'Forgive me?'

Cesare smiled, his eyes both sad and warm. 'Of course.'

'Grazie.' Vincenzo ushered him into an ufficio. 'My key is in here.'

Coltello saw Salvadori scuttle towards the Doge's palazzo, his black robes flapping around his legs. He muttered to the guards before going in, red-faced and puffing. She had stationed Marco outside the entrance to eavesdrop on conversations while seeming to hawk trips on his gondola to any passing patricians. After Salvadori went inside the contessa beckoned Marco back to her. 'What did the last man say to the guards?'

'I didn't hear much,' the gondolier admitted. 'Something about an urgent tribunal meeting. He was in a hurry. Apparently, he only got the summons this morning.'

Coltello rewarded Marco with a handful of coin before sending him away; she was likely to be with the tribunal some time. The contessa watched the gondola leave, her thoughts turning over this new morsel. Mastello already knew about Dandolo's murder, having discussed that with Bragadin at the masked ball. Why was Salvadori not told sooner? It suggested he was less trusted.

In this, at least, Bragadin's judgement was wise. Yes, Salvadori intervened to help her the previous day, but she had not asked him out loud to do so. It had been his own initiative, so Salvadori still owed her a favour to her mind, and the contessa suspected it would be needed soon.

Coltello marched to the palazzo entrance, announcing herself to the guards. One of the tribunal's dour assistants was waiting to escort her inside. He marched ahead of her, saying nothing. Soon they were back where she waited the previous morning, the assistant requesting the contessa remain there while the tribunal was told of her arrival.

Bragadin soon emerged with a thin smile of welcome. 'I hope you can help us with this unfortunate matter,' he said, leading her to the tribunal chamber. Bragadin was wearing the scarlet robes of a doge's advisor, but it seemed he had not taken the trouble of having his servants wash or clean them. The unpleasant aroma of stale body odour seeped from his presence, making her nose wrinkle.

'I'm not sure what assistance I can offer,' Coltello replied, 'but I am at your service.'

Bragadin smirked. 'Indeed.' He took his place between Mastello and a ruddy-cheeked Salvadori at the long table. The dour assistant was hunched over a small table in one corner, ink and paper ready to record the session. This time the tribunal had provided a high-backed wooden chair for Coltello. She settled onto it, nodding to each inquisitor in turn.

'Buon giorno.'

They returned her greeting, Mastello with brisk efficiency, Salvadori more breathless. His brow was furrowed with confusion. Whatever Bragadin was about to reveal would be a surprise to Salvadori, it seemed. That did not bode well. No matter, she was ready.

Bragadin smiled again in a way that reminded the contessa of a cat that enjoyed tormenting a trapped mouse. His arrogance was an unattractive quality – especially when it was so lacking in foundation or reason.

'Contessa,' he began, 'we hope you can help uncover those responsible for the murder of Armando Dandolo, one of this tribunal's most promising assistants. He was lured from his famiglia residence two nights ago, murdered, and the corpse hidden in a nearby canal. Had the body been washed out into the lagoon, the killer might have escaped justice. Fortunately – for us, at least – it was recovered before that happened.'

Coltello kept her face a mask of benign interest. 'And how may I assist?'

'We shall come to that,' Mastello replied. 'First, we need to hear from a witness.' He nodded to the assistant who ushered in a gaunt man wearing the garb of a servant for a rich famiglia. 'Signor Pignotti, grazie for joining us.'

Pignotti bowed his head, respectful and quiet. Definitely a servant. A patrician would feel obliged to speak, to announce himself in some way; a servant knew better than to give answers for questions which had not yet been asked.

'You are maggiordomo to the famiglia Dandolo, yes?'

Again, Pignotti nodded.

'Can you tell the tribunal and our guest what happened two nights ago?'

At last, the maggiordomo spoke. 'A servant came to the door

and asked that Signor Armando – the youngest son of the famiglia Dandolo – be summoned.'

'Can you describe this servant?' Bragadin asked.

'Only a little, a black Carnival mask covered much of his face. His clothes were well made but unremarkable. From what I could see, he was between thirty and fifty in age.'

Coltello doubted Aldo would appreciate anyone thinking him close to fifty, but he should be flattered to pass for thirty. The Carnival mask had done its job well.

Mastello leaned forwards. 'Did the servant give a reason for this summoning?'

'Yes,' he said. 'Contessa Coltello wished to see Signor Armando, and it was a matter of great urgency. I passed on this message and Signor Armando came to the door.'

'What happened after that?'

'The servant led Signor Armando away, and he never returned.'

'Did you see this Contessa Coltello whom the servant mentioned?'

Pignotti shook his head. 'And there was no gondola on the canal outside.'

'Is there anything further you can or wish to tell us about this encounter?'

'No, signori.'

'Very well, you may go,' Mastello concluded, gesturing for the assistant to take Pignotti away. Before they could leave, Bragadin interjected.

'One last thing, do you recognize this woman?' He indicated Coltello.

For a moment the contessa feared the maggiordomo might claim to know her, that Bragadin had pressured Pignotti into lying. But the servant shook his head.

'No, signor.'

Bragadin waited until the maggiordomo was gone before speaking again. 'It is clear now that Dandolo was lured from the safety of his famiglia residence to meet with you. Please, Contessa Coltello, tell us all you know about this. And remember, lying to the Inquisitori di Stato is a crime punishable by death.'

It took all of Aldo's will not to shout. Vincenzo had been searching the ufficio for more time than seemed possible, yet still had not found his key to the secret archive. 'I left it last night,' he insisted, 'so the key must be here. Somewhere.'

Aldo helped as best as he could, lifting piles of papers to see if they had been placed on top of the key, and shifting tables in case the key had fallen between them – all to no avail. 'Could it have been a different ufficio?'

'No, this is the chamber all assistants share. We—' Vincenzo stopped, his eyes widening. 'Last night, I was late. Signor Mastello was already locking the archive door when I got there. We secured it together and then –' He spun round and closed the ufficio door. A loop of cord hung from a hook on the back, the key glittering on it. 'And then I hung the key up here so I could find it again in the morning.'

Aldo reached inside his tunic, retrieving a leather pouch with a fresh block of sealing wax inside. 'May I?' Vincenzo gave him the key. Aldo looked around. 'I need heat to soften the wax.'

Vincenzo lit a candle. Working together, he and Aldo warmed the wax until it was pliable enough to press the key into it. Aldo examined the impression once it was made, knowing he wouldn't get a second chance to copy the key. 'Good.'

Vincenzo nodded. 'Do you have a copy of Signor Mastello's key?'

'Not with me. Why do you ask?'

'You could use it and my key to get into the archive.'

Aldo frowned. 'How did you know I have a copy of Mastello's key?'

'Because I told him,' a gruff voice said from behind Aldo.

He spun round to see the ufficio door swinging open.

'What are you doing here?'

Chapter Twenty-seven

Bragadin enjoyed watching the contessa squirm. She had escaped blame for his nephew's murder, but that had happened months ago in another city, without witnesses. The death of Dandolo was fresh, had taken place in Venice, and there was testimony directly linking Coltello to it. This time she would answer for her crime.

'Well, Contessa? Have you nothing to say?'

'Forgive me, signori,' she replied. 'I was simply considering how best to answer the question posed to me. But I must concur with what you said, Signor Bragadin.'

Knowing how devious this strega could be, he waited. Better to let the contessa dig her own grave; then there could be no argument that she was coerced or duped.

'It is clear that Dandolo was tricked into leaving his famiglia residence,' Coltello continued. 'I have no dispute with what Pignotti said, either. The masked servant who went to Palazzo Dandolo offered my good name as a lure.'

'Then you agree with our findings?' Mastello asked, much to Bragadin's frustration. Why did this fool seem obliged to insert himself into interrogations? Doing so offered the contessa an opportunity to gather her thoughts, a respite from pressure. Yet Mastello went on speaking, in love with his own words. 'You agree we have good reason to suspect you of being involved with Dandolo's murder?'

Coltello frowned. 'That is not what I said, Signor Mastello.'

'Isn't it?'

'No. This masked servant, whoever he was, used my name – but he has nothing to do with me. I was not there. My gondola was not seen outside the Dandolo residence. The fact that their famiglia maggiordomo did not recognize me is further proof of my innocence.'

'The evidence is not yet—' Bragadin began, but Mastello blundered on.

'Then why would the killer use your name?' Mastello asked. 'How did they know to employ that as a trick to bring Dandolo out of his home after dark?'

The contessa shrugged. 'I am quite at a loss to explain it, signor. Of course, if the tribunal was able to bring this masked servant before it, I might be able to offer more help.'

There was a knock at the door behind Coltello. Bragadin called for those outside to enter. A burly figure with a bushy red beard brought in another man. A gag across the second man's mouth kept him silent, while his arms were bound in front of him.

'Perhaps you will now have that chance,' Bragadin said. 'Contessa, this is Giovanni degli Scozzesi, the tribunal's investigator. I bring him here from Bologna on occasions when an outsider might be more effective in getting to the truth.' He glanced at Mastello and Salvadori. 'Unless you have any objections, of course?'

Both men shook their heads.

'I prefer to be called John,' Giovanni announced in his gruff foreign accent. Most of the time Bragadin could understand what he said, but not always.

'Be that as it may, you shall be known by this tribunal as Giovanni degli Scozzesi.' Bragadin glared at the captive in Giovanni's grasp. 'And who have you brought before us?'

'That is Cesare Aldo,' Coltello said, rising from her chair. 'He's a former mercenary who worked for the Otto, the most feared criminal court in Florence. Now he's an enforcer for Duke Cosimo de' Medici – and a very dangerous man.'

'She's no wrong,' Giovanni agreed. The prisoner struggled to free himself, without success. He was shouting into the gag, but the cloth muffled his words.

'And where did you find this very dangerous man?' Mastello asked.

'Where Signor Bragadin said I would,' Giovanni replied. 'Aldo threatened one of your assistants, Vincenzo Culmine, into bringing him inside the Doge's palazzo.'

'Culmine came to my palazzo late last night,' Bragadin said, smirking at Coltello. 'He told me about Aldo's stratagemma. It seems our Tuscan friend wished to access the secret archive and steal back certain documents Armando Dandolo brought here from Florence.'

'Opening the secret archive needs two keys,' Salvadori said, breaking his silence. 'Culmine has one of them, but the other is safeguarded by—'

'Dio in paradiso!' Mastello jabbed a finger at Aldo. 'This is the man who stole into my palazzo last night. We chased him but he escaped by leaping into the canal. When he did not come back up for air, we thought he had drowned. I searched my sanctum but found nothing missing.'

'He did not have to steal your key,' Bragadin observed. 'He merely needed to make an impression of it and then get a copy made. Giovanni, did you search our prisoner?'

'Aye, but there were no keys, only this.' He held up a block of red wax, the shape of a key pressed into it.

Coltello cleared her throat. 'Signori, may I make a suggestion?'

'Proceed,' Bragadin reluctantly agreed.

'Armando Dandolo came to my palazzo in Florence some days ago with your letter summoning me to appear before this tribunal. When he did so, Signor Dandolo sought my help with another matter. He said the Inquisitori di Stato was eager to retrieve a stolen book of Venetian ciphers. I gave him what assistance I could. However, I believe Signor Dandolo was guilty of exceeding the tasks given to him by your tribunal.'

Mastello glanced at Bragadin. 'What is she talking about? What tasks?'

The contessa smiled. 'Signor Dandolo created a diversione which enabled him to enter the ducal residence and steal private papers, along with a book of Venetian ciphers. The Medici sent Aldo after Dandolo with orders to reclaim those papers.'

'You're suggesting Aldo is the one who killed Dandolo?' Salvadori asked.

'Yes,' she replied. 'Why not bring Pignotti back and see if he recognizes Aldo as the masked servant who lured Dandolo to his death?'

Bragadin could not dispute the value of this. While the maggiordomo was fetched, the tribunal questioned how Coltello knew so much about Aldo and Dandolo.

'I've known Aldo for several months,' she said. 'Cosimo sent him to me, hoping I would be foolish enough to have Aldo as one of my informants, supplying lies to this tribunal about the Medici's plans and alliances.'

'But you saw through that stratagemma,' Salvadori said.

'Indeed. After Signor Dandolo's daring raid on Palazzo Medici, Aldo sought my help, which I refused to give. He stalked poor Armando all the way to Venice. Aldo approached me again when he arrived here. I allowed him to stay at my residence, believing it was better to have him close so I could keep watch on him. I'm sure my own maggiordomo Amaro can testify to the fact that Aldo has been in my palazzo the past two nights.'

Bragadin already knew this. Coltello's maggiordomo was waiting elsewhere in the palazzo, ready to give evidence. Coltello had made that worthless, but there was still an opportunity to question her judgement.

'You're telling the tribunal that Aldo has been your guest,' Bragadin said.

The contessa held up her hands. 'It was a foolish mistake,' she agreed. 'One which shames me. But I had no idea he would go to such lengths.' Coltello glared at Aldo. 'That he might resort to murder and extortion to achieve his Medici master's wishes.'

Aldo flung himself at her, hatred blazing in his eyes. Mastello shouted a warning and the contessa backed away from the prisoner. Giovanni kept hold of Aldo – just.

Bragadin wasn't sure how much of the tale Coltello was telling he should believe. If she and Aldo were allies, the way she had turned on him was quite ruthless.

The assistant returned, bringing Pignotti. The maggiordomo confirmed Aldo was the masked servant who had lured Dandolo. The tribunal thanked Pignotti before sending him back out. Bragadin conferred with Mastello and Salvadori, but their deliberations were swift. The three of them faced the accused, Giovanni still keeping Aldo under control, while the contessa stood to one side.

'Cesare Aldo,' Bragadin began, 'it is the judgement of this tribunal that you are guilty of murdering Signor Armando Dandolo, one of our most esteemed and respected associates. You will be taken to the cells at the bottom of this palazzo. There you shall be incarcerated to await execution. Tomorrow is Fat Thursday, a time of civic celebration. Your sentence will be carried out at dawn before those festivities begin.' Aldo roared at them from behind his gag, thrashing against Giovanni, but it did no good.

'Take him away,' Bragadin commanded, and the prisoner was dragged away.

It was difficult to hear most of the snarls and threats Aldo directed at Coltello, but Bragadin did make out three words: 'I'll kill you!'

Aldo fought and thrashed as he was dragged from the tribunal chamber, kicking at anyone who came close. John struggled to keep hold of him, and called for help. Two guards took a leg each, but not before Aldo kicked one in the belly and the second in his face. A third guard grabbed hold of an arm, while John grasped the other. They lifted Aldo into the air to carry him along the corridor, making patricians and servants step out of the way.

When the awkward procession reached a narrow stairwell leading downwards, John told the guards to put Aldo down. The mercenary stood in front of Aldo, grabbing his jaw with rough hands and staring into his eyes.

'We are taking you down these stairs. You can walk on your own legs, or we can throw you down them – it's your choice. But the walls and steps are solid stone, and I doubt you'd be alive by the time we reach the cells. Now, is this where you want to die?'

Aldo spat abuse at John, but the spit-soaked gag stole his words.

'Yes, you want to kill me,' John replied. 'Yes, I'm the motherless son of a merda, and whatever else you just said. Are you going to walk? Nod if you understand me. Otherwise, I'll throw you face-first down these steps myself.'

Aldo seethed and snarled but eventually nodded.

The guard Aldo had kicked in the face spat out a bloody tooth. 'I say we throw him down the steps anyway.' Another guard nodded in agreement.

'It's no more than this bastardo deserves,' John agreed. 'But the Inquisitori di Stato wishes to execute him. If Aldo dies on his way to the cells, we would all suffer for it.'

The guards grudgingly agreed. John sent two of them ahead before letting Aldo go down. The steps were very different from the wide, elegant staircases elsewhere in the Doge's palazzo. Those were made for patricians, officials and dignitaries, designed to be seen and admired. These were narrow and rough, the uneven steps worn by the boots of servants and guards. Aldo climbed down, struggling to keep his balance with both wrists bound. His shoulders scraped against stone walls on either side. When Aldo reached the bottom of one set of steps, he was led to another.

As they descended through the Doge's palazzo, the air became increasingly damp and fetid, filling Aldo's nostrils. There was a wooden trapdoor blocking entry to one set of steps which the guards had to prise open. 'One of the old doges had this put in after a prisoner overpowered a guard and came up into the palazzo,' John said. 'There's no way of opening the trapdoor from below.'

'That must be why they call it a trapdoor,' one of the guards said, laughing at his own brilliance. 'Anyone below this door is trapped down here!'

John laughed too, but there was mockery in his voice. 'Aye, very funny. You should get a job as a jester.'

Aldo struggled to breathe when they reached the cells, such was the foulness of the air, ripe with piss and rot and despair. Stagnant lagoon water covered much of the stone floor, splashing Aldo's legs and hose. The ceiling was so low he had to bend not to hit his head against the stonework.

'These are below the level of the canals,' a guard said, sounding proud of his knowledge. 'Water pours in when the tide rises, that's why we call these cells the pozzi. Count yourself fortunate you won't be here for the next acqua alta. Prisoners have drowned.'

A bolt was pulled back and the heavy wooden door to one of the cells opened. John had the guards surround Aldo, ready to hurt him if he lashed out again, before untying the rope binding his wrists. John reached for the gag in Aldo's mouth. 'Cover your ears, signori. We're about to hear every curse word in Tuscany!' But when the gag was removed Aldo did not shout abuse or threats. Instead, he whispered.

'What was that?' one of the guards asked.

Aldo whispered again, his words too quiet to be heard.

'Speak up, man!' John said, making the guards laugh. 'We cannae hear you.'

Aldo whispered once more, and John leaned closer—

Aldo smashed his forehead into John's face. The Scot staggered back, roaring with anger. The guards attacked Aldo, punching and kicking him. He collapsed into the cell, falling in a puddle of cold, foul water.

'Leave him,' John shouted, pulling the guards back. 'Don't follow him in there, that's what he wants.' Aldo got to his knees but before he could stand the cell door had been pulled shut and its bolt rammed home.

John sneered at him through a small, square opening in the sturdy woodwork. 'Don't get too comfortable, eh?'

Aldo spat a mouthful of abuse. John laughed while marching away with the guards. 'We can come back later and see if he wants a priest for his last rites.'

* * *

After Aldo was dragged away, Coltello thanked the tribunal for finding Armando Dandolo's killer. 'I am especially indebted to you, Signor Bragadin. I know we have not always been at peace with one another, but the leadership and perceptiveness you've shown here . . . It does you great credit. I see now how incorrect I was about you, and offer my humblest apologies for any foolish words in the past. You were right, and I was wrong. I pray you will find it in your heart one day to forgive me.' She bowed low, her face hidden.

'I appreciate your contrition,' Bragadin replied. 'I agree you have been foolish, in word and deed. Having a Florentine murderer as a guest at your palazzo . . . The tribunal might yet consider it proper to bring charges against you for this.'

'I will respect whatever judgement you make,' she said.

'I'm not sure we need punish the contessa for an honest error,' Mastello said. 'She provided valuable information as to why this Aldo murdered Signor Dandolo.'

'Very well,' Bragadin agreed. 'This tribunal thanks the contessa for her small part in these matters, and dismisses her.' He smirked at Coltello. 'You may go. I imagine you must be eager to return to Florence.'

'Grazie, Signori.' She pressed a hand to her heart before bowing again so Salvadori and Mastello could savour another glimpse of her bosom. 'Grazie mille.' Coltello went to the door, waiting for the tribunal's assistant to open it. She glanced back at the three men behind their long table. 'Signor Bragadin, I wonder, might it be possible to see Aldo before I leave Venice later today? I should like to tell this monstrous creature what I think of him. But I would only go if you agreed to accompany me. I imagine the cells are no place for a woman alone.'

Bragadin sank back in his chair, seeming perplexed. 'Condemned men are rarely allowed visitors, except famiglia and a priest to give them the last rites.'

'I understand. In this, as in all things, I respect your judgement.'

Coltello waited, knowing Bragadin would find it hard to resist. He still suspected her of being involved with Dandolo's murder. Taking her to Aldo offered a last chance to test that suspicion.

'I shall allow it,' he eventually announced.

'Grazie, Signor,' she simpered. 'Truly, you are a man of unique wisdom. There are few in Venice that are your equal in this.'

Bragadin nodded, accepting the compliment as a statement of truth, rather than the insult it was. 'Come back later and I shall escort you myself.'

Coltello withdrew from the tribunal chamber. As she strode away, the contessa realized Giovanni degli Scozzesi was marching towards her, probably on his way back from the basement. Rather than move so that they could pass unhindered, he seemed determined to confront her. She moved to the other side and he matched her, coming closer. Just before they collided, Coltello moved sideways and their arms brushed one another.

'Foreign fool,' she hissed. 'Why don't you look where you're going?'

'Aye, and you should mind the company you keep!'

The contessa stalked away.

Chapter Twenty-eight

Aretino could not decide if Contessa Coltello was a blessing or a curse. There were few women in Venice to match her for courtly intrigues or barbed comments, and she possessed a knowing beauty that could make the most unlikely of subjects quite besotted. Yet she had an uncanny ability to appear at moments of considerable inconvenience to his writing. If she were anyone else, he would have sent them away. Instead, Aretino found himself listening to an account of her latest adventure.

'And you are certain I cannot write about any of this?' he asked. The contessa had sworn him to secrecy when she arrived, but this glimpse into the workings of the Inquisitori di Stato was rich material for a future treatise.

'When I am dead, you may write what you wish about me,' Coltello replied. 'Indeed, I will be disappointed if my name does not appear in your letters one day. But for now, dear Pietro, I must ask you to keep ink and paper apart in this matter.'

'Very well,' he agreed, emptying his cup of wine. 'More for you?'

'Grazie, no. It is better I keep my thoughts sharp. Now, tell me, did your good friend Sansovino leave behind those drawings he promised?'

Aretino smiled. 'I will have a servant fetch them.' He sent his maid Cisti. 'Sansovino said he could not vouchsafe their accuracy, but was most intrigued by the request. What do you plan to do with them?'

Coltello gave a sly smile. 'I can tell you, but you must not share my answer with anyone, not your servants or whomever is warming your bed at the moment.'

'Alas, you need not fear me divulging your secrets in the aftermath of passion, Contessa. I am without a companion for such pleasures at present.'

'That is most regrettable,' she said. 'I know several women in this city who would welcome a witty writer with nimble fingers. Or perhaps you have other preferences?'

Cisti returned before Aretino could answer, bringing a sheath of sketches with copious notes around their edges. The contessa smoothed them out atop the dining table. 'These are excellent,' Coltello said. 'Please give my compliments to Signor Sansovino.'

'I will,' Aretino agreed. 'Now, where shall we begin?'

Vincenzo waited until early afternoon when most guards were dozing before he descended to the basement of the Doge's palazzo. He had been there once before to inform a prisoner they would be executed that night. The man's anguished howls and the dank, fetid aroma were good reasons not to return, but obligation forced Vincenzo back. He could not leave Cesare to die without saying what must be spoken.

The stench was as bad as Vincenzo recalled, if not worse: stagnant water and ripe body odour, rot and mould and hopelessness. Should anyone find a way of capturing all of this and unleashing it on a battlefield, every enemy would run. Vincenzo's eyes were watering and his nose running as he came down the last steps.

A surly guard, unhappy at being woken, agreed for a generous handful of coin to let Vincenzo speak with Cesare alone. 'Last cell on the left,' the guard sneered. 'Stay back, if you value your teeth.'

Vincenzo edged along the dank stone walkway, careful to avoid the low ceiling. Everything here was oppressive, from the narrow corridors to the insistent darkness. A few burning torches on the walls offered a little light but no warmth. Water splashed his boots, while the sound of scuttling vermin sent a chill up his back. No man would wish to spend an hour in this place, let alone the last day of his life.

Cesare was hunched in a cell. The walls were stone, unlike the wooden panels that lined and warmed the rooms where Vincenzo worked. The cell floor was awash with water, more leaking through small barred openings in the outer wall. A little light seeped in, enough to show despairing pleas that past inmates had clawed into the walls. Vincenzo pictured men losing their fingernails to leave behind a final message.

'What do you want?' Cesare demanded.

'I came to see how you are.'

'Imprisoned. Condemned. Waiting to die. And all because of you. Grazie.'

'You brought this on yourself,' Vincenzo replied, his temper rising. 'You came to Venice. You lured Armando Dandolo to his death.'

'You betrayed me,' Cesare hissed.

'I did my duty for the Serenissima!' Vincenzo stepped back. 'What happens now is your own folly. I have nothing more to say to you.'

'Good. Then go, leave me in peace.' Cesare turned away, arms folded.

Vincenzo stalked back to the entrance. 'Sounded like you two are the best of enemies,' the surly guard said, a satisfied grin splitting his face.

'You were listening to us?'

'We listen to everything that happens down here. Signor Bragadin wants to know if the prisoners or their visitors say anything important. Thought you would know that.'

Vincenzo gave the guard more coin for his trouble, and went back up the stairs. As he ascended the air became less acrid, and he found it easier to breathe. But the stench of that place seemed to linger on his clothes, as did the hatred in Cesare's face.

That stayed with Vincenzo, burning into his thoughts.

Bragadin received word midway through the afternoon that the contessa had returned to see the Florentine prisoner. He intended to hear every word that passed between her and Aldo. Reports from the guards were adequate in most cases, but Coltello was too cunning for that. Bragadin went to the courtyard to meet her. The contessa waited demurely by one of the wells. Bragadin beckoned her to his side. 'This way, Contessa.'

She hesitated before joining him, eyes cast down. 'Grazie. I know you must be much occupied by your duties.'

'True, but there are certain questions I must ask before taking you to the prisoner. What you will see there, what you will smell ... Strong men have been undone by that place, and women driven near to madness.'

'I understand,' the contessa replied. 'I am willing to take that risk.'

'And why is it that you wish to see the Florentine?'

'As I said earlier, I need to tell this monstrous creature what I think of him before the tribunal's righteous sentence is executed.'

Coltello lifted her gaze. 'I want Aldo to know my true feelings when death claims him.' Hatred blazed in her eyes, its vehemence such that Bragadin was almost sorry for the man who had angered her.

He led the contessa to the guards' staircase inside the palazzo, and down to the basement, having the trapdoor raised so they could reach the cells. Coltello said she admired the ingenuity of this simple measure to prevent prisoners from climbing up into the Doge's palazzo, should they escape the cells.

Bragadin laughed. 'No prisoner has ever escaped. One overpowered a guard while being taken to their cell, but none have found a way out. When a man is locked down there, all that awaits him is death.'

Aldo sat hunched on the stone bench in his cell, arms around his legs. It was the only way to keep his boots out of the freezing water. His hose were soaked through, but might dry out in time. Whether he would live long enough for that to happen remained unclear.

He knew the Inquisitori di Stato often chose to drown convicted men at night, especially if their crime was an embarrassment to the Doge. Hopefully the tribunal had no such plans for him. The prospect of execution was bad enough; to die by drowning was somehow worse. If his life was to be taken, let it be by a different death.

'You have a visitor,' a guard announced, trudging towards the cell. Aldo peered at the small opening in the door, expecting to see a priest outside it. Instead, the sneering face of Bragadin was there. He stepped aside to reveal a second arrival: the contessa.

She appeared ashen, overwhelmed by her surroundings, but

Aldo knew better. He had seen some of himself in her once. Now he knew without doubt she would sacrifice anyone and anything to ensure she faced no punishment or pain.

'What is this cagna doing here?'

'The contessa asked to see you,' Bragadin said, dismissing the guard.

'I've nothing to say to her.'

'That is of no consequence,' Coltello replied. 'The last thing I wish to hear is more lies from your mouth. I came to tell you exactly why I shall welcome your execution. My only regret is that I will not be present to watch.'

'Why not? I thought you enjoyed seeing the men of Florence humbled.'

The contessa dismissed his accusation with a waft of her hand. 'You shall not goad me into anger. I am leaving Venice today, as soon as my maid Agnese has finished packing. By nightfall I shall be on the mainland at Mestre. Tomorrow, I start the long journey back to Florence. Signor Bragadin and his colleagues have kindly made my position there permanent. The sooner I can return to that city, the sooner I can return to serving the tribunal.'

Aldo twisted his furious face away from the cell door. 'I have no interest in such matters,' he muttered. 'And no interest in you.'

'Nonetheless, you shall hear what the contessa has to say,' Bragadin insisted. 'She did her duty to Venice, so you will respect that and listen.'

Aldo spat curses at both of them.

Bragadin called for guards to punish Aldo's foul mouth, but Coltello interceded. 'It does not matter, signor. All the prisoner has left are vile words, but they are a mask for his fear. He knows death is coming for him, so he lashes out in that ugly Tuscan tongue. Tell me, when does the tribunal intend to carry out its sentence?'

'Tomorrow, probably not long after dawn.'

She smiled at Aldo. 'Good. The sooner this creature is gone, the better.' The contessa moved closer to the cell, leaning into the small opening. 'The sooner he—'

Aldo sprang across the cell, grabbing Coltello through the gap in the door. 'I've got you now, strega! Let's see how you like being caught!'

'Guards!' Bragadin shouted. He turned away, bellowed along the corridor for help. The guards came running and soon got the contessa free. She spat at Aldo.

'I pray you burn in hell,' Coltello snarled.

'Then I will see you there,' Aldo replied with a smirk.

The contessa stalked away, complaining about the safety of visitors. The guards followed her out, but Bragadin lingered behind.

'I warned the contessa against getting too close,' he said. 'But it will do her good to be reminded of the dangers in believing yourself above retribution.'

'If you ever find a way to punish her, do it,' Aldo urged.

Bragadin tapped a finger against his chin. 'Perhaps you can assist me. Is there anything you can tell me as evidence against the contessa? You were staying at her palazzo here in Venice. You must have seen things, overheard things?'

Aldo scowled. 'Coltello is too clever to let her guard slip. Be careful of her, signor. She cannot wait to see me dead. Be wary of what she might do to you next.'

Bragadin straightened his back. 'I am aware of how dangerous the contessa is. That is why I have not challenged her post in Florence being made permanent. Better to throw a poisonous snake into your neighbour's garden than keep it in your own.'

He marched away, leaving Aldo in the cell.

Waiting to die.

Chapter Twenty-nine

The contessa had her gondola make one last stop before going to Palazzo Coltello. 'Over there,' she said, pointing to a grand residence that had seen better days. The stonework and ornamentations were fine indeed, but the shutters showed signs of neglect. In Venice, it was not enough to own an impressive palazzo. Such buildings had to be maintained and protected against the lagoon, an expensive undertaking. The grander the residence, the costlier such measures became – as Coltello knew well. A palazzo showing neglect meant only two things: the famiglia was not there often, or lacked the coin to keep their residence as it should be.

The former was true of Palazzo Coltello.

The latter was certainly true of Palazzo Salvadori.

The contessa presented herself, asking the maggiordomo to fetch his master. She knew the tribunal was not in session, and had checked Salvadori was not busy gossiping on the broglio. That did not ensure he would be at his residence, but improved her chances. The maggiordomo returned with word his master would be happy to meet her.

She was ushered into a grand library to wait, the walls lined with volumes by great writers and philosophers. It amused her to find several volumes by Aretino. More notable was the fact that few, if any, of the books showed signs of being opened. Most bore a layer of dust, yet the bindings remained pristine. Coltello found several shelves had no books at all, only the spines of expensive volumes glued to blocks of wood. That said much about Salvadori's troubles and delusions.

He bustled in. 'Contessa, this is an unexpected surprise.' He took her hand in a clammy grasp. 'Ahh, I see you have been admiring my collection. These are my pride and joy.'

'Indeed? The late count and I were never blessed with sons or daughters, but I'm often told most parents consider children to be their greatest joy.'

'Well, yes, of course. I would say the same thing.'

'Then these books are not your proudest possession?'

'Well, yes. I mean, no. I mean . . .'

Coltello pressed a gentle hand to his perspiring face. 'Do not look so anxious, I am teasing you.' She brushed past him, moving to a nearby chair. 'May I?'

'Of course.' He brought another so they could sit facing each other. 'To what do I owe the pleasure of this visit?'

'I have come for the favour you promised me.'

'The favour?' Salvadori appeared confused, as if he were a dog asked to read Latin out loud. 'But I already repaid your favour.'

The contessa paused, as if this had slipped her mind. 'When?'

'When the tribunal was in session yesterday. I insisted Signor Bragadin ask your maid Agnese who had been in your bedchamber last October. And I helped secure you a permanent position in Florence, as well.'

'Yes, you did,' she agreed.

'So, my favour to you has been fully repaid.'

'I'm afraid not, signor.'

'But what I did was of enormous benefit to you—'

'It was.' She leaned forwards and patted a hand on his hose-covered thigh. 'But I never asked you to do either, and certainly not as payment for my favour.'

'But . . .' His mouth flapped uselessly.

'I have another task in mind for you that will satisfy me. Do not worry, signor, it requires little effort on your part.'

'It does?'

'Yes.' Coltello beckoned him closer and whispered in his left ear.

Salvadori listened intently. 'Is that all I must do?'

'Yes.' She let him sigh with relief before continuing. 'For now, at least.'

'You cannot keep holding this debt over me, Contessa,' he protested. 'If I do what you ask, I must insist on being freed from my obligation.'

'I don't think so. You have no coin, and the parlous state of this palazzo tells me how many other debts you have unpaid.' She cupped his palle in her hand. 'Being of service to me is a far easier way of paying what is owed, don't you agree?'

Salvadori's face flushed crimson. 'I . . .'

The contessa squeezed, making his eyes bulge. 'Don't you agree?'

'Y-yes,' he squeaked.

Coltello smiled. It was simple to control most men. All one needed was to know their vulnerabilities, and be ruthless enough to exploit them.

Aldo spent the afternoon contemplating what was to come. There must be some way out of the cells, some means of escaping this basement. But, if so, it was well hidden. The guards were eager to brag how no man had ever got away. That meant the only prospect of leaving was by being taken for execution.

He had been close to death before, yet always believed it could be cheated, outthought or outfought. This time was different. Sense told him he should write a letter to leave behind. But he had no property or wealth to pass on, no children to be cared for after his death.

Yes, there was a famiglia of sorts; his half-sister Teresa would probably mourn him, and her daughter might miss him. Isabella had seen him only a few days ago but any pain from his loss would likely be brief and soon forgotten – his stepmother Lucrezia would make certain of this. The realization that the vicious old strega would outlive him was infuriating.

Saul would grieve the most, Aldo believed – or at least hoped. He was sure the Jewish doctor loved him, yet in the handful of years they'd known one another their times together were all too brief. The laws of God and man had prevented more than that. Aldo did love Saul, in his own way, but a question clawed at his thoughts.

If there was nothing stopping him and Saul being as one, would they be together? If they could share a home, a full life, might that expose how different they were, how unsuited for one another? It was impossible to know. Their mutual attraction was clear, but could they have ever been a couple like men and women were? Aldo did not know, and it did not seem to matter now. Their last moments had been constrained by circumstance. What he wouldn't give for one last chance to kiss Saul, to be with him again.

But there seemed no chance of that.

Not now.

There was a rattling of keys, and Aldo heard footsteps approach, two sets – no, three. Where the guards bringing another prisoner to the cells? Or were they coming for him?

Aldo went to the door, water soaking through the joints in his boots. There were three guards, two of them armed with heavy clubs, the other carrying rope. The man with rope announced he was Ravini, leader of the guards. 'Step back from the door.'

Aldo did as he was told. Having been beaten once already, it was wiser to keep the strength he had left for whatever was to come.

'Has my execution been brought forwards?' Aldo asked. Bragadin was a petty, vindictive creature, the kind who would delight in stealing away a man's last hours.

Ravini ignored the question, unlocking the door instead. 'Turn around,' he commanded. 'Hands together behind your back.'

Aldo complied, and the other guards bound his wrists. 'In Florence we always have a priest present to hear a condemned man's confession.'

'You're not in Florence,' Ravini sneered. 'Bring him,' he told the others. They took Aldo from the cell, along the corridor and out of the basement. Four more guards waited by the narrow stone staircase up into the Doge's palazzo. 'He's all yours,' Ravini said.

Aldo was led upwards, two guards in front and two behind. The trapdoor was open, allowing them to reach the palazzo's first level. If he was to be executed, it would happen here . . . but the guards led him to another staircase, pushing Aldo further up. He asked questions but got no answers – just curt instructions to keep moving. Had the tribunal summoned him back for interrogation? Would Bragadin offer a deal in exchange for information to incriminate the contessa?

The journey continued, rising through the palazzo. The guards took him past the corridor that led to the secret archive, and by the doorway to the tribunal chamber without stopping. Instead, they went to a wooden staircase leading up into dark, murky shadows.

'What's up there?' Aldo asked.

'The piombi,' one guard replied. 'New cells are being built in the attic for when those in the basement are flooded. The piombi are not all finished yet, but there's one ready for you.'

'You won't drown up here,' another guard said, smirking.

'But you might freeze to death,' a third added.

'Gets very cold in the piombi at night, being so close to the palazzo roof,' the first agreed. He nodded to the others. 'Take him up.'

Aldo was dragged and pushed up to an attic. There was room to stand upright in the middle where the roof was at its highest, but that sloped down quickly on either side. A few skylights offered meagre illumination, allowing Aldo to see sturdy wooden cells tucked beneath the roof. Two guards led him to the nearest cell, but their leader told them to stop. 'That one isn't completely finished. Put him in the next one along.'

The door to another cell was opened, and the guards untied Aldo's wrists. He rubbed at the red raw skin, peering at the inky blackness beyond the doorway.

'Get in,' one of the guards snarled, shoving Aldo through the doorway.

When he tried to stand upright, his head thumped into the heavy wooden ceiling. Aldo cursed, using his hands to test the height of this new home while crouched over. It couldn't be taller than his shoulders. 'You can't leave me in here,' he protested. 'This isn't—'

The door slammed shut, and a bolt was rammed into place. 'Don't go anywhere,' a guard said through a small opening in the door, laughing at his own jest. He vanished, and Aldo heard the guards stamping across the floor before clattering down the staircase.

Then there was nothing but silence.

Aldo sat down with his back to the door, using what little light came through it to study his surroundings. The cell was made entirely of wood, being roughly twice as wide and long as it was high. A ripe smelling piss-pot lurked in one corner, while a thin mattress lay against a wall, straw poking out.

'Anyone up here?' Aldo called, but got no reply.

The other piombi were empty, unoccupied.

He was alone.

Vincenzo hesitated before entering Signor Bragadin's ufficio. He had never questioned the judgement of the tribunal before. But he wanted to be certain one particular decision accorded with the wishes of all its members.

'Scusi, signor,' Vincenzo said. 'May I have a moment of your time?'

Bragadin was working behind his table, hunched forwards in a high-backed chair to study an orderly stack of papers. 'Come in.'

Vincenzo ventured closer, perspiring hands clasped behind his back.

Bragadin held up a sheet of paper. 'I was reading what the cipher deputies found in the journal Dandolo brought back from Florence. There's nothing of great note here.'

'I have already placed the journal in the secret archive.'

'Very good. In fact, your work has been exemplary these last few days. Well done.'

Vincenzo bowed his head. 'Grazie, signor. I was only following your example.'

'Never apologize for being adept at what you do. And you must learn to accept praise, rather than attributing your success to others or to good fortune.'

'Yes, signor. I—' Vincenzo stopped, realizing he was about to do exactly what Bragadin advised against. 'I shall try.'

'Good. Now, what was it you wished to see me about?'

'The prisoner, Cesare Aldo, has been moved to one of the completed piombi in the attic. It happened without incident and I'm told he has been securely locked in a new cell. I wanted to confirm this met with your wishes.'

Bragadin was already examining the next document on his table. 'Mastello must have asked for this. He favours keeping prisoners in the piombi, forgetting they are directly above the tribunal chamber. The last thing we need is prisoners banging on our ceiling.'

'Indeed, signor.'

'You say the prisoner is secure?'

'Yes, signor.'

Bragadin glanced up. 'Then I confirm this meets the tribunal's wishes.'

'Very good, signor.' Vincenzo bowed before withdrawing.

'One last thing, Culmine. I'm calling a meeting of Inquisitori di Stato for tonight. Send word to Signori Mastello and Salvadori, please. We have urgent matters to discuss.'

Chapter Thirty

Aretino held his book open at the first few pages for the guard to inspect. It had taken all the writer's considerable powers of persuasion to get so far inside the Doge's palazzo, not to mention a generous selection of bribes. But this guard was proving far less helpful. 'See? It's a collection of my letters, which were published to considerable acclaim. I wish to give this volume to the prisoner, Cesare Aldo. I believe it may offer the condemned man some small measure of comfort before the tribunal has him executed tomorrow morning.'

The guard stared at the pages, but Aretino suspected they meant nothing to him. It was well known the Doge's palazzo employed men who could not read as sentries. 'Why would letters comfort a man waiting to die?' the guard asked.

He might not be a reader but that didn't make him a fool.

'These may help take his thoughts away from what is to come,' Aretino replied. 'Better to be distracted than spend your final hours dwelling on that imminent demise.'

Eventually the guard gave a disinterested shrug. 'Very well. I'll give him your book when he gets his final meal.'

'No, that won't do any good. I wish to give this to him myself,' Aretino said. He produced a large pouch from inside his tunic, pressing into the guard's hand. 'Please.'

Soon Aretino was being led to the attic, though he was gasping for breath when they approached it. Being a writer exercised the mind, but left the body ill prepared for most other exertions. Aretino promised himself he would take more walks and be more careful with what he ate – once his current project was complete.

The writing had to come first, obviously.

'He's up there.' The guard pointed to a steep wooden staircase.

'You're not coming with me?'

A quick shake of the head. 'The attic is haunted.'

Aretino wasn't sure if the guard was jesting. 'Haunted? By phantasma?'

'One of the men building the piombi died up there. At night, we hear his spirit moving around in the attic. The floor, it creaks and groans.'

More likely that was the palazzo adjusting as the warmth of day left the building. Aretino had observed this happening in his own residence, but chose not to say so. Better to let the man have his beliefs. 'Well, grazie for telling me. I will be careful.'

Aretino clambered up the wooden steps, his book under one arm. The attic was a bare chamber with low, sloping ceilings. Meagre light seeped in from outside, a few beams from the setting sun illuminating the sturdy wooden cells. Only one had its door closed and bolted.

'Cesare? Are you in there?'

A confused face appeared at the small opening. 'Aretino?'

'I brought you this.' He held up his book. 'It's a copy of my letters,' Aretino said, raising his voice so the guard below would hear. 'It may bring you some comfort in the hours ahead.' He pushed the book through the small opening.

Aldo took it with the bemusement of a nun clasping a cazzo. 'There is no light in here. How am I supposed to read this?'

'I believe you will find the answers you seek inside.' Aretino pretended he had the book in his own hands, opening it with surprise and delight on his face.

'I'm sure your writing is very good,' Aldo replied, 'but I'm not in the mood for this.'

It took all Aretino's strength not to shout at this obtuse man. 'I think you may find the later entries particularly useful. Do have a look.'

Finally, Aldo leafed through the closing pages. 'Ahh! I see what you mean. Grazie, signor. This shall be a great comfort. Grazie mille.'

'Prego.'

'Duke Cosimo was right about you,' Aldo said.

'Cosimo de' Medici?'

'Yes. He gave me a letter of introduction for you. Said I should come to you for help if I needed it here in Venice.'

Aretino smiled. 'How delightful. Do you still have this letter? I should like to read it.'

'No, it was lost, but I shall tell him of your assistance if I make it back to Florence.'

'Perhaps I shall write about you. Then you would be immortalized in print for ever.'

Aldo arched an eyebrow. 'You believe people will still read your words after both of us are dead?'

'I certainly hope so. Why? Do you think my works will be forgotten?'

'We are all forgotten, sooner or later.' Aldo beckoned Aretino closer. 'Before you leave, there's something I need you to do for me.'

Not long after Aretino left, Aldo heard more boots stamping up the wooden stairs to the attic. This time several people were coming. Two guards approached the cell before stepping aside to reveal

John of Scotland. 'I've come to ask what you want for your final meal,' he said.

'I'm not hungry,' Aldo replied. 'Waiting to die does that to a man.'

'What about drink? You must be thirsty.'

'I am, but that doesn't matter. I will be gone before morning comes.'

'Gone?' John laughed, pointing at Aldo. 'Did you hear that? This fool believes he's going to escape!' The guards joined in with his laughter, enjoying the impossibility of what Aldo was suggesting. 'What are you planning to do?' John asked, a smile splitting his bushy red beard. 'Climb out through a skylight and fly away like a bird?'

'Perhaps I will,' Aldo said.

'You need to get out of your cell first, idiota,' a guard sneered.

'Yes, that does make it more difficult.' Aldo smiled at their hilarity before mumbling something under his breath.

'What was that?' John asked, moving closer. 'I can't hear you, fool.'

Aldo shot an arm through the opening in his cell door, grabbing John by the beard. He pulled the burly Scotsman into the door, slamming John's face against the woodwork. 'That's for betraying me,' Aldo snarled. He let John lean away, then yanked him back into the door. 'And this is for working with that bastardo Bragadin!'

John bellowed at the guards to get him free. They tore him from Aldo's grasp, but left a handful of beard behind. John cursed in Tuscan, Venetian and English. Aldo's ear for the last was rusty but the meaning was still clear.

'Open that door,' John shouted. 'I'll kill him now, save the city doing it later.'

When they refused, John reached through the door to grab at Aldo's tunic. The two of them grappled with each other, fingers clawing at eyes and nostrils. Aldo leaned back –

– and smashed a fist straight into John's face.

The Scotsman staggered backwards and collapsed on the attic floor, his senses lost.

'Now who's the fool?' Aldo spat.

The two guards stared at John. 'What are we going to do?' one asked. 'We can't drag him down the stairs, Bragadin would have us executed.'

'Well, I'm not staying up here with him,' the other said. 'You know as well as I do this attic is haunted. It'll be dark soon. That's when the spirits come out.'

'Put him in here with me,' Aldo suggested. 'I haven't finished with him yet.'

'And have you two beat each other to death before the tribunal can execute you? Don't take us for fools,' one of the guards sneered.

'Then put him in the next cell. He can sleep it off in there.'

The guards pondered this. 'It would serve the mercenary right for ordering us around.'

'He's not a true Venetian. He's not even from Tuscany.'

One man took John by the legs, the other grabbed his arms. Working together, they dragged him into the cell beside that of Aldo before closing the door.

'You better bolt that shut,' Aldo said. 'He's stupid enough to come and have another fight with me once he wakes up.'

The guards muttered to each other before shoving the bolt across, locking John in.

'We'll be back to let him out in the morning,' they said.

'Doesn't matter,' Aldo replied. 'I'll have escaped by then.'

The guards laughed as they clambered down the staircase. 'Idiota still believes he's going to get away alive. Buona fortuna with that, signor – buona fortuna!'

The contessa watched Pozzo loading her gondola. The Florentine maggiordomo had been busy all day, making arrangements for their journey back to Tuscany along with certain other tasks. Coltello's maid Agnese was already in the gondola, finding homes for the bags before they crossed the lagoon. It would not do to lose something of importance in the water.

'I will make my own way across to the mainland,' Pozzo said when the task was complete. 'Your carriage is at the coaching house in Mestre. It will be ready to leave at dawn.'

'I am unlikely to be up that early,' the contessa replied. 'Grazie, both of you, for all you have done these past few days. I appreciate your efforts.'

Pozzo and Agnese bowed their heads, acknowledging the rare praise.

Coltello went back into her late husband's palazzo. It was a pity she had not resolved whether to have the damp, decaying building sold or repaired. She had hoped to find a buyer for it, someone sufficiently wealthy and besotted with her to overlook the many flaws. But Bragadin and his troublesome tribunal had occupied too much of her time.

The palazzo would have to endure a while longer.

Her Venetian maggiordomo Amaro made no effort to hide his pleasure at her leaving. 'It is a sadness to see you go,' he said, 'but I pray you return to Venice soon.'

'As do I,' Coltello agreed, her smile as false as his prayers. 'Until that day, I leave you in charge of this palazzo and its servants. I have told them all that you offered to increase by half what they are currently being paid.'

'I did?' Amaro's brow furrowed with confusion.

'Indeed. And that you will be paying them this from your own purse – a most generous decision, I must say. Well done, my dear Amaro.'

'But . . .'

'You are probably wondering how you can afford all of this,' the contessa said before leaning close to whisper in his ear. 'Use the coin Bragadin pays you to spy on my household. Did you honestly believe I would not discover that, you irredeemable *merda*? Count yourself lucky I am not staying longer, otherwise my punishment would be far worse.' She stepped back from Amaro. 'I hope that is agreeable with you, yes?'

The maggiordomo nodded, his face ashen.

Coltello smiled. 'Then I shall go. Farewell!'

It was past nightfall when Aldo heard groans of pain, followed by curses in different tongues. 'Did you have to hit me so hard?' John called. 'Think I lost a tooth.'

'It was a lucky punch,' Aldo replied in a whisper. 'And keep your voice down. The tribunal meets directly under these cells.'

'Aye, and Bragadin often has night sessions. Don't worry, I know.'

'Your *piombi* isn't finished yet, that's why I was put in this one. But when Aretino was here earlier, I had him look inside where you are. He told me there was a way out. Can you see it?'

John said something about holding his wheesht. Aldo didn't know what a wheesht was or how he should hold one, but guessed it was a plea for patience. He listened to John moving around in the next cell. 'Well?'

'It's no easy to see in here, and this place was made for a wee Venetian,' John replied. There were more noises, then silence. 'I'm not seeing anything.'

'Have you looked up? Sansovino told me one of the cells had a gap in its ceiling, and Aretino confirmed that when he visited.'

'The ceiling was the first place I looked. I'm sorry, Cesare, but there's nothing.'

Aldo slumped against the wall of his cell, sliding down to its wooden floor. He had been so certain there would be a way out, so long as he was up here in the attic. But Sansovino's information had been wrong, or too old to be of use.

A crooked square of light appeared on the floor in front of Aldo, fading into life before him. He bent down, trying to determine from where the light was coming. A faint beam was falling through the small hole in the cell door. Aldo scrambled to it, pressing his face into the gap, peering outside.

There, up in the palazzo roof – a skylight. Beyond it he could see the moon.

'John, look around again,' Aldo urged.

'I told you, I've already—'

'Look again!'

'Aye, I will, but I'm telling you . . .' His voice died away. 'There's a board missing in the roof. It was so dark before, I couldn't see that.'

'Can you get out through the gap?'

'Not yet, no. But maybe I can make it bigger.'

Aldo listened to John grunting and pushing and straining. There came the sound of wood splintering. First one piece, then another, and then a third. Eventually, Aldo heard John's voice more clearly. 'I'm out.' Aldo peered through the cell door opening to see John grinning as he strolled over.

'Serve you right if I left you in here.' John pulled back his upper lip to show the gap where a tooth was missing. 'Look what you did.'

'Bragadin would be happy to find me still here tomorrow,' Aldo said.

'Good thing your contessa paid me so handsomely to help get you out.' John eased back the bolt securing the cell and opened the door.

'Grazie,' Aldo replied, stepping out. He stretched his back, rubbing at his neck before placing Aretino's book of letters down on the attic floor.

'This is no time for reading,' John said. 'Thought you wanted to escape?'

'First I need to know the way out from here.' Aldo turned to the back of the book, and loose pieces of paper fell out. Lines had been made on these with red ink. Individually, they looked like nothing. But when Aldo rearranged them on the floor, they became one image: a drawing of the palazzo as if seen from the side with an outer wall removed.

'That's this place,' John whispered, jabbing at the map.

'And here's my way out.' Aldo traced a path down through the palazzo. He opened the book again, turning to its centre pages where a hole had been gouged. Nestling among the words of Aretino lay a key. Aldo recognized the distinctive shape as a copy of Mastello's key to the secret archive. Aretino had been right; his book was bringing great comfort.

John pulled the second archive key from his tunic. 'You'll be needing this.'

'How did you . . . ?'

'I slipped the wax block I took from you to the contessa earlier when we bumped into each other outside the tribunal room. She had that copy of Vincenzo's key made from it, and sent her man Pozzo to give it to me with the rest of the coin she'd promised.'

'Grazie,' Aldo said. He held out a hand for John to shake, but the burly Scotsman pulled him into a mighty embrace. 'You're crushing me.'

John put him down. 'Sorry. It's just . . . I doubt I'll see you again.'

'I won't be coming back to Venice, that's certain. But if you ever need my help, send a messenger. I owe you my life.'

'Don't you forget it,' John agreed. 'Now, let's get me locked back in my cell. I have to put these roof boards back in place so Bragadin can find me locked in when he comes for you in the morning, otherwise I'll be the one getting executed.'

Chapter Thirty-one

Aldo crept down the wooden steps from the attic, heat rising to welcome him. The Doge's palazzo was as quiet as a church after nightfall, so much so he could hear sea birds in the distance. How people lived with their constant cries was beyond Aldo. He supposed Venetians were used to them, probably did not even notice, but it set him on edge.

So far, the plan devised with Coltello was working. She had arranged his betrayal by Vincenzo, and paid John to assist with that. Her accusations in front of the tribunal helped convince Bragadin and the others of Aldo's guilt for the killing of Dandolo. The Inquisitori di Stato was part of a vast bureaucracy so the chances of immediate execution were slight, according to Coltello; the tribunal would need to complete considerable paperwork before having Aldo drowned or hanged. Of course, she wasn't the one risking her life.

Being imprisoned in the Doge's palazzo gave Aldo an opportunity to get inside the secret archive during the hours at night – the only time when that room wasn't guarded. He had proposed hiding himself in the palazzo until it was dark, but Coltello dismissed that. She needed him to be blamed for the killing of Dandolo to ensure her own future. Being locked in the basement had not been part of the plan, especially with its trapdoor mechanism to prevent anyone coming up from below. But when Aldo had grabbed her from inside his basement cell, Coltello had whispered two words of reassurance to him: 'Trust me.' She succeeded in getting him moved to the attic. Pozzo's skill in making keys and the assistance of Aretino and Sansovino were further pieces of the elaborate plan. Now all that remained was the task of retrieving Cosimo's journal and escaping the palazzo. Simple!

One floor down from the attic, Aldo strolled along a corridor. Better to look as if he had nothing to hide. Those who walked with self-assurance and purpose were seldom challenged, whereas the furtive always drew attention. Anyone who studied him closely would soon see he did not belong. Yes, he wore the clothes of a servant, but they were dirty and torn. Hopefully the dark hours of night would help conceal that.

Aldo's path to the secret archive took him by the door to the tribunal chamber. Approaching it, Aldo could hear Bragadin's voice, sneering and superior. What a pleasure it would be to see that haughty face when Bragadin discovered the empty cell, its door bolted shut. But that was better imagined than witnessed, like so many things.

Leaving the tribunal chamber behind him, Aldo reached the short corridor that led to the secret archive. Its door was shut, but unguarded. He strode to it, one key in each hand. The first – a copy of the key Mastello kept in his sanctum – slid into the lock easily. The second, Vincenzo's key, slid halfway in . . .

. . . but no further.

Palle!

Aldo pulled the key out, then slid it back in. The result was the same.

Had the impression he'd made of Vincenzo's key been flawed? Perhaps the wax did not get enough time to harden before John snatched it away? Had Pozzo rushed while making this copy, and failed to properly match the original? Aldo shook the key inside the lock but still it would go no further. He could force the key, but that risked the copy breaking.

Aldo stopped, willing himself to be patient. He filled his chest with breath. A musty smell caught in both nostrils, creating an urge to sneeze. He closed his eyes, determined not to give himself away. The archive would be full of old documents and dust. That aroma reminded him of a similar room in Palazzo Fioravanti, where the famiglia papers were kept. It was never locked because the mechanism was faulty, and his papa had insisted the papers had little value to anyone else. But he had shown Aldo how to open the door if someone was foolish enough to lock it: lifting the handle took pressure off the lock.

The solution couldn't work for this door, could it?

He eased the door upward in its frame.

The second key slid all the way in.

'Grazie, Papa,' Aldo whispered.

He turned both keys, each unlocking its mechanism.

The door to the secret archive of Venice swung open before him.

Aldo slipped inside, pushing the door back into position but not locking it. Moonlight coming in between a single set of shutters was his sole illumination. He dared not light a lantern or candle, even if he'd had a flint or flame to do so. Better to search fast, find the journal and leave; that was easy to decide, but far harder to achieve.

The secret archive was vast.

There were stacks upon stacks of papers. Open cupboards with more papers and books lined the walls, awaiting attention. The archive must date back decades, even centuries.

How could he find a single red journal amid all of this?

Dandolo had brought it to Venice a few days ago. Even if the journal had gone into the archive immediately, it was still likely to be on top of the piles in need of filing, rather than already hidden away. Best to search the least-dusty stacks first, checking the documents for any dates to show when they were brought here.

A brisk scour of the stacks nearest the door confirmed they were the latest additions to the archive, but no red journal was lurking among them. Aldo went on to the next pile of papers, and the next, and the next . . . without success. The date on the uppermost documents in these was several weeks in the past. The further he went, the older the papers became. It wasn't here. Cosimo's journal was not in the archive.

Had all of this been for nothing?

Aldo heard a creak, and swung round to see the archive door opening.

Vincenzo stood there, holding a plain red journal with a small black letter C on it.

'Looking for this?'

Vincenzo knew Coltello must have had a hidden reason for wanting Cesare brought before the tribunal. Cesare being held solely responsible for Dandolo's murder shifted accusations from her, but it was another mask, another ruse. She wanted Cesare inside the Doge's palazzo after nightfall. The contessa needed a way into the secret archive and had gambled on that as her best chance. The request that Cesare be moved to the attic confirmed Vincenzo's suspicions, but what was it Coltello wanted?

The answer was obvious: the journal Dandolo had brought from Florence. It was written in code but several pages inside mentioned

Coltello. Using the cipher key provided by the deputies, Vincenzo read those pages. Dandolo had been correct; it was the Florentine duke's own journal, full of his private thoughts about enemies and allies. Vincenzo realized Cesare planned to escape his cell after dark to reclaim it.

Once the tribunal's night session was underway, Vincenzo excused himself to wait and listen. Sure enough, Cesare came downstairs from the attic, producing two keys to unlock the secret archive's door. But Vincenzo had already removed the journal. Now he stood in the doorway, brandishing the red-leather volume.

'I'm not surprised you've gone to such lengths for this,' Vincenzo said. 'What your Medici duke writes in these pages . . . It could destroy him.'

'Wars have been started for less,' Cesare agreed.

'But what are you willing to do for this book? Would you kill me to get it?'

Cesare did not answer, but his silence spoke for him. Vincenzo could see now that this Cesare was very different from the young man he had known so long ago: harder, leaner, more bitter. Had what happened years ago changed him so much? Or was it an accumulation of wounds and scars built up over the years that brought out such ruthlessness in him?

'You would have to be swift,' Vincenzo said. 'If I call out, you will not escape. The guards would return you to the pozzi for execution tomorrow at dawn.'

'I will not kill you,' Cesare said, 'but I need that journal. I have come too far, been through too much to leave empty-handed. I cannot return to Florence without it.'

There was sorrow in his face, regret too. Cesare's sadness seemed honest . . .

'Why does going back to Florence matter so much?'

'It is my home. I belong there, much as you belong here in Venice.'

'Is someone waiting for you?'

Cesare nodded.

'Do you love him?'

'Why do you need to know?' Cesare asked. 'You insist that you love your wife, your famiglia. Why do you care about the contents of my heart?'

'Because I want you to be happy. After what happened, I would wish you to know what contentment is.' Vincenzo smiled. 'We all deserve that.'

'But few of us get it.' The wariness remained in Cesare's eyes, as if he expected guards to stalk into the archive at any moment. 'Will you give me the journal?' he asked.

'I might, but only if you agree to my conditions—'

A door slammed nearby, stilling the words in Vincenzo's mouth. Someone had come out of the tribunal room. 'Culmine, are you there?' a male voice called. 'Culmine?' Boots stamped away, fading into the distance.

'That was another of the tribunal assistants,' Vincenzo said. 'Bragadin must need something. We don't have long before someone comes here looking for me.'

'What are your conditions?' Cesare asked, haste in his voice.

'You must never return to Venice.'

'Happily. The tribunal is already eager to execute me.'

'You must never write to me or my famiglia, never contact them.'

'Agreed. I've no wish to hurt you, not now. I will make sure Coltello leaves you in peace.'

'I doubt you have such power over her, Cesare. That woman does as she wishes, or to amuse herself. But I have a means to shield myself from Coltello's retribution.' Vincenzo opened the journal, showing Cesare the torn edges of several missing pages.

'You've taken the entries that mention the contessa?'

'Yes. If she or anyone else denounces me, I will use those pages to destroy her in Venice. She seemed eager to get back to Florence, but being banished from this city would still hurt her, as would the Inquisitori di Stato sending men against her.'

'I'm sure the contessa will see the wisdom of accepting your terms.'

'Make certain she does.' Vincenzo proffered the journal. 'Now, take this and go.'

Cesare moved closer, one hand taking the book, the other on Vincenzo's arm. He stared into Vincenzo's eyes. 'I wanted to say—'

'Culmine!' The assistant's voice echoed along the corridor. 'Where are you?'

Vincenzo glanced out of the doorway, but there was nobody in sight. When he turned back, Cesare kissed him on both cheeks before they shared a last, lingering embrace.

'Be happy,' Vincenzo whispered.

'And you,' Cesare replied.

'Culmine!' the voice shouted again.

'Now go,' Vincenzo urged. 'Get out while you still can.'

Aldo tucked the journal inside his tunic as he strolled away from the secret archive. The urge to run was strong, but he resisted it. Instead, he followed the path mapped out by Sansovino's plan, down one staircase and a second. Along an empty corridor and on to the loggia. Another staircase, and then the vast courtyard was stretching out in front of Aldo.

This was where the real danger lurked.

Inside the palazzo there were few people to see him, so he had passed unnoticed. But in the courtyard his progress could be observed from hundreds of rooms in the moonlight. Even if he kept to the arcade on this side, he might still be visible to some. Better to brazen it out, move as if he had every right to be there.

But it didn't keep fear from clenching a fist inside his belly.

Aldo straightened his back, took a deep breath . . . and stepped into the moonlight.

No voice cried out, nobody shouted or accused him. On he went, expecting to be accosted or attacked or surrounded. But the silence remained, broken only by the distant cry of gulls and the sound of his own boots on the courtyard stones.

Aldo approached the tunnel that led out of the palazzo. There were three guards ahead of him. One was sleeping, slumped against a wall, but the other two were upright and awake, staring at the lagoon, weapons ready to repel an attack on the palazzo. This was to Aldo's advantage. All their focus was outwards. The guards had no reason to fear or suspect him – not unless they had been warned of his escape.

Vincenzo could have betrayed him. He did not want to believe it; Vincenzo appeared cautious and careful in the secret archive. But in Venice, anyone could wear a mask.

Aldo continued into the tunnel. It was too late to turn back now.

The guards turned to face him. 'Buona sera,' one called.

'Buona sera,' Aldo replied with the slight sibilance of a Venetian.

'Working late?' the other guard asked.

Aldo nodded, letting his shoulders slump a little. 'Always.' He showed a rueful smile as he passed, but kept going. 'Arrivederci.'

'Arrivederci,' the guards replied in unison.

Aldo strolled across the broglio, passing the tall columns beyond the Doge's palazzo. A boat bobbed up and down by the shoreline with Coltello's preferred gondolier, Luigi, inside it. He stood as Aldo approached. 'Wasn't sure if you would make it. The contessa said I should leave if you did not come before midnight.'

'Where is she?'

'At a coaching house on the mainland where her carriage stays when not in use. She's returning to Florence at dawn. You can go with her, she said, or make your own way.'

Spending several days in a carriage with the contessa . . . Who knew what intrigues she would devise on the way to amuse herself, or how dangerous the mischief she might drag him into? But Aldo had no coin for a horse and the further he could get away from Venice, and quickly, the better. 'Coltello's carriage it is. Let's go.'

Chapter Thirty-two

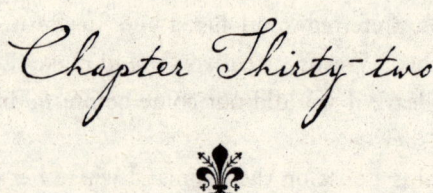

Thursday, February 15th 1539

Bragadin marched into the Doge's palazzo not long after dawn, despite the late conclusion of the tribunal session the previous night. He was eager to see Aldo executed, to see justice done for Dandolo's murder. To attack an assistant of the Inquisitori di Stato was to attack the tribunal; to murder that assistant was little short of a declaration of war upon the Serenissima.

Bragadin had expressed this to the Doge but the old fool Lando was reluctant to reach the same conclusion. The Doge's attention was all to the east, where enemies were massing to steal more maritime territories from the republic's control. Why could he not grasp that threats could also come from the west and south? Venice was founded on its dominion over land as well as sea, yet the Doge was blind to such dangers.

No matter. Once the golden robes had passed to the right man, Bragadin would ensure the city was protected on all sides. Until then, he must use the powers at his behest to show those who dared attack representatives of Venice the full cost of their folly. The swift and merciless execution of Aldo would demonstrate the potency of the tribunal and its leader. There must be nothing flaccid in their will or their resolve.

Bragadin had a messenger summon Ravini, the leader of the

guards, and three of his men to assist in bringing Aldo down from the piombi. Better too many guards than too few for such a task. A prisoner on the way to his execution had nothing to lose and was often the most dangerous of men. But when they reached the attic Bragadin noticed that doors to two of the piombi were bolted shut.

'There was a fight between the prisoner and Giovanni degli Scozzesi,' Ravini said when questioned. 'Aldo left the mercenary without his senses, so he was put in a piombi to sleep it off. The door was bolted to stop him attacking the prisoner in retaliation.'

Bragadin nodded his approval. 'Get Aldo out of his piombi.'

Ravini pulled back the bolt and opened the door, the other guards ready should Aldo attempt to escape or attack them. But nobody emerged.

'Come out,' Bragadin called, 'and face punishment for your crime.'

Still nothing happened.

'Get him out of there,' Bragadin snapped.

'Yes, signor.' Ravini went in, one hand on the hilt of a dagger at his side, a lantern in the other. Bragadin could see Ravini inside the piombi, looking about himself. Eventually he emerged – alone. 'Nobody's in there.'

'That's impossible.'

'I agree, signor, but it is true. See for yourself.'

Bragadin snatched the lantern and stalked into the piombi, crouching to avoid the low ceiling. The wooden cell was empty aside from a piss-pot and a discarded straw mattress. He scoured the walls and ceiling. There were no weaknesses, no missing boards, no way out. Yet the door had been bolted shut when they arrived, he had seen that with his own eyes. Bragadin straightened up and smashed his head into the ceiling.

He came out muttering curses and rubbing at his scalp. 'Check the other one, make sure Giovanni degli Scozzesi is still in there.'

Ravini pulled back the bolt on the second piombi, revealing a burly figure sprawled on the wooden floor, snoring gently. 'Wake up!' Bragadin shouted.

Giovanni jerked forwards. 'What's wrong?' he asked, looking around. 'Where am I?'

Ravini reminded the mercenary what had happened the previous evening as Giovanni clambered out, ducking low to avoid striking his head. 'Aye, that's right. Aldo has quite a fist when it hits you fair in the face.' The mercenary pulled back a lip to reveal the gap where a tooth had been the previous day. 'Where is Aldo?'

'That's what I wanted to hear from you,' Bragadin hissed.

'How would I know? I've been in that piombi all night.'

'Explain to me how a prisoner escaped a locked piombi?'

Giovanni shrugged. 'I can't.'

Bragadin wanted to slap the smile off his face. 'Ravini, you and your men shall make a complete search of the palazzo. If Aldo is still within these walls, I want him found. He may be hiding, waiting for an opportunity to slip out. Which guards were on duty at the broglio entrance last night?'

'I'm not sure,' Ravini said. 'But they will be asleep at home now.'

'Have them brought to my ufficio. If Aldo did leave, he must have passed by them.' Bragadin glared at Ravini. 'Well? What are you waiting for? Go!'

The guards stumbled down the wooden stairs. 'The contessa must have found a way to get Aldo out of the palazzo . . .' Bragadin muttered to himself.

'I thought Coltello was leaving Venice yesterday, before sunset,' Giovanni said. 'She would already have been on the mainland when Aldo escaped.'

The mercenary was correct, and that made it even more vexing. 'Go to her palazzo by Ponte del Diavolo, find out when she left,' Bragadin said. 'We need to be certain.'

Coltello could recall numerous occasions when she had been up to see the dawn, but those came after a night of enjoying herself. The hours before sunrise were her natural domain, after all, a world where she was at her finest. Being woken by Agnese this early was far less welcome, but it had seemed wise to make such arrangements.

Spending a night in the port town of Mestre on the mainland ensured that Bragadin and his tribunal could not blame her for Aldo's escape attempt. If it went awry, she was far enough away to avoid any accusations of complicity. In the unlikely event he succeeded, she could not be held responsible for that either. The blame would fall on Bragadin and his guards, not her.

'Well?' Coltello asked. 'Did Aldo make it?'

Agnese smiled. 'Luigi brought him across the lagoon during the night. Aldo slept at the stables behind the coaching house, as you directed.'

'Good.' The contessa had few trusted allies in Mestre, so it was wise for Aldo to keep his distance overnight. 'I wish to leave as early as possible. Tell Pozzo to wake Aldo, then return here and help me get ready. It will take several days to reach Florence, even with fresh horses. The sooner we put some distance between us and Venice, the better.'

'Very good, Contessa,' Agnese replied before withdrawing.

Coltello settled back in bed to savour the last few moments of comfort. Her carriage was sound enough, but long hours bumping along dirt tracks were far from a delight. At least on this journey she had fresh company; Agnese could ride outside with Pozzo and the driver. Teasing and tormenting Aldo on the way to Florence would be a treat, and her plans for where they would stay each evening made the contessa smirk.

She was going to enjoy testing his . . . flexibility.

All things considered, her trip to the Serenissima had been a success. The tiresome inquiry into who killed Grossolano was no more, and her position as Venice's spymaster in Florence had been confirmed. Ideally, she would have found a way to destroy Bragadin, but it was enough to have thoroughly bested him, and on his own territory.

His year on the tribunal would finish in autumn, removing Bragadin as a stone in her zoccoli. The man's blustering pomposity and need to dominate others meant he had few allies and fewer friends within the Doge's palazzo. Coltello doubted Bragadin would ever be elected Doge. It was more likely he would die thwarted and frustrated, always suspecting a woman had the better of him. All that righteous anger would come to nothing; Bragadin would be tortured by his own impotence.

'Good,' the contessa murmured to herself. It was what he deserved.

Aldo compared notes with the contessa as her carriage carried them away from Mestre. He had been party to much of her plan, but there were elements of it which she had withheld even from him. 'When did John start working for you?' Aldo asked.

'I employed him after my first meeting with the tribunal,' she replied. 'You said he could be persuaded to help for enough coin, and I needed someone close to Bragadin.'

'So, John was in your employ when he chased me through Palazzo Mastello?'

Coltello nodded. 'If he hadn't been, I doubt you would have escaped. And he made enough of a diversione that I was able to get you away from there with my gondola.'

'You couldn't have known what would happen when I was brought to the tribunal.'

'I couldn't be certain, but a man like Bragadin is quite predictable. Besides, I enjoy inventing a new stratagemma in the moment, especially when life and death are at stake.'

'Yes, but it was my life in danger,' Aldo said.

She shrugged before smiling at him. 'You survived, didn't you?'

'Just.'

'Then nothing more need be said.'

'Yes, but—'

Coltello pressed a finger to Aldo's lips, silencing him. 'Shush. There will be plenty of time for questions later. Now, settle back and get some rest. We have a long journey ahead of us. But don't worry, I have a stop or two planned along the way that should provide us both with some entertainment. You might even get the chance to show me your appreciation.'

Letter from Pietro Aretino to Contessa Valentine Coltello

Venice, February 15th 1539

My dearest Contessa,
Of all the days that fall during the festivities of Carnival, Fat Thursday is by far my favourite. This is when the city and its people celebrate most, a day during which patricians and workers mingle closely. It is the unifying moment of the year, bringing the people of this city together as one. Piazza San

Marco and the areas around it become places of wild activity, with almost anything possible and – more importantly – permissible. Lust, gluttony and outrageous spectacles abound, despite the best efforts of the dour Doge, his Council of Ten and the less playful among the patricians.

Week upon week of abstinence and chaste reserve loom ahead of us, so Fat Thursday is also one of the city's last chances for true indulgence. Men go dressed as women, courtesans dress as men without fear of arrest, and masks are even more common. It is a city turned upside down, you might say. Yes, attempts to civilize the festivities are taking hold – pigs are no longer allowed to enter the Doge's palazzo, for example – but the city still has bull hunts and a mighty beast is executed in front of the Doge's residence. There will be fireworks and music well into the night.

I always go early to the Piazza San Marco on Fat Thursday so I may enjoy every moment of the madness. But this year I went especially early to watch and listen on your behalf. You asked for a report of what was happening outside the Doge's palazzo, but also on whatever I could discover about events inside. I am still composing my full account of the day's outdoor festivities, but wished to send you this summary of more urgent events. (You should consider writing a journal of your own exploits one day, Contessa. You have a talent for capturing the essence of people in a few words, whereas my own writings tend to occupy rather more pages, as this letter demonstrates.)

The first person of note I encountered was Signor Vincenzo Culmine. Grazie mille for your description of him, it was most accurate and made finding this gentleman a simple task. I approached him as he was entering the Doge's palazzo midway through the morning, and spoke to Signor Culmine again a few hours later. He was happy to share what he had observed inside the grand building, and his account appeared to be honest and true. (It might be safer to say he believed his words to be true; we all have our own interpretations of events.)

I also spoke with that bear of a man you named as Giovanni degli Scozzesi, though he insisted on my calling him John. In truth, I struggled to understand all that came from his mouth. That bushy beard makes it difficult to see his lips and, as I get older, I find myself watching people's mouths more as they speak to understand what they say, especially in a noisy salone or amid a crowd of people. Giovanni – John – has a voice I would describe as well travelled. He uses the Venetian dialect, the Tuscan tongue and words of Inglesi, often all in the same breath. I grasped most of what he told me, but must confess my understanding of that is less assured.

Nonetheless, here are the essentials of what I learned.

Rather than admit Aldo has vanished, it seems the Inquisitori di Stato altered its records to state he was executed by drowning during the night for the murder of Armando Dandolo. This will satisfy the victim's famiglia, and spare the tribunal from admitting a Florentine agent somehow escaped from a locked cell inside the palazzo. The piombi in the attic are being broken down and removed to spare the tribunal any further embarrassment. Perhaps they will be rebuilt some day, but for now prisoners must suffer being kept in the basement.

Bragadin had the maggiordomo from your residence by the Ponte del Diavolo brought before the tribunal for questioning, as he did the gondolier who took you across the lagoon to Mestre. They both confirmed you left the Serenissima hours *before Aldo's disappearance and thus could have had no part in that. In this, you are above reproach.*

Bragadin has been raging at those who work for him and the tribunal. Whatever the official record might say – I hear any mention of Aldo may be removed from it – all the patricians know of Bragadin's duping, how he has been cuckolded. It seems the tribunal will be his last appointment of note; none will vote for him again.

It is a pity Aldo's exploits in escaping his imminent execution must remain unknown. Whispers of them may survive, however; they may even inspire others in the coming years to seek ways of escaping imprisonment within the Doge's palazzo.

Contessa, I hope to encounter you again one day.
Until then, I remain your friend,
Pietro Aretino

Chapter Thirty-three

Sunday, February 18th 1539

Aldo breathes in sandalwood and decay. One is the scent of his boyhood home, the other is the stench of death. He knows these aromas too well. He is back in Palazzo Fioravanti. He is waiting for Papa to die.

He ventures into the bedchamber. The room is barren, just a high bed and a dying figure atop it, facing away from Aldo. They are no more than a husk, skin yellow as a candle stretched taut across jutting bones.

Aldo edges nearer to the bed. He does not want to see, to have these dying remnants to be the last memory of his papa. But after growing up in this palazzo, he knows how to hide his feelings, whether they are love or fear or longing or shame.

A wizened hand reaches out to Aldo, and he puts his palm inside it. 'I'm here, Papa.'

'Papa?' The voice is harsh, sharp. 'I had nothing to do with bringing you into this world, bastardo.'

The head turns to Aldo, hate twisting its features.

He knows her all too well.

His stepmother.

Lucrezia.

Aldo pulls back, but she will not let go. Her grasp claws at him, jagged nails slicing into his skin. She hisses, her breath that of a serpent. 'If I die, you die with me.'

Aldo was woken by the carriage jolting to a halt. The contessa sat opposite, an eyebrow arched. 'I don't know who you were dreaming of,' she said, 'but I hope it wasn't your lover.'

'Why've we stopped?' Aldo asked. 'Where are we?'

'Approaching the north gate into Florence. See for yourself.'

Aldo opened the carriage door to look out. The city wall of Florence stretched into the distance. Ahead of them stood Porta San Gallo, its gates open to welcome arrivals.

He was nearly home, at last.

The journey from Venice had taken three days, thanks to Coltello's carriage stopping at the country estates of women who seemed delighted to welcome her. Each overnight stay had been eventful – the incident with the mongoose would not be easily forgotten – but Aldo was tired of the road, the carriage and even the company of the contessa. She was unlike any woman he'd known, yet even her presence palled after three days in close quarters.

'You should get out,' Coltello said. 'I can't enter Florence with one of Duke Cosimo's men as my travelling companion, and I imagine you have little wish to arrive alongside the spymaster for Venice. We are supposed to be adversaries, remember.'

'As if I could forget,' he replied. 'Grazie mille for the ride, Contessa, and for some . . . interesting stops along the way.'

She smirked. 'The road can be tiresome without a diversione or two.'

Aldo climbed from the carriage. Coltello called to her maggiordomo. 'Pozzo, our guest is leaving us. I believe you have something of his that needs returning.'

The maggiordomo reached into a satchel by his boots, pulling out Aldo's stiletto and hurling it into the long grass well away from the track. 'Fetch,' Pozzo sneered.

'No doubt we shall see each other again,' the contessa said. 'Until then, farewell.' She blew a kiss before closing her door. The carriage rolled on, leaving Aldo in a cloud of dust.

Retrieving his stiletto from the grass, Aldo slid it into his left boot. It was nine days since he had ridden out with Ottone in pursuit of the Dandolos, and that seemed a lifetime ago. All the others were dead now.

What was it Lucrezia had said in his nightmare? *If I die, you die with me.*

Aldo was happy to disappoint her.

Once inside the city, Aldo went first to Palazzo Medici. The sooner he returned the duke's private journal, the better. There was a lengthy wait to enter the ducal residence, five guards stationed outside. That gave Aldo a chance to savour Florence: the broadness of these streets, so unlike the narrow calle and canals of Venice; the sturdy stone of its palazzi, none of them slowly sinking into a lagoon; even the aromas of piss and merda left behind by cart horses were welcome, for a while.

When admitted to Palazzo Medici, Aldo was taken to the duke's private ufficio. Cosimo rose from behind the simple table to greet him. 'I had a wager with Campana on whether we would see you again. After not hearing from you for so long, I was beginning to fear losing my coin.'

'I feared I might never return, at times,' Aldo said.

'Where is Ottone?' Campana asked.

'Dead, along with his guards. But so are those who intruded on this residence.' Aldo gave a brisk report on what had occurred on the road to Venice, and within that city. He neglected to mention how much Coltello was a part of all this; the duke need not be troubled with such details. Aldo concluded by pulling the private journal from inside his tunic. 'You will see several pages have been torn out. These are in the possession of an assistant with the Inquisitori di Stato who helped me secure the journal.'

Cosimo leafed through the book, noting which pages were missing. 'I believe that I wrote about Contessa Coltello on those.'

'She was visiting Venice and extorted the assistant into ensuring her position as the Serenissima's spymaster here in Florence was made permanent. To get his help, I gave the assistant those pages on which you named the contessa – after ensuring there was nothing else of interest on them. He can use those to undo her should she ever threaten him. It seemed a small price to pay for the journal.'

The duke's eyes narrowed before he gave a quick nod. 'Agreed. You have done well, Aldo – very well indeed. I have a vacancy among my permanent staff now that Ottone is dead. Would you be willing to serve as my head of security?'

Aldo had not expected this. He considered the offer a few moments before shaking his head. 'I must decline, Your Grace. I am honoured to help you whenever I can, but my skills are best suited to working alone, not leading a company of men.'

After being paid a generous pouch of coin, Aldo left Palazzo Medici and went south. The weak wintry sun was already sinking behind buildings as he skirted the Duomo, heading towards the

Arno. Aldo crossed the river at Ponte alla Carraia, preferring not to use Ponte Vecchio while apprentices were washing blood and fish guts off the bridge. By the time Aldo reached via dei Giudei, the alley was in near darkness as twilight settled across the city. But the door to Saul's home was still open, his student ushering a patient out as Aldo approached.

Rebecca smiled at him. 'You're back. Dr Orvieto will be pleased.'
'Is he still seeing patients?'
'Yes, there are two left inside. Are you in need of a healer?'
'No, but I need his . . . opinion about something.'
'Let me ask when he hopes to be free.' Rebecca bustled back in, leaving Aldo on the doorstep. He nodded at an old Jewish couple as they shuffled by. Rebecca returned, shaking her head. 'Sorry, but both patients have complicated illnesses that require all of Dr Orvieto's attention.' She leaned closer to whisper in Aldo's ear. 'Come back after curfew.'

Aldo smiled. 'Grazie,' he said loudly. 'Buona notte.'
'Buona notte.'

It was a short stride to Piazza della Passera and Signora Robustelli's humble bordello. Aldo could not wait to shed the borrowed servants' clothes he was still wearing, to sleep in his own bed. After so long away, he craved simple comforts. But Aldo's shoulders slumped when he saw what lurked outside the bordello: a carriage bearing the Potenza famiglia emblem. His step-niece Isabella was hoping to lure him back to Palazzo Fioravanti. She had not achieved this before Armando Dandolo's fateful intervention took Aldo away from Florence, and she certainly wouldn't now he had finally returned.

Aldo recognized the sour-faced servant pacing by the carriage. 'Tell Signora Potenza I have no interest in going anywhere with her. Not while her nonna is still alive.'

'Signora Potenza is not here,' the servant said before introducing himself as Calabi, maggiordomo to Isabella. 'She sent me to find you. I am not allowed to return without you, Signor Aldo. I have been waiting all day.'

'You're fortunate to have only waited a day. I've been away more than a week.'

'Nonetheless, you must come with me,' Calabi replied. He took hold of Aldo's arm, pulling him towards the carriage door.

'Let go,' Aldo hissed, ripping himself free. 'I have sworn never to set foot in Palazzo Fioravanti until that vicious old cagna Lucrezia is dead. Events forced me to break another of my vows a few days ago, so nothing you can say or do will persuade me.'

'Lucrezia Fioravanti is dead.'

'What?'

'Lucrezia Fioravanti died last night. Signora Potenza is heartbroken, as is her mother, Teresa. They need you.' Calabi sniffed at Aldo. 'Those were her words, not mine.'

The urge to dismiss Calabi was strong. If he had been one of Lucrezia's own servants, Aldo would not trust a word of what Calabi said. But the maggiordomo worked for Isabella, not her nonna, and that made the message more believable.

'Very well,' he sighed. 'I must go inside and change. Wait here for me.'

'We have been,' Calabi replied. 'All day.'

Aldo stalked into the bordello and up the staircase to his room. He undressed and washed in a bowl of cold water, using the borrowed clothes to dry himself. After pulling on fresh hose, a tunic and his old boots, Aldo went downstairs. Robustelli was waiting for him, her face a mix of delight and anger.

'We've been worrying for days. Where have you been?' she asked.

'Venice.' Aldo held up a hand to stop any more questions. 'I'll tell you everything when I can, but not until tomorrow.'

The bordello's matrona pouted. 'Promise?'

He kissed her on the cheek. 'I do.'

Aldo stepped from Isabella's carriage. Palazzo Fioravanti had seen better days. Even in the last moments of daylight the palazzo betrayed a famiglia unable to maintain appearances. Shutters hung off their fixings, while plaster peeled from its walls. The residence was shabby and forlorn, a symptom of lost wealth and limited means.

He strode inside. 'Isabella? Teresa?' Aldo got no reply. Silence filled the inner courtyard. Aldo took the wide marble steps two at a time to the middle level.

Isabella emerged from a doorway. 'Cesare? What are you doing here?'

'You sent for me.'

'No. You told me not to, not until Nonna was dead and cold.'

'But your maggiordomo said—'

'He said what I paid him to,' a harsh voice called from below. Aldo looked into the courtyard and saw Lucrezia using two walking sticks to step from the shadows. 'Pay anyone enough and they will do whatever you wish.'

Aldo spat out a curse at being duped. On another day when he was not so exhausted, this would not have happened. He stalked down the marble steps towards Lucrezia. 'That's how you've always got your way: bribes and lies. Why tell the truth when you can twist and manipulate others to do your bidding?'

She sneered at him. 'You lie to the world about who you are every day, buggerone.'

'I protect myself,' Aldo replied, 'that's all.'

'And I protect my famiglia,' Lucrezia hissed back. 'That's all.'

He reached the courtyard but stopped short of her, not wanting to be within reach of the strega's malevolent claws. 'Why bring me here? We have nothing to say to each other.'

'I'm dying. But before I do, there is one thing you need to know. One truth.'

'I don't believe a word that comes from your twisted, vile mouth.'

Lucrezia laughed, but it became a hollow cough, wracking her body. She staggered to a chair, collapsing into it. Aldo did nothing but savour her distress.

Eventually, she found breath to speak again. 'It does not matter whether you believe me. This truth will haunt you, just as it has haunted me all these years.' Lucrezia wiped a clawed hand across the spittle on her lips before whispering one word: 'Ginevra.'

'Don't you speak my mama's name,' Aldo warned.

Lucrezia ignored him. 'What do you know of her?'

'I don't answer to you,' he replied. 'You lost any power over me when you banished me from this palazzo. I am not a servant you can bribe or a child you can bully.' He looked up to see Isabella watching from the middle level. Her mama, Teresa, appeared at Isabella's side, concern in her face. 'I'm leaving. You know when I'll come back.'

'When I'm dead?' Lucrezia rasped.

'Yes.' Aldo stalked towards the door.

'Don't you want to know what truly happened to your mama? To my sister?'

Aldo stopped. 'My mama was a servant in this palazzo. She died giving birth to me. You told everyone that a hundred times when I was a boy.'

Lucrezia gave an empty grunt of satisfaction. 'I lied.'

He should go. He should leave and not come back instead of listening to more tricks and falsehood. He should go. Yet Aldo stayed.

'Her name was Ginevra and yes, she was your mama,' Lucrezia went on. 'But she was also my sister. My beautiful little sister. And she lured my Aldo to her bed.'

'You're lying.'

'Ginevra taught me a valuable lesson: only those who care can be hurt, and only those who lie can ever win.'

'More lies, more self-justifications.'

'But I made certain my little sister paid the price of that lesson,' Lucrezia went on. 'I had her sent outside of the city to have her bambino – to have you. I could not let her shame the famiglia any further with what she'd done. After the birth, I insisted my Aldo lock Ginevra away in an ospedale for the incurabili. We told those who were in charge that she was dangerous, and not to believe a word she said.'

'My papa would never—'

'Your papa was ashamed of his weakness. That guilt made him do what I wanted, so long as I allowed you to be brought up alongside our legitimate children.'

'I don't believe you—'

'It doesn't matter what you believe,' Lucrezia spat. 'It only matters what—'

Her words stopped, replaced by a rattling sound in that wizened throat. Lucrezia's back arched outwards, her face stricken by agony. This was the moment Aldo had craved for so long.

The old cagna was finally dying . . .

. . . yet he needed her to live.

He needed the truth.

Aldo strode to Lucrezia, grabbing her by the arms. 'Which ospedale did you send her to? Where was it?' Lucrezia did not reply, her teeth clenched in a grimace, but her eyes glared at him with triumphant venom. 'Where, you old strega, where did you send her?'

Lucrezia spasmed and flinched, her body jerking and thrashing beneath his grasp.

Aldo could hear servants rushing down the marble steps.

'Cesare, let her go!' Teresa shouted from above.

'Which ospedale was it?'

Lucrezia drew in one last, pain-wracked breath. 'You'll . . . never . . . find . . . her . . .'

A final rattle slipped from the old woman—

– then she slumped back in the chair.

Dead.

'No,' Aldo snarled. 'No!'

But she was gone, only her corpse left behind.

Servants pulled Aldo away, though it took four of them.

A maid leaned over Lucrezia, listening for a breath before shaking her head.

Aldo paced the courtyard. It was hours since Lucrezia's corpse had been carried upstairs by servants, but he did not care. They could burn her body on the back steps of Palazzo Fioravanti and he would applaud. But Lucrezia's final few words . . .

She had lied so often, for so long, it was impossible to know whether what she said at the last was true. Even if Lucrezia was not false at the end, Aldo's mama had given birth to him more than forty years back. If Ginevra was still alive she would be sixty, if not older. The chances of her surviving all those decades in an ospedale were like a single star in the sky outside the palazzo, wagered against all the other stars in the night. And, if she had somehow endured that long inside such a place, what would it have done to her?

Teresa came down the marble stairs, clutching a shawl around her shoulders. 'You're still here,' she said, stopping short of him.

'Yes.'

'What happened with Mama—'

'Don't,' Aldo warned.

'I forgive you,' Teresa said.

'I've done nothing that needs forgiveness. And I can never forgive Lucrezia for what she did, let alone what she claimed was done to my mama.' Teresa nodded, sadness filling her face. 'Did you know about this?'

'No,' she replied. 'Mama never mentioned having a sister before, not in all these years.'

'And nobody else ever spoke of Ginevra as Lucrezia did?'

Teresa shook her head. 'You were born three years before me. If anyone was likely to have heard whispers about your mama, it was you, not me.'

That made a bitter sense to Aldo. 'Knowing Lucrezia, she probably forbade most of the servants from saying anything, and paid the rest for their silence.'

'But in the last few weeks, Mama was stricken as you saw her tonight. She survived, but it loosened her tongue. She said the most terrible things . . .'

'Worse than when we were children?'

'Far worse,' Teresa replied. 'She kept talking about Ginevra, and a bambino. I didn't realize that meant you.'

'It could be another of her lies,' Aldo insisted. 'One last twist of the knife to torment me, even when she was dead. You can't deny it is what Lucrezia would do, if she could.'

'It is. And yet . . .'

'And yet it seemed true.' Aldo went to Teresa, embracing her for the first time in more years than he could remember. 'I have to go,' he said after a while.

'Where?' Teresa asked.

'To bed. I'm tired to my bones, though I doubt I shall sleep after this.'

'Will you come to the funeral?'

Aldo stepped back. 'No. I have a friend, someone I care about, who has been waiting too many days to see me. But I'll return when Lucrezia is in her crypt – if you will let me.'

'Of course,' Teresa said.

'Grazie. I need to search the famiglia papers, every document inside this palazzo. Somewhere there may be a clue to discovering if what Lucrezia said was true.'

'But it was so long ago . . .'

'I have to try. If my mama is alive, I will find her. No matter how long it takes.'

Aldo strode from the palazzo, out into the cold night air.

Historical Note

Carnival of Lies is a work of fiction, but it features real places and people. For example, much of the information about Duke Cosimo de' Medici and his new wife Eleonora de Toledo comes from the Medici Archive Project: http://bia.medici.org. This online resource holds transcriptions and translations of documents from the period, including letters written to, from, and about the duke. Cosimo was awaiting the birth of his first child with Eleonora in the winter of 1539, and frequently went hunting outside the city walls. Eleonora went hunting with Cosimo in the early months of her first pregnancy. The attempt by exiles to murder the duke in this novel is fictional, yet inspired by multiple attempts on his life, such as the Pucci Plot.

Pietro Lando was in his late seventies when elected Doge of Venice in 1538. His time as leader was marked by losses of maritime territories and failed policies, such as forbidding courtesans and sex workers from wearing jewellery or silk clothes to help purify the city.

Signor Girolamo Bragadin is my own creation, but the Inquisitori di Stato was a real organization. Formed in 1539, the three-man tribunal was tasked by the Doge and his Council of Ten with running counterintelligence operations in rival territories, using complex ciphers to protect covert communications from beyond the Serenissima. For more on the Council of Ten and the

Historical Note

Inquisitori di Stato, I suggest *Venice's Secret Service: Organizing Intelligence in the Renaissance* by Dr Ioanna Iordanou.

Pietro Aretino was a real person in Venice during this period who counted among his friends the architect Sansovino and the painter Tiziano, better known these days as Titian. Aretino was a quite remarkable individual whose erotic sonnets The Sixteen Pleasures so enraged the Pope that the writer was forced to flee Rome.

Aretino was present at the death of Duke Cosimo's father Giovanni delle Bande Nere, and frequently sent letters to notable individuals. (You can find examples of his missives to King Henry VIII in online archives.) Aretino did reside in Palazzo Bollani, which still stands today on the Grand Canal in Venice, opposite the Rialto markets. A few years after the events depicted in *Carnival of Lies*, Aretino was chosen as one of three envoys from Venice to meet with the Holy Roman Emperor, Charles V, and impressed him mightily.

Despite Aldo's gloomy prediction in Chapter Thirty, the works of Aretino survived long after the writer himself died in 1556 and some remain in print to this day. For example, contemporary composer Michael Nyman adapted Aretino's notorious sonnets into the *8 Lust Songs* which got their debut in Venice during October 2007.

You can see the cells where Aldo is held prisoner by taking the secret itinerary tour inside the Doge's palazzo. The tour also visits the tribunal room where the contessa twice proves her mettle against the Inquisitori di Stato. The guide will take you to the basement cells of the Doge's palazzo, and all the way up the narrow stone staircase to the wooden piombi in the attic. Records indicate the piombi were not constructed until 1591, but I could not resist having Aldo escape from an earlier, fictional incarnation of the

Historical Note

piombi, doing so in the same manner as Giacomo Casanova in 1756. Hopefully you can forgive my trespasses.

Last but not least, the contessa's home in Venice is based on a real building. Palazzo Priuli does indeed stand next to Ponte del Diavolo, the Devil's Bridge. The building is now a luxury hotel, and is in much better condition than when Contessa Coltello owned it.

Acknowledgements

I am indebted as ever to my publisher, Pan Macmillan, without whom *Carnival of Lies* would neither read so well nor look so splendid. Special thanks are due to editors Alex Saunders, Raphaella Demetris, Celia Killen, Rebecca Needes and assistant Ellah Mwale; cover designer Neil Lang, publicist Lucy Doncaster, and everyone else at Pan Macmillan for believing in this series of historical thrillers.

I owe a debt of gratitude to booksellers and librarians everywhere for helping spread the word about Cesare Aldo. Special shout-out to my local independent Atkinson Pryce Books and many others for supporting the series including The Edinburgh Bookshop, Night Owl Books in East Linton, the Book Nook in Stewarton, Waterstones branches in Perth, Kirkcaldy, Braehead and many other places, Cogito Books in Hexham, The Bookhouse in Broughty Ferry, and Imagined Things Bookshop in Harrogate. Ngā mihi to Wardini Books, Unity Books, Page & Blackmore Booksellers and Time Out Bookstore in Aotearoa for pressing my tomes into the hands of readers across New Zealand.

A doff of my digital cap to the many bloggers and wonderful book cheerleaders on Instagram and other social media for raising me up; there are too many to name everyone, but I appreciate you all. Thank you to the literary festivals that have welcomed me since my last Acknowledgements – Theakston's Old Peculier Crime

Acknowledgements

Writing Festival in Harrogate, Bloody Scotland in Stirling, the Bookmark Festival in Blairgowrie, Stockport Noir and many more. Special thanks to the mighty Craig Sisterson, who champions so many crime writers from Aotearoa and beyond; without him, our wee corner of the world would be a lesser place.

I'm grateful to my Creative Writing colleagues past and present at Edinburgh Napier University – Sam, El, Dan, Noelle, Ally, Elizabeth and Nick – for their support and patience.

A special grazie is due to fellow author and Venetian resident Philip Gwynne Jones for saving me from more errors about that delightful city than I ultimately have in this novel.

I remain blessed to be represented by the wonderful literary agent Jenny Brown, who lifts so many writers up with her empathy and boundless enthusiasm.

Lastly, thank you to my better half, whose tolerance and forbearance is remarkable.

Shadow of Madness

By D. V. Bishop

Read on for an extract from the next book
in the Cesare Aldo series . . .

Chapter One

❦

Thursday, December 20th 1540

Cesare Aldo stared at the man opposite him as the cart bumped and jolted up the rough dirt track. Saul Orvieto was his friend, his lover and a good doctor to the Jews of Florence. When Aldo had still been investigating crimes for the Otto, the city's most powerful criminal court, Saul helped solve some of those with his expertise in bodies. But that did not mean they were always in agreement, and this was a moment when Saul was simply wrong.

'You don't believe in evil?'

'No,' Saul replied.

'But you've seen the things men do. Stabbings, rapes, even burning people alive, and all because of greed or hatred or lust. How can you not believe in evil?'

The doctor stroked his thick russet beard. Grey was gradually appearing in Saul's hair, and more wrinkles framed his warm hazel eyes, but somehow that only made him more handsome. 'I don't deny that men do evil things,' he said. 'Some more than others. But I'm not convinced this makes such men evil, or that they carry evil inside them.'

Aldo shook his head. 'Then how do you explain their actions?'

'No doubt each one had their reasons, and believed in those enough to do what they did. You said it yourself: violence is caused by greed, hatred and lust. Take those away and most men have no reason to kill, no cause to be cruel or inflict suffering.'

'Most men? So, you agree some men are outside these boundaries of yours.'

Saul's face saddened. 'There are always those who cannot control their actions, whose judgement is damaged or whose conscience is overcome by madness. But that is an illness of the mind, not proof of evil. Such people are suffering in their own anguish, and deserve our pity. We will probably find men and perhaps even women like that where we are going.'

Aldo and Saul were travelling north, high up into the Tuscan hills above Florence to visit Ospedale de' Pazzi. Years ago, it was where wealthy famiglie sent their daughters to spend the last months of an illegitimate pregnancy. The babies were born far from prying eyes and gossiping neighbours, shielding the parents from shame. Most of the infants were given to the Church for adoption or passed on to an orphanage for foundlings.

Over time the building's purpose had changed, becoming an institution where those who had lost their reason or were deemed incurabili could be locked away out of sight. Officially, it was called Ospedale de' Pazzi, but a nickname from decades past – La Macchia – still lingered, because anyone sent there was seen as a stain on their famiglia. In recent years the ospedale had changed again, becoming a place where the worst and the most dangerous of Florence's incurabili were sent – out of their minds, and out of sight.

Aldo had used a precious favour owed by Cosimo de' Medici, the ruler of Florence, to secure a letter of authority, signed by the duke, to make an official visit to the ospedale. The fact that La Macchia was administered by the Church with both monks and nuns present meant he had also required permission from the diocese of Florence. Monsignor Testardo had demanded a full report on the ospedale as the price for that. By rights, such a report should be made by a senior cleric, but Testardo had no wish to visit La Macchia in the dead of winter.

If securing authority to inspect the ospedale had been difficult, obtaining the means of getting there had proved even more so. If Aldo were travelling alone, he would have hired a horse and ridden up into the hills. But Saul had insisted on coming too, and he was far less comfortable in a saddle. Walking would take time the good doctor could not spare from his patients. The solution was finding the cart driver who took supplies to La Macchia each week and paying him handsomely for a ride. But the driver refused to have anyone sit alongside him, so they were stuck in the back of his cart amongst the sacks and barrels bound for the ospedale.

To pass the time, Aldo was debating Saul about morality. He agreed with much of what the doctor said and they shared a mutual respect, even when their beliefs diverged. It was one of the reasons he and Saul were close, despite the laws of God and man forbidding what they did together in bed. But Aldo had seen the worst of men during his youth on the streets of Florence, his time riding as a mercenary and his many years enforcing laws for the Otto. 'You cannot deny that a man such as Father Pagolo Zati was evil,' he said.

Saul shivered. The wintry air was cold and getting colder as they went higher into the hills, but Aldo knew that was not the reason for Saul's trembling. 'I saw only what Zati did,' the doctor replied. 'Yes, his crimes were evil in nature, but they may have been the work of a disordered mind. You were the one who spoke with him.'

Aldo had questioned Zati after the priest admitted garrotting two men, bisecting their tongues lengthways and writing holy words on their foreheads with ash. Zati had previously killed elderly parishioners in his care, though his crimes remained unproven. The priest himself had dismissed those as the work of a novice still learning his craft.

'Zati told me he had always known he was different, better than those around him,' Aldo recalled. 'To become who you truly are, he said, you must trust your judgement above all else. Zati believed there was beauty to be found in murder, and a purity in what he—'

'Enough.' Saul held up a hand. 'I will concede that there are some men whose acts are truly evil. Let us be thankful they are few and far between, and that Zati is dead.'

The priest had been banished from Florence for his crimes, protecting the Church from a scandal. Zati went to Venice, where he had famiglia, but drowned in a canal soon after arriving, his death an apparent accident. In truth, it had been arranged on Aldo's behalf, yet he bore no guilt for that. He took no pleasure from having another man killed, but sometimes it was necessary. Aldo had looked into Zati's eyes, seen the evil lurking there, and knew the priest would never stop killing. He had promised to seek Aldo out one day, and Zati was not a man to break his word. Stopping him for good was the safest way to protect Florence.

'Do you two ever cease talking?' the cart driver asked, glancing back at them while scratching at his thick black beard.

'It keeps us occupied,' Aldo replied. 'How much further?'

'You'll see La Macchia round the next bend.' The driver urged his horses on with a snap of the reins. 'If you're looking for evil, you are going to the right place.'

'Why do you say that?' Saul asked.

'Only been inside once, but it was enough. Made me cold to

my bones. The worst of the worst are kept there, but the guards and even the monks – they're all mad, bad or worse.'

'I was told there are nuns at the ospedale,' Aldo said.

'Four of them,' the driver confirmed, 'looking after the women inmates. Mostly the nuns stay in their part of the building, keep themselves to themselves. I don't blame them. People from the village who come up the hill to work at La Macchia always leave before dusk. That place does something to a person, changes them. Stay there a night, you'll see.'

'Then it's a good thing we are returning down the hill with you today.' Aldo gave Saul a reassuring smile. 'We should only be inside a few hours, at most.'

'Just make sure you're ready to leave when I am.' The driver jabbed a finger at the glowering sky. Heavy, grey-white clouds were gathering overhead. 'That's snow, and plenty of it. La Macchia has been cut off in the past when the weather closes in.'

'How strange,' Saul said. 'We're not that far from Florence, and the city rarely gets more than a dusting, even in the coldest of years.'

'That's because all the snow falls up here,' Aldo replied.

The driver scratched his beard again. 'One year was so bad, it took nine days for anyone to reach the ospedale. No wonder they all go strange, sooner or later.'

Aldo twisted back to stare at Florence in the distance. He could make out the curve of the Duomo standing proud above the rest of the city. It was some miles south of here, but still visible from this high up in the hills – for now, at least. Once the snow came, Florence would soon disappear from view. But he and Saul should be back home before nightfall.

The cart rounded a curve in the track to reveal a cold, grey building huddled against a sheer stone hillside. There was a sharp cliff near the western edge of the ospedale with a precipitous drop below it.

The building had two levels beneath a roof of weary, broken terracotta tiles. Arched openings cut into the walls resembled forlorn eyes, metal bars across them to prevent anyone getting out and wooden shutters inside those. Built in the shadow of the stone hillside, the ospedale's interior would be bitterly cold most of the year.

As the cart rolled closer, Aldo could see where parts of the plaster on the outer walls of the ospedale had surrendered to the weather, exposing the bricks behind it. Beyond the building on its eastern side was a small stable, while another path led round to the western side. There the ground gave way to a sheer drop, the cliff edge uncomfortably close.

He and Saul exchanged a wary look. 'Still glad you came?'

The doctor forced a smile. 'You take me to all the best places.'

One of the double doors at the ospedale's main entrance opened and a monk emerged, peering at the cart as it rolled closer. He wore a plain brown habit, a white cord tied round the waist. A sudden gust of wind blew back his hood, revealing the bare scalp of his tonsure. Aldo raised a hand in greeting and the monk frowned before scuttling back inside.

'Not much of a welcome,' Aldo observed.

'Don't expect anything more,' the driver said. 'Not from this lot.'

A fat flake of snow passed Aldo's gaze, followed by another and another.

'Told you it was going to snow,' the driver said, grim satisfaction in his voice.

'Then the sooner we complete our visitation, the better,' Aldo replied.

Fra Pandolfo resisted the urge to sigh while the abbot prayed out loud. It was the last weekly meeting at the ospedale before Christmas, but followed an all-too-familiar pattern: an opening prayer from the abbot, followed by desultory reports from everyone else and, finally, a feeble attempt to encourage and uplift all of those present. The results of this repetition were always the same: boredom or bickering, depending on who had chosen to attend. The days leading up to Christmas might be full of anticipation and joy in Florence, but here at the ospedale they were merely fragments amid a long, cold, bleak midwinter.

Part of the problem was Fra Gherado had no right or justification to call himself the Abbot of Ospedale de' Pazzi. Abbot was a title for those leading a large monastery or abbey, places of wealth or importance. This ospedale was small, poor and getting poorer. Sacrist Fra Egidio often detailed how little income was being received for looking after the incurabili. Meanwhile, urgent repairs to the roof were needed, the vestments had not been renewed in years and the upper level at the back of the building had been barricaded since the previous winter, deemed too unsafe to use after the ceiling gave way.

Yet Gherado insisted on being called abbot, and the others indulged his delusion. It was easier than dealing with his sulking and disappointment. To Pandolfo's eyes, the abbot was a weak man. He would dither and delay without direction from others, unable to make even the simplest of decisions. How had such a man come to be in charge? The ospedale's previous leader had died three years ago after a long illness and his then-deputy, Gherado, succeeded to the post when none of the other monks put themselves forward.

It had been a mistake, one whose consequences they were all now enduring.

The head guard belched loudly as the abbot finished his prayer, making no attempt to stifle the noise or apologize for the stench of stale garlic it brought. Lamberti was a brute of a man who never hid his contempt for anyone else. Pandolfo always sat as far from him as possible. 'You done yet?' Lamberti demanded.

'I . . .' The abbot frowned before nodding. 'I suppose so, yes. Why, do you have something you wish to share, signor?'

'How many times must I tell you? Lamberti is my name, that's all. I'm not one of those men who calls himself by a special title just to seem more important.'

Pandolfo pursed his lips. Bickering it would be.

'Of course,' the abbot agreed, offering a smile of appeasement to the burly figure. 'Forgive me, Sig— Forgive me, Lamberti. It is hard to overcome the dutiful habits of a lifetime. When you have been raised to treat everyone with the same respect—'

'Yes, yes,' Lamberti cut in. 'We all know about your noble upbringing, the politeness you were taught from the cradle. Some of us didn't have that.'

'No, I suppose not—'

'Can we get on? I have men to supervise.'

'Of course, of course.' The abbot hesitated, his brow furrowing. 'Where was I?'

Fra Bernardo leaned forward, a solicitous smile on his thin lips. 'Just finishing your prayer, abbot. It was most well said.'

'Ahh, grazie,' the abbot murmured.

'Now it is time for the reports,' Bernardo added.

'Very good, very good. Well, who wishes to go first?'

Bernardo looked round the table, his face a mask of eager expectancy. He had been at the ospedale since spring, a replacement for the abbot's previous deputy. Where the abbot was withered and weary, a man in the winter of his years, Bernardo had all the sharpness of a newly honed blade. His dark brown beard was neatly trimmed and tended, his gaze never less than piercing, and his manner was far from Pandolfo's liking. The prospect of Fra Bernardo succeeding the abbot one day, perhaps soon, was not appealing.

Lamberti scowled. 'There's little to report. Ulivo refuses to wear anything and keeps smearing himself in his own merda. He'll freeze to death if he's not careful. We've emptied the cell beside the Monsignor – he upsets the other inmates too much. And Isola got hold of a needle from somewhere and has been sewing cockroaches together with loose threads.'

'Should he have something sharp in his possession like that?' Bernardo asked.

The head guard shrugged. 'He's never attacked any of my men.'

The abbot nodded. 'Good, good.'

Bernardo turned his attention to Pandolfo. 'And how goes the infirmary?'

'All is well. One of the female inmates, Seta, has been in my care. Her humours are far worse this time of year, which leads to melancholy and howling. You probably heard her.'

'Cagna never shuts up,' Lamberti muttered.

'My remedies have helped her recover enough that she is returning to the women's area. Suor Ortenza and Suor Cecilia are taking Seta back to her cell now.'

'Congratulations, Fra Pandolfo,' Bernardo said. 'How fortunate the ospedale is to have a skilled apothecary and infirmarian among its monks.'

Pandolfo acknowledged the praise with a nod, though it was as insincere as everything else about Bernardo – aside from his ambition. 'The nuns asked me to pass on their regrets at not being here,' Pandolfo said. It was a lie, but only a small one and for a good cause. He could always seek forgiveness from the Almighty later for bearing false witness.

'That explains why none of our sisters in God are present,' the abbot said, 'but not the absence of Fra Egidio. Does anyone know where our sacrist is—'

The ufficio door burst open, Fra Egidio tumbling in. 'Forgive me for being late, abbot, but I have been waiting for the cart to arrive. I wanted to be sure it had all of our supplies. Snow is coming, and we don't wish to be left short.' The sacrist was in his forties, yet still had a boyish quality to his face, despite the tonsure. Egidio pursued his responsibilities with a fervour Pandolfo considered close to unhealthy, as if keeping a close account of everything would deflect any and all other concerns. If only Egidio had that same fervour when it came to washing; alas, the sacrist was always ripe with the stench of body odour. Despite all of that, Pandolfo had a kinship of sorts with Egidio; everyone needed an ally, however awkward.

'This explains why you were not here for the abbot's prayer,' Bernardo observed, 'but not the reason for entering with such abandon.'

'Forgive me,' Egidio replied. 'But the driver has brought two men with him.'

'We're not expecting anyone,' the abbot said before turning to his deputy. 'Are we?'

'No, Abbot,' Bernardo agreed, rising from his seat. 'What do they look like?'

'Men,' Egidio spluttered. 'They look like men.'

'We'd get more sense from Ulivo,' Lamberti sneered.

'Perhaps the cart was not yet close enough to properly see the faces of these visitors,' Pandolfo suggested, wanting to support the sacrist.

'That's right,' Egidio said, giving him a grateful nod. 'But it will be here soon.'

'What should we do about this?' the abbot wondered aloud. 'Bernardo?'

His deputy smiled. 'You and I will go to meet them, Abbot.' Bernardo helped the older man up from his chair. 'We shall welcome them to Ospedale de' Pazzi, and enquire as to why they have decided to grace us with this unexpected visitation.'

Suor Ortenza fought the urge to laugh while holding out her hand to the wild-eyed woman in the corner of the infirmary. Four years ago, she could not have foreseen herself doing so and yet, here she was. 'Try these mulberry leaves, Seta – they're your favourite, yes?' Ortenza lifted one of the dried leaves to her nose, inhaling its subtle scent. 'Hmm, wonderful.'

Seta stared back, both hands bunched in front of her face. 'M-Mulberry?'

'That's right. I've five of them, all for you, if you come with Suor Cecilia and I.' Ortenza held up the leaves, spreading them out so Seta could see. 'Would you like one?'

Seta nodded, quick and nervous.

Ortenza offered a leaf to the nun beside her. 'Suor Cecilia, could you give this leaf to our friend Seta please?'

The other nun had only arrived at the ospedale a month earlier. Cecilia was young but no novice; she wore the dark blue habit and white wimple of a chapter nun. But she was still learning about the female inmates and their individual peculiarities. She had an open, friendly face that did not carry a lifetime of cares. Ortenza almost envied that innocence, but knew it would not last long at La Macchia. Quite what Cecilia had done to get herself banished from Florence to this hope-forsaken place remained unclear, and Ortenza had chosen not to pry. In the past, she would have pressed the young nun until Cecilia surrendered her secrets. But that Ortenza was no more; no longer did unworthy concerns usurp her duty to the Almighty.

'You want me to feed her a mulberry leaf?' Cecilia asked.

'Seta can feed herself,' Ortenza replied. 'All you need do is hand it over.'

Still Cecilia hesitated, seeming bewildered by the notion.

Ortenza leaned closer, lowering her voice to a whisper. 'Seta often believes she has been turned into a silkworm. When that happens, we give her mulberry leaves until the belief passes. Don't worry, they do no harm. If anything, these help to loosen her bowels.'

'Truly?'

Ortenza smiled at the inmate. 'We have nothing to fear from Seta, especially now that Fra Pandolfo has balanced her humours. Go on.'

Cecilia took the leaf and edged closer to Seta. The inmate had a disordered look, her pale face pasty and her hair a greasy mess of knots. She was little older than Cecilia, thirty at the most. The shift she wore was stained and creased, the bones of her narrow frame jutting against it. A strong wind could carry Seta away, but she had not set foot outside in years.

The inmate snatched the mulberry leaf from Cecilia, making the nun jump back, but Seta did nothing more except nibble on its edges. Joy filled her red-spotted face.

'Good,' Ortenza said, making her voice a warm murmur. 'Now, let's get you back to your cell, shall we?' Seta nodded her agreement, still nibbling at the leaf. 'Suor Cecilia, if you take Seta's left arm, I'll take her right.'

Working together, the two nuns guided the inmate out of the infirmary and along the hallway, passing Pandolfo's workshop and the chapel. Turning the corner, Ortenza saw three monks clustered at the ospedale entrance: the abbot, his deputy and the sacrist. Freezing air was blowing in through the open doors, making the corridor even colder than usual.

'Scusi,' Ortenza called as she and Cecilia led Seta toward the monks. Still the men did not move, their attention outside the entrance. 'Scusi!' she repeated, raising her voice.

At last Egidio looked round. 'Forgive us,' he said, ushering Bernardo and the abbot out of the way. Ortenza led Seta and Cecilia by, glancing out of the doors to see what was so fascinating. At first there was nothing remarkable: simply a horse-drawn cart laden with provisions and snow falling around it. Then she saw two men clambering from the cart. One was a Jew, the yarmulke on his hair denoting the man's faith. That was unusual; no Jew had come to the ospedale before. But it was the second man that brought Ortenza to a standstill.

Why in the name of God had Cesare Aldo come to La Macchia?

*SHORTLISTED FOR
THE 2021 WILBUR SMITH
ADVENTURE WRITING PRIZE*

'An impressive and immersive debut set in a beautifully realized sixteenth-century Florence'
Antonia Hodgson

'A first-class historical thriller . . . Bishop's spirited and richly detailed story is a tour de force'
David Baldacci

'Richly atmospheric . . . transports you to another time and place'
Ambrose Parry, author of
The Way of All Flesh

Discover the explosive first novel in the Cesare Aldo series today – available in paperback, ebook and audiobook

WINNER OF THE CRIME WRITERS'
ASSOCIATION HISTORICAL DAGGER

'A great insight into Renaissance Florence. What I love
about these books is the seamless weaving of factual history
with a great story'
Abir Mukherjee

'He is fast becoming a serious rival to C. J. Sansom and
S. J. Parris with his page-turning novels. Highly recommended'
Historical Novel Society

'D. V. Bishop transports you to an utterly convincing sixteenth-
century Florence, where the best and worst of human nature
constantly circle each other in this tense mystery'
S. G. MacLean

**Discover the second novel in the Cesare Aldo series
today – available in paperback, ebook and audiobook**

'It's hard to think of a better guide than D. V. Bishop to the brutality and glamour of Renaissance Florence. Religion and lust? Money and politics? It's all here, combined into a murderous brew'
Andrew Taylor

'A deft and engrossing historical thriller set in Renaissance Florence drawing on the fascinating and troubling legacy of Girolamo Savonarola. I thoroughly enjoyed the latest – and I think best – in D. V. Bishop's brilliant series'
Anna Mazzola

'In *Ritual of Fire*, the third scintillating Cesare Aldo novel, D. V. Bishop once again immerses us in sixteenth-century Florence and the heady intrigues of Renaissance Italy. Aldo is a magnificent creation'
Vaseem Khan

Discover the third novel in the Cesare Aldo series today – available in paperback, ebook and audiobook

'In *A Divine Fury*, D. V. Bishop leads us on another darkly atmospheric journey through Medici Florence, keeping us constantly on our toes. Who can we trust and whom should we run from? I look forward to finding out what Cesare Aldo does next'
S. G. MacLean

'D. V. Bishop has such tremendous flair for a thrilling plot, a gruesome mystery, and engaging, relatable characters. It keeps you hooked and guessing all the way to its conclusion. With contemporary relevance about secrecy, hidden lives and cover-ups, Bishop's books are stories to lose yourself in, with all the sights, sounds and smells of sixteenth-century Florence. But above all, this is the very finest in historical thriller storytelling'
Kate Foster

'In Cesare Aldo Bishop gives us a Florentine Shardlake, and this is his best escapade yet'
David Hewson

Discover the fourth novel in the Cesare Aldo series today – available in paperback, ebook and audiobook